DISCARD

continued . . .

Praise for

Death Comes Silently

"Sparkling . . . A bucolic setting, colorful characters, and frequent knowledgeable recommendations of mystery authors and books old and new help make this another winning entry in a cozy series that shows no sign of age."

—*Publishers Weekly*

"Fans of this popular cozy series will not be disappointed with Hart's latest entry. It is always a pleasure to read about the current obsession of Annie's well-meaning mother-in-law, Laurel Darling Roethke, and the competition between Henny and resident mystery writer, Emma Clyde, over the bookstore's monthly mystery contest. Recommended for all cozy mystery fans, especially those who like to read Joan Hess, Leslie Meier, and Jill Churchill."   —*Library Journal*

"[Hart] serves up a beautifully constructed puzzle mystery."
—*The Connecticut Post*

"The latest Death on Demand cozy is a superb entry that keeps the series fresh . . . Carolyn Hart has written another strong whodunit."   —*Genre Go Round Reviews*

"There are lots of reasons Carolyn Hart's books are all national bestsellers. They are just great."   —*Cozy Library*

"*Death Comes Silently* does not disappoint. I was immediately engaged . . . As usual, Hart's story line flows."
—MyShelf.com

"Any book by Hart is guaranteed to include a top-notch mystery delivering an enjoyable reading experience. Hart is a master storyteller and her popular Death on Demand series continues to include strong plotlines and characterizations."   —*RT Book Reviews*

Cry in the Night

CAROLYN HART

BERKLEY PRIME CRIME, NEW YORK

THE BERKLEY PUBLISHING GROUP
Published by the Penguin Group
Penguin Group (USA) LLC
375 Hudson Street, New York, New York 10014

USA • Canada • UK • Ireland • Australia • New Zealand • India • South Africa • China

A Penguin Random House Company

CRY IN THE NIGHT

A Berkley Prime Crime Book / published by arrangement with the author

Berkley Prime Crime Books are published by The Berkley Publishing Group.
BERKLEY® PRIME CRIME and the PRIME CRIME logo are trademarks of
Penguin Group (USA) LLC.

ISBN: 978-1-61129-027-1

PRINTED IN THE UNITED STATES OF AMERICA

Cover photo © Shutterstock/gary718.
Cover design by Jason Gill.
Interior text design by Laura K. Corless.

To the memory of Henrietta Von Tunglen

Author's Note

This story occurred in 1982. At that time the location of the missing treasure found in the novel was among the great mysteries of archeology. In 1993, it was learned that much of the treasure had been taken by the Russians as war booty and placed in the Pushkin State Museum of Fine Arts. But it is always possible that some of the treasure followed another path to Mexico and that in 1982, a young museum curator was caught up in a deadly search for gold.

1

The first time I ever saw him, he was furious.

He leaned forward, his right hand jabbing toward us. His words were harsh, clipped, uncompromising: "You are responsible, you and you and you"—he pointed at one and then another—"for murders and theft, pillage and bribery."

I was surprised and a little shaken at the anger I sensed among his listeners. Though I don't know why, really. Violence begets violence and certainly he was laying it on us.

"You talk on the phone to an art dealer and in Guatemala a forest guard is shot, in Greece a customs officer bribed, in Italy the *tombaroli* rifle another tomb." He slammed his hand down hard on the lectern. "The reason why is you."

His vivid blue eyes glared at us.

In the space before he spoke again, I looked at him and at his audience and saw them frozen in a moment of time. Perhaps I sometimes see things this way because, as an assistant museum curator, I have planned and arranged so many exhibits, everything from dioramas to tomb reconstructions. I never consciously decide to see anyone or anything in a timeless way, but sometimes, unexpectedly, everything comes to a standstill and, for an instant, I see a scene as distinctly and three-dimensionally as if it were carved in high relief.

It happened now.

Across the aisle, the director of a California museum smiled slightly, his cherubic face bland and unperturbed. Smoke wreathed gently upward from his pipe. Everything about him was plump and satisfied and indolent—his hands, the knobby bowl of his pipe, his slightly humped shoulders. Two rows forward, her haughty face in profile, a well-known curator from a southern museum reddened with indignation. Her chin lifted, her thin bloodless lips parted. She almost spoke.

But mostly, in that moment out of time, I saw him, those electric blue eyes, that shock of straw-colored hair, the bony face with a beaked nose and sunken cheeks. The collar of his shirt was frayed and he had nicked under his chin when he shaved.

As quickly as it had stopped, time moved on, the reel turned, the Californian drew on his pipe, the southern curator grimaced, and he began to speak again, his voice urgent and angry.

I wasn't listening. Instead, I watched him, wondering at my response to him.

Every woman, if she's honest, will own to a private and personal picture of the man she would like to meet. The angry man standing on the auditorium stage had nothing in common with my imagined man. That idealized portrait, though dim and a little obscure, was surely of a more pleasant-mannered, equable man, the kind of man who liked to walk a spaniel in autumn woods and talk quietly over a candlelit dinner.

That portrait didn't fit this violent, iconoclastic, skinny fighter. He would be lucky if he got out of the auditorium without a punch in the nose, though museum curators are more likely to fight with words than fists. Maybe. There was a huge fellow in the left front row who kept moving impatiently as if he would like to jump up and lunge at the speaker.

It wasn't that I wanted peace at any price. Just almost any price. I wanted no part of quarrels, controversies, or battles. No hassles, please. That was why, I admit it, I had chosen to become an Egyptologist. One reason, at least. There are few scholarly disputes over ancient Egypt's art and history. There aren't many revisionists in the ranks. It's all there, as vivid and clear on limestone walls as it was four thousand years ago. The ancient Egyptians were an attractive people, confident, secure, joyous, supremely sure of their place in a well-ordered world. I admired that confidence, envied it, because I lived in a precarious, uncertain world where you couldn't be sure the verities of one decade would even be in the ballpark the next. I took comfort in long settled history during the turbulent decade of the seventies, happy to immerse myself in the past.

I was, then, orderly, reasonable, temperate. Why did I feel an immediate attraction to an obviously intemperate, vituperative man?

His cheeks curved inward, emphasizing the long line of his mouth. . . . I shook myself mentally. Okay, Sheila, he's obviously undernourished. Probably too busy scrapping with people to eat regular meals. Big deal. But my eyes lingered on his mouth until I forced them down to the notebook in my lap.

It was heavily scored with doodles—interlocking black circles bordering the title of his talk, "Museum Responsibility in the Art Trade." An innocuous title for an explosive topic. The speaker was a visiting curator at the National Museum of Anthropology, Mexico City. His name was Jeremiah Elliot. I raised an eyebrow at that, wondering if his parents had a presentiment. Jeremiah, indeed.

With some measure of objectivity restored, I looked at him once again and began to listen, making an occasional note. I was, after all, expected to submit a report on the different sessions I had attended at this conference.

This was the closing day. I would catch the Metroliner home to New York this evening.

I probably wouldn't make too detailed a report on Jeremiah Elliot's topic. It wouldn't be well received at my museum, this equating of murder and mayhem with an open acquisition policy.

I wondered suddenly if he had read my mind when he said bitingly, "At some museums, they call it an open acquisition policy. That's a fancy name for receiving stolen goods."

I must have moved in protest in my seat because those cold blue eyes fastened on me. "Every illicit sale fuels the market. Interpol periodically lists the most wanted missing art. Recently the list included about two dozen paintings, some of them worth a million dollars each. That doesn't even hint at the real market. Right now, today, there is at least a hundred million dollars' worth of stolen art at large."

He paused to let us mull over that figure, then said emphatically, "This figure is for art stolen from churches and private collections and small museums—art of record. It doesn't even count the artifacts plundered from Etruscan tombs or jungle-hidden sites in Mexico and Guatemala. These last are the worst losses of all because they include pottery and stelae that archeologists haven't seen in place. The minute an artifact is taken from its original site it's no longer of any value in piecing together a picture of the past. This art sells like hotcakes at diamond prices to American museums."

He shoved a hand through his unruly hair, then stared in turn at each person in the small auditorium. He was gentler when he spoke again. "This convention has drawn almost three hundred museum people. I see"—he paused, totting up the figure—"twenty-seven people in here. Now, all of you knew what my topic was when you came in here this morning because you chose to attend this session. I'm hoping that some of you, maybe all of you, really listened, because you are the only ones who can make a difference. All the laws, all the international agreements, won't help if museum directors keep on buying art and artifacts that don't have an honest pedigree."

He stepped out from behind the lectern and moved to the edge of the stage. "You are the ones who can wipe out the international art thefts. You can start by having your museum adopt the policy of prohibiting purchase of pilfered artifacts. The Field Museum has done it. So have the museums of the University of Pennsylvania, Harvard University, and Southern Illinois University at Carbondale."

He looked at each of us in turn.

"What has your museum done?"

That, of course, was his wrap-up, and I thought, I hoped (but why should I care?), that the program was going to end pleasantly. There was a general rustle, notebooks snapping shut, the click of attaché cases closing.

The big fellow in the front row stood. He was imposing and he knew it—tall, husky, thick gray hair, fashionable wire glasses. He had a big voice to match, the kind of voice that echoes comfortably from a rostrum.

"I can tell you what my museum does, Dr. Elliot." His tone was bluff and hearty. "It's in the business of protecting the art of the world for the present and the future. When we are offered a magnificent object, we don't look at it and say, 'Oh, that's Etruscan; that belongs to Italy.' Art does not *belong* to anybody. The finest works of man can be appreciated by all peoples."

The rustling stopped. The wait for Dr. Elliot's answer was amused and expectant.

Jeremiah Elliot nodded slowly, then asked, "Your museum has one of the finest collections of pre-Columbian artifacts, doesn't it?"

The big man nodded.

"So that's an interest of yours. If someone offers you a Mayan stele in excellent condition but without provenance, would you buy it?"

"Young man, if an artwork has reached the hands of a dealer and it is of great beauty, I see it as the responsibility of my museum to offer sanctuary."

"You don't care where it came from or how the piece got to you?"

The museum director shrugged. "We have to deal with the world as it is, young man."

Elliot responded sharply, "It's not the way the world is.

7

It's the way we've made it. If nobody bought stolen art, crooks wouldn't move in. They do it for money, not to share art with the world. The going prices for great works of art are ten times higher today than they were twenty years ago. Art today is one of the best investments in the world. It attracts people who will do anything for money."

He looked away from the museum director for a moment and seemed not to be looking at anything. When he spoke his voice was angry again. "I had the good luck, when I was first getting started in my field, to work at Tikal in Guatemala. It was great work and I met some great people. One of them was a forest guard, Pedro Arturo Sierra, who was very serious, very dedicated to helping protect his country's past. In 1971, he interrupted some looting at La Naya, an isolated site. He identified some suspects, helped send them to jail. Some weeks later, he led a visiting archeologist to the same site. It was dusk. They set up camp, got a fire started to fix supper. Without warning, two shots rang out. The first one hit Sierra in the back. It knocked him around. The second shot caught him in the chest. He bled to death, there in the jungle. The killers gunned him down in reprisal because he had identified suspects in the earlier looting."

Elliot turned away from the audience and gathered up a small sheaf of papers from the rostrum. He put the papers in his briefcase. "It's a dirty game you play when you buy stolen art."

This time he was finished, and a general disorderly exodus began. I was caught up behind a slow-moving clot of older women who were trying to decide where to go for lunch.

One of them twittered, "Edna, if you think we have the time, I would so like to have lunch at the Capitol restaurant. This is our last day and I've never had the bean soup and I promised myself I would, this trip."

Edna was a massive lady in a picture hat. I wondered if she found it in the forties. She was obviously the leader of the group.

The little bank of women stopped, blocking the aisle, waiting for Edna to speak.

As a display of power and pecking order, it was fascinating.

A younger woman in wire-framed glasses with long straight hair said briskly, "Oh, we've plenty of time, Catherine. It's just now a quarter to twelve. We're free until one."

But Catherine waited, half turned, for Edna to speak.

Edna scarcely even took pleasure in her dominance, it was so easy. She smiled at the younger woman. "Dear Key, I can tell this is your first visit to Washington in the summer. Why, it would take almost to one o'clock just to find a cab and, of course, it's too far to walk in this heat. No, we've just time for a quick sandwich." And then she was shepherding her flock through the doorway.

The younger woman hung back for an instant before she followed the others up the hall.

Delayed by this exchange, I reached the doorway just before Jeremiah Elliot. Head down, he was walking slowly as he arranged some papers in his briefcase.

And he heard, as clearly as I did, a laughing voice behind him: "Silly young fool; what does he think a museum is for?"

The "silly young fool" stopped him for an instant. His face reddened, his chin lifted, and he started to turn around. Instead, he lunged toward the doorway, furious, oblivious to anything in his way.

He cannoned into me, his briefcase still open. It spilled, of course, and his papers tumbled out. The impact of our collision bumped my purse off my arm. It snapped open and the contents clattered to the floor. "Sorry," he muttered brusquely. He crouched and began to stuff loose papers back into his case.

He didn't sound very damned sorry.

I glared at him and hoped uncharitably that the patches of sunburn on his bony face itched.

I managed to retrieve my billfold and key chain and compact, but I was just an instant too late to save my lipstick from crunching under the foot of the California museum director, who walked on with his companion, not even noticing.

As Jeremiah Elliot and I gathered up our loose possessions, the two of us were the only ones left in the auditorium.

Quite soon he had his precious papers all together and was closing his case.

I couldn't find my lucky sixpence.

The floor was speckled gray marble that hides a multitude of sins, like mud from dirty shoes, scratches from the moving of chairs and tables, and any small objects that aren't brightly colored.

I am a bit nearsighted, but I only use glasses for reading. I peered at the floor and my hands patted the marble in ever-widening circles.

He was getting up.

"You could at least help," I said bitterly. "I mean, if you barrel ahead, knocking down everything in your path, you should at least be willing to help pick up."

"What's lost?"

I said stiffly, "My lucky sixpence." My tone dared him to laugh.

He didn't laugh. In fact, he bent down, looked carefully back and forth, back and forth, then pointed. "There it is."

The coin had rolled across the aisle and lodged at the end of a row of seats.

He stepped over, picked it up, and held it out to me. "I'm sorry I bumped you," he said apologetically. "I didn't intend to spill your things."

"It's quite all right," I said quickly. I was surprised to find myself smiling at him. I liked him, bony face, self-absorption, and all.

He put out his hand. "I'm Jerry Elliot."

I took it. "Sheila Ramsay."

We walked out of the auditorium and down the hall together as if it were the most natural thing in the world.

"I did a study once, on amulets," he offered.

"Did you?"

"Yes. They serve several functions, many of a magico-religious nature."

"Is that so?"

"In this particular tribe, in the interior of Peru, there is an especial fondness for small, bright metal objects." He grinned and it was a surprisingly attractive grin that creased his bony face into unexpectedly pleasant lines.

I laughed and somehow found myself telling him all about the battered little sixpence.

"It belonged to my mother and she truly believed it was *lucky*. You see, she was at the Café de Paris the night it was bombed. . . ."

It turned out, of course, that he had never heard of the Café de Paris, so I told him about the London nightclub and how excited my mother had been to be asked there that Saturday night in 1941. She was nineteen and fresh to London from a country vicarage. Newly joined up in the WAAFs, she had just received her orders and this would be her last night in London. The music was bright and gay, the latest swing. Everywhere there were uniforms, but many of the girls wore chiffon and satin. Costume jewelry sparkled in the spotlights.

There was no warning.

She was dancing with an RAF lieutenant and she always remembered the song "Oh Johnny, Oh!" Her partner was a vigorous dancer who loped around the small floor. They had been right in front of the bandstand one moment and the next they were at the back of the floor, which was crowded with dancers. As her partner swung her about, she saw something glitter bright as a star on the floor. They stopped and she reached down.

She could never, later, remember that actual moment of the blast but it must have been just then for, when she next could see, it was smoky gray everywhere and there was a choking smell of cordite in the air and someone very near her screamed and screamed. She was looking up at her partner. He had not bent down and shards from the mirrored walls were lodged in his throat. Blood spurted everywhere and he was quite dead. As she watched, he fell slowly to the littered floor. In her hand she was clutching the bent little sixpence that had glittered at her feet.

"I believe I'd carry it, too," Jerry agreed. "I'm only surprised that she's let go—"

We were up from the basement of that branch of the Smithsonian and pushing out a side door into the heavy hot air of Washington, DC, on an August noon. He was holding the door and we were on the sidewalk when his words cut off sharply. He knew from my face that Mother was dead. She had given me the sixpence two years before when she knew her time was almost gone. I've always been bitter that her doctor didn't tell me the truth, that he connived with her to keep me in ignorance. Because there were weekends I had not come home from college to see her, and I would have come if only I had known.

I blinked against the bright Washington sunlight and reached out impulsively to touch his hand. "It's all right. She laughed when she gave it to me and said it was my turn to have a talisman, that it had only failed her once." It was my turn to break off. I wasn't going to tell this bony-faced stranger everything in my life this hot summer day. Not that the little sixpence had fallen from her purse once at an airfield and a young American had helped her find it, the young man who would be my father and who would fly until the day nine years later when his plane slammed into a North Korean mountainside. After his death, Mother put away the sixpence and only brought it out years later to give to me.

I knew in my heart that she had not actually believed it had magical properties—though there was a strain of Irish in my mother's blood—but it had saved her once and brought her my father, and it was something real she could give me and there was little enough of that. Something to remember her by, to remember her gay blue eyes and the courage and good humor that never failed her, even when my father was killed.

She once told me, "If you survived the Blitz, you can survive anything."

So I smiled up at the straw-haired young man. "It's

just a coin, really." I dropped the sixpence into my purse and stepped back a pace from him, showing that I was making no claim on his time, that this pleasant interlude was over. "Thanks so much for helping find it. How do they put it? It has great sentimental value." I held out my hand to him.

He ignored it, tugged at my elbow, and pulled me along with him. "You haven't had lunch."

Since his lecture had started at ten, obviously I hadn't lunched. "No."

"Let's go eat."

I don't remember what we ate or where. It was a small café. He discovered before we had half finished our sandwiches that this was my first trip to Washington and I hadn't had time to see more than the White House and two branches of the Smithsonian. So we downed our iced tea in a gulp and he took me on a tour of Washington.

We walked for miles. It was hot, as only that beautiful city can be hot in August, but the sky was vividly blue, the buildings a gleaming, shining white. He knew his Washington so I saw it not only as it is today but as it was when it first began. Then the White House sat in a naked field overlooking the Potomac and the half-built Capitol was visible a mile and a half away across a swamp. We tramped all the way from the Capitol to the White House on Pennsylvania Avenue (it was still a dirt road in Lincoln's day), and Jerry explained why the Treasury Building butted into the famous street, preventing the clear view from Capitol Hill to the White House that had been L'Enfant's intent. President Andrew Jackson was so irritated about the wrangling over the department's site that, when badgered while out waking one day, he had banged down his sword cane and said, "Right here!" and that's where the Treasury now stands.

We ended up in Georgetown and along the way I learned quite a bit about Jerry Elliot: ". . . came to Georgetown on a scholarship. I'm the sixth of seven in a long line of scholarly but poor Elliots. My dad teaches at Western Reserve and . . ."

He showed me many of the famous beautiful houses of the small and elegant district, the Dumbarton House on Q Street, where Dolley Madison sought refuge, clutching state papers and a portrait of Washington, when the British burned the White House in 1814, and the townhouse on N Street where John Kennedy and his young family lived when he started his presidential campaign.

". . . always spot the early Federal architecture by the fanlight over the front door and the long lintel stones above the windows. The brick is bright red and the shutters . . ."

I managed to keep up with his long strides and his swiftly paced, eager descriptions. It was a hot, exhausting, but exciting afternoon.

It ended as abruptly as it had begun.

We were standing outside a Georgetown bookstore, looking through the rack of old dusty ten-cents-each books, because, of course, you never know, when he looked through the shop window, saw a clock, and exclaimed, "Oh, good grief!"

He glanced up at the sky and the late-afternoon sun confirmed the time. "Hey, Sheila, I'm sorry; I've got to rush. I'm supposed to make a presentation to an old professor of mine and I'm almost late."

A cab was stopping two doors down and he hurried toward it, calling back over his shoulder, "I'll look for you at the banquet tonight."

I waved after him.

Tonight I would be on the train to New York.

But I didn't mind his abrupt leave-taking. I wandered slowly out of Georgetown, tired but smiling. It had been a marvelous afternoon.

It was a long way from the sharp sound of shots and blood seeping into the rich green grass of the jungle. It was a world away from murder.

2

That should have been the end of it. In my neat and tidy fashion, that week was catalogued as past, done, finished. But, at odd moments, I would see his face so vividly that I almost felt if I were to look around he would be standing there. Once, in fact, the feeling that he was near was so intense that I deserted a group I was leading through the first gallery with its Old Kingdom exhibits, tossing a hurried "Excuse me, please" over my shoulder and chasing around a model of the Sphinx to catch up with a slender, bony man who turned in surprise at my hand on his sleeve—and of course, it wasn't Jerry at all. I had hurried back to my patient group, my face flushed with embarrassment, and tried to pick up my spiel where I'd dropped it. As I led them through the galleries, answering questions, describing art and customs and manners, I was amused at myself. What is up, Sheila?

I managed for a full week to squelch any light-minded memories of Washington, dwelling instead on other sessions I had attended there. I finished my report on the conference and made no mention of Dr. Elliot and his topic. I had myself well in hand.

Then I received my quarterly copy of *Expedition* and there he was, or at least a thumbnail picture of him, with an article on "Plunder and the Art Trade." I studied the small biographical sketch. It didn't tell much about him, only his degrees, his publications, and his formal title with the museum in Mexico City.

Mexico City.

It might as well be Bangkok or Calcutta. That was the first thought that came into my mind and a very revealing one.

I had never in my life deliberately set out to place myself within the ambit of any man, and here I was, admitting that I would like to go to Mexico City to see him again. On the strength of what? An afternoon.

There was no danger on my following through on that wild inclination, however. I didn't have an extra penny. Literally. I could write an article on "Penury and the Museum Game." There are a lot more willing workers than jobs. To the delight of most museums, there are hordes (I see them in my mind, exquisitely dressed, artistically coifed) of well-educated, well-to-do women who are delighted to volunteer their time. This practice, of course, cuts down on the number of paying jobs. The jobs that offer a salary pay the least possible amount because most museum directors are much more interested in beefing up their exhibits than in fattening their staff.

Ideally, to work for a museum and live, you also need to teach, have a working spouse or independent means, or write for money.

I don't qualify so I'm genteelly poor, which means that every cent of my income is allocated to meet expenses—rent, food, insurance, et cetera. There isn't any give. Anywhere.

In this swinging age, it is possible to fly now and pay later, but my mother, in addition to a trace of Irish, had a broad stripe of Scot, and I learned early that it is immoral to spend money you don't have. As for borrowing, that is the work of the Devil.

So I settled down to work and stopped mooning about. I had plenty to do. There is always plenty to do in a big museum. I was working up an exhibit to be trucked around the state to high schools, trying to refine a radio script into an allotted five minutes, and, in my spare time, making an item-by-item inventory of a storeroom, which is much more complicated than it sounds. Also, since I was the low woman on the totem pole, I was the natural recipient of all stray tasks bucked downward by my superiors—that is, entertain generous donors, prod suppliers into delivering the new shipment of acrylics, compile a weekly summary of scholarly publications, train volunteer guides, block out the basic copy for a new guidebook, and on and on.

Every day there was something new and unexpected and challenging. But the trip to Washington, DC, did make a difference in my life in the museum and it was to be a profound one.

I began to visit the pre-Columbian wing. I won't go so far as to say I haunted the place, but I went often enough to meet my opposite number in that section, Timothy Simmons. It was fun to have a new friend, to hear gossip about august section chairmen, to be a little scandalized by Timothy's irreverence.

All innocent fun, and, too, I was learning something about Jerry Elliot's field, beginning to understand some of the Mesoamerican cultures.

It never occurred to me when I first walked up the stairs to the Mesoamerican floor, my sandals slapping lightly on the worn marble steps, that the entire direction of my life would be affected by those visits, by the manner in which that section's secretary sorted the morning mail, and by the readiness of one member of that staff to seize on a particular set of circumstances, betting his future and my life, on a wild, inside-straight, one-card-draw kind of gamble.

One morning late in November, I wandered slowly through the Olmec room. That was when I met Timothy.

"Lost a sarcophagus?"

I had thought the room empty so I jumped a little, then

smiled into friendly brown eyes. Before I could answer, he held out his hand. "I'm Timothy Simmons, and you're the new girl among the wonders of the Nile. Right?"

That was the start of our friendship. Soon, I would hurry up the stairs or he would come down my way at least once a day and we would share our lowly assistants' view of our world. Timothy was, no doubt about it, a bad influence, but it's possible to take a job too seriously and I knew I had been a little intense about this one. I was feminine enough, careful enough, never to forget that a malicious coffee-break companion is not one to be trusted with any words you wouldn't want repeated.

Timothy accused me of as much one day. "Sheila, you must break out of the mold or the visitors won't be able to tell you from the mummies."

I laughed. "I'm not that old and desiccated yet, Timothy."

"No, but you are too deadly damn serious and reverent about all of it. You know as well as I do that Hadley's barely better than a hack and Lassiter's a pompous ass."

I covered his mouth with a hand. "Hush, Timothy, they may not be much but they are senior staff." Then I was suddenly serious. "And that's not true about Dr. Hadley. Or Dr. Lassiter, either." I put my head on one side and studied Timothy's darkly frowning face. "Do you know, Tim, I don't understand you. Why did you work hard enough to get a museum job if you don't like it? I mean, what do you want out of it all?"

He stared at me and his brown eyes were, for the moment, neither malicious nor sardonic but blazingly alive and hungry and angry.

"What do I want?" He wasn't looking at me, wasn't seeing me at all. "I want to find a fantastic ruin like Stephenson or Thompson." He took a deep, hard breath. "But that takes more money or influence than I'll ever have."

"Your chance will come in time."

His mouth curled in a smile that wasn't a smile at all.

I reached across the table to touch his hand. "I mean it. You're good. I'm sure you are. You'll win recognition, be asked to head an expedition."

He jammed a hand through his thick black hair. "When? Twenty years from now? Thirty? When I'm an old man? I ought to have an expedition now."

So that was what made Timothy run. It explained his bitter humor and sharp criticisms. He was too impatient to inch his way up a rung at a time, an article here, an outstanding display there, a book eventually—the steady accomplishments that would win acclaim. I wanted to urge him to be patient and respectful, to do what he needed to do. But I didn't because his eyes were too dark, too hungry, too angry.

We were better friends after that and sometimes he dropped his mocking manner and patiently explained a new display to me. I began to gain an appreciation of the multifaceted cultures of Mexico. I always felt a little uncomfortable among the brooding inhuman sculptures of the Toltecs, but I loved the beauty and skill of the Mixtec jewelry. I even admitted the Aztec feathered headdresses were magnificent, though I didn't tell Timothy how loathsome I found the Aztec blood and death cult.

He liked to tease me.

"Do you know about the Flower Wars?"

"Flower Wars," I repeated, thinking, of course, of flowers. His eyes glinted with amusement as he explained how the finest warriors, the flower of manhood, would be captured to be sacrificed to the insatiable bloodthirst of Huitzilopochtli, the Aztec war god.

I knew that the Aztecs were Johnnies-come-lately to the central plateau of Mexico and that it was they who had subverted human sacrifice into a monstrous bloodletting. It shocked me that the Aztecs were, of all the tribes, Timothy's favorite.

I asked him once, "Timothy, why do you like the Aztecs so well? Their temples actually smelled of blood."

His answer came slowly and once again I glimpsed the true Timothy, the mind that hid itself behind jibes and jokes.

"It's the very perfection, the full circle of their culture that fascinates me, Sheila. It was so simple to them. The more sacrifices, the more blood they offered to the gods, the more they prospered. Until the Spaniards came, they never doubted that those sacrificed hearts were cause and effect. It is fascinating to see how a people's entire rationale can be reasonable and yet wrong. It proves, you see, that instinct can't be trusted, that empirical judgments can be absolutely wrong." Then he laughed and asked slyly, "Now, tell me, doesn't it make you question even a little bit some of our verities?"

I wondered what Jerry Elliot would think of this appraisal.

But Jerry was becoming a little dimmer in my memory with each day that passed. I had no positive idea what his response would be because I didn't know the man. I just thought I might like to know him.

I didn't actually pay too much attention to all that Timothy and I talked about. So much of it was frivolous, unimportant.

Later, when it became important to remember everything he had told me about his department, I only remembered snatches, odd bits of fact or fancy, not nearly enough to help when it mattered.

Later, I would try hard to recall exactly what he had said about the nut mail. I remember being chagrined when I discovered that he, unlike I, did not have to handle all of it for his department.

Nut mail. All museums receive it. Practically every day. You know the kind of thing—the writer knows the hiding place of a treasure to rival Tutankhamen's or has a map that will prove the Vikings reached Texas.

Some of contents are only mildly nutty. Someone wants to know how many rune stones have been found. Or who invented barbed wire. Or insists Shakespeare didn't exist. There is never any guessing what the next mail delivery will bring. In many departments, certainly in mine, the youngest, newest member of the staff is tapped to answer all such letters. I had, in my short time at the museum, answered some lulus. So I was outraged when Timothy showed no sympathy at my complaints and, instead, jibed that it was only another proof that New World civilizations were superior to the old in all respects, including the manner in which their departments were run. In the Mesoamerican section, all staff members took turns with the nut mail.

It was such an inconsequential conversation to later matter so much.

I did remember very clearly the spring morning, a Friday in April, that I wearied of my work, the final listing of all items in Storeroom 3-B, and pushed back my chair in my tiny office and decided to go find Timothy. I felt in need of cheer.

Instead, I walked right into the midst of a first-class row.

Unfortunately, the doors that screen staff sections from the museum display areas fit perfectly. I don't suppose the rattle of a jackhammer would filter through into the sacred precincts of the collections. I had no warning, no chance to slink gracefully away as one would from a family quarrel when a guest was in the house.

I opened the door labeled MESOAMERICAN SECTION and found myself in the middle of an old-fashioned shoot out. All it lacked was guns.

I stepped into a reception area opposite a conference room. The conference room was open. I saw a table and a circle of faces. Standing in the conference room doorway, a letter clutched in his hand, was the section director, Dr. Rodriguez. He was frowning after the man who was stalking up the hall, his back straight and angry.

"Karl," Dr. Rodriguez called, "I'm sure there was no intent to be disrespectful."

Karl Freidheim, second in the department, swung around and glared at Rodriguez. "It is an insult. They have no right to do this."

Dr. Rodriguez's reply was stiff. "They have every right. I agree that it is thoughtless of them to ask for the manuscript's return before you have completed your analysis. But we must remember that the manuscript belongs to the Ortega family. If they wish for the material to be returned, it must be returned."

Freidheim's blunt face, one cheek disfigured by a scar, was rigid with fury. He grimaced, turned away, barged into his office and slammed the door.

Dr. Rodriguez shook his head tiredly.

I was, as unobtrusively as possible, opening the door out into the main hall. Just as I slipped through, Dr. Rodriguez noticed me and looked inquiring, but I kept right on going. Five lions couldn't have pulled me back in there.

All the way to the museum's basement café, I was thinking gratefully how charming almost everyone was in Egyptology. Even those who weren't charming were certainly civil. Good grief, what an uncomfortable place the Mesoamerican section must be to work in.

I said as much to Timothy when he joined me a few minutes later. But he thought the whole scene hilarious, which made Timothy himself seem less than charming to me. He was obviously delighted by the quarrel between the two men. He took great pleasure in recounting it.

"That bastard Freidheim—it's time someone knocked him down. He's always leaning on everybody. It's fun to see him thwarted. You should have seen his face when Rodriguez told him the manuscript had to be returned."

"What's it all about?"

"Some rich Mexicans loaned Freidheim a valuable manuscript dating from early Colonial days. They wrote this week and said they wanted it back pronto and they wanted it hand delivered. Our Teutonic friend is beside himself. He hasn't finished with the manuscript; plus he likes to give orders, not get them. In his view, it's adding insult to injury to insist that someone bring the manuscript hat in hand."

Timothy laughed out loud. I shushed him when others in the café turned to look at us. But he wouldn't be shamed.

I didn't seek him out for coffee for more than a week. When he dropped by my office, he was at his most charming. He didn't mention the manuscript and the trouble it had caused and neither did I.

Oddly enough, I never connected the manuscript with

the notice that appeared a week later on the staff bulletin board in the main office. This bulletin board, which every museum employee probably passed at least once a day, is a hodgepodge of miscellany: brochures announcing conferences, notices offering items for sale, letters from staff members visiting afar. Anything and everything that might be of interest.

I saw this particular notice immediately. The all-capital first line couldn't have attracted me more quickly if it had flashed alternately red and green.

FREE TRIP MEXICO CITY

Wanted: Reliable person to deliver package.
Inquire: Museum ext. 41.

I was back at my desk, my hand on my telephone, in less than two minutes.

Just for an instant, I hesitated.

Surely, this was not I, Sheila Ramsay, pursuing, literally, a man I had met but once?

I dialed extension 41. I had been sensible all my life, every day in every way. Why shouldn't I go to Mexico City?

The phone was answered on the second ring.

"Freidheim here."

Again I hesitated. That bastard Freidheim, Timothy

had called him. But what difference did it make to me, the personalities in the Mesoamerican section?

"This is Sheila Ramsay. In Egyptology. I wanted to inquire about the notice, the trip to Mexico City."

"Ah yes, very good." There was only the slightest hint of gut in his pronunciation. "Let me see." He paused.

I waited, breath held, sure he would say he was sorry but I was calling too late. It was only then, as my fingers gripped the phone, that I knew how badly I wanted to go.

"Miss Ramsay"—and I was impressed that he retained my name—"I can meet with you at three this afternoon. Is that agreeable to you?"

"Yes, of course."

It was a quarter to ten. Time crept. But when, at last, it was ten minutes to three and I left my office and began to walk toward the Mesoamerican wing, my steps lagged.

Did I really want to chase thousands of miles after a man I had met only once? An abrasive, quick-tempered man. But his smile was unexpectedly likeable, and life would never be dull near him.

Besides, I lied to myself, it committed me to nothing to go to Mexico City. After all, I needn't even go see him. I wouldn't even think of that until I was there. I knocked on Dr. Freidheim's door and entered on command.

I'm not good, really, at meeting people. Especially not people like Dr. Freidheim. I took one look at him and immediately felt possessed of three left feet. I stumbled

31

as I sat down in the chair in front of his desk and, worst of all, felt my face flame with embarrassment. When you are sandy-haired and freckled a red face is noticeable.

He was big. Even sitting behind a desk, he looked big, heavy shouldered, huge handed. But it was his eyes that caught and held my attention, Alpine blue eyes that looked as cold and bright as a shallow lake on a winter day. His blond hair, well mixed with white, was cut short. He would have looked at home on a ski slope or in a financier's office or in a yellowing photograph from World War II.

It was a strained interview.

Very quickly he elicited a summary of my past, where I was born, my schooling, jobs, family background.

I was aware throughout that he either didn't like me or my answers or the interview itself. He was abrupt, cold, and very nearly rude.

Then came the question I had dreaded.

"Do you speak Spanish, Miss Ramsay?"

I shook my head apologetically. "No, I'm afraid not, Dr. Freidheim. I speak French and some German, but no Spanish."

"German," he repeated.

I could tell nothing from his face. It gave no hint how he judged me. He straightened the page upon which he had made notes as we talked.

"Interest has been expressed by several persons in making the trip, Miss Ramsay." He smiled, a humorless smile that did not reach those icy blue eyes. "Something for nothing is always attractive, am I right?"

I felt suddenly grasping and small. He was right, of course. The trip was a freebie on a giant scale and I had always prided myself on having too much style to go to openings for free baubles.

He looked down at the sheet then, viciously, gouged a check mark at the bottom of the page with his pen.

I shrank a little in my chair.

"I will check your background," he said curtly, rustling the paper. "We must, you understand, have someone who is responsible."

I nodded quickly, not understanding any of it.

"The return of the manuscript has been ordered." He glared at me. "I am not finished with my study of it."

If there was a reply to make, I couldn't think of it.

"The Ortegas," he continued, and the name was ugly on his lips, "have insisted that the manuscript be returned. Dr. Rodriguez says there must be a reason. But they have not given it."

I nodded again, mutely, finally realizing that the trip was part and parcel of the angry scene I had stumbled into.

A muscle twitched in his scarred cheek. "The manuscript belongs to them so we must return it. But I will not permit a member of this department to carry it to them."

"I see," I said tentatively.

"It is an insult, you understand."

I had no idea who was insulting whom, but I could tell well enough that Dr. Freidheim had worked it out in his own mind that sending a museum employee from another section took some of the sting out of having to return the manuscript.

"It is one of the few extant documents from the period directly following the Conquest so it is highly prized, you understand."

I leaned forward in my chair, curious to see what might make it possible for me to go to Mexico.

He pushed back his chair and stood. Turning, he lifted down a leather-bound book from a shelf behind his desk. Covered in protective plastic, the book was massive—a foot in width, a foot and a quarter in length, and several inches thick. His huge hands touched it gently. He laid the book on a nearby table and began turning its golden-toned vellum pages.

As Freidheim spoke, I learned a good deal about its author, one Father Sanchez, and his work among the *indios*, as the Spaniards called the natives. Freidheim described the priest's work among his charges, how he had learned Nahuatl—the Aztec language—and translated many codices, the painted fig-bark books in which the Aztecs wrote their histories.

I also laid to rest, as Freidheim droned on and on, the niggling little worry about the advisability of accepting free passage anywhere, a carryover from those long-ago days when I was warned never to accept a ride from strangers.

What could be safer, more respectable than serving as a messenger for my museum?

3

One week passed, then a second. The chill days of April slipped into the teasing warmth of May.

I would hope, and then I would despair. One moment I would feel confident that Dr. Freidheim would be impressed with my respectable background. The next I would be sure that he wouldn't even seriously consider an applicant who didn't speak Spanish.

Just in case, I scurried about, got my clothes clean, checked on getting a tourist card, even bought (an extravagance) a new spring coat. It was, the guidebooks assured, eternal spring in Mexico City.

I avoided Timothy for a full week, and then, when he ran me down and we went for coffee, I confessed all in one breath.

"I don't blame you if it makes you mad. After all, a trip like this should go to someone in the department, but when I saw the notice on the board, I couldn't resist trying for it."

He was surprised. "It never occurred to me that you'd try to go."

"I'm sorry, Timothy—" I began, but he held up his hands.

"It's fine with me," he interrupted. "Don't worry about it. It's no skin off my nose if you get the gold ring. Freidheim would see us all in hell before he'd let any member of the department make the trip."

"Why? That doesn't make sense."

"It doesn't," Timothy replied, "but Freidheim thinks it will put the Ortegas down if just any old museum employee lugs it back. No one else sees it that way but Rodriguez is going along with it because it soothes Freidheim."

Then he said, almost uncertainly, "But I never expected—I mean, I'm surprised you checked into the notice. Why do you want to go to Mexico City?"

I drank a big gulp of iced tea. I would never, of course, admit to Timothy why I wanted to make the trip. But the questions caught me unprepared.

"I don't know exactly," I said. "It's time for my vacation and I didn't have anything special planned and it sounds like fun."

He frowned. "I kind of wish . . ." he said slowly, then he ended in a rush, "It's not really the kind of place for a woman traveling alone. It's a huge city, millions, and it's always open season on a woman alone."

"Why, Timothy," I said, smiling, "I can't believe it's you talking. I didn't know you harbored such male chauvinist views. I'll have you know it's a brave new world out there. If I wanted to, I'd go to Tibet alone if somebody would offer to pay my way."

He laughed. "So you have a streak of adventure. Well, so be it."

I didn't see Timothy again the next week. When the week was almost done, I began to lose what little hope I still had that I might be the lucky one. After all, why should Freidheim choose me?

It was Thursday afternoon when I answered my phone and recognized his faintly guttural voice.

"Freidheim here. Are you still interested in the trip to Mexico City, Miss Ramsay?"

It was like winning the sweepstakes or graduating cum laude or seeing for a fabulous instant the shimmer of a rainbow.

"Oh yes, Dr. Freidheim."

"Good. You said when we talked that you had vacation coming. If it is agreeable with your department, I will obtain your tickets and you can leave Monday."

"Monday."

"Is that not convenient?"

"That will be fine."

It was arranged that I should come to the museum

Monday morning and pick up the boxed manuscript and my plane ticket.

Just before he rang off, Dr. Freidheim said brusquely, "You have been invited to stay with the Ortegas while you are in Mexico City. I assume that is agreeable to you?"

There is nothing quite as unattractive as the gaping spread when a gift horse opens its mouth.

I hesitated and, before I could answer, he continued. "It would not be polite to decline the invitation."

"Oh, of course not," I said hurriedly. "But wouldn't it be an imposition?"

"Not at all. The Ortegas are a very old and wealthy family. The house is large and quite easily accommodates guests." He paused, then said, "It would be very interesting to know why the return of the manuscript was requested. Although," he added quickly, "you must certainly not ask."

"I won't ask."

"It is settled then."

If I stayed with the Ortegas, I wouldn't have to use my slender resources for a hotel room and, of course, it would be very interesting to stay in a Mexican home.

I wondered over the weekend if Timothy would call to wish me luck. He didn't, and I didn't call him. I didn't see him on Monday morning when I picked up the manuscript, but I thought it was as well because he couldn't help but be jealous over my trip.

It was on the bus out to Kennedy that I realized that the

manuscript, packaged in a cumbersome Styrofoam container, was going to be an unwieldy and exhausting burden. It took both arms around it to carry the oblong box; plus I had to manage a lumpy manila envelope containing the papers proving Mexican ownership, and my purse.

I almost didn't make it past the first screening table at Kennedy.

Since everything carried aboard an airliner must be searched, Freidheim had tied the box shut with nylon cord in neat bows that could be pulled and retied.

I was, after my final brief talk with him, aware of just how valuable and irreplaceable the manuscript was and what a grave responsibility I had accepted.

When the guard yanked the bow, I said sharply, "Please, be very careful."

His hand jerked back from the cord. Before I could say another word, I was staring at the small black hole in the barrel of his automatic.

I don't know which of us was the more frightened. His hand, holding the gun, shook. I held up equally shaking hands.

"Please, there's nothing wrong with the box." I didn't dare say that prohibited word, or I might end up in jail before my trip even began. I tried again. "It's an extremely valuable old book. I asked you to be careful because it is very old, very delicate. Look, I'll open it for you."

He waggled the gun at me as I started to lower my hands.

I promptly raised them again.

We finally straightened it out, but I came within a quarter hour of missing my plane. The other passengers eyed me strangely and my day certainly lost its original fine savor.

However, the rest of the trip, except for my continuing tussle with the awkward box, was a lot of fun. I'd never flown often and only once as far. When I was fourteen Mother and I went to England, my first trip, her last.

It was evening when we reached Mexico City. I don't think I will ever again be so caught up in the magic of flying into a huge metropolis as I was that spring evening. The sky was clear. A pale quarter moon hung low on the horizon. Stars glittered in the night sky, but they didn't gleam and glisten with half the sparkle of the millions of lights that spread across the valley floor as the plane curved in to land. No diamonds in a tiara could match the breath-catching beauty of those millions of glittering, twinkling lights.

I had filled out the customs form on the plane. The manuscript was the only item of value that I carried. But, of course, it was very valuable so I wasn't surprised when the customs officer studied my form, looked at the letters of authorization I carried, frowned at my passport, and then said politely, "Señorita, if you will please be seated, this may take a little moment."

I didn't worry about the eventual outcome. After all, I had the proper papers and I had, too, the stature and respectability of my museum behind me. But I knew it would probably take more than a little moment.

The customs and immigration area was quite utilitarian. Polite inspectors sat behind wooden desks and briskly funneled passengers through. Soon I was the only passenger left. The area was restricted to incoming passengers and Mexican officials. Those waiting for arriving travelers had to stay beyond the exit in the airport proper. This exit was a wide doorway. When we had first arrived, there was a crowd bunched beyond the exit, waiting for travelers to clear customs. As the passengers passed through, the crowd dwindled until there was just one man standing there. He was in a uniform of sorts, black pants, white shirt, and black-billed cap. When I looked at him he lifted his hand to his cap. When I made no response, he looked worried, then looked past me and called out to one of the officials.

The man behind the desk listened politely enough and then turned to look at me. He frowned, slowly got out of this chair, crossed the room, and found the official who was holding my papers and passport and the box. Again, there was a rapid flurry of conversation.

I regretted the day I had chosen French over Spanish. What was going on? What were they talking about? What were they saying?

I was standing now, clutching my purse, too intent upon this colloquy that I knew concerned me to feign polite indifference. Finally, the two officials stopped talking. One turned and walked toward the door and the man who waited there. When he was even with me and saw my openly worried face, he paused. "Señorita Ramsay?"

I nodded.

"The chauffeur who is here to meet you"—and he pointed toward the man waiting on the doorway—"was afraid when you did not come through customs that he had missed you."

I looked toward the doorway and the chauffeur smiled.

A huge feeling of relief swept over me. It was wonderful to know that I wouldn't have to struggle out into the night, armed only with an address. I thanked the official, who smiled kindly at me, and settled back to wait.

There was nothing to do but watch the doorway. The passing scene was very entertaining. At one point, a haughty family group, everyone dressed in black, moved by, walking as though no one near them even existed. A lissome girl in a tiny miniskirt swayed past. A very drunk American, prosperous in a flashy way, leaned heavily on his companion, a streaked blonde who had been traveling for too many years.

Although I was watching that doorway closely, I almost didn't see the man in the shadow. I don't know how long he had stood there just to the left of the door before I noticed him. I think his immobility attracted my eye.

Everything else moved and there was an unending vivid stream of color past that open doorway and the half-heard tantalizing murmur of a language I didn't speak. I loved the sound of Spanish, though, liquid, rolling, and soft.

I saw the watching figure only for an instant. He stood in profile to me and I glimpsed his face and shoulder. I had only a fleeting look at him for when our eyes met, they held for a tiny space of time, and then he was gone. I stared, wondering if someone had actually stood there, as still and poised as a watching animal, or if it had been a trick of light and shadow.

I had an impression of power and strength, a force to be reckoned with. Yet all I had seen was a half-glimpsed profile, a high cheekbone and broad jaw. It was only as I stared where that face had been that a picture formed in my mind's eye and I saw straight black hair, a flaring sideburn, taut coppery skin, a jaw that jutted forward. Then that vivid momentary picture faded.

Still I stared at the now empty place. I blinked and rubbed my eyes. I was very tired. Impatiently, I turned to look at the official who held my papers. I saw him, my passport in his hand, talking on the telephone. How long now? I wondered.

I looked back at the doorway but listlessly now. It was beginning to be the same old story, travelers and porters, bursts of noise and movement, periods of quiet. That face that I had glimpsed (imagined so briefly?) was nowhere to be seen.

I don't know how long it was, five minutes, perhaps ten,

when a man passed the doorway, moving with the quiet grace of a big cat. He gave the customs room a cursory glance, an offhand, almost disinterested glance.

I wasn't fooled. I knew him immediately. This was the face that had watched me intently from the shadow, disappeared quickly when I noticed.

It was his very nonchalance, his studied indifference that heralded a warning. That atavistic sense that lies near the surface stirred, warning: Danger near, danger.

I kept my face as bland, as disinterested as his. I looked at him briefly, almost as if I didn't see him. But I saw and I would remember. A dark face, black eyebrows that slashed sharply upward, a thin tough mouth, powerful shoulders.

When he was past, I sat in that red leatherette chair with every nerve end alert, watchful, poised to react. Five minutes passed, twenty. Still that sense of danger throbbed within me. But he didn't come back.

I was so absorbed in watching the doorway that the official had to call my name twice before I heard. I went to the desk hesitantly, hating to turn my back to that doorway. My feeling of unease colored that interview. I felt that the customs official was eyeing me too carefully, too closely. This, in turn, made me stiff and awkward. He led me into a separate office where he painstakingly filled out three separate forms and showed me where to sign on each, which I did a little hesitantly—they all were in Spanish and I had no idea what I was signing. A confession to a double ax-murder? The smuggling of gold? The over-throw of the government?

Finally, though, he nodded in satisfaction and we were finished. I received my passport, papers, box, and suit-case. I thanked the official. He listened and finally, grudg-ingly, unsmilingly, he nodded.

I felt rebuffed. Then I decided my imagination was going overtime. I'm frightened by a man who walks past a doorway. I see a change of attitude because an official doesn't smile.

I was walking toward the doorway, finally free, and then I stopped to turn and smile farewell to my official because I had, undoubtedly, put him to a lot of extra work. But the smile never reached my lips. The official was watching me go and his eyes were suspicious and cold.

Hurriedly, I swung around and moved to the doorway where the chauffeur was waiting. He at least was smiling as he took my suitcase. Once out in the bustle of the airport proper, things seemed more normal and my trip once again took on a holiday glow.

While the chauffeur went for the car, I exchanged some traveler's checks, then went out to the sidewalk. I was watching travelers, listening to the soft murmur of Span-ish, when there was a tug on my arm. I looked down in surprise.

A shoeshine boy, barefoot, raggedly dressed, held out an envelope to me.

I shook my head. Whatever it was, I didn't want any.

"Por favor, señorita, para usted." He thrust the white envelope into my hand.

I looked down at the envelope, but it was empty of inscription. When I looked for him to hand it back, he was gone. Just then a horn sounded lightly and a cream-colored Mercedes pulled up to the curb and I recognized the chauffeur.

I looked again for the boy but nowhere did I see his sharp little face or ragged shorts. The chauffeur was holding the door for me now. I hesitated.

"Señorita," the chauffeur said.

The boy obviously had made a mistake, I thought, shrugging. It couldn't be very important, an envelope without a name on it. I dropped the envelope into my purse and stepped into the car.

Even though it was night, I saw enough of Mexico City to fall in love with it as the heavy, quiet car sped down broad boulevards. There were the trappings of a metropolis—industry and tumbledown tenements and faceless apartment developments—but there were also glimpses of colonial churches and tiled roofs and iron-grilled gates and balconies. The car would swing around a gardened circle in the middle of a street, the headlights briefly caressing an iron horse in its eternal gallop, giving an illusion of movement and life.

But nothing in what I saw or what little I knew of Mexico prepared me for the Jardines del Pedregal where the Ortega family lived.

I was peering through the window to my left at a huge amphitheater when the Mercedes slowed and turned off the main road.

Suddenly we were swinging down a wide, quiet street. In the spaced light of the street lamps, I saw an architectural wonderland. Although Mexican homes stand secure behind walls or iron fences, I could see enough to be exhilarated by the artistry that had combined nature's handiwork with man's. Everywhere great jagged black clumps of volcanic stone thrust up in every imaginable shape. On these primeval humps spread graceful soaring houses that seemed to breathe a spirit of freedom. Take your old ideas, they seemed to say, we've none of them here. Whatever man can imagine can be built.

The street curved and turned. The Mercedes, a twentieth-century creation, moved as a rightful inhabitant of this utterly modern world. Yet, even as I thought it, I knew these beautiful homes were neither old nor new but timeless in a way I was to find typical of Mexico. There is always the past, yes, the vivid lingering blood-and-bone substance of Mexico, but there is also a freedom of spirit, a willingness to experiment that forbids the boring, the colorless, and the imitative.

But this first evening, I had much yet to see and absorb. I only knew I was in a magical country.

The Mercedes slowed at the end of the block and turned into a drive of sultry pink stone. A high stone wall, spike-topped and covered with vines, curved away from a highly ornamented bronze gate. The car paused as the gates pulled apart, slowly, silently. I knew it had to be triggered by some sort of electric apparatus but it all seemed a part of the exotic turn the night had taken, the sleek expensive car, the mansions so secure on their lava outcroppings. Then the gates were open and the Mercedes nosed through.

I leaned forward, eager now for my first glimpse of the Ortega home. The car purred up the pink stone drive.

I looked back over my shoulder as the driveway began to curve. I don't know just why. The tall spiked gates were closing, smoothly, noiselessly. I saw the two halves meet and lock, and, just for a moment, I felt a sudden plunging breathlessness.

There was no turning back now.

4

I felt ill at ease in the blue tiled entryway, clutching the cumbersome Styrofoam box, terribly aware of the travel wrinkles in my dress, overwhelmed by the elegance of this walled and gated home.

A cool and airy hall stretched ahead to a wide stone stairway. Opening off the hall to my left was a huge room with wicker furniture, a billiards table, and a square swimming pool whose underwater lights illuminated emerald green water.

Straight down the hall I looked up at the open second floor that seemed to float behind a balcony hung with exquisitely woven rugs, bright red patterned on white, vivid blue on gray.

To the right of the hall another great shadowy room opened. In its center was one of the longest dining tables I had ever seen and, even from this distance, I could recognize the massive grace of a refectory table. Gilt-framed paintings hung on the walls.

The only sound was the whishing murmur of water slashing softly in the fountain near the base of stone steps that led up to the balcony. The fountain and the gleaming green swimming pool and the wide shadowy expanse of the huge rooms created a feeling of enchantment as if I were in the heart of a great forest amid trees so tall and so thickly leaved that all beneath was dim and quiet.

I stood very still scarcely daring to breath, I felt so much an intruder. Quiet as I was, I did not hear the woman coming. Rather, I realized suddenly that I was not alone.

I looked toward the stairway, but it lay empty. I watched where the hall turned, just past the fountain. At the very edge of my vision, something moved. I whirled around to stare into the dimness of the shadowy dining room.

I watched her cross that great space and I was surprised. She was not what I would have expected in this house. I felt for a moment that I was a child again and I could almost smell the disinfectant they had used to swab the school halls, and I remembered so clearly the mother superior, her face pale beneath her cowl, and the way her black habit swayed as she walked and the sharp click of her black shoes on the marbled floor. Then, as the woman moved out of the darker shadows and the light from the hall touched her, the illusion vanished. I saw a middle-aged woman, dressed, it is true, all in black but not the flowing lines of a habit—though the shirt was full and did reach almost to the floor. She wore her hair in thick coronet braids and walked with her hands folded together.

But I felt my instincts weren't wrong. This woman did not belong to this house. It could not be Señora Ortega.

She walked up to me with a great dignity, her lined face unsmiling.

"Señorita Ramsay?"

I nodded, then began uncertainly, "Señora . . ."

"I am Maria, the housekeeper. Señora Ortega asked me to welcome you and to explain that she and the señor were very sorry to miss you. They waited a long time, but then they had to leave for a dinner."

I glanced down at my watch. It was almost eleven.

"I'm sorry to be late," I apologized. "I had some difficulty coming through customs."

Maria nodded gravely.

"The señora feared you would be very tired. Have you had dinner?"

"Yes. On the plane."

"Then, if you like, I will take you to your room. The señora said they would look forward to meeting you in the morning."

I followed Maria, still lugging the manuscript box.

Maria didn't ask for it and I felt it was my responsibility to deliver the book personally, although it appeared that the Ortegas were clearly in no great hurry to receive it.

I scolded myself for feeling irritated. Why should they alter their evening plans to greet a stranger, even one bearing a valued family possession? Besides, I was just as happy not to have to face meeting the owners of this rather overwhelming house tonight.

I followed Maria down the hall, past the fountain and up the wide stone steps. The balcony held a magnificent family living room with two wide fireplaces, soft thick carpets, a wall of reddish wood, books, Steuben glass, and a painting that I did not recognize but that had the power to catch and hold my eye for a long moment.

Maria moved at an even pace along the balcony railing to turn into a long hall. We passed a series of closed doors. I assumed they were bedrooms. She turned right into a narrower corridor. The plan of the house certainly wasn't clear in my mind, but I guessed that we had come around and were now above the room with the pool and the wicker furniture.

My guest room was lovely, even if impersonal. Maria showed me the adjoining bath and I learned how to use the electric heater. She did everything efficiently and quickly.

"Would you like for me to unpack for you, señorita?"

I was putting the box down on a window seat and turned

in surprise at her words, but yes, there was my suitcase, duly delivered, I suppose, by the chauffeur.

"No, thank you."

Then she was gone and I was, blessedly, alone. I sank down into a wicker chair near the window and just sat. I was too tired to do one single thing more, though the bed looked terribly inviting. Still, I sat.

The knock at my door was so soft I thought I'd imagined it. When it came again, I called out, "Yes."

The door opened and a dark girl about seventeen slipped in, smiled shyly at me, and set down a tray on a nearby table.

She said something in Spanish and I spread my hands to show I didn't understand.

She pantomimed pouring, and I shook my head. "No, but thank you. *Gracias*."

She nodded and turned to leave but at the door she paused, pointed at a button near the light switch, and once again spoke.

Again I shook my head.

She frowned, pointed at herself, then at the button. I nodded to show I understood, and she left.

I lifted up the lid of the pot she had left and sniffed. Hot chocolate. The plate held two sweet rolls. I suddenly felt a lot more welcome and cheerful. How thoughtful of Maria. I started to pour a cup and then decided I would really feel marvelous if I had a bath first. The chocolate would still be hot if I hurried.

Five minutes later, my skin warm and rosy from the bath, I curled up in the chair, comfortable in my gown and robe, and had a delightful midnight feast.

I was content as a cat, warm, full, clean. I flicked off the overhead light, leaving on the bedside lamp, and turned down the covers. I was sitting on the big bed, ready to snuggle beneath the cold sheets, when I remembered I had neglected to jot down the day's expenses in a small spiral notebook that I carried in my purse especially for that purpose.

I would do it tomorrow.

I rolled between the cold silk sheets, then reached out and pulled down the chain to switch off the bedside lamp.

What a marvelous, magnificent, comfortable bed. I closed my eyes and prepared to tumble into sleep.

I had, of course, vowed that I would keep each day's expense without fail because it is impossible to remember small items after several days pass. Stubbornly, I burrowed my face deeper into the pillow. Not surprisingly, my mind as stubbornly began to recite the day's expenditures: coffee at Kennedy, fifty cents; Gothic pocketbook, Kennedy, a dollar twenty-five; coffee, Dallas–Fort Worth, twenty-five cents . . .

Resignedly, I pushed back the covers, turned on the light, and sat up. My purse was across the room, atop the chest of drawers. I swung out of bed. The tile floor was cold to my bare feet. Hurrying, I ran across the room, scooped up the purse, and ran back to bed.

I fumbled inside my purse for the little spiral notebook. My fingers brushed against an envelope. For a moment, I was puzzled. I pulled it out and then I remembered the ragged shoeshine boy. I turned the envelope over. It was sealed. I studied the blank face again.

I felt that quick surge of discomfort that comes when you know you've done the wrong thing. This wasn't meant for me. I should have gone after the boy, found him, somehow made it clear that he had made a mistake.

What if this letter was important, really important to someone? I slipped my finger beneath the sealed flap, worked it loose. Perhaps, if it really mattered, I could find out for whom the message was meant. The addressee's name might well be in the salutation.

I looked at a cream-colored sheet of paper and at the words neatly printed in the center of the page.

GO BACK TO NEW YORK
OR DIE

After the first startled instant, I almost laughed. Almost, but not quite. There is nothing laughable about threats, even those made, I had to assume, in fun. I must have stumbled into the middle of someone's idea of a joke. People who wished others ill did not pass them notes in a schoolboy fashion. It could be nothing more than a rather unfunny joke.

But the joke was on the writer since I had interrupted

a message that couldn't be meant for me. I crumpled up the sheet and envelope and tossed them into the wastebasket. Then I fished the little account book out of my purse and dutifully made my entries.

Now, conscience at rest, I could sleep. I turned off the light, stretched happily in the luxuriously comfortable bed, and slipped swiftly into sleep, down, down, down, deep into thick, swirling, enveloping folds of sleep.

The cry cut sharply through my sleep.

I woke, heart pounding, eyes wide, straining to see through the unfamiliar dark. My hands gripped the thin silk sheet, pulling it tight against me as if to ward off danger.

For a terrifying instant, I did not know where I was. My sleep-dulled mind tried frantically to recognize the different shapes of darkness in the wide, shadowy room. Nothing was familiar, nothing, not the great heavy mass of darkness that loomed beside the bed, not the bed itself, not the strange slickness of silk sheets. A faint oblong luminescence to the left was surely a window but my bedroom window was to the right of the bed. Then I was fully awake and fumbling to turn on the bedside lamp and remembering that I was a guest in the Ortega home.

The elegant home in which someone screamed in the night.

I sat up in bed, the covers drawn close to me, and knew

I was waiting for that cry to sound again, that thin desolate wail, full of loss and heartbreak, lonelier than a child's desperate call, hopeless as silent tears beside a grave.

It didn't come. There is a pattern, a timing, in all things. I felt suddenly that I would not hear that cry again. Whatever it was, whoever it was, there would not be another call for help.

For help? Was it that kind of cry? I tried again to hear the sound in my mind. A shiver rippled through me. The cry had been such a despairing lament. I shivered again, then quickly lifted my head to listen.

I heard something outside.

I pushed back the covers and swung out of bed. The tile floor was cold to my feet. I hurried to the window. With my eyes adjusted to the lamplight, I could see absolutely nothing. Whirling around, I ran to the lamp, turned it off, and then felt my way back across the room. I pulled up the wide window and shivered against the rush of cold night air.

I stared down into the patio. Slowly my eyes adjusted to the darkness. I was almost sure I had heard something from this direction. Nothing moved. Iron benches gleamed palely in the moonlight. Darker masses of bushes curved with the paths. The dominant volcanic stone rose jaggedly at the far back of the lot.

A door opened briefly beneath the colonnade on a ground-floor wing across the way. The house was apparently L-shaped. My room was on the second floor of the base of the L.

I leaned as far out my window as I could, pressing hard against the iron grillwork. Faintly I heard a muted sobbing, a soft murmur of Spanish. The door closed and, once again, the night was quiet.

I watched where the light had shown so briefly until I was cold to the bone. Finally, I pulled down the window and hurried back to the big bed. The slick silk sheets were icy against my thin cotton gown. I wished fervently for flannel. Pulling up a wool blanket, I huddled beneath the covers.

What should I have done about that single piercing cry that had startled me from sleep?

Nothing, obviously.

Oh sure, Sheila, walk right by, close your eyes, go back to sleep and pretend you didn't hear.

You can't carry the world on your shoulders, another voice countered. Do your best, but don't be a fool.

Wearily, I pushed back the covers and sat up. My life would be simpler by far if I didn't have such a pushy, officious conscience. But I was already out of bed and padding back toward the window, my feet once again cringing at the bitter chill of the tiled floor. I cupped my hands around my eyes and peered out into the night. The patio lay as empty and quiet as before. There was not even a faint glimmer of light beneath the colonnade.

What if someone lay injured, unconscious, in the garden?

What an absurd fancy, I told myself firmly.

But was it? The cry had been loud enough, sharp enough, to wake me from an exhausted sleep. I knew I'd heard a cry of need.

Why hadn't anyone else heard it?

I shrugged that off. Who knew why only I had heard? A trick of the wind, perhaps. The point was that apparently I was the only person who had heard it and who, therefore, could do something about it.

All right, all right, Sheila Ramsay to the rescue and to hell with looking like a fool. I turned away from the window, hurried to the lamp, and switched it on.

The light was a sharp reminder, if I needed one, that I was out of my element. Instead of my small but cheerful bedroom with its single bed topped with a down comfort, there was the rich glow of a fruitwood bed and matching ornate dresser. The tile, so cold underfoot, was of bright and charming blue and gold patterns. I knew instinctively that it wasn't just any old tile. I hesitated, then slipped on my dressing gown. I was determined now. I would not be put off by grandeur. I fumbled in my hurry to tie the sash, driven by an urgency that puzzled then frightened me. It took only a second more to find and step into my slippers.

The doorknob was a long iron handle, cold to touch,

heavy to pull. The door swung smoothly in and I stood in the threshold, daunted by the dark and silence of the hall.

Did I dare to move blindly down that hall, perhaps to stumble into some irreplaceable heirloom vase?

Someone had cried out. It had already been a long time since that cry. Too long.

I stepped out into the hall and shut the door behind me. The darkness was an assault on my eyes and on my nerves. I hesitated. I could ring the bell the girl had shown me. But that would waken her and perhaps there was no need. I had no idea of the time but it felt late, that middle watch of the night when dreams terrify and all manner of evil seems possible.

No, I would carefully find my way out to the garden and take a quick look in the pale moonlight, lay my worry to rest, and slip quietly back to my room without bothering anyone. Gradually I could see well enough to move cautiously down the middle of the hall.

I reached the balcony without difficulty and was able to differentiate shapes in the living room. I stopped at the head of the stone stairs. For some reason it was darker below and I looked down into a pool of black. I glanced back at the living room and realized it was lighter there because a faint sheen of moonlight seeped through the glass wall that overlooked the patio. Which meant that once I made it downstairs and to the pool room, I should be able to see quite well because there were glass windows there, too.

This gave me courage to start down the stone steps, to move into that cold darkness, my hand sliding along the rough stuccoed wall to my right.

I heard the scuff of my slippers on the stone steps, the soft splash of water in the fountain below, and, shockingly, the click of a closing door.

I stopped still, my breath held tight in my chest, and listened.

I remembered that moment with absolute clarity, the tiny click of that closing door and how surreptitious it sounded, the faint eddy of cold air, the ache in my chest.

Someone moved quietly in the deep pit of blackness at the base of the stairs.

That did it.

I remembered only one other time in my life when I was scared absolutely frantic. I was new to New York and my date—equally green at subways—had mistaken the station, and late one hot summer night we had walked up subway steps to a street of darkened tenements. I could sense danger as instinctively as a gazelle when a tiger nears. Our footsteps echoed loudly. A man stumbled out of the shadows of an alley. We passed him. A heartbeat later, he turned and followed us, his footsteps loud. We ran and reached a lighted street and, thankfully, a bus lumbered up and we climbed aboard.

I stood on that dark stairway and felt again the same mixture of panic and incredulous dismay and sheer hopelessness.

Whirling around, I tried to run back up the stairs, but my slipper caught in the long folds of my dressing gown and I stumbled and fell and cried out as my knee cracked painfully against a stone step.

I don't know what I expected, but my first feeling as I crouched on the hard steps was one of surprise that no one raced up the steps after me. Someone stood beneath me in that well of darkness and looked up. I felt sure of that. Then, so quickly that my initial impression was overlaid and distorted, there was, oddly, a splashing sound, a quizzical call, and one by one lights rippled on beneath me. I was half turned now, staring down the hall. Light spilled out from the poolroom. The crystal chandeliers in the entryway sparkled to life.

No one stood in the hall below me. No one.

A man came through the doorway from the poolroom, moving easily, unhurriedly. Most men would be diminished if they stood at the base of stairs, looking up, clad in a soft blue terrycloth robe, barefooted, hair plastered wetly down.

He was not diminished.

He looked up at me and slowly a smile spread on his face.

"What a nice surprise."

He was coming up the stairs now and reaching out to

pull me up, and I liked the firm grip of his hand and the good-humored smile on his face and the definite interest in his eyes.

"Hello. I'm Tony Ortega. I don't know when I've had the pleasure of meeting a beautiful blonde on the family steps in the middle of the night. In fact, I'd go so far as to say it was a first."

"You've been swimming," I managed. "I'm sorry I disturbed you.

"You haven't disturbed me at all."

I freed my hand and moved back a pace from him, but he was still close enough to touch and I was very aware of him. I realized as I looked at him that Dr. Freidheim had told me nothing about the Ortega family. I hadn't known there was anyone other than Señor and Señora Ortega.

"I'm Sheila Ramsay. I arrived this evening. From New York."

"New York," he repeated. "Are you the museum lady?"

I smiled at that. "Yes," I said agreeably, "I am the museum lady."

"No one told me the museum lady would be beautiful."

I didn't know what to say to this so I didn't say anything. I'm afraid I've never sparkled at this kind of repartee. Yet, even though it wasn't my kind of conversation, I didn't feel awkward or embarrassed. He had charm enough, kindliness enough, that I felt devilishly attractive, infinitely desirable. But I didn't lose my perspective enough to be swept off my feet. I had sense enough to realize that to be so effective he must have had lots of practice.

"Will you join me in a swim?" He smiled. "The water is heated."

"I'd like that sometime." I hesitated, then asked, "Have you been swimming long?"

It would have been understandable if he had been a little surprised at my questions, even a little irritated. After all, what business was it of mine? But his manners were impeccable. Not a trace of curiosity did he show.

"A quarter of an hour, perhaps. I'd just come home and decided I would swim before bed."

"You must think me terribly rude. But, you see, I was awakened by a cry and I wondered if anyone else heard it."

"A cry?" he repeated. For the first time, there was a reserve in his manner. His face changed, became smooth and unreadable.

"It woke me." I shivered. "I couldn't imagine what it was. I got up and listened, but it didn't come again. I tried to sleep but I couldn't. I was afraid that perhaps someone had fallen in the garden and might be lying there now. I was coming down to check."

He frowned. "But you must have been going up the stairs to have fallen as you did."

I nodded, feeling foolish, but I said steadily, "When I was coming down, I heard someone moving in the hall below, and it was so dark and the sound was so stealthy and I'm afraid I'm not very brave. It frightened me."

"I'm sorry you were frightened. There is nothing to fear in the Casa Ortega. I think you must have dreamed badly." He looked down the stairs into the empty hall. "As you see, there in no one here but us. I was alone in the pool."

I looked down the stairs toward the dark opening into the dining room. He followed my glance and gave an almost imperceptible shrug, as if to say, certainly, someone could have gone in there, but why?

I had my own thoughts, too. I could have been wrong that someone stood below me. Looking up. But I heard the click of a closing door and, before that, a cry in the night.

I said so. Nicely, but determinedly.

"There are always noises at night," he rejoined. "In all houses. As for a scream or a cry, about that I can set your mind at rest."

His tone was relaxed, untroubled. And unconvincing.

"Yes," he continued, "you must have heard one of the peacocks. Come, I'll show you."

I followed, of course. He might have been going to show me peacocks, but I was going to look at the patio.

I did wonder if we would rouse the entire household when he opened a door in the glass wall beyond the pool and touched a switch.

The lights that clicked on weren't harsh; they were

gentle, floating wisps of light in delicate filigree iron lampposts. Each light was a different color, rose and aqua, lemon and orange. The effect was enchanting.

Even in the brief moment that I surveyed the patio, I knew it was a work of art, as imposing in its way as the house. Here the lava was tamed. The cost must have been enormous, much like quarrying rock. A gently sloping lawn with graveled paths spread down to the rugged cliff of lava. The lights, the occasional wrought-iron benches, the paths and fountains, all were in perfect harmony. Vines flowed over trellises and clung to the lava cliff. Flowers spread apparently without plan but on second glance were artfully sown. All the paths led to a central tiled fountain where water fell in a graceful circle from what I later realized was a miniaturized version of Tlaloc, the great water god. Dominating the whole was the cliff of lava. The cliff emphasized the delicacy and perfection of the garden and, at the same time, reminded how insubstantial is man's handiwork. The garden was both beautiful and disturbing. I wondered if that had been its creator's intent.

All of the garden, neat and perfect, could be seen from where we stood. Whatever the cause of that cry in the night, it had left no trace here. The benches sat empty. The paths lay smooth and unmarred. The central fountain splashed softly in its tiled circle.

"Look there," he urged, pointing toward a bush behind

the nearest bench. He bent down and scooped up a smooth stone and flung it.

The bush quivered and broke apart. In its shadow were sleeping peacocks. They stirred and ran. Two of them spread their magnificent tails. Feathers with huge eyes shone like ripples of quicksilver in the soft lamplight. Two outraged cries sounded, high and shrill and near enough to a scream to satisfy anyone.

Tony Ortega watched them scurry away.

"You see?"

I nodded. The peacocks cried, yes, but that was not the cry I heard. I nodded without answering. We turned and moved back into the house. He touched the switch and the lovely lights behind us faded and dimmed.

I thanked him and again turned down an offer to swim and once more apologize for disturbing him, but I was quickly reassured. It was all very pleasant and civilized. I felt let down because I liked him very much and felt very strongly, deep in my bones, that he was hiding something in this elegant house, hiding something both sad and frightening.

My vague feeling of disappointment crystallized abruptly when we reached the stairs and I looked up. I felt, confusedly, that his exclamation when we met must have been patently phony for there, standing at the top of the stone steps, was a truly beautiful blonde. I felt not only disappointed but like a fool. I am a garden-variety honey blonde with regular-enough features and a sprinkle of freckles. I have always been a little proud of my green eyes because they are nicely shaped and a bright, clear sea green, but I know they aren't anything spectacular.

The blonde standing at the head of the stairs was spectacular in any language, English, Spanish, what have you. Most men probably wouldn't care whether she spoke anything at all.

Tony Ortega stopped at the foot of the stairs. The hand politely guiding my arm gripped it harshly for one fleeting moment, then dropped away.

She was one of those women who can make every other woman in a room feel like a drudge. She stood gracefully, one hand clasping the folds of her ice blue dressing gown, and her soft golden hair swirled to her shoulders, shining like moonlight.

She spoke Spanish and her voice was low and husky and sounded like the smoke that wreathes gently upward in a cocktail bar.

Tony replied in English, "Miss Ramsay, our guest from New York, was wakened by one of the peacocks. She mistook the cry for a person and hurried to see if anyone was hurt."

He turned to me. "Miss Ramsay, I don't believe you have met Señora Ortega." He paused, then added expressionlessly, "My father's wife."

I said hello as gracefully as I could.

She stood motionless for a long moment, then her cool, husky voice floated down. She spoke English with a German accent.

"How courageous of you, Miss Ramsay, to brave the dark. I hope Tony has managed to set your mind at rest."

It wasn't what she said that rankled; it was the way she said it. It did have the effect of bringing Tony Ortega quickly to my defense, but I still felt an inch and a half tall and wished I were anywhere else in the world at that moment. Even the warmth of his hand once again on my arm didn't help.

I was in the midst of yet another apology when she yawned, delicately, like a cat. "It's quite all right, Miss Ramsay. As Tony so eloquently says, you surely meant well. But it is late, isn't it? I'm sure we'll have a good laugh about it at breakfast. Good night, you two."

Her parting words made it sound as if he and I planned an immediate tryst on the nearest couch. My face flamed again and I decided I would certainly move to a hotel tomorrow. Then my feelings of embarrassment and humiliation faded as I sensed Tony Ortega's fury. He lowered his head and bunched his shoulders. I was afraid he was going to run up the stone steps after her. Instinctively, I reached out and caught his arm. I felt anger and outrage in its rigidity.

"Mr. Ortega," I said sharply.

He took a deep breath and another. Slowly his arm relaxed. He looked down at my hand on the sleeve of his terrycloth robe.

I quickly pulled my hand away.

As quickly, he caught my hand but his touch was as gentle as a summer wind. "I beg your pardon," he said simply.

They were not casual words, not the unthinking use of social formula. He meant every syllable.

I shook my head. "There's no need."

"There is every need. You have been made uncomfortable in my family's house."

"It's all right now." I meant every word.

He looked at me for a long moment, then nodded slowly. He smiled. "Very well, Sheila Ramsay. If you are sure."

"Very sure." I gathered up the skirt of my dressing gown to go up the stairs. "Good night, Mr. Ortega."

He reached out to stop me. "Tony."

"All right. Good night, Tony."

He was still standing at the foot of the stairs, watching me, his face somber again, as I turned and hurried down the hall toward my room. I hurried because I wanted to take no chance of meeting my hostess.

In my room, I lay in bed and tried to sleep but sleep was long in coming. Like a litany, I kept saying over and over, *Tomorrow I'll see Jerry, Tomorrow I'll see Jerry*, but somehow, his sharp and bony face was indistinct, and clearer by far was another face, smooth and charming, then dark and angry. I fell into a troubled sleep where I searched and called for Jerry but at every turn saw Tony Ortega, and now his face was no longer charming or threatening but aloof, unreadable, and alien.

5

Fear is spawned in the dark. Fear is a nocturnal creature, arrogant and assured in the folds of night. Fear dwindles, collapsing like a night-blooming flower, in the sharp, clear light of day.

I awoke early, heard the cooing of pigeons not far from my window. I followed the pattern on my wall where the sun slanted through the drilled window; it seemed absurd that I had confused the call of a peacock with a scream or that I had stumbled and fallen trying to run up steps, too frightened to face the darkness in the downstairs hall.

My fears seemed absurd on a beautiful, crisp morning. I stood for a long moment beside my window and knew that I had never seen a sky that particular soft shade of blue.

I was looking forward to a happy day. I would see Jerry. Everything was going to work out. I felt sure of it, absolutely certain. I would present the Styrofoam case with the enclosed manuscript to the Ortegas, thank them for their hospitality, gracefully gather up my suitcase, and leave. If anyone protested, saying I had been expected to remain a guest throughout my stay in Mexico City, I could easily plead surprise. I would manage to shake free. Surely I could find someplace inexpensive to stay. Perhaps Jerry would help me.

It all seemed easily arranged as I stood in the lovely room, making up the script in my mind, directing the players one way, then another.

I picked out my prettiest dress and slipped it on. I stood for a moment in front of the mirror, admiring its pale lemon shade and the way the skirt swirled when I turned. I was almost ready to go when there was a soft knock on my door and in came the little maid who had brought me hot chocolate the night before. With a good many giggles and much gesturing, she managed to make it clear that Don Tony awaited me at breakfast.

That was luck, I decided. I could return the manuscript to Tony and perhaps have the good fortune not to have to face my hostess again. Yes, everything was working out. Soon I would see Jerry.

I grabbed up the Styrofoam box and followed the maid downstairs. The patio had been beautiful last night beneath pale pastel lights. This morning it was breathtaking.

Bougainvillea blossomed pale pink and soft white and bright red. Carnations swept in a circle around the central pool. The sweet scent of honeysuckle mingled with the musky smell of roses. A waterfall trickled languorously over a hump of lava near the round wicker table that was set for breakfast.

Tony rose from the table and came to greet me. I held out the Styrofoam box and Tony, a little surprised, took it.

I smiled at him. "This is my reason for coming to Mexico, to return this manuscript that your family very graciously loaned to the museum."

"Which manuscript is it?"

It was my turn to be surprised. "The Sanchez manuscript."

"Oh yes, of course," he replied. "Well, it is certainly good of the museum to send it by hand, very thoughtful." As he spoke, he was turning away from me.

I frowned, puzzled. Hadn't the family insisted that the manuscript be hand delivered? I almost asked, but Tony was speaking to the housekeeper and handing her the boxed manuscript to be put away. There was a clatter and scuffle and two little girls skidded from behind a willow tree to fetch up, panting and laughing, at the table. Tony introduced me to his ten-year-old twin sisters, Rita and Francesca.

Breakfast was a buffet. I tried papaya and mango, fruits I'd only read about before. There were sweet rolls and eggs fried and placed on tortillas, hot chocolate, and a sweet dark coffee.

The twins, after an initial shyness, were friendly and charming and told me about their school and the club where they played tennis and their piano lessons. They spoke fluent English. Tony watched them indulgently.

We were halfway through breakfast, and I was wondering just how to most gracefully ask for someone to call me a taxi, when Tony pushed back his chair and rose.

"Good morning, Father." There was great respect and affection in his voice.

I pushed back my chair and started to rise, too, but Señor Ortega hurried to my side. "Don't get up, my dear. I understand we owe you great thanks for burdening yourself with an old book of ours."

I liked Tony's father immediately, liked the firm clasp of his hand and the way he made an unimportant guest feel welcome. I was surprised, though, at how little resemblance there was between father and son. Where Tony was tall and broad, his father was not much taller than I and slightly built. They both did have the beautiful olive skin and crisp curling black hair, but Tony's face was blunt, his father's narrow.

It was a cheerful, happy half hour, that breakfast, and I was regretting my decision to leave the Ortega house and go to a hotel because they were all so friendly and kind, and then, as suddenly as a cloud passing over the sun and chilling the land below, the atmosphere changed on that beautiful terrace.

The twins, like two little dark barometers, gave the first warning. Their loud chatter fell away abruptly and their faces took on that look of stupidity that children assume when they want to escape notice.

Tony looked up. His change in demeanor was, of course, far more subtle but in its way equally revealing. Even adults can't truly hide dislike, no matter how hard they try. Tony rose and smiled and pulled out another chair, but his eyes were cold.

The only person happy to see her was Señor Ortega. He called out, "Gerda, my dear, what a delight to have you come down so early. Have you met our lovely guest, who most thoughtfully delivered El Viejito's book?"

In the clear, sharp light of morning, Gerda Ortega was not as young as I had thought the night before. She was still breathtakingly beautiful, her thick golden hair again in coronet braids this morning, her delicate pale face perfectly made up. She smiled at her husband, a cool lovely smile, and his face reflected pride and delight in her. She nodded offhandedly to the rest of us but paused beside her husband to touch him lightly on the shoulder. "Yes, Luis"—and she, too, spoke in English—"I met Miss Ramsay last night."

I stiffened, expecting her to continue in that husky, compelling voice with some slighting reference.

She took her place at the breakfast table and was, most obviously, the lady of the house, when she continued, "We are very grateful to you, Miss Ramsay, for your trouble. We want to do everything we can to make your visit to Mexico a happy one."

The twins watched her carefully from under lowered lashes. Tony's expression was an interesting combination of surprise and puzzlement. Señor Ortega was nodding warmly. "Yes, we want to do that."

"I have already instructed Manuel, our chauffeur, that he is at your service, Miss Ramsay," she said with a charming smile.

Señor Ortega beamed at her. "How thoughtful of you, Gerda."

"Oh, thank you very much, señora," I said quickly, "but I couldn't impose on you in that fashion. I appreciate staying with you last night but I will move to my hotel today. I want to thank all of—"

Everyone interrupted at once. I wasn't moving to a hotel; they wouldn't hear of it. No one who had performed such a service for the Ortega family could possibly spend any time in a hotel. I tried to move against the tide, but they overwhelmed me. Gerda Ortega protested as strongly, as firmly, as any of them. Finally, I gave in.

By the end of breakfast, I had almost decided that I had misjudged Gerda Ortega (perhaps it made her surly to be awakened at night) when there was an odd exchange. I was finishing the hot, sweet coffee when I said, "I plan to spend the day at the National Museum of Anthropology,

Señor Ortega, so I won't need for the car to stay with me. I will, though, certainly appreciate a ride to the museum."

"The National Museum of Anthropology?" he repeated.

I nodded happily. "Yes, I have a friend who works there."

"Are you interested in Mexican artifacts?" asked Señor Ortega.

I smiled. "I'm interested, yes, sir, but it isn't my field. I'm an Egyptologist."

Tony glanced down at his watch. "I can give you a lift."

Gerda Ortega smiled. "That won't be necessary, Tony. Manuel can take Miss Ramsay. You needn't be late to the office."

Tony laughed. "One of the advantages of ownership, Gerda, is the privilege of coming when you wish and if you wish."

I knew her opposition only made him more determined to take me. I wondered, as I pushed back my chair and made my good mornings, how such a perceptive woman could fall so far short in accomplishing her objectives.

But my last glimpse of her surprised me yet again. She looked utterly satisfied.

Tony said he would meet me in the drive. I hurried up to my room for my purse and guidebook. Once there, I paused long enough to brush my hair and redo my lipstick. I glanced toward my suitcase but decided against unpacking now since Tony was waiting. I had been too tired the evening before to do more than fish out my nightclothes.

I was almost to the door when I stopped and turned. Frowning, I crossed to the suitcase and stood looking down at it. It was closed, but at one side a tiny tip of lingerie poked out. Slowly, I reached down and opened the case. It was packed as I had left it.

Wasn't it?

I touched the little bulge of silk that had shown through the crack. It was a new slip. I had worn the slip only once before and had carefully laundered it. When I had folded and packed it, I had tucked it down at the side so that it would be in no danger of being caught by the lid and perhaps snagged.

I looked through the suitcase but everything was there. Did I really think a house of this sort could harbor a sneak thief?

Thief? I whirled around and snatched up my purse. If anyone wanted to steal something . . . Everything was there—my tourist card, my letter of authorization from Dr. Freidheim as courier for borrowed property, my bill-fold bulging with the pesos I'd purchased at the airport.

No thief had walked in my room.

Could the pretty little maid have been curious about the American lady's pretties? Perhaps. But, living in a house such as this, she had often seen much finer.

I took one last look about the room. I could be wrong, of course. Perhaps the clothes had shifted and the slip popped up as I was closing the lid.

I didn't think so.

I shook my head impatiently. Tony was waiting. I would think about it later. What difference did it make, after all? Nothing had been taken.

I hurried downstairs and found Tony outside on the drive, standing beside a black classic MG. I was glad, when we had started, that I had tucked a scarf into my purse.

He told me the area where they lived was called the Pedregal and that many of the homes had been designed and built by Mexico's most famous architects.

"Architecture is as much an art as painting in Mexico," he explained.

One spectacular house succeeded another. I thought nothing else could possibly impress me as much, but we had scarcely left the Pedregal when I call out excitedly, "Tony, what is that? Over there."

So we made our first stop and I began to be caught up on the magic that is Mexico.

It was the campus of the University of Mexico. The building that had caught my eye was the university's Central Library, which, incredibly to me, was one gigantic mosaic, each wall of the building entirely utilized to tell some part of the story of Mexico in bright and glittering patterns of colored stone.

Tony delighted in my response.

"Haven't you ever even seen a picture of it?"

I shook my head. "Never. I've never seen anything like it." As much as the Egyptians liked wall decorations, they had done nothing like this.

The fire and the color, the passion of the intricate design overwhelmed. Tony led me the whole way round the library, explaining the beautiful mosaic as we walked.

"This is the north wall. There, do you see the sun? That represented the most ancient symbol of matter. The eagle symbolizes the building of Tenochtitlán. There is Quetzalcoatl and Tlaloc."

I followed his pointing finger, sometimes understanding, often not, but the power of the great mosaic thrilled me.

"The south wall represents the Spanish Colonial occupation."

Yes, there were the quaintly dressed figures of sixteenth-century Spaniards and there the hands of the Church.

When we came full circle and stopped and once again I looked up, I knew that I would never again see things as simply as I had before. There was a more profound, subtler spirit at work here than any I had encountered before. I knew, of course—what archeologist doesn't?— that the world of man can be many things, all different, all as individually conceived as the infinitely variable mind of man can devise. My background and training were in classical archeology. I had once taken a survey course on Middle America, but knowing intellectually that Mexico was the product of a fusion of cultures and actually seeing the results of that fusion in living, glowing color was quite another thing.

I turned and impulsively touched Tony's arm. "Thank you, Tony."

He took my hand and smiled, and then he, too, looked back at the lovely building. "So much of Mexico is there, on those walls, Sheila." There was pride and love and more than a little awe in his voice.

As we walked back to the car, he told me of other murals. "You must see *Sueño de una tarde dominical en la Alameda* Central, Dream of a Sunday Afternoon in Alameda Park, by Diego Rivera in the Del Prado lobby. In that mural, you can see all that is Mexico."

I hurried to keep up with him. He was so absorbed in his subject that he had lost formality and reserve. It was now, his gestures as eager as a schoolboy's, that I realized he was an older man than I had thought in the dim lights of last night and on the shaded patio at breakfast. Lines fanned out from his dark, deep-set eyes. There was even a touch, the merest hint, of gray at the edge of his thick black hair.

He was so informed, so authoritative, that I made a mistake. I should, of course, have remembered Gerda Ortega's reference to an office, but I didn't think. Instead I said, "Tony, you must be an artist to know so much."

Eagerness seeped out of his face. We were at the car now. He opened my door for me.

"No," he said shortly. "No, I am not an artist."

We were well under way, swinging up onto a freeway, before he spoke again. "No, Sheila, I am no artist. I am a member of the Ortega trading company. Ortegas are always traders." His voice was dry and hard.

The MG roared like a wild thing along the concrete expressway. I watched him and wondered at this man with his many moods. I wished I hadn't driven the happiness from his face.

"I didn't mean to say the wrong thing," I offered hesitantly.

The car slowed immediately. "Don't be sorry. I am the one who must apologize. It is only that sometimes a man must regret the choice he didn't make. You have a poet who speaks of the fork in the road and that the way he chose made all the difference." Then he laughed, a good-humored, relaxed laugh. "I should probably have been a very poor architect."

"But if that's what you wanted to be . . ." I broke off. It wasn't any business of mine.

He frowned and for a moment I was afraid that again I had said the wrong thing. But no, he was only thinking how to make it clear to me.

"I do not believe in the United States that you have the same feeling for family that we have here." He shrugged. "When I said that Ortegas have always been traders, I meant it. For almost four hundred years there has been an Ortega trading house in Mexico City." The car slowed a little more to wing onto an exit ramp. He added quietly, "I have a great affection for my father."

I liked Tony Ortega very much. It might not be, it certainly wasn't, the approach to life in the United States. But I admired him for his choice.

"Now," he said briskly, and I knew the discussion was closed, "straight ahead is Chapultepec Park. The loveliest park in the world. This is our Hyde Park and Bois de Boulogne and Central Park. It has everything—a zoo, children's playground, roller-skating, lakes, rowboats, restaurants, theaters, a castle, a polo field, and several museums, including the Museum of Anthropology."

He turned into the main drive through the park. The drive wound past huge stately trees with gray-green leaves and rough bark. You could tell the trees were old by their size. Tony called them *ahuehuete* trees and explained they were a kind of cypress native to Mexico.

"Some of them are two hundred feet tall," he said. "There is one in the park that is forty-four feet around. It's called Moctezuma's Tree after the Aztec emperor who was in power when Cortés came."

He pointed up through a grove of the beautiful old trees at the castle crowning Chapultepec Hill, the castle where Maximilian and Carlota lived during their turbulent fateful years in Mexico. We passed a monument with six gleaming white pillars of marble and Tony told me the touching story of the boy heroes. In 1847, the castle housed a school for military cadets. When the United States invaded Mexico and tried to take the castle, the cadets fought to the death. When only one still lived, he wrapped himself in a Mexican flag and flung himself over the side of the steep hill rather than surrender.

Next we passed the Museum of Modern Art, and then

we turned left into a wide avenue, which I later learned was Reforma Avenue, the most famous and loveliest in the city.

Reforma passed through the huge park and, beyond the traffic on either side, there rose old trees and rolling hilly land. Tony pointed ahead to an enormous monolithic sculpture that marked the entrance to the Museum of Anthropology. Huge, squat, massive, the statue was a brooding embodiment of power.

As we turned in, Tony said he was Tlaloc, the rain god, and that he had assured himself of undying popularity among Mexicans by performing as a god should. The huge statue, discovered in a ravine not far from San Miguel Coatlinchán, was brought into Mexico City in August 1964 a few days before the museum was to be officially opened. The statue weighed 168 tons and was carried on a huge truck with twenty wheels. People lined the streets to watch him pass and some taunted him for bringing no rain. However, the moment he arrived at his destination, there was the greatest cloudburst of the year.

"So the old gods are not entirely out of power in Mexico even today," he concluded.

We were at the beautiful white stone steps that swept up toward the museum.

"I wish I could come with you," he said as I started opening the passenger door. I knew that if urged, he would. But that wouldn't do at all.

"I've taken too much of your morning as it is," I said

quickly. "But thank you so much, Tony, for stopping at the university, for all the marvelous things you've told me, and for bringing me here."

I was out of the MG now and leaning down to say good-bye.

"Do you intend to be long at the museum?" he asked.

"I've several people to look up. On behalf of my museum. I've no idea how long it will take."

He nodded understandingly.

I saw disappointment in his eyes and hoped he didn't think I was rude.

"If you should be free in time for lunch, call me." A car tooted behind us. Tony ignored it and wrote a number on a card and handed it to me.

"I will if I can."

The MG bucketed off and I turned to climb the gleaming, shallow white steps and I no longer thought about Tony or any of the Ortegas.

In only a few minutes, I would see Jerry.

6

Water drummed steadily down. A fine spray gently touched my face. A sparkling curtain of water fell in a ring around a huge carved gray stone column that supported an immense glistening aluminum canopy.

Water that washes away our sins, water that breathes life to growing things, water that can save, water that can destroy. Elemental. Essential. The water slapped endlessly against the gray volcanic stone blocks of the courtyard, impervious to man though falling at man's design.

I looked slowly around the long enclosed courtyard—at the silver-colored canopy that soared above the water-circled column, at stone latticework decorating the walls at a pool near the far end—and marveled at the imagination that had conceived this open, airy, sunlit setting for a museum.

I had inquired for Jerry when I first entered the museum but was told he was not in his office. He was expected back soon, so I left my name and said I would be looking through the exhibits. I bought a ticket and a guidebook and walked out into the courtyard, around which the display halls were built, and was caught and held by the power of the falling water.

When I finally left the courtyard and entered the first hall, I found that the grace of the falling water typified the museum. Every exhibit seemed touched with light and color and I had never seen a better exposition of man's beginnings than the introduction to general anthropology in the first room.

I didn't try to absorb everything at one. I wandered a little haphazardly from one area to the next, admiring a figurine here, a vase there, a monumental sculpture along the way. I had a nice busman's holiday in the Egyptian section.

I was halfway around the rooms off the courtyard, among the relics of the Mayas, when I spotted doors leading out to a garden. Through the glass walls, bright green ferns beckoned. There was a reconstructed temple in the garden, but I had seen enough of ancient monuments for the moment and instead delighted in the feathery light green leaves of tall, slender trees. I moved out of the shadow of the temple to sit upon a retaining wall and enjoy the soft warmth of the sunlight.

It was very quiet in the small garden. I was alone. I

could hear, and it seemed far away, the smooth flowing spiel of a guide. Children laughed somewhere nearby, but in this small sun-dappled enclosure it was quiet and still.

I heard someone coming fast. He exploded into that oasis of serenity. I turned and saw him and began to back away until I came up against a wall and was trapped.

Jerry caught my wrist in a painful grip. He leaned so close I saw a nerve flicker in the hard, ridged muscle along his cheek. Through the pain that burned along my arm and the shock of this totally unexpected reception, I scarcely heard his harsh, angry words.

"When they said you were the courier, I didn't believe it, couldn't believe it. Not the girl I'd met in Washington. I asked twice if they had the right name."

He shook with anger.

I felt a sudden wash of panic. I tried to pull away, but he held me tighter, pulled me closer. "You've got a hell of a nerve, that's for sure, to come here." He glared at me. "Did you think nobody knew? Well, you and your stinking museum ought to know that somebody always talks. Always. It's like dead meat and buzzards. That kind of money makes talk."

Abruptly he let go of me and I thumped back hard against the edge of the retaining wall. He turned away and crossed the small grassy plot. He stopped at the exit and looked back at me, a look so filled with contempt that I felt shriveled and shaken.

His bony face was hard and bleak. "If you know what's

good for you, you'll get out of Mexico. Today. Because no matter how clever you are, no matter how you plan and scheme, you aren't going to succeed." He clenched his hand into a fist and raised it. "I'll see you in hell first."

Then he was gone.

Once again it was peaceful and still in that small pocket of greenery. Only the buzz of a bee and the ragged sound of my breathing broke the quiet. I rubbed my arm, up and down, trying to erase the imprint of that hard hand, the bruises that I knew would darken, staining my arm.

Damn him. Damn his priggish, self-righteous, hateful arrogance. Damn him. Damn him and his museum.

Later, I never could remember how I made my way out of the museum, never remember passing through the courtyard and the lobby to the wide esplanade outside.

Tears slipped down my face. People turned to look as I went by. Somehow I left the museum behind and walked, head down, oblivious to traffic and passersby, until I was a long, long way up Reforma. Slowly, slowly, my breathing came back to normal and the tears dried on my face.

I stopped finally and sat down on a wide stone bench in the shade of an elm. Traffic, spewing fumes, hurtled past. I sat and tried to make some kind of sense out of that frightful scene in the museum.

Jerry, obviously, believed I was involved in some kind of illegal trafficking on behalf of my museum. He was, of course, wrong. That didn't stop the hot prick of tears behind my eyes. It didn't matter that he was wrong or even that I could prove he was wrong. What hurt was that he would believe an accusation against me without even asking to hear my side of it. No matter what he had been told, why hadn't he felt inside that I wasn't that kind of person?

He had said that he "didn't believe it, couldn't believe it."

But he had believed it, whatever it was. Believed it and hated me for it.

I was still too shaken, too upset to feel anything but a great emptiness. I had looked forward too long to seeing him again. Deep inside it had meant so much to me. I had liked him, violent, irascible, and quarrelsome as he was. No matter that he wasn't the kind of man I had ever envisioned caring for. In a silly, childish way, I had taken the happiness of one out-of-context afternoon and pinned my dreams on it.

So dreams don't come true. I was old enough to know that, old enough not to be crushed by disappointment. Old enough, surely, not to let an irrational, ugly happening ruin my visit to a beautiful and fascinating country.

It wasn't the fault of Mexico, after all, that I had come on such a foolish quest.

I sat up straight on the hard bench and opened my purse. The little hand mirror showed a wan face with powder-smeared cheeks and red eyes. I brushed my hair and put on fresh lipstick and powder.

All right, Jerry Elliot was a clod. I had only imagined

a bond, a current of empathy between us. It was lucky that I had learned the truth. I had nothing to be unhappy about.

I touched the card where Tony had scrawled his number in bold, clear figures.

I looked about me purposefully. Skyscrapers, sunlight glittering on their glass expanses, rose all along the broad boulevard. Interspersed were small buildings, apartments, shops, restaurants. I found a restaurant with a kind proprietor who telephoned for me.

Tony was there in ten minutes. One look at his eager face, his dark eyes smiling, and I put the morning behind me.

We lunched at the Chalet Suizo, dipping bread bits into Swiss cheese melted in white wine. We walked through the Zona Rosa, the Pink Zone shopping area of small, excellent specialty shops. I couldn't resist a new leather purse, soft as a gardenia petal to the touch.

I was always to remember that afternoon as a perfect span of hours. Tony was utterly carefree.

"Are you up to a walk, a real walk?" he asked, when I had finished my shopping.

I nodded of course, and so we started up Reforma, that broad and lovely tree-lined avenue that Maximilian planned.

We walked from *El Ángel* to *El Caballito* and it took us the afternoon, but what a happy afternoon it was. The graceful gilded angel, poised atop a 150-foot-tall marble column, is the monument to Mexico's independence. Much of Mexico's fierce and blood-drenched history is commemorated on that shaded avenue. There is a monument to Cuauhtémoc, last of the Aztec emperors, who fell fighting Cortés. There is *El Caballito*, which is considered one of the finest statues of a horse in the world. It is only incidental to Mexicans that weak, muddleheaded Charles IV, Cortés's king, is astride the horse.

We walked and Tony told me all of this and much more. We stopped often to rest a moment on a stone bench and watch the people pass. We did not, of course, talk of history and statues all that afternoon. We talked about tennis (we both loved it; we would play one day soon) and flowers (yes, they are beautiful but what are their names?) and New York (plays and the Staten Island Ferry) and our families.

There was only one awkward moment.

"Why did you come to Mexico, Sheila?"

I hesitated, then finally answered with a shrug. "I'd never been here before and there was the opportunity to come. So I did." I was happier when I could turn the conversation back to him.

He told me, surprisingly, a good deal about his family and about his father's second wife. His mother had died eight years earlier. "At first Father was so busy with the twins, but then they began to grow up. I think he was lonely. I was busy at the bank and the twins and Juan, my brother, were involved in their own activities. It was last spring that he met Gerda." Tony shook his head. "I know how they met but it still seems so out of character, Gerda hiking."

The story came in bits and puzzling pieces.

"Father was out riding one day last spring—we have a hacienda in the mountains near Tlaxcala—and he rescued Gerda. She had been hiking and had fallen and sprained her ankle."

We were both quiet for a moment, pondering the unlikely vision of golden-blond, husky-voiced Gerda clambering around on a rocky mountainside.

"It was love at first sight for him," Tony said dryly. He added grudgingly, "She is beautiful."

Her background, so far as Tony had been able to discover, was enough out of focus to make him wonder. "Though, to be fair, she's probably not hiding anything more disgraceful than the fact that her parents were Nazis."

I must have looked shocked at that because he smiled. "Don't you know how the story goes? A nice German couple moves to Mexico in 'forty-four or 'forty-five and, of course, they came from Venezuela and they had fled that dreadful Hitler years earlier. The funny thing is that they can scarcely speak a word of Spanish for all the years presumably spent in Venezuela."

He shrugged. "Not that it really matters but old memories die hard, and there are a lot of Germans in this part of the world who don't want anyone snooping too closely into when they came to Mexico. Or why."

So Gerda was of German parentage and still spoke with something of a German accent though she had grown up in Mexico. According to her, she had been orphaned as a baby and taken in by a German couple in Puebla. The years after she left her convent school and before she showed up on a mountainside in Tlaxcala were a little fuzzy.

"The first I knew about it, that he had married her, was a telephone call," Tony said. "I couldn't believe it. When I met her, it didn't take me a week to see it for what it was. She married a man twice her age and it was only for money." He shook his head. "I asked him for God's sake why had he *married* her?" He smiled but it wasn't a happy smile. "That's the only time in my life that my father ever struck me."

The sun was beginning to curve down in the west now and the light was slanting low through the huge gray-green trees. Tony shaded his eyes when he stopped talking and looked at me with a kind of wonder.

"I don't believe I've ever told anyone else about that." He paused. "You are very easy to talk to."

Perhaps then he felt he had said too much, revealed too much of himself. He looked at his watch and said abruptly, "I've made too long a day of it for you. Come, we'll take a cab back to the car."

The late-afternoon traffic had thickened on Reforma,

but he did get us a cab and soon we were hurtling back to where we had left the MG.

We didn't say much on our drive to the Pedregal. I was tired. Tony, of course, was a Mexican driver, so we fairly flew out Reforma and onto the freeway.

It was almost six o'clock when we got there. The house was very quiet. I hesitated, once in my room, but decided I probably had time to bathe before dinner. As it turned out, I had plenty of time because Mexican families traditionally dine late, about eight. I bathed, then lay down to rest for a moment and didn't waken until a hand touched me lightly on the shoulder. It was the little maid, and she showed me on my watch that it was a half hour until dinnertime.

It was at dinner that I met Tony's younger brother, Juan.

I would never have taken them for brothers. Where Tony was substantial, Juan had a quicksilver quality. He was tall, thin, gangling, somehow unfinished. I calculated quickly from all that Tony had told me about the Ortegas that afternoon. I judged Juan to be nineteen, but there was about him a very adult aura. His face was mocking and weary, his eyes knowing. Something a little wild glittered deep in their black depths. His glance shifted from one to another at the table in quick, probing little looks, searching, testing, taunting. I didn't at all like the way he looked at me. There was nothing the least bit boyish about Juan's appraisal.

It was a strained meal.

Señor Ortega was abstracted and only roused himself once to smile down the table at me. "What do you think of Mexico, young lady?"

I began to tell him and then realized, midway through my paean, that he wasn't listening. To my surprise, it was Gerda who took up my answer and adroitly drew me out about my day. Again I felt I must have misjudged her. She was being kind, keeping a relaxed flow of conversation going to make her guest feel at ease. But her lovely violet eyes were cold and empty when they looked at me. Once again I felt confused and uncertain.

Abruptly I wished I were out of this house, luxurious and impressive though it was. We were dining in a small dining room just past the family living room. We could look down through long French windows and see the pale pastel colors of the patio lights. Here, where we ate, the lighting was subdued and candles gleamed at either end of the table.

I was a stranger here. I didn't belong.

All the faces around the table seemed masklike in the dim candlelight. Señor Ortega, his eyebrows bunched in a frown, sat at the head of the table. He stared down at a plate I knew he didn't see. Gerda's face was smooth, lovely, and empty of expression. The twins had said scarcely a word the entire meal and those only in subdued whispers. Tony watched his brother grimly.

Only Juan seemed alive. There was an aura of excitement and, yes, even of danger. It was so strong that I almost felt I could reach out and touch it. His face was long and narrow, his nose aquiline. His thick black mustache curved with his mouth. All the while he smiled; as he ate, as he talked, as he watched us all with those quick, darting black eyes, he smiled.

He smiled at me.

Tony raised his head and watched him carefully.

Gerda broke off a sentence in mid-phrase, stumbling over a word.

The twins' eyes fastened on Juan.

Only Señor Ortega was oblivious, his thoughts turned inward.

Juan smiled at me and caught and held and exploited the sudden pause. His teeth flashed as he laughed, a soft happy laugh.

"Miss Ramsay, do you know that death is always near in Mexico?"

I must have looked utterly puzzled because he laughed again in great good humor.

I began uncertainly, "I don't think I—"

Gerda interrupted, her voice sharp and hard. "Don't be absurd, Juan. Don't try to frighten our guest."

"Frighten?" His voice was all innocence. His bony shoulders lifted and fell in an exaggerated shrug. Then he leaned across the table. "You'll see, Miss Ramsay." And he was smiling again, and I knew it was the same smile a buccaneer would have worn when the white sails of his prey lifted in view over the horizon, a smile of anticipation and excitement. The kind of smile that would light the face of a highwayman as he urged his horse on faster and faster and felt the straining muscles between his legs and knew that in only a moment he would thunder beside the carriage and force it toward the ditch, gambling all the while that he would live and others die. "Death is a bony lady in Mexico, Miss Ramsay. She is certain and faithful. All others will betray you. But not Death."

I watched him spellbound. The shadowy corners of the room seemed suddenly cold and threatening. He was looking deep into my eyes now and his voice was high and soft and hypnotic. "Do you know the best way to die, Miss Ramsay?"

"Juan, we all must help Miss Ramsay plan her excursion for tomorrow," Gerda said firmly. She turned toward me. "Have you thought what you might like to see?"

Tony and the twins all spoke at once.

"Xochimilco," Rita suggested.

"The Bellas Artes," Francesca said.

"It would be a good day to visit the pyramids," Tony said decisively. "We'll pack a picnic lunch and spend the day. Did you know, Sheila, that the Pyramid of the Sun is the third largest pyramid in the world?"

"Aren't these pyramids shaped differently from those in Egypt?" I asked.

"Yes," Tony agreed. "These have flat tops instead of rising to a point. You see, a temple always sat atop the pyramid, but over the centuries the temples have not survived."

"It's all dusty and ugly," Rita said.

"I'll bet you won't climb all the way to the top of the Pyramid of the Sun," Francesca teased.

The rest of dinner passed pleasantly and everyone was cheerful and talkative as we finished dessert, an apricot sherbet. But I knew all the while that it was a surface calm, and I was aware that I avoided looking directly at Juan.

After dinner, Tony asked if I would like to go dancing. I was tempted but I also knew I was tired. If I was going to clamber up the sides of a pyramid the next day, I knew I'd better get some rest. I thanked him, said no, and excused myself from the family.

I was to wonder later if it made any difference that I did not go dancing with Tony. We would have come in late, I know, and if we had, I would have stumbled directly into the shock that I was to face that night.

7

The stealthy opening of the door woke me.

One moment I was sleeping. The next I was wide awake, aware of the cool feel of the silk sheets, the impenetrable deepwater darkness of the room and, more strongly every second, conscious of something alien near me.

I learned more about myself in the next five seconds than I ever wanted to know, learned that when I am terrified to the core my mind can twist and turn frantically, seeking safety, but that my body goes as limp and flaccid.

Something frightful was near me. I knew with sick certainty. Stiffly, I turned my head toward the door and tried to see through murky shadows. My throat closed with fear, my heart thumped, my chest ached. All the while, I strained to see and couldn't. Something was there.

Was it coming toward me?

Scream, scream, Sheila, scream, my mind implored. I tried. I opened my mouth and tried to scream. I couldn't make a sound.

Turn on a light. Run. Hide. My mind scrambled frantically, but I felt as though my body were pinned to the bed, caught and held, unable to move. It was too dark to see but I heard the unmistakable creak of the door opening ever wider.

That homely sound steadied me, gave me strength to translate thought into action. That creak was the seal of reality. The door was opening. Unless I meant to lie there spinelessly, accepting whatever came, I must move now.

I still could not find breath enough to scream, but my hand obeyed my brain and slipped from beneath the cover and reached out to the bedside lamp and yanked at the little chain.

Nothing happened.

I yanked again and the sound seemed explosively loud as the chain pulled the switch. Nothing. I was half sitting up in bed now. I grabbed the lamp by its neck and raised it above my head, ready to strike.

I heard a light rustle, clattering sounds, a flurry of movement, a piercing scream. The cry rose, abruptly cut off.

I listened over the thudding of my heart, thought I heard running steps, but quickly the sound was gone. As suddenly as I had sensed the presence of danger, I felt equally certain no one was near. The threat was gone, but an intruder had come and opened my door and flung something on the floor, and a scream had scarred the night's silence.

In a rush, I slammed the lamp onto the bedside table and rolled from the bed. By the time I was on my feet, light flooded the hallway. I reached for my robe and slipped into it.

The hall light confirmed the fact that the intruder was gone. The doorway was empty. I moved around the end of the bed.

Everything happened at once. Calls and shouts echoed in the hallway. Juan was the first to come. Barefooted, in shorts, he ran to the open doorway, skidding to a halt to look down at the strange display on my floor.

I, too, stared in puzzlement at the remnants of a Barbie doll that had been ripped apart, the head chopped free to lie by itself, the arms and legs broken from the torso. A bunched serape lay a foot away.

Juan reached out and flicked a switch. The overhead light came on. I turned to look toward the bedside lamp and saw the cord lying loose on the floor. Someone had pulled the plug from the socket so that I would have no light when I awoke.

More running steps. Tony came around Juan and hurried toward me. "What's wrong? Why did you scream?" Tony, too, wore boxer shorts. He was muscular and looked powerful and very attractive.

Juan was now leaning against the doorframe, dark eyebrows raised. "Some kind of ritual, maybe? Do you always scream when you kill a doll?"

Kill a doll . . . The words lodged in my mind and I felt an inward lurch of sickness. That's what it looked like. Someone had killed a doll. A blond doll. I was blond. Gerda was blond.

"Don't be absurd." My voice was crisp. I knew my anger was evident. "I did not scream. I had nothing to do with the destruction of the doll. I was asleep. A noise woke me, the creak of the door opening. Someone stood there, threw things on the floor, screamed, and ran away."

"Really." Juan's tone was silky, his disbelief evident. "Well, funny how things happen when there's a stranger in the house."

"*Suficiente, Juan.*" Tony's voice had a hard edge.

Juan gave an elaborate shrug. He reached down to pick up the serape. As he shook it out, something clanked to the floor. Juan stepped over the doll remnants, reached down, and picked up something dark. He held it cupped in his hand. He came upright and spoke rapidly in Spanish.

Tony moved toward him, held out his hand, and spoke sharply.

Juan frowned, shrugged again, and handed the dark object to Tony.

Tony looked down, slowly turning toward me.

His demeanor changed as if from light to dark. When he had hurried from the hall, holding out his hands to me, he was all sympathy and concern. Now that he held that dark object, his face turned secretive, speculative.

"What's wrong?" I took a step toward him.

"Have you seen this before?" On his palm rested a blade of rock—hand-formed obsidian. His eyes were dark with worry.

I didn't doubt for a moment that the sharp edge had efficiently dismembered the doll. The blond doll. Again I felt a wash of sickness. "I know nothing about it."

"What"—it seemed to take effort for him to push out the words—"did you see in the doorway?" He waited too tensely for my answer.

I looked at him in dismay. "I didn't see anything. It was too dark."

It was as if he'd been handed a reprieve. "Well, then, let's pick these things up. Come downstairs and we'll have a drink."

"What about the doll? What about that knife? Someone came in my room tonight. Shouldn't you call the police?"

"Police?" A deep voice sounded dismayed.

We turned to see Señor Ortega. He was fully dressed. Perhaps he saw the surprise in our faces and possibly a question in my eyes. He said pleasantly, "I was in the garden taking a walk and saw the lights. Is there some difficulty?"

Tony took a deep breath. "Someone was playing a joke on our guest." He nodded at the floor.

Señor Ortega's face changed from polite inquiry to inscrutable blankness.

"What's going on?" The throaty voice was demanding.

Tony's father swung around to face his wife. He moved to intercept her, but she had stopped short, gazing down at the dismembered doll. Her lovely face looked stricken. And frightened.

"Who did that?" Her voice shook.

I spoke up. "Someone opened my door and threw in the pieces of the doll and screamed. Did you hear the scream?"

She shook her head.

I turned again to Tony. "It seems clear someone gained entrance to the house tonight. Surely you want the police to come."

Tony shook his head. "That wouldn't be helpful."

I wanted to demand why an investigation wasn't going to be made. I knew he wouldn't answer. And, after all, I was a guest. This was not my house. But it was my room that had been entered.

"I'll pick up the doll." There was an avid gleam in Juan's eyes.

Tony reached the pieces first and scooped them up.

The housekeeper came, pulling a robe around her.

Tony questioned her sharply in Spanish. I had no idea what he asked, but she made a vigorous denial, her voice firm.

Señor Ortega chimed in, his face anxious.

Maria looked from Tony to his father and replied vehemently.

Whatever the conversation between Maria, Tony, and Señor Ortega, it appeared to reassure Gerda. She watched her husband and stepson, her gaze swinging from one to the other. Some color seeped back into her face.

Obviously everyone knew something that I didn't know, and closed me out.

Juan finally said something to me. "You are very lucky," he said softly. His brown eyes glistened with excitement and something more, a kind of expectancy.

"Lucky?"

Everyone turned to watch Juan and me.

He liked being the center of attention. But there was more than a bad boy's tendency to show off, to shock. It was more frightening than that. "You were in the same room with Death tonight, death of a doll," Juan said softly, so softly. "You were so close, you might have reached out and touched him."

They all came down on him at once, his father, Tony, Gerda. Don Ortega's command was abrupt. "Bastante." Tony's eyes blazed. "Stop the nonsense, Juan."

Gerda's voice was high. "Don't talk about death."

Juan fell silent with a little shrug, but the smile and the eagerness never left his eyes.

Juan's response wasn't normal, but were his words any stranger than the way the rest of the family was acting? No one had reacted as I would have expected.

Why weren't the police called? Who would throw a dismembered doll onto the floor and scream? Why had it happened in my room? Who had unplugged my lamp? Why had Tony's face suddenly become secretive, inward, withdrawn?

As suddenly as everyone had gathered, they dispersed. Tony did have the decency to pause a moment after the exodus and ask, "Sheila, would you like to move to another room? I can have Maria see to it quite easily."

I said briskly, "No, it's all right, Tony."

"If you're sure."

"Yes."

He turned to leave.

I said quickly, "Tony, please, who would do a thing like that? Why?"

I could not have felt more shut away if he had physically closed the door between us. His face was utterly expressionless. "I have no idea, Sheila, none at all."

He was lying.

When he was gone and I was alone in the room, I wedged a straight chair beneath the door handle. I plugged the lamp in and this time light shone when I pulled the chain. I was glad to know light was near. As for the chair at the door, I don't suppose it would have stopped anyone who really wanted in, but the barrier gave me a sense of security.

Was it any wonder that I couldn't sleep? I lay rigid on

that comfortable mattress and stared sightlessly into darkness.

Tony Ortega had reached out to me until he saw that sharp-edged obsidian ax.

I turned restlessly.

What difference should it make how the doll was cut apart? Whether it was a kitchen knife or a machete or a hand-shaped stone weapon? What possible difference?

I bunched up my pillow and buried my face in it. I couldn't bury my thoughts.

Finally I gave up trying to sleep and got up and crossed the room to the window. I rested my head against the cool glass and stared down into the garden, which lay, cold and stark, in the pale moonlight. It looked just as it had last night, the wrought-iron benches sharply black, the paths smooth ribbons of swept gravel, the upthrust cliff of volcanic stone oppressive. Nothing marred the utter stillness.

A shadow moved.

I tried hard to distinguish one patch of shadow from another. I was sure, almost sure, that something had moved near the entrance to the poolroom.

As quietly as possible, I slid up the window and leaned out to press against the iron grille that barred my window. I heard the scrape of gravel beneath a shoe. I strained harder to see.

At the same time, I wondered frantically how best to

rouse the household, how to call Tony, without warning the intruder. For whoever it was, whoever walked so softly across the patio, must be an intruder, or he would not be so careful to stay in the shadows.

My breath expelled in a sigh.

There was only an arm's length of space that lay bare in the moonlight that the figure had to cross to reach the darkness of the colonnade.

I saw him for that instant, for the fraction of time it took him to move in the pale hard light of the moon until he reached the sanctuary of the colonnade. I didn't see his face. I didn't need to see it. I knew the shape of his head, the set of his shoulders.

Why should Tony Ortega move as quietly as a thief in the garden of his own home?

And, if he did, why should I care?

But I did care. I liked him. I liked the way he smiled and the way he moved. I liked the good humor in his eyes and the gentleness of his hands when he touched me. I stared down into the dark garden, puzzled and disappointed.

A door opened. In a brief flash of light, I saw Tony step inside the room and softly shut the door behind him.

That was the same door that had opened last night after the cry woke me. I had watched the patio and that door had opened, and I had heard a murmur of Spanish and the muted sound of sobbing.

I turned away from the window, crossed to the chair

beside my bed, and found my dressing gown and slipped into it.

There was something both sinister and frightening happening at the Casa Ortega, and somehow, it involved me.

I was going to find out what it was.

8

I slipped like a ghost past the living room where embers glowed in the fireplace and tiptoed down the stone stairs and paused beside the splashing fountain to listen. Knowing myself to be an intruder now, I crept to the door of the poolroom and watched a long moment to be sure the glimmering green water was empty, that the tables and chairs waited silently for players who would not come this night.

My soft slippers slapped against the tile floor. I stopped twice more to listen. The night seemed full of movement and sound, but each time there was nothing but the soft ripple of water, distant barking of dogs, and, once, the faint trill of a whistle.

I reached the sliding door and cautiously stepped out

onto volcanic flagstones. The colonnaded wing loomed darkly to my left.

It must have taken me some few minutes to make that journey, to slip on a dressing gown and move uncertainly down the dark hall, to pass the living room and then to step quietly down the stairs, pausing to make sure no one was about.

It was only when I was outside, shivering in the chill air, that I realized I was not alone in the garden. First I strained to see into the shadows beneath the colonnade, where Tony had entered a room. The faint murmur of voices wasn't coming from that direction. No, somewhere deep in the garden voices whispered as lightly as leaves rustling in a gentle breeze.

Now it was I who stepped from shadow to shadow, moving ever deeper into the garden. The deep, sweet scent of the roses and freshly turned damp earth mingled. Water fell softly in the central fountain. Once I stepped on a magnolia leaf and it crackled so sharply I knew the whisperers must hear. I waited, breath held, but the soft light whispers continued. Then it was silent. Footfall by footfall, I crept on. I was almost upon them when they spoke again. They were hidden deep inside the concealing shadow of an arbor thickly vined with honeysuckle. I was so close I could have reached out and touched them.

Somehow it didn't shock me to recognize Gerda's voice. She was anxious, frightened. I could not understand the Spanish but I could hear the fear.

Then the man spoke. He whispered, too, and his voice was soft and gentle. I could not believe my ears. Did not want to believe my ears.

Oh please, no. It mustn't be Tony. Not Tony.

But I had seen him in the garden only a little while before. Had it been Gerda's door that had opened and closed so quickly?

Surely not. Somehow that did not seem a likely spot for the bedroom of the mistress of the house.

"My father's wife." That was how he had introduced her to me that first night on the stairs. I had thought he did not like her. Was it, instead, that he liked his father's wife all too well? As for the things he had told me this afternoon, was it on his father's account that they rankled?

Unable to leave, but hating to listen, I stayed beside the arbor a moment longer. I could not see them, could only hear them behind their curtain of vines. But I heard his voice, a soft and tender voice, and it was the timbre of Tony's though lighter than I remembered. But that would be the lightness of love, of intimacy.

She started to speak again and then her voice fell away and I knew his mouth had closed on hers.

I did turn then and moved blindly away, somehow managing not to make any noise. I regained my room without being seen. I no longer cared whose room he had stepped into earlier. He was nothing that he had seemed to be.

I must have slept. It didn't seem that my eyes ever closed that long, miserable night, but darkness shaded to dawn, pigeons cooed a welcome to a cool shining morning, and the house awoke.

I dressed slowly, heavily. I tried to analyze why I felt so bereft. Why should I care what Tony Ortega did? I brushed my hair, one stroke after another, and remembered the unfeigned admiration in his eyes when he looked up the steps at me that first night. That had been real. I knew it. I felt it. I was sure of it.

But Sheila, a dry sardonic voice inquired, you've been wrong on everything so far, haven't you?

I laid down the brush and leaned close to the mirror. Coral-toned lipstick and a delicate touch of eye shadow, but the green eyes I stared into were somber, the green of hanging moss, still and lifeless.

When I was dressed, when I had taken all the time over it that I could, I stood for a moment and stared at my closed door. I could hear, outside on the patio, the rhythmic whish of a broom as one of the maids swept the terrace. The morning had started and I could not stay forever in this room. At dinner last night, a lifetime ago, they all had tried to help me plan today and we had settled, Tony and I, on a trip to Teotihuacán, the city "where god was offered prayers."

I could not possibly spend the day with Tony.

I would, at the moment, have done almost anything to escape the Casa Ortega. But I had accepted the big freebie and I was committed, for good or ill.

I straightened my belt one last time, smoothed my hair and, face schooled, opened my door and began the day. I realized, even before I reached the stone stairs, that the house itself had an air of uneasiness. It was too quiet, a house listening to itself, waiting, wondering.

When I reached the patio, I turned reluctantly toward the breakfast table, expecting to see some member of the family, dreading to see Tony.

The table was set, each place setting a gay spot of color with mats of yellow straw and napkins of pale lime. No one was there. I looked down at my watch. It was half past eight, the same hour I had breakfasted with everyone the morning before.

I walked slowly toward that empty table. If no one else came, no one at all, it could only mean that they were avoiding me. Did all of them, every last one of them, know or guess why the dismembered doll was thrown in my room? What did they think?

I stopped at the place where I had sat yesterday and there was an envelope waiting there. It was addressed to me in a heavy sloping script that I did not know.

I read the message:

Dear Sheila,

A business matter requires my attention today so I must forego our trip to Teotihuacán. Maria is

*fixing you a box lunch and Manuel will be ready
to leave at your pleasure.
I hope you find the pyramids interesting.*

Tony

Signed *Tony* and that was all. Nothing about tonight
or tomorrow. I should have been delighted that I would
not have to face him. Instead my disappointment was
sharp and startling.

I ate alone. The little maid who had brought me chocolate the first night waited the table. Twice I caught her
watching me, her eyes huge and frightened. I tried once,
in a pidgin sort of Spanish dredged up from guidebook
studies, to ask where the family was but when she
answered I could not understand a word.

I wasn't hungry. There is nothing quite like the feeling
of being a pariah to discourage appetite. I picked at my
papaya and drank one cup of the hot sweet coffee, and
then I dropped the napkin beside my plate and left the
table. I stopped on the terrace to look across the beautiful
garden and to wonder what I was going to do next.

It was very still, still and cool in the early-morning
quiet. At the far end of the garden, near the sudden stark
uplift of lava, the glossy bright green leaves of a huge
magnolia rustled, were still, rustled again.

I began to walk that way, down a graveled path that
curved among gladiolas then around a fountain with iron

frogs spewing water in never-ending streams. The leaves rustled again on this one particular low branch and I heard a quickly smothered giggle and I knew my guess was correct.

The girls, in blue shorts and bright orange T-shirts, clung like locusts to a broad low-hanging branch and were, from only a few feet away, well hidden by the broad glossy leaves of the magnolia.

"Rita? Francesca?" I called softly.

"Shh," they whispered.

"We aren't supposed to be out. Maria told us—" Rita nudged her sister. There was an instant of sharp silence.

Told them what? Not to talk to the American visitor?

I knew better than to ask a direct question. But I felt sure they could tell me what was happening or, at least, some of it. Sometimes children don't understand what they see, but they always see more than anyone thinks.

I sat down on a wrought-iron bench beside the magnolia. "I won't tell anyone I spoke to you or saw you here. We'll keep it a secret between us."

They liked that. They had, like healthy kittens, a hungry curiosity. I let them in their artless fashion work around to last night.

"Couldn't you see anything?" Rita asked.

"Not a thing. Tell me, girls, I'll bet you have some ideas about it. What do you think it means?"

They backed and filled, interrupted each other, bubbling with excitement.

"Maria said it was spite, a mean trick by Lorenzo," Francesca explained.

"Who's Lorenzo?"

"He was Pancho's assistant in the garden and Gerda fired him last week," Rita said importantly.

"Juan laughed when Gerda wondered if it was Lorenzo. Juan said it was meant to scare you, a sacrifice," Francesca said quickly.

"A sacrifice?" I repeated.

"You know," Rita said, "like the Aztecs."

I remembered too clearly the sundered arms and legs, the torn chest of the torso.

"The Aztecs," I said faintly.

The little girl nodded casually. "They had to have sacrifices all the time so the sun would come up."

I must have looked shocked at that.

Childlike, she took it as a lack of belief. "I mean it," she insisted, forgetting to whisper. "They took people up to the top of the pyramid and they say it was almost at the Zócalo and when they got them up to the top, they had to stretch out on this sort of stone slab—"

"Then the priests, and they were all dirty and smelly because they didn't bathe," Francesca interrupted, "they took a knife, just like the one Juan found on your floor last night, and made a kind of big *X* on their chests and pulled out the heart and it was all pumping blood and they put it in this special stone holder."

"I see." I paused and looked at the two earnest little faces above me. "Juan said someone hurt the doll to frighten me?"

They both looked scared at that and whispered again and said I mustn't repeat what they had told me because they just happened to overhear Juan and Gerda and they would be in lots of trouble if anyone knew they had heard.

They had been eavesdropping. It was as clear as the suddenly distinct freckles on their noses. Obviously, they were scared witless of Gerda and Juan. I wondered why. I reassured them and reminded them again that everything we had talked about was a secret between us. They were relieved, but still nervous and ready to slip away.

It was then, and somehow I kept my voice steady, that I asked them what Tony thought.

"He is afraid it's El Viejito," Francesca said.

Rita hissed in Spanish at her sister like an angry little duck.

Francesca clapped her hand to her mouth, then said hurriedly, "It couldn't be him. Maria said it was much more likely to be Lorenzo. She said El Viejito doesn't do strange things, that it was only Gerda who wanted everyone to think he was crazy."

This time Rita clapped her own hand over Francesca's mouth and stared defiantly at me. "It isn't El Viejito."

I had no idea who El Viejito was, but I knew what to say. "I'm sure it isn't. I can't imagine why anyone would think that."

My fishing expedition was so successful that I felt a quick rush of shame.

Rita smiled, grateful for those comforting words. "It is only, señorita, that he is old now and Gerda would like for him to be sent away. She says he watches her and that he is too much taken up with the old gods and the old ways." Her small brown face furrowed in a frown. "He has been very upset lately, but he won't tell us why."

"Rita. Francesca."

Maria stood at the top of the terrace, shading her eyes, staring this way.

"She mustn't know we talked to you," Rita said frantically.

I knew then I was not mistaken in thinking the family was trying to shut me out of what was happening. "I won't tell her. I promise."

I left the twins clinging to their branch, still invisible to anyone walking in the garden. Maria watched me come up the path, her dark face impassive, but before I reached the terrace she turned and went back into the house.

Was she avoiding me purposely? Or was she busy about her own tasks and I wasn't one of them?

I walked slowly up the path toward the house. I was uncertain what to do next. I had made one attempt to leave the house and go to a hotel. It would be awkward to try again. I couldn't as a representative of my museum afford to offend such important benefactors.

I paused on the terrace, looking up at the house. Its

stucco gleamed a soft apricot. It was utterly beautiful in the soft morning light and I hated it and wished I were back in sooty, smelly New York, passing by glass-fronted shops near my apartment, nodding to old Mr. Kaber sweeping out his grocery, stopping on my way to the subway to buy my morning paper.

I should have never come to Mexico. It was only what I deserved, chasing all this way after a man I had met but once. But I was here and it would be humiliating to run home to New York, not even staying a week.

I began to walk briskly toward the house. I was here. I would see Mexico. I wouldn't let a mutilated doll or a strange family or anything else make me run away.

9

I lingered at the Temple of Quetzalcoatl, fascinated by the flowing line of plumed serpents carved in relief, and fell behind the group. I didn't care. I had an excellent guidebook in hand, and there is nothing more destructive to absorbing any sense of past grandeur than to be one of a milling throng of tourists. I didn't hurry after the group. Instead I took my time in the citadel. When I stepped out onto the Avenue of the Dead, the wide avenue stretched deserted and dusty, a long two-mile walk to the Pyramid of the Moon. I occasionally paused, read a bit, then moved ahead. Until I actually began to walk up the avenue, I had not realized how far flung and separated were the ruins of the pyramids of Teotihuacán.

I was alone on the dusty, pebbled avenue. Far ahead

and to the right, tiny antlike figures toiled up the steep steps toward the top of the Pyramid of the Sun. On either side of the long avenue rose wild, hilly country with thick green brush.

I wondered what the pyramids had looked like when Teotihuacán was a living city, the hub of a people's world. No one knew who had built the immense complex. The buildings had long been abandoned when the Aztecs ruled the Valley of Mexico. Once there must have been festivals and processions moving at a stately pace up this long, wide avenue. Had the priests and nobles led the way and the people followed? Or had family groups and visiting villagers lined either side of the avenue to watch the passing procession? Had wide-eyed children been lifted high to glimpse the chief priest?

I could almost see the passing shadowy throng, high-colored people and magnificent feathered headdresses, and hear the soft shuffle as thousands walked along the wide way.

I was listening so hard to the past, hearing the muted thump of drums and the steady beat of marching feet, that a sudden popping sound scarcely registered. Dust spurted as something struck the ground in front of me. I saw the puff and realized incredulously that a bullet had whizzed past me. I ran, knowing as my sandals slapped against the gritty street that I couldn't run fast enough.

Pop.

I wouldn't hear the shot that hit me; wasn't that how it worked? Like bombs?

Where was everybody? Where had that disorganized group of visitors gone? Where were the two teachers who watched everyone so carefully and the honeymooners who were oblivious to the pyramids, to the tourists, to everything but each other? Where were the college kids in their crumpled, stained Levis and brightly colored T-shirts?

The street was uneven. One sandal caught on a half-buried rock. I fell headlong and hard, but even as I slammed onto the ground I was rolling, trying to get up. Again I heard the ominous light pop. Dust plumed by my hand. I scrambled up and veered to my left, running when there was little breath left, hoping for safety as the muscles in my back tightened in anticipation of pain.

I saw the drop-off in front of me just an instant before I jumped. I didn't hesitate. I hadn't realized that the long Avenue of the Dead was interrupted by this large square depression. I wondered even as I dropped the five feet to the floor whether it had at one time been an underground water chamber or perhaps part of an elaborate drainage system. I had no idea but I was terribly grateful for the feeling of safety when I landed on the floor and pressed against the stonework. I crouched, trembling, sweat spreading down my face, my back, my legs.

I looked around and realized almost immediately, with

heart-stopping shock, that I was trapped. Whoever hunted me, loaded gun in hand, could be moving behind the hilly, uneven ground that rose on either side of the Avenue of the Dead, moving until I was in clear view pressed against the side of the depression.

If I climbed out, I would be vulnerable the instant that I rose over the edge. If I didn't climb out, if I stayed here pressed against the side, I was doomed. But I couldn't remain here. I was particularly easy to spot in my white double-knit dress with pink patch pockets.

Not so white now, I thought irrelevantly while I scanned the edges of my trap. Not very white at all after my tumble onto the gritty avenue and scramble to get up again.

Quickly, make up your mind. But still I cowered beside the wall, clinging to the illusion of protection, knowing it was illusory.

Should I climb up here, try to run the width of the street and scramble up the hillside and dart behind a clump of green brush? Should I zigzag across this depression, hoping to reach the opposite side, climb up, race past the second depression, and be close enough to some tourists to cry for help?

The huge Pyramid of the Sun rose off to the right. The figures climbing the steps were tiny, far away. If anyone heard a shout, a cry for help, could they possibly know it for what it was?

My shoulder pressed hard against the rock. I strained to see any movement alongside the depression. My heart hammered when something flickered in the corner of my sight. My head jerked around. Panic ebbed. A lizard. Only a lizard. He was black-and-white striped. I watched, fascinated, as bright red loose flesh beneath his neck ballooned out, held for moment, collapsed, ballooned again. Was he warning me? Or was that his means of trying to frighten off enemies? He and I, in that event, had equally ineffective defenses.

I still hesitated, hoping. Would someone come? Please, would someone walk briskly up to peer interestedly into this sunken square? Then I would be safe. Seconds slithered away and with every one that passed my danger grew. Whoever shot at me would have me in sight again soon. It was hot and still against the rough stone wall. No whisper of a breeze stirred here. There was no welcome crunch of nearing footsteps, no amiable chitchat between sightseers.

Shame made me move. I had to try. I owed myself that much. It was better surely to be shot on the run than to cower against a wall. Up, then, and running, no more time for thinking. I rushed to a corner of the depression, reached up, clawed at the top of the wall, pulled myself up, scraping my elbows and knees against the rough rock side. I was up and out of the depression. I lunged to my feet and ran up uneven ground. Five, ten, twenty feet and I reached a line of green bushes that sprouted irregularly alongside the ruins. I dodged behind the first clump of bushes but I kept on running until I couldn't run another step. I dropped behind a thickly leaved bush and tried, over the whistling rush of my breathing, to hear if anyone moved near, if anyone followed.

I couldn't be farther than a stone's throw from the Avenue of the Dead but I might have been a hundred miles distant. I was alone on dusty, rock-strewn ground in the midst of a thick clump of bushes in a small hollow. I couldn't even see the huge hump of the Pyramid of the Sun, which I knew was to my right across the Avenue of the Dead. There was not a voice, not a footstep, nothing but the ragged dry sound of my breathing as I tried to draw air into starving lungs.

The gunman was on the other side of the street. Since no other shots had come, I had either moved out of his sight or he had lost me when I jumped into the depression.

Was he hunting for me now?

With hands that trembled, I opened my guidebook to the centerfold and studied the map of the pyramids. I should be just there. My finger stopped on pale green paper. I looked around me and all I saw was a small, rough bowl of ground ringed by dusty, dry, gray-green bushes. I didn't dare go back to the Avenue of the Dead. But how could I find my way back to the road that circled Teotihuacán?

I lost my way almost at once stumbling up one hill and down another, watching for snakes and lizards, stopping often to listen. The luck of lost children must have been with me for I found the parking lot near the museum and that was where Manuel had parked.

I hesitated at the edge of the lot. Only a few cars and buses were parked on the far side of the log near the museum entrance. I saw the soft cream of the Mercedes. I hoped Manuel was waiting in the front seat.

I would be vulnerable when I crossed that almost empty parking log. How far to the Mercedes? One hundred and fifty yards? At least that.

I stood at the edge of the lot in the sparse cover of the brush, afraid again.

I hesitated and so I lived.

Rocks slithered underfoot off to my right. Brush crackled.

I drew back deeper into my little patch of shadow, felt the pinprick sharpness of the gray-green leaves, smelled the musky dryness of the bush. I listened and looked, looked hard, but still I almost missed him.

He, too, waited in shadow, watching the almost empty lot. His faded blue denim shirt was barely discernible in the brush, his gray trousers merged with the shadow. He looked toward the Mercedes.

I saw his face, sharply, clearly, and prayed that he would not sense my nearness.

His face was memorable, black eyebrows that slashed sharply upward, a thin, tough mouth, taut coppery skin, straight black hair and flaring sideburns, powerful shoulders. I recognized him. He had watched me at the airport. I stared at his dark and dangerous face and saw a pattern.

The letter pushed into my hand at the airport.

The dismembered doll.

Shots on the Avenue of the Dead.

Jerry Elliot's angry insistence that I leave Mexico. At once.

I don't know how long we stood, each of us taut and still. Then he shrugged off a backpack. I saw a gun in the hand. He put the gun in the pack, slipped the pack back on his shoulder, then moved, stepping as softly as a pad-footed animal. He was moving away from me, his back to me now, crossing the parking lot. He walked to a motorcycle near the far edge of the lot. He handed a coin to the boy who had watched it. He swung the cycle in a slow half circle and passed the Mercedes. If I had doubted before, I had no doubt now. He hung for a moment beside the beautiful cream-colored car, then, abruptly, dust and gravel spitting beneath his wheels, he gunned the cycle and was gone.

I was sure now. He had shot at me. I no longer wondered who had directed the ragged shoeshine boy to thrust a letter in my hand at the airport. Somehow, who knew how, it must have been he who tore a doll into pieces.

Everything was done with one objective, to drive me out of Mexico. To kill me if necessary. Why? At whose direction?

I shivered, though it was warm in the soft heat of the midday sun. I was afraid that I knew the answer. I had run to Mexico to see Jerry Elliot. I had built on one summer afternoon and, obviously, built upon sand.

Who had sworn at me? Who had bruised my arm? Ordered me out of Mexico?

Jerry Elliot.

I saw his thin, intense face in my mind, remembered the ugly twist of his mouth as he shouted at me, the hard pressure of his hand on my arm.

Hot tears slid down my face as the last tiny, hopeful twist of a dream crumbled to nothing. I swiped my hand against my face. I was abruptly consumed by fury. I was a living, breathing, seething mass of anger, disappointment, and outraged pride. So Jerry Elliot would send a gunman after me, make me run and stumble, fall, scrape my knees, ruin my dress, frighten me out of my wits. I began to run again, this time toward the Mercedes. I'd show him.

Manuel was stretched out comfortably on the front seat of the car, drinking a beer. He obviously thought the señorita a little unhinged. I didn't blame him. My dress was a mess, my legs and elbows scratched, my face flushed with exertion and anger.

"Señorita, what is wrong?"

I hesitated. I almost told him. But he wouldn't believe me. I knew with a bitter certainty that no one would believe a gunman had stalked me on the Avenue of the Dead, that bullets had popped into the dust beside me. If I tried to tell the guards about it, they would think I was making it up. No one had seen me run and no one apparently heard the shots or an alarm would have been sounded.

I spread my hands wide and shrugged. "I fell down.

The ground is rough." I made some attempt to brush the dust from my dress. I knew the brown stains would never come out.

Manuel opened the back door for me.

Before we started, I told him where I wanted to go.

"Sí, señorita. The Museum of Anthropology. Sí."

I leaned forward, willing the car to hurry, though, in truth, Manuel certainly drove fast enough. Still I wished he went faster. All the way back to the district, I never wavered in my conviction that Jerry was responsible for every ugly thing that had happened to me since I arrived in Mexico. My first furious anger had hardened into implacable resolution.

At the museum, I opened the door for myself, forestalling Manuel. I told him he need not wait. I would find my own way back to the Ortega house.

I had no eyes for the beauty of the museum today, for the graceful sweep of the shining white steps. No eyes for the grace of the children, dark eyed and eager, as they played near the outside fountain.

I pushed through the door, determined to face him. He couldn't shoot me down in his office. I would effectively block any further attempts by his agent once I confronted Jerry.

He was in his office and he obviously didn't expect me. He looked up as I stepped inside. The immediate flicker of distaste on his face infuriated me.

I closed the door behind me with a sharp, hard slam. "You certainly didn't expect me, did you?"

Before he could say anything, I rushed ahead.

"You obviously think any means are justified to achieve what you think is important. But there are limits and you are damn well going to find out what they are. You picked the wrong person to lean on, buster."

He pushed back his chair and started to get up.

"Oh, that's all right," I said angrily, "you needn't stand for me. After all, your henchman just finished shooting at me. I think the time for any courtesies had passed."

He took off his glasses and watched me unblinkingly with his sharp blue eyes.

"I don't know what you're talking about."

"Of course you don't," I agreed smoothly. "You don't know a thing about somebody shooting at me on the Avenue of the Dead. Or the doll. Or the letter. Nothing at all." I was so angry I could scarcely talk. "How stupid do you think I am? You are disgustingly self-righteous. I'd like to know what's so fine about scaring someone with a gun; that's what I'd like to know. If you do one more thing, just one, I'm going to the American embassy."

With that I turned and banged out of his office, slamming the door so hard it rocked in its frame, and ran down the hall. I was outside in the clear bright air, running past balloon vendors, when I heard my name shouted.

"Sheila, stop! Stop!"

I didn't stop.

I hurtled down the wide, shallow steps and plunged toward Reforma, three lanes each way and the cars moving so fast only a fool would cross without a light.

I reached the center median. Horns squalled. Tires screeched. Then he was beside me, grabbing my arm. "Wait a minute. You're going to get run over."

I yanked my arm away and ran on. There was a lull. Just time enough to cross.

He had my arm again when we reached the other side. I pulled away and said through clenched teeth, "If you touch me once more, just once, I'll scream."

He didn't touch me again but he stayed right beside me, following me down an asphalt path into Chapultepec Park. I walked quickly past a kiosk with a green plaster top and bright orange-backed chairs. I hurried a little faster and turned onto the walk that skirted the soft green waters of the lake.

I stopped and faced him where a huge boulder jutted out into the lake, narrowing the walk. "I'll scream if you try anything."

He shoved a hand through his thick hair. "Dammit, will you relax?"

I started to turn away, but he reached past me to touch the boulder and his arm barred the way. "Who shot at you?" he demanded.

I glared at him. "Your man."

"Don't be a fool. I'm an archeologist. Not the local Mafia chieftain."

"You threatened me yesterday. Warned me to get out of Mexico. The note at the airport didn't work. Or the doll. Today you sent someone after me with a gun."

I ducked down, slipped under his arm. I was around the boulder, almost back to where the walk widened, when my sandal slipped on a wet rock. I stopped and stood on one foot to massage my ankle.

He was right behind me and reaching out to help. I shook him off impatiently. "Thanks, I'll do it myself."

"I need to talk to you."

I faced him again.

"It's a little late for talk. But, if you'll leave me alone, promise not to set me up for target practice, we'll call it quits. I won't complain to the embassy and you can pursue whoever is after your precious artifacts because, in case you still have any doubts, it isn't me."

"It isn't that easy."

I glared at him. "Why not?"

"I didn't send anybody after you with a gun."

"Oh, no, of course you didn't." I tried again to slip past him but this time he half pushed half pulled me off the path and plumped me down on a low stone wall and did a little glaring of his own.

"Listen, Sheila, I lost my temper when I found you in my museum yesterday. We are pretty sure someone from a

U.S. museum was in Mexico this week to pick up one of the most fabulous archeological treasures in the world. When Mexico customs told me you were at the Ortegas', well, it had to be you." His vivid blue eyes held mine, questioning, seeking. Slowly his face changed. "By damn, I don't believe it's you after all."

"No. It's not me. So you can call off your dogs."

"If you aren't the one . . ."—he spoke slowly, almost to himself—"why would anyone shoot at you? Unless, of course"—and his voice quickened with excitement—"they made the same mistake. That means . . ." His words fell away. He was figuring, thinking hard, and I didn't understand any of it.

"What are you talking about?" My voice was sharp and thin.

Those blue eyes looked back at me, focused on me. He shook his head a little. "The Ortega Treasure, of course. Don't you see, someone else thinks you are in Mexico to buy it. And they are willing to kill to stop you."

10

The Ortega Treasure.
   I suppose ever since that frightful scene yesterday in Jerry's museum that I had expected something like this. Still, my heart twisted at his words. The Ortega Treasure.

Jerry had me by the arm now and he was hustling me along the sidewalk. "You'd better get out of Mexico today. I'll get you to the airport. You can tell me everything you know on the way."

I stopped, braced myself, and refused to move. "I'm not running away. Not for you or anyone."

His hand tightened on my arm. "By how far did the bullet miss you?"

"Bullets," I corrected. I remembered the ominous,

chilling popping sounds and dust spurting near me. So near. I remembered the sound of the bullets and the savaged pieces of the doll on my bedroom floor. Fear squeezed air from my lungs. If it wasn't Jerry Elliot's man who had shot at me, who was it? Why?

"Come on," he commanded. "We've got to talk."

This time I didn't pull away or hang back. He rented a rowboat, all the while watching sharply around us. Before we stepped in, he took off his coat and, without a word, handed it to me to hold. When we were settled in the boat, he rowed rhythmically and swiftly. The hair on his arms glistened like gold in the sunlight. He rowed easily and somehow that surprised me. But, of course, there were many things I didn't know about Jerry Elliot.

A dozen pulls on the oars and we were in the center of the shallow lake. There could not have been a more peaceful or private spot in all of Mexico City. The green water was as smooth as a pottery glaze.

"All right, Sheila. Tell me everything."

I described my shock at that first light pop, my frantic scramble down into and up out of the depression, my breathless dash for the safety of the hills, and my relief at finding the parking lot. And then the man who half circled the Mercedes before riding off on his motorcycle.

"He must be the one who shot at me." I told of the gun in his hand and that he was the same man who had watched me from the shadows at the airport.

Jerry shook his head slowly. "You certainly stirred up somebody. That's very interesting."

"Interesting is one way to describe it," I said dryly.

Jerry, with characteristic single-mindedness, nodded in agreement. "Right. It puts everything in a different perspective. Of course," he mused, "it's probably all to the good that it happened. Otherwise, we might never have known there was a third party after the treasure until it was too late."

I looked at his attractively ugly face and knew that here was a man who had his priorities clearly in order and I surely had not made the ranking.

"But you've made me waste a lot of time," he said abruptly.

I stared at him in disbelief. Then I sputtered, "There's just no pleasing you, is there? Look, this boat ride isn't my idea. I'll be glad to be on my way."

He looked puzzled. "You take everything too personally."

"I don't know how else I should respond."

"I meant that we've wasted a lot of time on you, checking up on you, thinking you were in Mexico to buy the treasure."

"I'm sure sorry."

"Yeah, so am I," he agreed.

I could cheerfully have strangled him.

"We'll have to adjust all our thinking," he continued.

"Let's take it from the first so I can get everything clearly in mind. To begin, why are you in Mexico?"

"I'll be damned if I know," I said bitterly.

He didn't understand that, of course.

I spread my hands helplessly. "I almost mean what I said, Jerry. One day, about a month ago, there was a notice on our main office bulletin board. It announced a free trip to Mexico in exchange for delivery of a package for the museum."

He was watching me closely now. "Didn't that seem odd to you?"

I shook my head quickly. "Not at all. The Ortegas requested return of a manuscript they had loaned to the museum. The only reason I got to make the trip was because the request made Dr. Freidheim mad and he didn't want anyone from the Mesoamerican section serving as the courier."

He wanted to know everything I could tell him about Karl Freidheim. It wasn't much. Freidheim was second in the department. He was an autocrat.

"Ambitious?" Jerry asked.

I shrugged. "I suppose so. I don't know much about him."

Jerry frowned. "That all sounds on the level. Why did the Ortegas want the manuscript back now?"

"I don't see how the manuscript has anything to do with a man shooting at me or some lost treasure," I said irritably.

"It must," Jerry insisted. "I don't believe in coincidences. Don't you see? It's all too pat. At the very time that we think an American museum is hooked up with the Ortegas to smuggle out a treasure, you show up with a manuscript as an excuse for a visit."

"But I'm not here to smuggle anything. It has to be a coincidence. Now it's time for you to tell me what I've stumbled into. What treasure? How does a treasure link up with the Ortegas? And with my museum?"

"Treasure," he repeated softly. "It's quite a word, isn't it? You see pirate chests filled with shiny doubloons and a Jolly Roger flapping in the wind. It's still an accurate picture. Every treasure brings out the pirates. The only difference today is that a rogue wears a well-cut suit and has soft hands and probably has a suite of offices with a Vermeer in the waiting room."

"What kind of treasure?" I looked at him skeptically.

"The Treasure of Axayacatl."

It didn't mean a thing to me.

He smiled a little. "Mexican history isn't your thing."

"No. I did a little reading before I came. Cortés arrived in 1519 and marched across the country, hunting for gold. Cortés moved into Tenochtitlán, the Aztec capital. Moctezuma deferred to him because he thought the bearded white man might be the god Quetzalcoatl returning. The Aztec people finally had enough of it and, after Moctezuma was killed, they drove the Spaniards out of their city. Cortés eventually came back and fought. Before it was over, most of the Aztecs were dead and the city was a heap of rubble."

"Right. The shining white city that the conquistadors first saw was razed and Mexico City rose on the same site."

"How does that concern the Ortegas and me four hundred and fifty years later?"

"The Ortegas have a huge sheep ranch near Tlaxcala in a little mountain village, east of Mexico City."

"What does Tlaxcala have to do with this treasure?"

"Everything. Cortés's main allies were the Tlaxcalans. Without them he might never have defeated the Aztecs. The night the Aztecs drove the Spaniards out of Tenochtitlán, the survivors struggled and fought their way toward Tlaxcala. They holed up there and licked their wounds and planned the attack on Tenochtitlán."

"That still doesn't spell treasure."

"But it does," he said earnestly. "That night, called the Noche Triste, some of Cortés's men grabbed up as much treasure as they could carry. The Tlaxcalans carried, literally, the king's fifth, the share that was intended for Charles V. This treasure had belonged to Moctezuma's father, Axayacatl. None of it survived. Most was lost in the lake as the Spaniards and Tlaxcalans tried to fight their way across the causeway to safety. What little was salvaged was used by Cortés or melted down. There has always been a secret hope that some of that load of gold survived and will be found, perhaps when a tunnel is dug in construction in the part of the city that rests on the old lake bottom. Perhaps it will be found somewhere along the line of retreat that the Spaniards took to Tlaxcala."

His vivid blue eyes shone with excitement.

He had my attention now. Four hundred and fifty years is a long time. Not nearly as long a time elapsed from the burial of the Egyptian boy-king Tutankhamen to the discovery of his tomb. As every archeologist knows, nothing survives better than gold.

Gold is not destroyed by age or weather like wood and leather and cloth. Gold glistens as brightly, shines as brilliantly whether it was worked five years ago or five thousand years ago.

I thought quickly of some of the most famous golden treasures that had survived the ages. There was the incredibly fabulous Treasure of Tutankhamen, which enthralled the world when Howard Carter found the tomb in 1922. There was Schliemann's Treasure of Troy, discovered in one of archeology's most exciting moments only to be lost to history in the closing days of World War II. Some said it was once hidden in Pomerania. Others were sure it was put for safekeeping in a huge bunker in the Berlin Zoo and destroyed when the bunker was hit by bombs. Others said no, the gold disappeared when the Russians captured Berlin. There was the Treasure of Dorak, a collection of delicate and elegant ancient jewelry, which briefly came to light in Turkey, then disappeared again.

The Treasure of Axayacatl. Had anything like it ever

been discovered in the Americas? "There is quite a field of study in Mesoamerican metalwork, isn't there? Some of it must have survived."

"Only a little. There was a good find at Monte Albán. A lot has been learned from written sources in the early Colonial days. But of actual pieces of Aztec gold, we have just a handful."

"So, if someone found a secret cache of jewelry from the days of Moctezuma, it would be a huge achievement."

"The archeological discovery of the century," he exclaimed.

"It would be worth a lot of money?"

He laughed a little. "More money than you and I will ever see in a lifetime. Enough money to bring out the pirates."

"You think the treasure has been found? Near Tlaxcala?"

"I'm sure of it." Then he hedged a little. "At least something has been found, something damned valuable."

"How do you know?"

He hesitated. He pulled a pack of cigarettes from his pocket and took one, then absently offered them to me. I shook my head and waited while he struck the little wax match against the box and lit his cigarette. He pulled on it, then asked obliquely, "How well do you know the Ortegas?"

"Not at all," I said quickly. "They asked me to be their guest because I delivered the manuscript. I was invited because I came from the museum. The invitation had nothing to do with me personally." I hesitated, then explained. "I accepted because I didn't really have enough money to stay very long in Mexico if I had to pay my way at a hotel."

He understood that. He worked for a museum, too.

"I almost moved out after the first night, though."

"Why?"

"I'm still not sure what happened. I heard a scream." I told him about the cry that had brought me out of my sleep, how I had waited for it to sound again, and my decision finally to go and make sure that no one lay injured in the patio. I hated telling him the rest of it for it certainly revealed me as less than brave. But I did. I explained how I started down the stairs and heard the click of a closing door and how I turned to run back up the stairs only to sprawl ignominiously. It was, of course, a little anticlimactic to describe how the light came on and Tony introduced himself and showed me the peacocks.

"You don't think it was a peacock?"

"I'm sure it wasn't."

"What was it?"

"I can't imagine. It certainly wasn't Tony or Señora Ortega or Señor Ortega or Juan or the twins. I can't imagine a servant in that household making that kind of noise and, if they had, why would Tony have lied about it? Pretended it was a peacock?"

Jerry was watching me intently. "What about the old gentleman?"

"What old gentleman?" I asked blankly.

"Señor Herrera."

"There's no one of that name there."

"Oh yes," Jerry said quickly. "If you haven't met him, then someone is keeping him under wraps, and that means a hell of a lot."

"Who is he? Why should he cry out in the night?"

"He is Tony Ortega's grandfather, his mother's father. He is a retired professor of Mexican history, an authority on the Aztecs. He may have cried out in the night because of you."

"That doesn't follow at all. I've told you, I've never seen him."

"It follows beautifully. They may be keeping him hidden, but that doesn't mean he may not know what is happening in the house. You arrived late that evening and when the word finally reached him of the visitor's identity, he wanted to see you."

"Look, Jerry," I said as patiently as I could, "I've never met this man, never even heard of him, so why should he care a fig if I'm visiting his family's house?"

"You represent your museum. He knows or suspects that someone in the family is trying to sell something immensely valuable. He's afraid it's the Treasure of Axayacatl."

I looked at Jerry doubtfully. "If he's there in the house but sort of being kept a prisoner, how can you know whether he suspects something like that?"

"No one has seen him alone since Christmas. Not one

of his old friends has been permitted to visit him. He is *not well*, they are told when they call. He has not spoken to anyone."

"Why are you sure he isn't sick? How can you claim that he suspects anything at all?"

"There was a dinner in his honor," Jerry said quietly, "shortly after the Feast of the Epiphany. He came to that and made a short speech in response to a plaque presented to him. He shook hands with the man who handed it to him."

"Then I suppose he whispered, 'Help, I'm a prisoner in my own home.'"

Jerry was far too close to all of it to think that was funny.

"No, we'd have a lot more to go on if he had," Jerry said seriously. "But he slipped a small piece of paper into the man's hand. That man is my boss and that was the first hint of something happening up near Tlaxcala."

"What did he write?"

Jerry looked around the lake. Other boats floated peacefully on the placid green water. No one paid any attention to us.

Still, Jerry spoke softly. "I remember it word for word, I've studied it so often. He wrote: 'I suffer from an anguished heart, old friend, torn between loyalty to my family and my duty to my country. Perhaps the weakness of age will excuse my lack of resolution. Beware foreign museum agents near Tlaxcala. Request thorough study of all jewelries leaving

Mexico. I have appealed to my old friend, Vicente Rodriguez, but I have heard nothing. God grant that I am wrong.
Yours in sorrow, Tomas Herrera.' "

We were both quiet for a moment. Lake water slapped
gently against the boat. From the shore we heard happy
shouts of children kicking a ball. But both of us were
listening to the words just spoken, sorrow-laden words.

An old man, fearing for his country's past. An old . . .
I reached out abruptly and touched Jerry's knee. "What
does it mean in Spanish, *El Viejito*?"

"The old gentlemen. Often that's what Mexicans call
a grandfather."

El Viejito. Yes, of course. Tony was afraid it was he
who had torn apart the doll. The girls were trying to
protect their grandfather and they had been warned not
to speak of him.

I had a sudden picture of an old man, worried, fearful,
trying to do his duty as he saw it, but even he did not know
who it was in his family that he should fear.

Gerda? Juan? Tony? Señor Ortega?

Señor Herrera didn't know. Was he trying to find out
when he wrote Dr. Rodriguez, the head of the Mesoamerican section in my museum? Señor Herrera had received
no answer.

Why?

I recalled Dr. Rodriguez, plump, smiling, amiable.
Could he connive to smuggle a treasure out of Mexico?

"I can't believe it," I said suddenly. "Dr. Rodriguez

wouldn't set me up to come down here and be in danger. It's too fantastic."

Jerry shook his head. "Nothing's too fantastic when a fortune in gold is at stake. There's not much gentility beneath the surface of the museum trade."

"You talk in terms of someone being willing to kill me to keep me from getting the treasure." I remembered the bullets but it still seemed impossible. "That's murder."

"Yes," Jerry agreed. "It wouldn't be the first murder."

11

Jerry told me of the short life and violent death of Raúl
Muñoz. I listened, appalled, and knew that I had stumbled into or deliberately been thrust into a dangerously
grim business. It was doubly chilling to realize how the
death of Raúl Muñoz had almost passed unnoticed.

People in villages don't talk to outsiders. If Jerry or an
inspector of police had gone to Tlaxcala to ask about rumors
of treasure, they would have learned very little. But people
talk among themselves and if an unobtrusive stranger listens
and never presses, he may learn many things.

It was in midwinter, not long after the old gentleman
had pressed his note of distress into a friend's hand, that
a young man, a quiet young man from Orizaba, or so he
said, came to Tlaxcala. He was an assistant to Inspector

Enrique Gonzales of the antiquities divisional. But no one there knew that.

The young man learned a good many things about the Ortegas. One of the first interesting facts was of the death of a young ranch employee, Raúl Muñoz. The stranger thought hard about this. Policemen have a feel for unexpected deaths.

Raúl died at the end of November. That would have been shortly before El Viejito, Tony's grandfather, wrote his sad, disturbing letter to my museum, the letter that was never answered.

Raúl had been different in November, some of the villagers remembered. No one, to be truthful, liked Raúl much. He was too ambitious, too self-serving. But you had to give him his due. Orphaned at seven, raised by an older brother, he had done well. Some of the credit belongs to his older brother Lorenzo, who had worked for years for the Ortegas and found a job for his little brother. Raúl had managed on his own to impress the foreman of the Ortega ranch and to come to the attention of the family. Everyone felt, though, that he had gotten above himself when he began riding with the señora. If he hadn't reached too far, they seemed to think, he would still be alive. For it was on a horseback ride that he had apparently fallen to his death. He had grown up riding mules up and down the treacherous trails. But horses and mules are different animals altogether.

No one knew what happened that bleak November day.

He had gone out alone. The horse came back late that afternoon, riderless. It took a week to find his body.

Had anyone else ridden out on the Ortega ranch that afternoon?

No one knew; it was such a time ago. Anyway, what difference did it make? No one had mentioned seeing Raúl.

A word here, a phrase there, a slowly assembled picture of an agile, eager young man trying hard to please. A flashing smile, quick nervous gestures, but ultimately there was more to him than that. Beneath the surface effort to please was a tough, hungry spirit.

It was after he had been a month in Tlaxcala that the quiet young man from Orizaba first heard the word *gold* and heard it in conjunction with Raúl.

The quiet young man had picked up a day's work as a casual laborer, loading hand-quarried rock onto a truck. When the work was done, he and the driver sat beneath a scrubby tree. It had been a warm day for February and the quiet young man had shared his beer and listened, impassive, as the driver, at his ease and expansive, pointed to a lightning-shattered tree, just barely in view from the dusty road, and said, "It was there, in an arroyo, that they found the body of Raúl Muñoz." The old man had paused and stared at the rugged rocky terrain, fit only for nimble goats and sheep. "He ran up and down those trails as a boy. They say the horse must have thrown him. Funny, though—he'd ridden that same horse all year." The old man's voice dropped almost to a whisper. "He was thrown the day after he spoke up in the bar and said he was going to be rich, that he'd found gold in the hills." The old man's eyes were dark, unreadable. "If there is gold in the hill, it doesn't belong to any man; the gold belongs to the gods."

The old man wouldn't say more. Not a word. But now, with something definite to go on, the quiet young man unobtrusively asked more questions, a few of this one, a few of that one. Very slowly he recreated Raúl Muñoz's last night to live.

Raúl had swaggered into the little tavern in midafternoon. He drank tequila. He drank as the sun slipped behind the mountain. He made no friends that last night. From men who had been present in the tavern, the story emerged piece by piece.

"He was full of himself. So big, you understand."

"He laughed at us. He laughed and said we were poor because we did not look for riches."

"He said he would be as rich as a king because he knew when to act."

Finally, his words so thick they could barely be understood, Raúl Muñoz said he had seen with his own eyes the gleam of gold softer than the shine of the sun on an angel's wing.

Some of the men taunted him for they were angry at his drunken arrogance. If he had found treasure, he must prove it. Where was this gold?

The very tequila that loosened his tongue now cloaked him with the cunning of the drunk. He shook his head slowly from side to side. Someday they would know he spoke the truth. He was going to be richer than a king.

None of them ever saw him again. In little more than a week, the church bells tolled his farewell.

He was nineteen when he died.

The men in Tlaxcala have often talked about treasure and hunted it. Some wondered after Raúl's death, but soon the talk fell away. So many had hunted treasure and no one had ever found it. Once they were sure that gold was hidden in an overgrown mound not far from town. They dug all one long night, hoping to see the bright gleam of gold, and there was nothing but the worn remains of an ancient temple.

It was warm in the drifting boat in the middle of the smooth green lake, but coldness touched me. The sunlight did nothing to dispel it.

"You think it was murder?" I asked.

"Don't you?"

"Why?"

"Gold," he said softly.

"Someone found the treasure," I said slowly, thinking it out, "and Raúl discovered it?" I shook my head and answered my own question. "That doesn't make sense. If anyone found some fabulous treasure, they'd make sure no one came upon them with it. It's all too fantastic."

Jerry rubbed his cheekbone thoughtfully. "I have a feeling that nothing in all of this has happened accidentally. I don't absolutely discount coincidence, but I think a very careful mind is at work. I don't, for example, think you are involved in this by chance."

I jerked up my head.

He shook his head quickly. "We are always talking at cross-purposes, aren't we? I don't mean I'm still suspicious of you, Sheila, but think about it for a minute. This must be the sequence." He ticked them off on his fingers. "Someone, some member of the Ortega family, discovers a treasure and contacts someone in your museum. Señor Herrera finds out. He writes his old friend, Dr. Rodriguez, who has often spoken out against antiquities smuggling." Jerry glanced at me. "Not all your people are bad."

I bristled a little at that. There is the other side of the coin in this question of protecting archeological treasures. But I knew that I would never again be able to argue it, not when I remembered the murder of Raúl Muñoz.

"So we have someone at Tlaxcala and someone in New York making plans," Jerry continued. "Now, if it's the usual situation, neither one will trust the other. They will have to meet and make the exchange. The museum person knows very well the danger of gossip and how word can leak out and the spoor bring the sharks. That's where you come in, Sheila."

I must have looked absolutely blank.

"Don't you see?" Jerry asked impatiently. "You are the decoy, the stalking horse." He nodded, sure he had hit on it. "A cat's-paw."

I almost laughed at the quaint, old-fashioned word.

Cat's-paw. I could imagine this gray-and-black-striped paw with pale pink pads, claws neatly sheathed.

Jerry didn't see my quick smile. Head bent, tousled hair falling down over that high forehead, he was intent upon his thoughts. "That's it, of course. One of the Ortegas requests the return of the manuscript. You bring it down and you are so publicly, so blatantly linked with your museum that you are bound to be noticed. It worked." He nodded, admiring the skill of it. "It worked like a charm. We noticed you, suspected you. More important, it brought out his competition, the other seeker after the treasure." Jerry's blue eyes narrowed. "It showed that word had leaked out, that they would have to be very careful indeed about the ultimate transfer of the treasure."

Cat's-paw. One person used as a tool by another, a decoy. Suddenly it didn't seem funny at all.

"Do you have your tourist card with you?"

I looked at him blankly. He must have thought I was dim-witted, but his grasshopper leaps from one topic to another always left me floundering. "My tourist card?"

"Your tourist card, is it with you?" he repeated impatiently.

I nodded. Yes, my tourist card and traveler's checks were in my purse.

"Good. The thing to do, right now, is get you on a plane to New York. Out of Mexico. There's no need for you to stay here and be in danger."

I didn't say anything for a minute. Go home now? A

part of me welcomed that thought, hungered for the comforting anonymity of New York. But, almost to my own surprise, I was shaking my head.

"No," I said sharply.

"Look, Sheila, you're lucky those shots on the Avenue of the Dead missed you."

I shook my head stubbornly.

"He might be luckier next time."

"I want to know. I have to know." For the first time I knew I was angry.

"Know what?" He was lost now.

"A cat's-paw, you said. Someone at my museum moved me like a chess piece, set me up to draw fire. I can't walk away, pretend nothing happened."

"Don't worry," he said reassuringly. "We'll catch whoever it is."

Would they? Right now, right this minute, one of the Ortegas could be meeting someone from my museum. Who was it? What familiar face would I see if I were at the cautious meeting?

"We're keeping watch on the family. The most likely person is Antonio Ortega."

"Not Tony. I can't believe that."

"Why not?" Jerry asked, surprised and a little wary.

Why not, indeed? Hadn't I been wrong about him once? But he was kind and respectful to his father (what about Gerda, though?) and gentle with his sisters and there was no taint of cruelty in his darkly handsome face.

Cruelty. I saw again Juan's narrow face and the wild light in his eyes.

"Gossip has it that the Ortega trading company is in trouble. An extra million or so might make the difference," Jerry said.

Gossip is more often wrong than right, I thought defensively. And wasn't all business a gamble? Down one minute, up the next?

But I was slowly nodding my head. "I see." Yes, reluctantly, I could believe that Tony would go to great lengths to save the family firm. Not for personal gain, but for family salvation. But murder? I recoiled at that. No, not Tony. If the boy, Raúl, had been murdered to protect the treasure, Tony could not be involved.

I held on to that certainty as Jerry continued to talk. ". . . a bad time for some of the smaller trading companies. There are shortages everywhere, breakdowns in manufacturing, lack of raw materials—"

"You can't be sure it's Tony." I had to interrupt finally.

Jerry shrugged. "No, but who else is there? Who especially that Señor Herrera would wish to protect?"

Juan, I thought quickly. Tony's father. Even Gerda.

"We'll watch all of them," Jerry said soothingly. "That's our job. You don't need to worry any more. Now, I'll get you out to the airport. We won't go by the house for your suitcase. You can call from the airport and ask them to ship your things, explaining an emergency made it necessary for you to return to New York."

165

"The exchange could be taking place right now," I said abruptly.

Jerry's bony face tightened. "Right. So I need to hurry." And he began to row swiftly toward shore.

"But if it hasn't happened," I said smoothly, "and I'm there in the house, watching all of them, there's a better chance we might be able to stop it."

He paused in midstroke. The boat swerved a little to the left. He straightened it, but his eyes never left my face.

"It could be very dangerous," he said slowly.

I'm not sure even now what my true reasons were. Anger at being used? Stiff Scot pride that forbade running? Determination to root out banditry from my museum?

Or was it a muddled attempt to help Tony even though I had no real reason to believe him innocent? I had nothing more than an instinctive, stubborn faith that he could not be the one.

12

The gate to the Ortega drive was a work of art. In the soft light of afternoon, the bars gleamed a rich bronze. As my cab pulled away, I touched the button to activate the intercom system and spoke my name firmly. As the gates slid open and I stepped inside, I still felt confident of my course. It was only as I heard the sharp click behind me as the gate inexorably closed that I felt once again the breathlessness of that first night when I had looked back over my shoulder and watched them shut.

Trapped.

Nonsense. If I wanted to, I could turn around and call on the intercom and walk free into the street. I looked up the drive as it began to curve, at lush greenery crowding close to each side of the pink stone drive, and battled my fear.

I forced myself to move forward. I was committed. I might well be able to discover the truth and save a national treasure. It didn't appear we were going to be able to find out much in New York, though Jerry made every effort. After returning to the pier, Jerry led me out of the park in a circuitous fashion and then by cab and subway we reached his apartment. It was my idea that we call Dr. Rodriguez and ask him directly about the letter from El Viejito.

The call was a disappointment. The connection was poor, but finally we understood: Dr. Rodriguez wasn't in and would not be back for two weeks.

I had to decide quickly whether to try to talk to anyone else on the staff. Reluctantly, I decided not to chance it. I might talk to the very person who had used me as a decoy.

There would be no help from New York. It was up to me.

I continued up the drive toward the house, deep in thought. I took one steady step after another. Pick 'em up and put 'em down—that's all I had to do. And come into my parlor, said the spider to the fly, come right ahead, walk up this way and I'll be waiting. One step, another. The sudden thud of running steps startled me and then the twins erupted around the curve.

". . . said you were here and . . ."

". . . been waiting all day. Will you swim with us?"

"Please, please?"

I wondered at their urgency, and then with the artlessness of children, Rita said, "No one's here at all. We can't swim alone and grouchy old Manuel said he's too busy to watch us."

"The water's heated," Francesca added. "You'll like it. Please, Miss Ramsay?"

I said yes, and not with any ulterior motive. I liked the twins, liked them a lot, and whatever strange shadow hung over the Ortegas, it couldn't be a good thing for them. It would be better, surely, if the person who had killed Raúl was discovered. If someone kills once, they are forever a danger to any near them.

The pool was heated and it was fun. We played keep-away with a soccer ball until I was panting and clinging to the side, crying, "Too much, too much."

We each tipped ourselves up onto huge inflatable floating chairs and I took the first step on a road that would lead to terror on a star-spangled night.

"Is your grandfather well enough for me to visit with him for a few minutes?"

Their silence was absolute and revealing. Before my question, their laughter and the splash of water as they kicked and paddled in their floating chairs had muted all other sounds. In the sudden quiet, the water from the fountain fell into the pool and each drop sounded as it struck.

Rita said not a word. One twin is always the strongest. It was Francesca who asked, her face guarded, "I did not know you were the friend of my grandfather?" Her formality reflected her fear.

I looked at her gravely. "I would like to be his friend, Francesca, but you are right, I have not met him yet. He is the good friend, though, of a man who works at my museum in New York, Dr. Rodriguez."

Her small brown face, so like Tony's, relaxed a little, but she was still puzzled and suspicious. "But grandfather cried when—"

Rita interrupted then, speaking in Spanish.

Francesca listened, but before she answered, I took a chance.

"Girls." I spoke in a low, soft voice that caught their attention immediately. "Please, I know you don't understand, but tell your grandfather that I am on his side. Tell him that. Then, if he wishes, I would be very happy to talk with him."

They stared at me solemnly, wanting to trust me, afraid to.

My heart ached for them. "That's all we'll say about it. Don't worry. If he doesn't want to talk to me, that's all right, too."

We had a race then, but their hearts weren't in it. The fun was gone. I wished I could bring the happiness back to their faces.

I worried later, as I bathed and dressed for dinner, that I had put too heavy a burden on them. But surely I had not put them in danger. After all, Señor Herrera had not been harmed, so the twins should be safe enough.

The twins were not at dinner that evening. I almost asked after them, but decided against it. There was one other empty chair. Señor Ortega had flown to Veracruz to bid on some coffee. So Tony, Juan, Gerda, and I sat down to dinner.

Midway through the meal, I took my second step on the doom-fated road.

Gerda asked how I liked the pyramids.

I didn't answer at once. It happened that every face turned toward me and there was a lull in the conversation. Everyone waited for me to answer.

If I had thought about it, estimated what effect my words might have, I might have answered differently. Instead, I felt a flicker of anger. I looked around the table. "Someone shot at me."

Each face reflected shock in a different way.

Tony stared at me. "What do you mean?"

"I was walking up the Avenue of the Dead. I was alone. No one was near me. Someone shot at me. Three times."

He didn't accuse me of lying, but his disbelief was obvious. "Did you call the guards, ask for help?"

I described my frantic scramble for safety, how I stumbled into the lot where Manuel waited, and my decision not to tell anyone.

"Why not?" Tony demanded, darkly frowning, his hand tight on the stem of his crystal wine glass.

It was utterly quiet as they waited for my answer. Gerda scarcely breathed. Her lovely face, always pale, seemed paler yet. Juan leaned across the table. His dark eyes glistened. Was it excitement, pleasure, or something darker, harder to define?

"I should have told someone," I admitted. "I wanted to tell someone. But I knew what would happen."

"What?" Tony again, his voice hard, cold.

My lips trembled, but I managed to speak steadily. "No one would believe me. But it happened."

Tony put everyone's question into words. "Why would anyone shoot at you?"

Now it was I who sat silent. What could I say? Someone here in your house, your father, your brother, your stepmother, one of them has connived to put me in danger, has used me as a decoy to flush out treasure seekers.

I looked down the table at Tony's face, heavier, older in the flickering light of the candle, and wondered with a sad painful catch, *One of them or . . . oh Tony, was it you?*

Finally, tiredly, my voice drained, I answered. "I don't know."

No one, of course, believed that.

Certainly not Tony. His face was as closed as it was that night after he picked up the obsidian knife near the mutilated doll.

I excused myself immediately after dinner. I could not gather with them in the luxurious living room and hold a cup of coffee in my hand and idly chat. I said good night. As I reached the hall, I heard a swift murmur of

Spanish from Juan. Tony made an angry reply. I was sure the exchange concerned me.

I walked so quickly I almost ran. Footsteps came after me, but I didn't slow. I was almost to my door when Tony's voice stopped me.

"Sheila."

I turned to face him.

The hall was dimly lit. What little light there was came from behind him. His face was in shadow. He was only a few feet from me but he seemed far away. "Sheila, I went to Tlaxcala today." He spoke very tiredly.

I wished that he had not followed me up the hall, that he had not told me. I hadn't wanted to know. I looked at him, but I could scarcely see through a mist of tears.

He lifted his hand, stretched it out toward me, then shook his head and let it fall.

"Please go back to New York. Go back." He turned and was gone.

Once in my room, I closed the door behind me and leaned against the hard panel. I had my answer now. There could no longer be any doubt.

Feeling numb and empty, I slipped on my gown, brushed my teeth, and made ready for bed. Tomorrow, I would leave the Casa Ortega. I lay in that high strange bed and ticked off in my mind the things I must do: make my excuses to the Ortegas, exchange my plane tickets, pack. I would go home to New York and be free of fear and safe.

Safe? In New York? If I went back, reported to my boss all that had happened here, I would not be safe. It wasn't going to be that easy. I couldn't just walk away.

But I could not, would not bring trouble to Tony.

No matter what he had done?

A small, still voice answered, *No matter what.*

Still, I didn't dare go home unless I knew from whom to expect danger.

The danger lay in the Mesoamerican Department; that seemed almost certain. The first week in January, Dr. Herrera had alerted Mexican authorities to expect a smuggling attempt. Just before that, he wrote to Dr. Rodriguez but received no answer. In January there were six members of the Mesoamerican section: Dr. Rodriguez, Cecilia Edwards, J. Thomas Wood, Michael Taylor, Karl Freidheim, and Timothy Simmons.

Cecilia Edwards and J. Thomas Wood were in Peru in January, directing an expedition.

That left four.

I was sitting up in bed now. I reached out and pulled on the light. In only a moment, I had retrieved a notebook and was propped up in bed and writing.

Dr. Rodriguez. Michael Taylor, Karl Freidheim. Timothy Simmons.

I stared at those four names. One of them. It had to be.

Michael Taylor. A small, dark, spare man. Black hair streaked with gray, horn-rim glasses, head usually bent in thought.

Freidheim. That bastard Freidheim, Timothy had called him. He was vice chairman of the department. He had been furious that the Ortegas had requested the return of the Sanchez manuscript. Had Dr. Freidheim's anger been clever camouflage? Who could have been in a better position to suggest to one of the Ortegas (say it, Sheila, say Tony) that the manuscript be recalled, providing a reason to send an innocent museum employee to Mexico City, thereby attracting any official attention plus, as it turned out, decoying another treasure seeker?

Last of all, Timothy Simmons. My friend Timothy. I remembered Timothy without any false shadings. I didn't trust Timothy. There was little I'd put past him. But could he possibly have the stroke for this kind of caper? Timothy, after all, was as new to the museum as I was. It was his first job and he, like I, was at the bottom of the heap.

I shook my head. I didn't see how it could be Timothy. Whoever was coming to Mexico (or perhaps was already here) had to be someone with a measure of importance at the museum, someone who had wangled the necessary money (and a million or so takes a little talent to find) either from a museum patron or from the board.

Of course, it was always possible that the seller was going to be cheated by the buyer, somehow, someway. Perhaps the crime was a venture independent of the museum.

I looked up from my notepad, drew in a quick breath. I hadn't locked my door. The handle was moving, slowly, so slowly. The door began to open. . .

13

The twins slipped into my room, fingers to their lips, brown eyes huge in their pretty rounded faces, their cotton gowns a cheerful pink.

"Shh, don't make any noise," Rita instructed in a feather-soft whisper.

"Grandfather will see you now," Francesca explained. "But we must be very quiet."

Rita nodded. "Juan isn't home yet, so it should be safe enough."

The reality of life at the Casa Ortega slipped into sharper, harder focus. They were afraid of Juan. Juan. I was afraid of Juan myself.

I put on my dressing gown, doused my light, and followed them into the hall. They led me down the main hall toward the living room but stopped short of it to take me down a narrow, twisting staircase that opened out into an equally narrow hall to the kitchen. We slipped through an immaculate kitchen to a door that opened onto the patio near the breakfast table.

The patio lights were on, glowing softly, making pools of pastel color on the terrace and down into the garden. Francesca led me into the shadows along a wall that ran along this side of the patio. Midway the length of the wall, she guided me out into the garden and we paused in the shadow of a hibiscus. I saw that she intended to lead us the long way around the garden, from one dark shadow to another, to the colonnaded wing.

We were almost at the end of the garden, still avoiding pools of soft light, when Francesca clutched my arm, jerking me to a stop. I heard voices the same instant. Rita stumbled into us. The three of us stood rigid.

We were near wooden steps that led down a sharp incline to a hidden level of the property and the garages. The figures came up the steps, quarreling in low angry voices. Gerda was pleading. They stopped at the top of the stairs. They were well hidden from the house by the hump of the vine-covered trellis. They felt safe from view. They could not be seen or heard from the house. They would scarcely expect anyone to be out in the lower garden at this late hour.

Gerda was facing us, moonlight full on her face. He stood with his back to us. She clung to his arm, all soft femininity. In the sharp white light of the moon, her hair shone like silver.

I looked down at Francesca and wished for her sake and for Rita's that they were not here beside me. There was no surprise on the twins' brown expressionless faces. No surprise at all.

Gerda said something more. He shook his head and started to turn, pulling away from her hand.

My heart stood still. I knew that head, the shape of it. The man standing there wasn't Tony.

"Juan." Her voice was imploring.

Juan swung around, his face hard, angular, dangerous. His mouth twisted contemptuously.

Of course the man was Juan, not Tony. One brother's voice can certainly sound like another's. Juan's lips had closed on Gerda's. Not Tony's. Never Tony's.

Gerda clung to Juan's arm.

He said something in a mocking tone.

Gerda moved closer to him, pressed against him, slipped her hands up and around his neck. He hesitated for an instant, shrugged, murmured something, and bent his head to hers.

It was dreadful how glad I was. I didn't at that moment care at all that they were lovers. At least, not until I looked at the girls again. I hated for them to see this passionate encounter. It seemed hours before that embrace ended.

When Gerda and Juan had gone, when it was utterly

quiet in the garden again, Francesca gently touched my arm. We moved on. None of us said anything. I didn't know what I could say. Perhaps they knew better than I that there was nothing to say.

They led me to the door that had opened so briefly my first night. It was this door that Tony entered last night. He had been there while Juan and Gerda were whispering in the vine-covered bower.

The twins tapped on the door softly. Maria answered. She hurried us inside and latched the door after us.

This room did not match the rest of the house. There was no hint of luxury here. Instead there was simplicity and dignity and a sense of place. It was an austere room furnished with a narrow, dark wooden bed, a chest of drawers, a rolltop desk, two leather chairs. The crucifix above the bed dominated the room. Christ in his agony was here.

Señor Herrera was propped up in the bed. He held out his hand and I hurried to take it. I was shocked at its lack of substance. He was very old, his hair a wispy white, his creased and wrinkled face a faded khaki color. His black eyes were vivid and alive and fearful.

"You have come"—and his voice was as faint as the faraway murmur of wind chimes—"from Vicente?"

I realized after an instant's pause that he meant Dr. Rodriguez. I hesitated.

He saw that hesitation and struggled up on one elbow. "If you did not come from Vicente, how can you be here to help me? Did the girls make a mistake, misunder-stand?"

I smiled reassuringly. "I am here to help. There is no mistake. I will help you if I can."

He rested back on his pillow and listened. I explained how I had come to Casa Ortega to return the Sanchez manuscript.

He interrupted me. "Why did you bring it back?"

"The Ortega family requested the return of the manuscript."

His weak voice was emphatic. "That is not right, not right at all. The manuscript is mine. I loaned it. I did not ask for its return."

So the return of the manuscript had been an excuse to decoy a member of the museum staff to the Ortega house. Since Señor Herrera had not asked for the manuscript, he suspected the worst when I arrived. It had been he who cried out in the night upon learning of my arrival.

I told him how he had not been alone in suspecting me, of the warning thrust on me at the airport and of the torn-apart doll.

Maria interrupted here to say something in Spanish. He listened and nodded, then urged me to continue. His dark eyes were shocked when I described the shooting on the Avenue of the Dead. I told him of Jerry Elliot and the concern by the Department of Antiquities and he seemed both elated and at the same time grieved.

He looked past me to speak to Maria. "I put everything

in God's hands. I wrote out the message, asking for help. I thought I had done my duty."

I wished I had not had to tell the tale I told, obviously implicating a member of his family. It was intolerable to him that the antiquities he had spent his life studying should be spirited out of Mexico. But that he should bring disgrace upon some member of his family was intolerable, too. I understood his dilemma. I squeezed his hand gently.

"I wasn't sure," he said sadly. "But I was afraid."

Here was the heart of it. Now I would learn what had prompted him to write Dr. Rodriguez, what had forged the chain of death that linked New York and Tlaxcala.

His story was a simple one. Maria had come to him in early winter and told him of Raúl's death and of the whispers of gold and treasure and how Raúl had boasted the evening before he died of gold that would make him richer than a king.

He dismissed the tales as gossip and nothing more. He didn't connect rumors of gold with his grandson Juan's visit to his room the next week. He was pleased, excited Juan had come to see him.

"It had been since midsummer since I had seen him," the old man said apologetically.

The visit had been such a pleasant one. Somehow the conversation had turned to the antiquities trade and museums reputed to buy stolen goods. He and Juan spoke of my museum, one of the worst offenders.

"I see," I said tiredly. I did. I saw more than the old

gentleman could imagine. The sequence was clear now. A treasure, a fabulous treasure, discovered by an unscrupulous young man. What then? Chests of gold can't be hawked on the street corner. A little discreet investigation, a letter to the museum, perhaps describing the treasure well enough that the recipient knew that here was the find of the century.

"Did you mention a particular person at the museum?" I asked tensely.

He shook his head gently.

The letter had gone blind to the museum. It would have been received in the main office, that same office where I saw the fateful notice on the bulletin board. The secretary there would open and forward it to the appropriate section. The letter must, of course, have been guarded, but some hint must have been made about gold—that and the letter's origin in Mexico would be enough to direct it to the Mesoamerican section. Received there, it would be part of the nut mail and with that section's egalitarian system the letter went to the next staff member in line to answer nut mail.

Who had read that letter and sensed its authenticity?

Dr. Rodriguez? Michael Taylor? Karl Freidheim? Timothy Simmons?

One of them.

Dr. Herrera, of course, knew none of this. He didn't think at all about his conversation with Juan. At least, not until his son-in-law, Tony and Juan's father, spent an evening with him in early December.

Señor Ortega often came in the evenings to play a game of chess and share a glass of wine with his first wife's father. They talked of family and the hacienda, of the grandchildren's plans. Toward the end of this particular evening, Dr. Herrera remembered the moment perfectly, his son-in-law asked if he had started a new project, a paper perhaps for a scholarly magazine?

Señor Herrera was puzzled. It had been several years since he had worked. He had ideas, yes, but he no longer had strength. His son-in-law knew this so Señor Herrera was surprised and asked, "Why did you think I was writing again?"

His son-in-law told him how pleased he had been when he paid his telephone bill for the month to see three calls to New York. To the museum.

Señor Ortega told of the calls tactfully for he knew the old gentleman, El Viejito, sometimes forgot things.

The old man knew that sometimes he did forget so he didn't make an issue of the phone calls. The conversation moved on to other things. Days passed but Señor Herrera worried about the calls, felt uneasy. He had Maria get a copy of the bill. He checked the number. The calls were to the museum, to the extension that belonged to the Mesoamerican Department.

A warning bell clamored in his mind. Gold in Tlaxcala. Juan's visit. The museum in New York, a museum that in the past had not been too fastidious in the sources of its treasures. But surely his old friend Vicente Rodriguez would not permit the finest of Mexico's art to be stolen.

On the one hand, the old man feared the loss of a great treasure from its homeland. On the other, he dreaded the discovery that one of his daughter's children was conniving to smuggle away his heritage.

Señor Herrera lay very still when he had finished, his hand limp in mine. I feared for a moment that the strain had been too great on his heart. Maria was frightened, too, for she pushed in beside me and took that limp, shadow-light hand in her own and called to him.

He opened his eyes after a moment and smiled up at her and murmured something in Spanish.

She answered him soothingly, then turned to me. "Enough. He has spoken enough."

"I know," I said quickly. I looked down once again for that aged hand was plucking at mine. He was tired, very tired now, but still he whispered, "I am so sorry."

I held his hand in mine. "You have no reason to be sorry, señor."

He nodded. "Last night, Tony came and he was so worried. I told him everything, but I told him you were here to take the treasure away. You must tell him I was wrong." His voice faded away.

I held his hand and my heart sang. That was why Tony had gone to Tlaxcala; that was why he had urged me to go back to New York.

Not because he was guilty.

"Please," Maria urged. "You must go now. El Viejito must rest."

"Thank you, Maria. I will go. Reassure him that I will protect the treasure." I looked down at his shadowed face. "Tell him not to worry." Then I said, and the words were out before I weighed them, "tell him Tony and I will see to everything."

Her face softened a little, warmed to me. "He has been so afraid."

"We will make sure the treasure is saved."

But was it a promise I could keep?

All the way back to my room, the girls and I slipping from the safety of one dark shadow to another, I tried to decide what to do. There was no question in my mind that I must do something. Up to now, I had been buffeted this way and that by events. Now I had committed myself to act. The strain had eased in the old man's face at my promise. It was time I made things happen.

Once at my room, I beckoned the girls inside.

"Francesca"—and I made no excuse for my question—"what did Juan and Gerda say to each other?"

"In the garden?"

I nodded.

She frowned. "I couldn't hear all of it. When they came up the steps, she was asking him to"—Rita paused, then said carefully and slowly, and I knew she was trying to remember the exact words—"to 'move it tonight,' my stepmother said. 'Please, Juan. Do it for me.' Juan said something I didn't hear, and then she kissed him and I didn't hear the rest."

Move it tonight.

Move what tonight?

My heart gave a funny little leap. Was she asking Juan to go out in the cold light of the moon and swoop over a mountain road, covering in an hour or so the hard, rugged country that had taken Cortés's soldiers four days to cross when they fled Tenochtitlán? Could Juan hurry to a hidden cache and gather up gold that had been lost for four hundred and fifty years?

Jerry had described to me what might be in the Treasure of Axayacatl, intricate works of the softest hammered gold, ear spools and pendants, nose plugs and whistles, headdresses, breastplates, discs. Each piece would likely reflect the highly original mythology of the Aztec people. Jaguar heads and feathered serpents, a writhing skirt of snakes, the soft teardrops of falling rain—all of these and more might be captured in gold.

Tonight?

I don't know that I consciously made a choice. Jerry had given me his home and office telephone numbers and told me to call at once should I discover anything.

I may, as I stood there, have remembered that and remembered also when he put me into the cab and said,

"For God's sake, be careful, Sheila." If I thought about it at all, it was only in passing for there was really no choice to be made.

"Francesca," I said urgently, "get Tony for me. Quickly. Tell him that I've talked to your grandfather, that I'm on his side. Please hurry. It's very important."

When she left, Rita close behind her, I dropped my robe and gown on a chair and slipped into a navy double-knit dress and white sandals. I don't really know exactly what I had in mind. I do know that I never questioned my decision to call Tony, to tell him everything. I hoped that perhaps he and I might be able to put everything back together again. If we could find the treasure—perhaps we could follow Juan or demand that he show it to us—if we could find the gold, get it to safety, then we could see what might be salvaged out of the mess.

I didn't think about Raúl, the clever, boastful young man, so ambitious, so early dead.

I was brushing my hair back, twisting it into a bun, when there was a soft knock at my door. I snatched up my sweater and ran to the door. I opened it and was startled to find the little maid there, the one who had brought me hot chocolate the first night.

She looked nervously over her shoulder, then gestured to me to follow her. Somehow I had expected the twins to return with Tony, but perhaps he felt the children had been through enough for one night and sent them on to bed.

To my surprise she led me downstairs—her finger to

her lips—and out onto the terrace by the poolroom. I half expected her to turn toward the colonnaded wing. Instead she hurried me down the center path of the garden, then veered off to the right to scurry down the wooden steps that led toward the garages.

She didn't stop at the garages. I paused and asked in my guidebook Spanish, "¿Donde está Tony?"

She clapped her small, warm hand over my mouth, whispered something I didn't understand, and tugged at my sleeve. We started off again. We passed the garages, dark and barnlike, and turned down a narrow brick walk that ran beside a tall, prickly cedar hedge. It was utterly secluded with scarcely enough space between the garage wall and the hedge to look up and see the stars.

I slowed down again.

She yanked on my arm, whispering.

When I stubbornly stopped, she gestured ahead at a huge wooden door. She stepped in front of me and lifted the heavy crossbeam. The door slowly swung out. She paused to let me go first. "He must talk to you, señorita. My brother is waiting for you."

I tried to see ahead of me but that sweet-smelling hedge grew tall enough to block out the moonlight, making shadows as thick and black as a pool of oil.

I stepped hesitantly to the opening. Her brother? Someone who needed to see me? Midway through the door, something moved at the periphery of my vision. I swung around as arms reached for me.

14

He was incredibly strong. One arm held me pinioned against him. The other crooked about my neck, pulling my chin high and my head back against his chest. I couldn't move.

The wooden door slammed shut behind me. I heard the crossbar drop into place.

If he pulled my head any higher, my neck would break.

There is a point beyond fear where terror envelops you and the world is reduced to a frantic struggle to survive. Nothing existed in the world but the agonizing strain as my neck arched back and back. I was held in a hard, unrelenting grip, unable to move.

His voice was a harsh, hot breath against my cheek. "Be quiet and you will be safe."

My heart thudded erratically. My head throbbed from pain and fear. I knew I was even nearer death than I had been when the bullets pitted that ages-old pavement on the Avenue of the Dead. I trembled, but I no longer fought to be free. Gradually he loosed his grip, easing the strain on my throat. Quickly, before I realized his intent, he pulled my hands behind me, twisted a leather strap around them, and tied the ends in two quick twists.

I was still frightened, terribly frightened, but I had wit enough to realize that I was not hurt. He could easily have strangled me if that had been his intent.

He herded me down the alley. The way was rough and rocky. His hand was hard on my arm. Far ahead a lamp marked the alley's entry into the street. We were not far from the street when a flashlight beam danced around the opening into the alley and a musical whistle trilled.

My captor lifted me as if I weighed no more than a pillow and plunged half a dozen steps back into the obscurity of the alley, pressing both of us against another wooden gate recessed in a wall.

I knew better than to make even the tiniest of noises. The man holding me signaled his intent clearly. Menace emanated from him in waves.

The watchman almost passed us.

His flashlight was loose in his hand. He hummed a tuneless hum. His shoes scuffed leisurely along the rocky ground. He was in no hurry. A few feet from us, he paused and swung the light up to run along the rim of the wall. The light illuminated him for a moment, gray cap tipped to the back of his head, shirt a bright striped pink and yellow.

I don't know what alerted him. Perhaps he saw the white of my sandals. I hope not. Perhaps it was the glint of my captor's knife blade. He saw something. He stopped and swung the beam of the flashlight toward us. At the same moment, he lifted his whistle to his lips.

My captor moved quickly, yet one strong hand still gripped me. The knife in his other hand swung up to slash the watchman's throat. The arc of blood from the severed vein was visible for an instant in the light of the flashlight. The light clattered to the ground, its beam trained on nothing.

The watchman fell heavily forward. There was a hideous noise in his throat, then silence.

I knew who my captor was now. I saw his face for a moment in the watchman's light. It was that memorable face glimpsed at the airport and once again in the shadow of a bush at Teotihuacán, straight black hair and flaring sideburns, taut coppery skin, black eyebrows slashing sharply upward, thin, tough mouth. I knew who he was and now I knew what he was, a killer. One of life's pirates. As vicious as a piranha. I was his prisoner.

Mercifully, I don't remember too much about that horror-filled encounter. It was over quickly and we were running, his hand once again tight on my arm, down the alleyway. I do remember thinking gratefully that it was his other hand that gripped me, not the hand that had killed.

We left the watchman slumped on the ground, smaller in death than he had been in life.

When we reached the end of the alley, he stopped. I stumbled to a halt beside him, my breathing ragged and loud. No one moved on the broad, empty street. Vine-covered walls rose on both sides. Not a house could be seen. If I screamed, if I called out for help, no one would hear.

The knife was no longer in his hand, but he could draw it quickly, more quickly than the watchman had been able to lift the whistle to his lips.

We paused for an instant at the street, and then he hurried me across the cobbled stones and into the oppo-site alleyway. This time we didn't go far. His motorcycle was well hidden in the deepest shadows.

He untied the leather strip from my wrists then, astride the motorcycle, he gestured to me to climb on behind him. I debated. Could I possibly run? I knew the answer. I couldn't outrun a motorcycle or a knife. I climbed on behind him.

He grabbed my wrists, then pulled my hands around his waist and tied them. He kicked down on the starter and the cycle roared and began to lurch down the alley. Quickly the cycle picked up speed and turned into the street.

The ride was a nightmare. We hurtled down streets I'd never seen, past billboards that were meaningless. All was strange, the buildings, the road signs, the parks.

I had never before ridden on a motorcycle. The speed sucked my breath away, pressed against my face, pulled at my eyes. I could see only in a blur. Each swerve of the machine seemed perilously near disaster.

When we reached the highway and the city began to fall behind, the road swooped and curved and turned back on itself in sometimes shallow and sometimes steep ascents. The speed plucked at my will, tore at my mind. We rode on and on, occasionally roaring through a little village with only one light or two to mark huddled buildings clinging to the hillside. The air grew colder and colder and soon there was nothing in the world but the hard sweep of the wind and hurtling machine. I don't know how long we rode. An hour at least. Perhaps two.

My face was pressed against his back. The rough cotton of his shirt rubbed my cheek. Finally, the cycle slowed. We plunged off the narrow road onto a one-lane dirt road that wound still higher among stubby pine trees. We rode perhaps another quarter mile and stopped. After the seemingly endless, wind-whipped journey, the sudden quiet jolted me out of my passive acceptance.

An owl hooted not far away. The man turned his head to listen. There was a faint crackling as some animal moved along the hillside. I saw patches of sky through the trees. Stars glittered bright as sequins, but there was little light among the pines. I dimly made out tumbled boulders and rough, uneven ground with trees clinging tenaciously to the hillside.

He untied my hands and helped me off the cycle.

I was so numb and stiff, I was scarcely able to stand.

He turned away, rolling the cycle off the road.

Stiff as I was, unsteady on my feet, I didn't hesitate. I turned and ran.

He didn't hear me for a moment. When he started after me, I swerved off the road and blundered down a steep slope, slipping and sliding on hoof-sized rocks. There was no place to go, but I kept on running, stubbornly, hopelessly, twisting and turning, stumbling on.

As frightening as anything was the utter silence of his pursuit. He didn't shout at me to stop. There was no sound but the slap of his feet, the rattle of rocks as he jumped down a slope.

The angle of descent sharpened. He was close behind me. I dodged to my left and my ankle twisted under me. I fell, rolling over and over, rocks poking and jabbing against me until I brought up hard against the trunk of a pine tree and fell beside it. The sharp, clean smell of the pines reminded of a summer my mother and I spent in Minnesota, a happy, carefree summer. Now I huddled beneath the low-hanging boughs of a pine tree. Fallen needles were sharp against my face. Somewhere near, so near, a killer hunted me. I lay as still as the fallen needles. I waited.

He stopped, too. He knew I couldn't be far from him. I heard his heavy breaths and then they quieted. He was so close to my tree that, if I crawled a half yard forward, I would be able to reach out and touch his shoe.

"I won't hurt you." He spoke softly.

I wondered if we might be near a house. I knew in the same instant that it wouldn't matter if there were people only yards way. Long before I could rouse anyone with a cry, he would be upon me. I lay as still as the waxy, sharp-tipped needles beneath me and waited.

"Miss, miss, listen to me, miss."

If it weren't so horrible, it would be funny. Miss, indeed.

"I only want to talk to you."

I took a delight in how quiet I could be. Not the lightest breath, not the faintest rustle would betray me.

"I know you can hear me. I know all about you. I've known since before you came to Mexico."

Have you now? I thought, but I lay unmoving in my needle-lined depression.

"Listen." Anger flickered in his voice. "You can't fool me. You are here to buy the treasure for your museum. You have brought much money with you." He paused and pine trees sighed in the gentle wind and night creatures scurried about on their nocturnal rounds. "Much money."

Now I understood that there was no hope for me. I had no money. When he knew I couldn't give him the riches he had killed for, he would dispose of me as easily as a housewife swats a wasp.

"I will have the money. It is mine. The treasure belongs to me."

To you and to the Ortegas and to the Mexican government and to the shades of Aztec gods and Lord knows who all else.

"My brother found the gold . . ."

His brother. I listened hard to that soft voice.

". . . so they killed him. They killed Raúl."

Everybody loves somebody. He loved his brother. The bitterness in his voice made the hair prickle on my back.

He told me all he knew, how Raúl had realized that the señora did not ride aimlessly in the hills. Rather, that she searched for something and, when Señor Ortega was not at the hacienda, she rode all day, up and down the hills, the horse brought in lathered with sweat. One cool November day, Raúl followed Gerda.

"There are some, how do you say it, old places?"

Ruins? I thought to myself.

"Big humps that look like hills but it is said that once they were temples. There was a dried stream bed that curved around the hill. It was near here that the señora hunted every day. She had looked long that afternoon and she was resting, sitting in the shade of a pine when Raúl found her."

I had trouble picturing blond and beautiful Gerda scrambling up and down rocky hills. After months passed, the hunt must have seemed hopeless to her. But that afternoon, Raúl found her. Gerda liked young men and Raúl was both handsome and ingenious. She shared her wine with him and told him an interesting story.

Raúl's brother obviously didn't question what Gerda had told Raúl, but I could scarcely believe my ears. She was hunting, Gerda told Raúl, for a cave. She had a map. She showed him the map.

"I didn't see the map, you understand," Raúl's brother confided in that soft, whispering voice, "but Raúl told me that as soon as he saw the map, he knew why the señora's search had failed."

My captor didn't doubt what he was telling me, but I was sure Raúl had lied to him. I could believe in gold. I could even believe in a treasure trove. I couldn't believe in a map with an X marking the spot. A map four hundred and fifty years old?

His next words confirmed my skepticism.

"The cave was marked on the map, but it shows so many paces from the road and Raúl knew the map meant the old road. This the señora did not know. She had come to Tlaxcala this past summer and knew only the fine new road. She didn't know the old road."

Neither did Cortés's soldiers know the old road, buddy. But I didn't say a word. I lay quietly in my burrow. Raúl has sold his brother a bill of goods. I wondered why.

Raúl's brother described what he knew of the map, the funny writing—what would be the romance of a treasure map without an exotic inscription?—the number of paces from an overhanging rock to the mouth of the cave.

"He told the señora. He showed her the old road. They went together and together they found the gold so the treasure is as much his as hers, do you not think, miss?"

It was cold on the hillside. The pine needles were like slick pieces of ice against my skin. I felt sure there was no treasure. It was all a mad fantasy, the treasure, this cold damp hillside, the eerily soft voice of the killer trying to coax me to come out of my hiding place, demanding money that I didn't have.

If he found me, I would soon not feel cold. I wouldn't feel anything ever again. The touch of Tony's hand . . . The killer would find me. There was no escape possible. What could I do? How could I persuade him that I had no money?

I forced myself to face the truth. Even if I persuaded him that I had no money, he wouldn't let me go free. I had seen him kill, watched his hand plunge a knife into a man's throat.

I pressed harder against the pine carpet, felt again the breathless emptiness of fear, so like the sensation of falling. I missed some of what he said but when I heard again, he was insisting, "The treasure belongs to me now because my brother found the cave for the señora. He told me about the gold that last night. He was drunk and I didn't believe him. He told me how the gold looked, soft and shiny, bright as butter, he said."

For a moment that soft voice fell away. There was nothing but the gentle rustle of the pine trees and the clatter of rocks as he moved a step or so farther down the incline, ever closer to me.

Even in the dimness beneath the pine tree I could now see something of the terrain, tumbled heaps of rocks and wind-bent trees. If I could see better, he could see better. No frightened creature of the night could lie more still than I. I might have been a part of the ground.

"You come with me now," he pled. "I will show the treasure to you. We will take the gold with us and go together for you to get the money. Once I have the money, you will have the treasure. Please, come now."

He assumed that somewhere I had access to money, much money. He must believe the money was in another place, waiting. That meant he was sure I had no money in my room at the Ortega house. I remembered the edge of slip that had shown from my suitcase. Someone had searched my room, must have told him there was no money hidden there. I thought of the little maid who had brought me hot chocolate and who had led me through the night to the gate into the alley and him. He kidnapped me to show me the treasure and then he was sure I would give the money to him, not to Gerda or Juan. He was so confident, but I was sure that there could be no treasure. No map and no treasure.

Yet, he had killed for this treasure and he would kill again.

My mind rebelled. Ancient Aztec gold would not be hidden in a cave marked upon a map by the "old" road. That road might be a hundred years, but not four hundred and fifty years old. Had it all been a dreadful mistake? Had Raúl fallen accidentally and his imaginings triggered his brother to murder for nothing?

"Listen to me." He was angry now, angry and determined that I should do his bidding. "I tell you, I followed Juan. I saw him today creeping like a shadow, hiding a suitcase in the cellars. It must be the treasure."

Today. He saw Juan move something today. That was why he had taken me captive tonight. At first, he had tried to frighten me, the note at the airport, the doll flung on my floor. When I didn't go back to New York, he shot at me on the Avenue of the Dead. Now I realized he had intentionally missed. His plan then had been to prevent the transfer of the gold to a courier from the museum. His focus had been on finding the gold. Today when he followed Juan, he was sure that he could take possession of the treasure. He arranged with his sister, the little maid, to persuade me to come to the alley. He wanted to deal with me. I had money, he had gold, the transfer could be made.

I had no money. I doubted, as I lay shivering on that cold hillside, that he had a treasure.

If I moved, if I tried to run again, he would hear and catch me. If I lay still all night long, the sun would rise, its bright rays slipping down the hillside. Eventually, he would find me.

I was cold. And angry. I did not want to die on a rock-strewn hillside in Mexico.

I hated the sound of his voice. Now it rose as he implored me. In a dreadful fashion, the cadence was reminiscent of vendors everywhere in Mexico trying to sell you something—a ring, a horse made of straw, a serape, moccasins, balloons, postcards, necklaces, lace scarves, baskets, leather purses.

"Please, miss, you come now, you will see. My brother, he told me the gold was soft and warm to the touch. Please, miss."

I wanted to shut away his voice, shut away the picture of hands lifted up, filled with gold, cajoling, bartering.

"Miss, you come now. We will look at it together—" His words broke off.

I heard the roar at the same instant, the growl of an MG changing gears as it climbed the hill. The road was just above us. The lights from the car whipped across the top of the pines. Loose gravel spun beneath the wheels as the car careened around a sharp curve. The lights flickered in the treetops only for an instant. The screech of the tires sounded scarcely longer. But the whine of the motor could be heard when the car was long on its way around the curving, twisting road.

It was an MG. I knew it. I never questioned it. This road, this narrow twisting road, must belong to the Ortegas.

Tony's MG?

When it was very quiet again, the sound of the car only a memory, I realized I was alone on the cold, silent hillside.

Raúl's brother had gone.

15

It was much later that I learned why things happened as they did that frightful night, learned that Tony woke up the house, stormed up and down stairs, shouted when the twins led him to my room and I was gone, my purse on the desk, the bedcovers thrown back, my gown and robe a silken heap on the chair.

Lights had flooded the Casa Ortega. When everything had been searched, when they were sure I could not be found, the twins, white-faced, told Tony all that they knew, and the bits and pieces and patches of information—the hint of gold, Juan and Gerda, my disclaimer to the old gentleman that I was involved—all added up to danger. It was then that Tony stormed up to Juan's room.

Juan was gone, too.

I knew none of this as I ran, stumbled, fought my way against fear and the night and the deep-rutted road, knowing that ahead of me raced a killer, a killer who could move like a deer through the trees, a killer who would stop at nothing to claim what he felt was his. If only I could reach Tony first, if I could have the strength and breath to warn him, to shout, to save him from the danger he faced on my account.

There is no time to dissemble when you are running for someone's life. I didn't question that I cared so much, that I would run until I dropped, that I would kick and claw and battle to save him. It wasn't sensible. It wasn't rational. I had lived my life being sensible and rational. Tonight that caution fell away.

I remembered the way his hair glistened in the moonlight, black as a raven's wing. I remembered the eagerness in his voice when he showed me the mosaics at the university. I remembered the way he laughed and took my hand the afternoon we walked up Reforma. Simple things, nothing to set the pulses racing, nothing but kindness and grace and good humor, qualities to build a life on.

Hot stabbing pain in my side clawed like a live thing. I gasped for breath and sweat slipped down my face and back. More frightening than shouts or footfalls or racing motors was the silence. I might have been the only person in the world as I ran up the steep curving road.

I rounded a bend and saw a dark sprawl of buildings that had to be the Ortega hacienda. No light shone. No one moved in the dusty foreyard in front of an immense wooden door.

Where was the MG?

Where was Raúl's brother?

I stopped and stared at the dark hacienda. It was utterly quiet. I hesitated, uncertain what to do. Every passing second brought danger closer to Tony. Should I batter on that huge wooden door? Hope that someone would hear and come and help?

Struggling for breath, trying to think, I started for the door, then, at the last instant, turned away. Where was the MG? That was what mattered. Tony would not be far from the MG. The hacienda, like a huge sleeping animal, loomed above me. I ran to the right and passed a dozen dark oval openings beneath massive arches. Then I was at the end of the house. A dusty road angled up the hillside, away from the darkness of the hacienda. I saw the MG a hundred yards away. It looked as though the car had skidded to a stop. The driver's door hung open. Light spilled out onto hard-packed earth. The headlights gleamed brightly, throwing into sharp relief the thick rank of pine trees that crowded up the hillside. The lights angled away from the tiled-roof building just past the car. A barn? Stables converted to a garage? Storerooms? Square cut pillars curved into big graceful arches to support pale whitewashed walls. The arched openings were even darker than the night. Somehow, though, the lights from the MG seemed more threatening than the dark arches because the headlight beams aimed pointlessly up the hillside.

I reached the car and stopped to stare at the Saint Christopher medal dangling from the rearview mirror. I had noticed the medal the first morning when Tony took me to the museum. Saint Christopher had lost his place in the calendar of saints, but not in the hearts of travelers. I reached in and slipped the chain from the mirror and wrapped it around my hand until the round medal was in my closed palm. Then I turned and walked toward that big dark building. Gravel crunched beneath my shoes. My labored breathing was a rasping sound in the stillness. My lungs still strained from my wild run up the steep road.

"Tony." I said his name aloud. How could it be so silent? There should be some sort of sound. There was nothing.

When I stepped beneath the central arch it was like sliding into subterranean water, into total darkness. I felt before me, both hands outstretched, and took one cautious step after another. Finally, my fingers touched weathered wood. Splinters pricked my skin. I patted the wood gently. I touched the cold metal of a bolt. I slid the bolt free and pulled the door out. The door moved with a feathery, sighing creak.

I looked inside and was surprised that I could see. The door opened onto a courtyard. Bright shining stars showed, once again, hard-packed dirt and black walls broken only by an occasional door. It was so barren and lay so quietly in the chill light of the stars that the courtyard might have lain undisturbed for a hundred years.

Desperately I looked back at the MG. The abandoned car was there so Tony must be somewhere near. If I shouted, if I called to him, would he hear? Raúl's brother was somewhere near also, a killer who moved as quietly as a deer.

My throat closed upon the call I wanted to make.

I saw a faint luminous patch on the ground on the far side of the courtyard. The area of light was so small and indistinct that I blinked and squeezed my tired eyes and looked again. The small patch was there.

I stared, puzzled and uncertain. Why should there be a square of light in the ground? But the light was the only hint of human presence. I began to move across the hard dirt of the courtyard. With every step I took, the small square of light became more distinct. I was so tired, and my mind had been buffeted by so many shocks, that I was mystified by that patch of light, unable to guess what it could be.

When I was close enough to see a trapdoor thrown back and the protruding rungs of a ladder, I realized I was looking at an opening to a tunnel of some sort. I knelt beside the square opening and smelled musty dryness of long-closeted air.

Now, for the first time, I heard sounds.

Someone spoke softly in Spanish. The tone was unmistakable, a taunting, daring sound. Shoes scuffed against dirt and there was the noise of struggle, thumps and grunts and wheezing breaths. I swung over the side of the opening and started down the ladder. I dropped the last half dozen feet to land in a painful heap on hard earth. I pushed myself up and ran down a curving tunnel toward a gleam of light and sounds of combat.

The tunnel opened out into a cavernous room dimly lighted by a single bulb dangling from the center of the vaulted ceiling. On the far side of the cellar were several rows of wine racks. In the shadows of the first and second row, I saw them. I stumbled to a halt and my hands reached out to the cool plastered wall of the tunnel for support.

Raúl's brother, one hand held stiffly against his side, leaned against the end of the first wooden rack. Blood dripped down from that stiff arm, ran in a thick red rivulet to spatter onto the earthen floor. He stood between me and his unmoving victim. I could see the bright shine of black shoes, the dark gray limpness of trousers.

I was too late, too late, forever too late. I turned away and pressed against the curving wall of the tunnel. The wall itself seemed insubstantial. The mind and body can absorb only so much and I was far beyond the limit of my endurance. I had tried hard, very hard, and my struggle had been for nothing. I had found warmth in Tony's black eyes and the touch of his hand. Now, because of me, his body lay limp on a dirt floor. He would never again look up curving stairs and smile at a woman. He would never again sit at his desk and pit his judgment against his competitor's. He would never again pour wine into his companion's glass and look across the table, his dark eyes intent and measuring.

Sick at heart, I raised my head to look back into the cellar. I looked, then strained harder to see. Those shoes, that crumpled length of cloth. Did it really look like Tony?

But it had to be Tony. His MG sat outside. I held tightly in my right hand his medal of Saint Christopher. It was foolish to hope, hideous to open myself again to the shock of finality.

Raúl's brother moved, stiffly, doggedly. I realized with vindictive delight that he was seriously wounded. He dragged his right leg across the floor as if any movement were painful. He clasped his left arm against his side.

I now saw the fallen man clearly. Suddenly I knew who lay there. I edged back into the tunnel, trying to move like a shadow. I eased back one step, another.

If he turned his head he could see me.

I saw his right hand then. Bloodied fingers gripped the knife. Blood rushed down his arm, splashing onto the floor.

I was almost safe in the darkness of the tunnel when the shout came.

So much had happened that I had thought I was beyond feeling anything. I was wrong. Vivid joy swept me. Then, sheer horror.

The shout was hoarse with fear. "Sheila! Sheila!"

Running feet thudded. The sounds came from another tunnel opening on the other side of the cellar, an opening near the wine racks and the body. And the killer.

Raúl's brother stared at the dark mouth of that tunnel opening, head lifted, watching as an animal watches. He hunched his shoulders, slowly lifted his right hand, the hand with the knife.

"Sheila, are you here? Juan, where are you? Answer me."

I screamed his name.

At first the words were thick in my throat, my voice a ragged whisper. Fear sucks breath out of your lungs. I pushed out the words. My voice grew stronger and stronger. "Tony, go back. Get out of here. Get the police. He has a knife. He killed Juan and he will kill you. Tony, get out, get out, get—" I ran across the earthen floor, stumbling and crying and screaming. I caught the killer's arm, heard his gasp of pain. I tried to bend back his hand.

He grabbed me and flung me at the ground.

I slammed down and there was no air left to scream a warning. As I landed, I struggled to get on my feet. I scrambled toward him and managed to catch one leg, clawing at his ankle, crooking my arm around his legs.

He stumbled.

For one wild victorious moment, I felt him flail for balance.

He almost fell, but then he steadied, catching himself. One hand plunged down, grabbed my hair, a great thick handful, and yanked viciously.

My head snapped back. I let go of his legs and he was free.

He didn't look down at me. He shouted. The hand with the knife swung down toward my face.

I saw the silver flash of the blade and, sharp and painful, the point of the knife snagged below my ear. I didn't dare struggle.

Tony skidded to a stop no more than five feet away, a look of desperate fear etching deep lines in his haggard face.

The three of us froze into deadly tableau.

The point of the knife moved back to my ear. I felt a prick and the warmth of blood on my throat.

Tony yelled and started to move.

The knife moved from my ear, touched my throat.

The soft voice of the killer stopped Tony a foot away.

Tony answered and held up his hands.

Raúl's brother nodded and pulled the knife away from my throat. He let me go and I tumbled back on the floor. I lay on that hard-packed earth, raised up on one elbow.

Tony spoke, quickly, emphatically. "Sheila, listen carefully."

Raúl's brother interrupted. "I will tell her. So she will make no mistake." It was an effort for him to speak. But any hope that we might be able to overcome him were shredded by his words. "Miss, you understand, if you give me trouble, I kill you. I already tell Tony, I kill you quick if he tries to get me. You understand?"

"I understand." My voice was faint but steady.

"Take your belt"—he pointed to my navy blue patent-leather belt—"and tie Tony's hands. Tie them in front so I can see."

As I took off the belt, I realized the right side of my dress was wet and sticky. I couldn't see the blood against the navy blue, but I felt sick. I knew he had cut only my earlobe, and earlobes bleed furiously, but still I felt sick. What would he do once I tied Tony's hands? Would he push me aside and stab Tony? I held the belt in my hands, hands smeared with blood.

There was blood everywhere around me. Blood on my neck and shoulder and hands. Blood on the man who stood, knife in hand, so near me. Blood on the floor.

I held the belt and looked at Tony.

He understood my fears without any words at all. "It's all right, Sheila. Do as Lorenzo says. He has promised not to hurt us if we do as he says."

I looked behind Tony at the long crumpled length that was his dead brother. "How can we trust him?"

Lorenzo saw my glance. "I told Juan the treasure was mine. I told him. But Juan laughed and said he had warned Raúl away and now he was warning me." Lorenzo's face was suddenly implacable. "Juan killed my brother."

And tonight Lorenzo's sister brought me to the alley-way. Did she know what he planned? Or did she think she was simply arranging a meeting?

Juan had killed Raúl. Lorenzo had killed Juan, not for treasure alone, but to avenge his brother's murder.

Tony stretched out his hands and nodded at me.

I stepped close to him and wrapped the belt around his wrists. When it was fastened, I slipped my hands up his arms to his shoulders. There was a faint tinkle of metal.

He reached up awkwardly, his hands together, to clasp my right hand. He loosened my fingers and touched the Saint Christopher medal.

"I found the MG and I took the medal. Because it was yours." My fingers closed around his. "I was trying to warn you."

"You thought I had come in the MG?"

I nodded.

"Juan took my car," Tony explained. "He apparently headed for Tlaxcala the minute we realized you were missing. It took me a little while to get the story straight. The twins told me everything when we couldn't find you, but by that time Juan was already gone. I shook the story out of Gerda." His face was dark and angry. "She told me you were sent to Mexico so that it would appear you were the buyer."

"That's why Lorenzo grabbed me. Tony, what are we going to do? He thinks I have money to buy the treasure. He brought me here to show it to me, but I managed to slip away when we got off the motorcycle. He followed. I hid and he tried to persuade me to come out. He never stopped talking about the money. He kept calling to me.

Then the MG came. Both of us heard it. That was when he ran away. He was afraid someone had come for the treasure."

Lorenzo spoke then, but neither of us answered. I think he had been listening hard trying to follow, but his English was not quite good enough to catch and understand all we said.

"I didn't know it was Juan in the MG," I said. "I thought somehow you had come for me. So I ran. I was terrified for you. I knew he was a killer. He killed the night watchman in the alley behind your house."

"You knew that?" Tony demanded. "Yet you came after him?"

"I thought it was you in the MG," I said simply.

I looked up at him. I made no attempt to mask how I felt. For a moment, we saw in each other's eyes more than words say. For that magical space in time, we were alone together and nothing around us mattered, not the poor crumpled body of Juan, not the dangerous wounded hulk of Lorenzo, not the dim, musty, cavernous room where Death, that grinning bony lady, was in command.

16

The knife parted us, the knife and Lorenzo's angry, desperate voice, ragged with strain.

We did as he commanded for we knew he was very near to slashing us down. He had nothing to lose.

He motioned for Tony to sit down with his back against the wall. He had me lash Tony's feet with a dog's leash he'd found nearby.

When I was done, he said, "I will show you now, miss. You will see that I tell the truth."

I stared at him stupidly and could not imagine what he meant.

Impatience and a hot, desperate anger flickered in his eyes. "The gold; when you see the gold, you will give me the money."

The gold, and money, much money, money I didn't have. If I could persuade him that I had the money somewhere else, perhaps I could entice him away from here, away from Tony. When he discovered I had lied, I would die. There would be a final moment when he would know he'd been tricked.

But Tony would be safe.

My tongue edged out to wet dry lips. I nodded. "Gold," I repeated. "Yes, the gold."

He relaxed and almost managed a smile. His lifeblood still dripped steadily down. How could anyone lose so much blood and still live? If we held on, time and blood might run out for Lorenzo.

His chest pulled in and out, in and out. He stepped back a pace and leaned on the wine rack, hiding Juan's body. I was grateful for that. Poor Juan, who had flirted with death, teased death, and finally been claimed. He had danced too near the edge of the precipice, beckoned on by a fascination he could not deny.

"Now, miss"—and I wondered if Lorenzo knew his voice was weakening—"go past Juan, all the way to the end of the casks. I followed him today, saw him go that way. After he left, I checked and found the suitcase." He pointed to the opening between two wine racks.

I had to step over Juan to enter that space. I didn't let myself look closely at him. Even so, I saw too much, saw one hand twisted, lying palm up as though relaxed in sleep, saw the glisten of the earth by his head and knew his blood spread there.

Nineteen years old and brought down because he dared to taunt death. But I knew, as I stepped past him, that if it had not been Lorenzo's knife, Death would have found him in a fast car or on a hurtling motorcycle or while challenging wild surf. That thought helped me walk down the darkening passage between the wine racks, helped me find a suitcase deep in the last shadow, gave me strength to pull and tug the heavy case all the way back to the light. I hefted the case over Juan and pushed it all the way to Lorenzo.

Lorenzo leaned against the wine rack, his face gray now. Blood still ran down his arm to drip on his pants, pattering into an ever-widening stain at his feet.

Tony and I needed time.

"Open it," Lorenzo directed.

I knelt beside the suitcase. Seeing it in the light, I felt a little twist of surprise. The suitcase was big, perhaps four feet tall and a hand's breadth in width, but it was made out of some kind of cardboard. The bag was scuffed and dirty. A huge water stain discolored one side. The suitcase had originally been a brownish cardboard. Dirt and mildew had colored it an overall dingy gray.

I wondered why Juan and Gerda had put the treasure in such a messy container. It never occurred to me that the treasure might have been hidden in this flimsy cardboard grip. Not if it were the fabled store of Aztec gold. *Cheap.*

That was the word for this suitcase. Imitation leather straps buckled at the top. They were rotted and frayed. The big clasp in the center was tarnished yellow-green.

It was easy to open, however. The old straps slipped free quickly and the clasp snapped up. It must have been opened and closed a good deal recently. I laid the case on its side, lifted the lid, and looked down at yellowing humps of old newsprint. A queer electric tingle raced up my back as I saw old yellowed newspaper and recognized distinctive, unmistakable typescript.

I didn't know what the clumps of old newspaper held, but I knew that nothing I had guessed was right.

My hands shook a little as I picked up a rounded lump and began to unwrap the decaying newspaper. My excitement must have communicated itself to Tony and Lorenzo. They both watched intently as I unwrapped and unwrapped. I was reminded of the child's game where something quite small is swathed again and again. The last sheet of newspaper fell away, its small German print barely discernible.

A bracelet fell into my hand.

My breath caught and held for an instant. I looked at a simple but spectacularly beautiful piece of jewelry and knew it at once. At the same time, sure as I was of its origin, I felt it couldn't possibly be so.

The gold was the color of butter. Even in the dim light of that cellar, the bracelet glowed with the unmistakable fire of gold.

"You see, miss, Raúl spoke truly, did he not? This must be the gold of the gods."

I shook my head.

Before I could speak, he yanked me around and the knife was sharp against my throat. His face was drawn, his shirt wet with sweat and blood. "It is gold!" he shouted. "It is gold!"

"Yes," I breathed.

Slowly the prick against my skin eased.

The knife fell away, but still he loomed above me, his eyes angry and desperate and sick.

"Yes, Lorenzo," I said slowly, soothingly. "Yes, it is gold. Very valuable gold."

That calmed him. He moved slowly back to lean once again against the wine rack. He moved slowly, tiredly, as a wounded animal when the end of the hunt is near.

"If this treasure"—I waved my hand at paper-wrapped lumps in the suitcase—"is what I think it is, it is even more valuable than anyone knew."

I spoke calmly enough, but I was far from calm. Valuable. How do you set a worth on treasure thought lost forever? How do you put a money value on one of the oldest, most incredible finds in archeology?

To find Aztec gold would be to reach back four hundred and fifty years into the past and touch a craftsman's work. But this bracelet linked me to a goldsmith in the third millennium BC. If I was right, I held in my hand a piece from one of the world's most ancient and beautiful treasures.

When I saw more, I would know. I laid down the spiral bracelet, a heavy shining wire of gold that looped around a wrist three times to end in conical knobs, and reached into the cheap suitcase for another clump of yellowing newsprint.

This time I looked at the dateline and once again that queer tingle of excitement ran through me. The date was April 8, 1945.

My mind ran back like a skittering mouse, back through mounds of dates, and placed this particular time. April 8, 1945. The Russians were battering toward Berlin in the grim spring of 1945. Russians were coming from one direction, the Allies from the other. In Berlin itself, bombs fell day and night. Ordinary Berliners were dying by the thousands. Luckier ones, important Nazis and the last-ditch defenders, had some protection. Objects valued more than people had the most protection. The world's deepest, safest bunker had been built in the Berlin Zoo. Atop it were placed powerful guns. The Allies' bombs sought that bunker and the animals of the zoo began to die like their fellow Berliners.

After the war, long after the war, when one thing and another was sorted out, when this survivor's reflections and that one's memories were added together, a good deal was known about the bunker beneath the zoo and its last days before it was destroyed in the rain of bombs that washed over Berlin.

It was known for a fact that the Treasure of Priam had at one time been moved to the bunker for safekeeping. The Treasure of Priam, Heinrich Schliemann's triumphant proof that Homer's Troy was historic and rich. It didn't matter that the golden baubles were later attributed to an earlier age than Priam's—the treasure bore his name, for this jewelry was fit for a king.

There was no more stirring account in all of archeology than Schliemann's discovery of the Treasure of Priam. Schliemann always believed that Homer wrote the truth about Helen and Menelaus, about Priam and Hector. No one else believed the stories to be true. Scholars deemed the *Iliad* a pretty story, an exercise in classic Greek, nothing more. But a German grocer's assistant heard the stories as a boy and determined that one day he would go to Troy. By Zeus, he did. With extraordinary talents, he learned five languages fluently and secured the wealth he felt he needed to pursue his dream. He set out to find Troy. At a huge mound in Turkey called Hissarlik, he excavated and found proof of many settlements there.

He didn't find gold.

Schliemann had a good many frustrations as an excavator, including almost continual harassment by Turkish authorities. He was nearing the end of excavation and there were only a few days left to dig before the ruin would be closed. He and his young Greek wife, Sophia, were in one of the excavation's deepest cuts when Schliemann spied the soft gleam of gold in one of the walls. Quickly, he told his wife to call a rest for the workmen, though it was only midmorning.

When they were alone in the ruins, he hacked at the wall with his knife, every moment fearing that the great stones hanging above him would dislodge and tumble down to crush them. But he had not come so far and toiled so long to lose his treasure now. Later he claimed his wife Sophia wrapped pieces of the golden hoard in her red shawl.

I crouched by that cheap suitcase and shared in Schliemann's delight across the span of a century. In my hand I held a pin that a Trojan queen must have worn. It was three inches wide and absolutely exquisite. As the newsprint fell away, there was no longer any doubt in my mind what treasure I had found. I had seen too many pictures of this particular pin to be wrong. The head of the pin, an ornamented rectangular plate, was framed between two slender strips of gold. The bottom strip ended in curling upswept spirals. Six tiny golden jugs were attached to the top strip, perfect little jugs.

"Tony, come and look."

I had forgotten he was bound, but he managed to struggle and roll close enough to see. Lorenzo still rested against the wine rack, but he leaned forward, listening.

I held up the pin. "Do you know what this is?"

Tony looked and surprise flickered in his face. Aztec gold had never looked like this.

Before he could answer, I was telling Tony and Lorenzo, my voice wobbling with excitement, that we were looking at the most fantastic treasure imaginable. ". . . and the bunker at the zoo was demolished. Someone escaped with the treasure, smuggled it out before that last day."

Running steps clattered across the earth floor of the cellar. Gerda came at me like a wild thing, snatching at the pin, crying and shouting, clawing and pulling. Every word that spewed from the perfect mouth was in German so I was the only one in the cellar who understood.

"How did you know?" she screamed. "You have no right. This is mine. All mine." She had the pin now and I saw the metal bend in her clawlike grasp. "All mine, do you hear? My father saved the gold from the Russians. You have no right."

It was hard to catch every word. Her husky voice cracked as she screamed at me. She seemed oblivious to Tony and Lorenzo. She never once looked past me and back into the shadows that held Juan. She couldn't see beyond the gleam of the gold.

Her story came out in bits and pieces. A young German private assigned to guard duty at the bunker saw the end coming. He knew what would happen when the Russians reached Berlin. He was young and tough and clever. He and his new bride, a nurse, smuggled the treasure out among the refuse of amputated limbs from the air force hospital in the bunker. Their clever plan was discovered by a fellow soldier, Hans, who became a part of the effort. The three of them fled Berlin and took the treasure to Portugal and finally reached the New World. It was hard to follow Gerda here for she railed on about Hans, and I wasn't quite sure who Hans was or what he had done or how he was involved, but the three of them reached Mexico with the treasure.

Why the gold remained hidden all these years and why Gerda began her search so recently wasn't clear.

She paused and opened her purse. She pulled out a small black notebook. "It is all here," she cried. "My proof. This all belongs to me."

I didn't think Schliemann's Treasure of Priam qualified as war booty, but at this point what did it matter what I or anyone else thought?

She was quiet suddenly. She stood there, breathing hard, the small gold pin clasped tightly in her hand. Her eyes flicked back and forth, from me to the suitcase, from me to Tony, from Tony to Lorenzo.

"Juan?" she cried.

I think that was the first moment she had realized he was not there.

"Juan?"

Her cry chilled all of us.

Her face, already haggard and strained, blanched an icy gray. "Juan."

No one moved. There was no sound in that huge, dim room but her ragged breathing.

She took a step nearer, another. Her eyes moved past us, swept the shadows. Then she saw him. Her lips parted and she gave a deep moan, the bereft cry of a broken spirit. She moved slowly toward him, one beaten step dragging after another. She had cared. Juan had been more to her, much more, than just a handsome young man.

She moved into the shadow thrown by the wine racks, dropped to her knees, and pulled his poor lolling head up onto her lap. Her hands held him and once again came that stricken cry. Her face, old and ravaged, turned toward us. *"¿Por qué?"*

Lorenzo stood a little straighter. "I told Juan. I warned him." His face was hard. "He killed Raúl."

She was on her feet, flinging herself at him, one arm upraised. She had Juan's knife. She said nothing. There was nothing left in her but fury. The knife began its downward sweep.

I watched, paralyzed with shock.

Her hand faltered. The knife fell from nerveless fingers.

I closed my eyes but I had already seen too much, the great gaping wound, the welling blood on her white silk blouse. Lorenzo had been quicker. She crumpled at his feet.

I lost all hope. It didn't matter that he was wounded. He

still survived, clung tenaciously to life. Why should he spare us? Too many had died this night for us to survive.

I pushed the suitcase out of my way. I didn't care what the shabby old suitcase held, what might be damaged now. I wanted in these last moments to be near Tony, to touch warm hands and to kiss, for the first and last time, loving lips. Nothing mattered to me but Tony. I was so set in my purpose, so determined in my course that I paid no attention to a commanding whisper behind us.

Tony frowned. "Sheila, wait. Listen."

A harsh whisper sounded. I heard my name and stood still. The circle was complete now, the final evil link in place.

"Don't turn around, Sheila Ramsay. Not if you want to live."

The whisper was deliberately hoarse and uninflected so I wouldn't recognize a voice. Someone I knew whispered my name. If I turned I would see a familiar face. I understood that I must not turn.

Lorenzo moved away from the support of the wine rack, straightening to meet one more challenge. I heard him speak sharply in Spanish.

I knew the answer even if I couldn't translate the questions.

"It's all right, Lorenzo," I said bitterly. "This is the man you wanted in the first place. This is the man from the museum. The man with much money. Gerda must have brought him here tonight."

Lorenzo crossed the floor behind us, moving in a heavy, tired shuffle. "Is it true," he was asking, "are you the man who has come to buy the treasure?"

Whoever it was must have nodded without speaking. I wondered what he thought, the man from my museum, as he looked across that huge, dim room at Gerda's body. Did he see Juan lying there, too? Why should he care? He had sent me, defenseless, to shield him from view, to protect him from interlopers such as Lorenzo. Everything had worked out for him. Juan was dead and Gerda, too, but why should it matter to him? The treasure was within his reach.

Who stood there, watching to be sure I did not turn? Was it my contemporary, Timothy Simmons, clever Timothy? Was it small, dark, careful Michael Taylor? Could the whisperer be Karl Freidheim? Had he, years ago, been a soldier with Gerda's father? Was he Hans? Could the shadowy figure be plump-faced Dr. Rodriguez?

I tried to swallow and couldn't. Would he order me to stay turned away if he intended to kill me? I stood still and tried to hear what the man was telling Lorenzo, but they spoke so softly I couldn't make out a word.

A flicker of movement in front of me caught my eye. Tony was edging imperceptibly nearer Gerda. I saw his determined eyes on the knife that lay near Gerda's hand.

"No," I breathed, "no."

He looked at me and I read his eyes so well. If a man must die, he must die well, his implacable gaze said.

229

"Wait," I whispered. "Please, Tony, for my sake, wait."

He hesitated and the moment was past because Lorenzo was shuffling slowly, heavily back toward us. He came up behind me. "Now, miss, everything is going to be all right."

Tony yelled as pain exploded on the back of my head—fiery, unendurable pain—and then there was nothing at all.

17

They found Lorenzo's body early the next morning, on Reforma, slumped in the backseat of Gerda's car. He had bled to death. There was no trace of the car's driver. Or of an outsized, shabby cardboard suitcase.

It was some days later before I knew this. Much of what had happened was pieced together by Tony and the police.

Tony spent most of his time at the hospital with me. "I've never been so scared," he told me later. "One minute you would open those misty green eyes and smile and then you would just fade away. I kept calling to you."

Later I remembered some of that, remembered Tony's dark worried eyes, the soft voice of the nurse, and, of course, bell clear in my mind was the last time I saw Jerry

Elliot. He was furious. He bent over the hospital bed, his bony face red with anger. He even shook his fist at me. "Dammit, why didn't you call me that night? You could have. If you'd been at all concerned about saving the treasure, if you'd thought about anything but the Ortegas, we could have saved the gold. Now who knows where it is? The world may never see any of it again."

The irascible voice faded away. I slipped free of that angry, quarrelsome spirit. I wondered, even as I swept down into unconsciousness, how I ever could have thought him attractive. I had not only thought him handsome, but I had crossed a continent to see him again—but my last thought was quick and grateful for he brought me to Mexico and to Tony.

I was conscious, awake and weak, when the funerals were held. Tony came to the hospital when they were done, still in his stark black suit, his face weary. He sat by the bed and held my hand.

"How is your father?"

"It is a heavy burden," Tony said quietly, "but he doesn't know, he'll never know about Gerda and Juan."

I touched his lips with one finger. "Of course not."

He nodded, glad I understood. "We told him that Gerda was so grief stricken at Juan's death that she attacked Lorenzo before we could stop her. The truth, you see, but not all the truth."

"It is better that way."

We were both quiet for a moment. I couldn't fault

Gerda altogether. True, she had started a fateful chain of events when she came to Tlaxcala. But she had felt within her rights. Who of us could be sure that she hadn't cared for Tony's father? She had yet to meet Juan.

Tony had searched Gerda's papers and probed back to her days in Puebla, where she was raised by the Reinhardts. Mrs. Reinhardt, a dour, thin-lipped sixty, had little to say. No, she had not known Gerda's parents, had only heard by word of mouth of the little German left an orphan when her parents were killed in an accident in the mountains.

What kind of accident?

Their car skidded off a mountain road late one night. Near Tlaxcala. There was a baby left alone. The Reinhardts had taken the baby and swept into a box the miscellaneous papers Gerda's parents left behind. There wasn't much. Nothing of value. It wasn't until Mrs. Reinhardt was leaving her own house many years later, to live with a married son, that she sorted through that small box of clutter and found a leather diary. She thumbed the first few pages and realized it was Gerda's father's record of his war years. The old lady thought Gerda might be pleased to see the journal and had mailed it to her. Gerda received the diary in the spring. She had read it and come straight to Tlaxcala and hiked in the hills. It was then that she fell and twisted her ankle and was found by Señor Ortega. She had married him and who knew what was her strongest motivation. He was kindly and rich and she was alone. Too, the marriage made it easy to keep on hunting in the hills. She couldn't have known when she married him that she was going to fall in love with Juan.

Tony brought the diary to me because it was written in German. I read the letter, too, from Mrs. Reinhardt and wondered at the workings of fate. If the diary had been thrown away years before or if it had never been written so much grief could have been avoided.

Everything was recorded in the diary, including those last fateful days in Berlin.

Gerhardt Prosser's duty was to guard the Treasure of Priam. He knew the gold would be taken by the Russians when they came. He decided to smuggle out the treasure and try to escape Berlin. Another solider caught him at it and, of necessity, became a conspirator, too. The diary told how Gerhardt and his pregnant wife and the sergeant, Hans Rieger, traveled over war-convulsed Germany, fleeing all the armies. Their trip almost ended in disaster a dozen times—when a stolen staff car wrecked, when the Americans blockaded the best road south, when other deserters cornered Gerda's father and Hans in a burned-out farmhouse. Her mother had gone for water and came up quietly from the back and shot the deserters dead.

They stole food and fresh clothes in Lisbon and sold two golden earrings to get money enough to book passage on a rotten old freighter to Buenos Aires. The trip took four months and Gerda was born on the ship. They had hoped to settle in Argentina but they were too frightened to try to sell the treasure, and they became increasingly afraid of Hans. Late one January night, they crept out of their rooming house and began the long run that would end in death on a mountainside in Mexico.

The last few pages of the diary were the happiest. They were in Puebla and Gerda's father had found a job with a wool broker. It was on a buying trip to Tlaxcala that Gerda's father found the cave. The directions to it were on the next to the last page. With the treasure hidden until a good opportunity came to sell it, with a good steady job, with Hans left far behind in Argentina, the two refugees began to feel safe, began to look forward to the future.

I closed the little leather volume with a snap and wondered if the gold had caused as many deaths, as much misery, millenniums ago when it first was hammered into beauty by a Trojan goldsmith.

Probably. And the trail of death and tears had not yet ended. The husky whisperer from my museum was still unknown, still uncaught.

It should have been easy. As first everyone was sure it would be a simple matter to catch him, even though Tony couldn't describe him. All Tony had seen was dark trousers and black shoes. The man had stood well back in the shadows of the tunnel. Tony never saw his face.

After Lorenzo struck me down, he slammed shut the suitcase and struggled across the broad room to the waiting man. Lorenzo and the whisperer left together. Tony didn't care what happened to them or to the treasure. He was terrified I was dead. There he was, tied hand and foot, Juan dead, Gerda dead, and, more than likely, I was dead, too. He rolled close enough to Gerda to get the knife and managed to saw through the belt around his wrists.

He hurried to me. "You were lying facedown. All I could see was the blood on the back of your head."

But I was breathing. He had run then, run down the nearest tunnel, the one that led underground to the main house. There he roused Francisco, the old servant who stayed at the hacienda year round. Francisco heard thunderous pounding on the cellar door and opened it, a candle flickering in one hand, a shotgun ready in the other.

It had not been long before an ambulance arrived and then the police. Minutes after that, the alert was sounded, the border warned, a description of Gerda's car broadcast.

By the time I was able to hear about it, a week had passed and we realized we had been outwitted.

"But surely," I protested to Tony, "all they have to do is find out which of the four men from the museum was in Mexico."

That sounded easy. It wasn't.

Not one of the men had been in New York that week.

Michael Taylor was in Chicago, attending a seminar.

Karl Freidheim, a bachelor, was home, ill with the flu.

Timothy Simmons was on a hunting trip in Maine. Alone.

Dr. Rodriguez was driving to Los Angeles to bid on a rare collection of pottery at an estate sale. As for the warning message from Señor Herrera, Rodriguez claimed the letter never arrived.

Any one of them could have flown to Mexico, slipping in and out of the country for a day or two. As for tracing them, it was child's play to obtain an appropriate birth certificate and use that name to get a tourist card.

Each man denied involvement. Then came the real surprise. What, after all, could be proved against that unseen whisperer?

Stolen goods?

Stolen from whom? The golden artifacts didn't belong to the Ortegas. Or to the Mexican government. If they could be traced without question to Heinrich Schliemann, they should be returned to the Royal Museums of Berlin.

Who could prove that? Certainly not I. I had seen two pieces, in a dim cellar, and I was by no means an authority on Trojan jewelry.

If the man wasn't a thief, wasn't a dealer in smuggled goods, then, after all, he was responsible for what?

Juan murdered Raúl.

Lorenzo murdered Juan and Gerda.

The whisperer had done nothing beyond instructing Lorenzo to strike me down. How could that be proved? The man left with Lorenzo, but Tony and I knew how desperately Lorenzo was wounded and it was those wounds that killed him. After an initial flurry of excitement, the case was closed. Lorenzo was dead, and it was he who had left behind such a visible trail of blood.

Jerry, of course, was still furious with both Tony and me. It would have been a fantastic coup if he had been able to find the Treasure of Priam and reclaim for archeology the gold, which shone like butter. He still felt, I thought unfairly, that the loss of the treasure was my fault.

As for me, well, I was glad on several counts that I would not be returning to my museum to work, even though I had loved it. I didn't think I would ever feel comfortable there again.

18

After that night in the cellar, I don't think I ever questioned what the future would bring. But Tony is a very methodical man. My first evening out of the hospital, back in the Casa Ortega, he rather gravely asked me to walk in the garden with him. Amid the luxuriant flame-colored flowers and rustling leaves of palm and pepper trees, he asked me to marry him.

I didn't hesitate. I didn't need, either, to touch my lucky sixpence to remember that my mother had left her home and gone to a new land and had always counted her decision as a joy. There would be challenges because he was a complex person from a background different from mine, but, more important, he was the man I could picture with me walking in a park, smiling across the table, reaching out at night, laughing and living and loving, and growing old together.

We were married quietly, as is proper in a family that had so recently suffered such losses.

We went to Acapulco to the Ortega villa for our honeymoon. Acapulco is made for lovers. Sea-fresh breezes and the rustle of coconut palms and the vivid, brilliant colors of bird and flowers surround you and there is never a thought for tomorrow. Only for now.

We found an apartment when we came home to Mexico City. We had fun picking out colors, deciding on furniture and pictures. We were busy, Tony at the office and I with plans for a biography of Nefertiti.

Our lives were settling into a happy pattern, one singular to us, when the postman brought a small package, and, in my own mind, the truth about the Treasure of Priam became absolutely clear.

Thursday morning when I kissed Tony good-bye, I thought my day would follow the plans I had made, a morning of research, lunch with one of Tony's cousins, some pleasant shopping in the Zona Rosa, a late-afternoon game of tennis with Tony, dinner at eight.

Perhaps one of life's more bittersweet charms is its unpredictability. You never know how a day will go or what will happen.

The maid brought the mail to me. Cristina's youthful face reminded me of Lorenzo's sister who had led me into danger at the Ortega house. She fled when she learned of

Lorenzo's death and the grisly night at the hacienda. The police found no trace of her.

I flicked through the letters, then balanced on one palm a small brown paper-wrapped package.

It was addressed to Mrs. Antonio Ortega. It was postmarked New York and had no return address. I began to unwrap it. I dropped the brown paper and lifted the lid on a small white box. I pulled free a square of cotton padding and stared down in disbelief.

Two exquisite butter-bright shell earrings lay on another pad of cotton. A white card was tucked in the side of the box. I picked up the card and read the single typewritten line:

```
Thought you deserved a little something
            for your trouble.
```

I knew then who the schemer was, knew who had gambled and won an incredible treasure. I recognized in the laconic line a daredevil gambler with a sardonic sense of humor. He had put me to a little trouble, yes. Used me as a decoy and scared me to death, and here was a little something to make it right.

I picked up one of the earrings and was surprised at its weight and delighted in its smooth, silky feel.

I could never prove my hunch. To be honest, I wouldn't try. But I knew his name and face now as certainly as if he'd signed that card. It wasn't careful Mr. Taylor. Or stern-faced Karl Freidheim. Or cheerful Dr. Rodriguez.

Oddly enough, I'd been almost sure Timothy Simmons wasn't the man. He was, after all, my age. A beginner. But now, as I felt the smoothness of the gold, I remembered his restiveness and his contempt for conventions.

I dropped the earring back onto the cotton pad beside its mate. Training urged me to alert the Mexican archeological authorities. But what good were two alone? They could not be proven to belong to the Trojan hoard. The same period, the same area, right. But nothing more from two alone.

Prudence counseled calling the police. Again what crime could be proven?

I wondered what Timothy was going to do with his golden hoard. Ransom it to the Royal Museums of Berlin? Or was a queen's necklace even now smooth against the milky white skin of some oilman's Sophia?

No matter what I did, I wouldn't affect the fate of the treasure.

I laid the little box on the coffee table in front of me and watched as the soft sunlight shone through the window and touched them with fire.

Gold could bring, perhaps most often brought, great misery and danger. Priam's Treasure would likely cause more grief before the gold ever came to rest, if it ever did.

Slowly I reached out a finger to lightly touch a golden coil.

Should I keep them? Or should I not?

Personajes de la
BIBLIA

Pablo Martín Ávila

LIBSA

© 2013, Editorial LIBSA
c/ San Rafael, 4
28108 Alcobendas. Madrid
Tel. (34) 91 657 25 80
Fax (34) 91 657 25 83
e-mail: libsa@libsa.es
www.libsa.es

ISBN: 978-84-662-2687-5

Colaboración en textos: Pablo Martín Ávila
Edición: equipo editorial LIBSA
Diseño de cubierta: equipo de diseño LIBSA
Maquetación: Julián Casas y equipo de maquetación LIBSA
Documentación y fotografías: archivo LIBSA

PRESENTACIÓN

La Biblia es el libro que más veces ha sido impreso en toda la historia de la humanidad. Ha sido traducido total o parcialmente a más de 2.300 lenguas y es el más extenso de los libros sagrados de las principales religiones. Su contenido sirve de guía espiritual para más de 2.800 millones de cristianos del mundo, y sus primeros libros, la antigua Tanaj, son el compendio religioso que sirve de base para el judaísmo. Haremos un estudio de las Sagradas Escrituras a través de sus personajes más destacados. El contenido de este libro ha sido dividido en dos partes bien diferenciadas, como Antiguo y Nuevo Testamento, además de una especial atención a la figura de Cristo:

- **Jesús de Nazaret,** personaje de especial relevancia, páginas 10-35
- **Antiguo Testamento,** páginas 36-111
- **Nuevo Testamento,** páginas 112-183

Conocida también como el «Libro de los libros», la Biblia es una recopilación de decenas de volúmenes. Formalmente, la Biblia se compone de dos partes bien diferenciadas. El Antiguo Testamento, o Tanaj judío, que incluye entre 46 y 54 libros; esta diferencia emana de los matices dentro del cristianismo y principalmente de la tradición judía que es más amplia en esta parte de la Biblia. En esta primera parte se recoge desde la creación del mundo y la relación de Dios con los primeros hombres hasta los episodios más históricos de la vida del pueblo de Israel. La segunda parte, el Nuevo Testamento, es solo aceptada por los cristianos puesto que únicamente recoge la vida de Jesús de Nazaret y los primeros escritos de sus seguidores. Aquí también existen diferencias entre los cristianos y el número de libros que cada iglesia acepta. Algunas iglesias cristianas menores restringen el Nuevo Testamento a 20 volúmenes, pero la Iglesia católica aceptó informalmente en el Concilio de Hipona (año 393) y definitivamente en el Concilio de Trento (siglo XVI) el listado canónico

que todavía a día de hoy se mantiene como oficial por parte del Vaticano. Para los creyentes, en todos los libros que componen la Biblia hay una directa inspiración divina, por lo que no son simples relatos históricos o bellos poemas que mueven nuestro corazón hacia la bondad del alma. Dios inspiró a cada uno de los autores de los relatos bíblicos para reflejar unos hechos que encierran la verdad de la fe. Por lo que la diferencia de estilos no debe enmascarar el carácter eminentemente religioso que emana de sus textos. Existen infinitas posibilidades de abordar la lectura de la Biblia. Hemos visto que el carácter religioso prima sobre el resto de interpretaciones, pero la Biblia también es un libro histórico. Escrita durante un milenio (entre el año 900 a.C. hasta el año 100 d.C. aproximadamente), refleja con gran exactitud las múltiples vivencias del pueblo de Israel a lo largo de ese tiempo. Religión, moral, cultura, historia, poesía... y lenguas como el hebreo, arameo o griego se dan la mano en unos textos que abarcan muy diferentes épocas, autores y estilos literarios.

La Biblia ha sido estudiada, diseccionada y analizada en decenas de ocasiones por historiadores, teólogos, expertos en literatura... Con este volumen proponemos realizar un recorrido diferente por las páginas del libro más importante de todos los tiempos. El orden en el que son presentados los diversos personajes responde al de su aparición en la Biblia, a excepción de Jesús, con el que se inicia este libro por su evidente importancia en los textos sagrados. Los lectores pueden acompañar su lectura con una Biblia al lado para ir encontrando las alusiones a los relatos presentados según se indica al final de cada entrada a los personajes con una referencia a un versículo determinado.

Conociendo a los personajes que protagonizan las historias de la Biblia, podemos ir descubriendo la epopeya misma de la humanidad. Las siguientes páginas están pensadas para que tanto los lectores que ya conozcan la Biblia en profundidad, como los que se han acercado a ella por primera vez, puedan descubrir nuevos matices históricos, religiosos y artísticos gracias a los personajes que con sus vidas han servido para establecer los cimientos de la cultura judeocristiana.

Los personajes de la Biblia:
el mito y la historia

La Real Academia Española nos indica que un mito es una narración maravillosa situada fuera del tiempo histórico y protagonizada por personajes de carácter divino o heroico. Continúa la Academia indicando que con frecuencia estos relatos sirven para interpretar el origen del mundo o de los grandes acontecimientos de la humanidad. Todos tenemos en mente los grandes mitos de las culturas egipcia, griega u oriental, pero al repasar las páginas de la Biblia surge una duda: ¿sus personajes son mitos o responden a una realidad histórica? Esta cuestión sigue generando ríos de tinta en diversos libros y publicaciones.

Desde un punto de vista científico, no hay datos que puedan ratificar la existencia de algunos personajes bíblicos. Por el contrario, los historiadores y arqueólogos han podido descubrir evidencias certeras que corroboran los datos que la Biblia nos ofrece sobre los principales personajes que en ella aparecen. La ciencia ha experimentado un inmenso desarrollo en los dos últimos siglos. Hasta ese momento no siempre ha encontrado los medios necesarios para poder discernir la realidad histórica de un determinado hecho. Durante siglos la existencia del rey David, Moisés u otros grandes personajes bíblicos no estaba refrendada por restos arqueológicos ni escritos no religiosos que apoyaran con más fuentes su existencia, pero eso no menoscababa la realidad de estos personajes. Siguiendo esta lógica, la Iglesia católica ha preferido centrarse en la vertiente moral y teológica de los primeros escritos bíblicos y no centrar la carga de la prueba en la realidad literal de relatos como el de la Creación. Un claro ejemplo de la doble vertiente mitológica y científica lo encontramos en el relato del Diluvio Universal: hoy en día apenas se discute que su narración concreta se acerca más a la idea de un mito que a un relato histórico, pero al mismo tiempo los historiadores han descubierto mitos similares en diferentes culturas, así

como pruebas arqueológicas que evidencian la existencia en los anales de la Historia de un cataclismo relacionado con una gran inundación, lo que lleva a pensar que el relato bíblico, si bien narrado de una manera literaria que pretende servir de enseñanza religiosa basada en la fe profunda, sí que describe un hecho cierto ocurrido hace milenios.

Durante siglos ha existido una gran controversia sobre la existencia de mitos (figuras no reales) dentro de las páginas de la Biblia. Hoy en día teólogos e historiadores han elaborado teorías conjuntas que permiten dejar a un lado esta confrontación. Esta controversia ha tenido una fácil solución: la religión indica que la Biblia es un compendio de relatos de «inspiración divina», lo que no equivale a afirmar que todo lo que en ella se relata responda a una realidad literal, puesto que el objetivo de los autores no es retratar históricamente un hecho, sino dar una explicación religiosa que transmita una teología accesible a los creyentes. Se puede afirmar que los personajes bíblicos constituyen un conjunto heterogéneo de mitos y de realidades históricas que ha servido de hilo conductor del mensaje religioso judeocristiano. En las siguientes páginas vamos a profundizar en ambas categorías: tanto en los mitos que durante siglos han dado explicación a las grandes preguntas de la humanidad, como en los personajes históricos que protagonizaron los hechos religiosos más importantes del judaísmo y del cristianismo.

PERSONAJES BÍBLICOS CLAVE

Se analizará primero la vida de Cristo (las etapas de la vida del pilar de la fe), para pasar después a desgranar los personajes más relevantes del Antiguo Testamento y del Nuevo Testamento siguiendo un orden cronológico y de su aparición en los textos sagrados.

JESÚS DE NAZARET

El Hijo de Dios

Los teólogos coinciden en indicar que la Biblia no es una sucesión aleatoria de volúmenes y relatos, sino que todos sus textos tienen un hilo argumental común: la historia de la salvación del hombre. Jesús de Nazaret es el protagonista absoluto de esta salvación que sirve de nexo de unión a toda la teología que se desprende de los textos bíblicos. El Jesús de Nazaret histórico fue un hebreo de la región de Galilea, descendiente del rey David e hijo de José y María, nacido en el año 4 a.C. Jesús fue carpintero de profesión hasta que abandonó todo trabajo para dedicarse íntegramente a la predicación de la Palabra de Dios y del mensaje de salvación del amor. Las intrigas políticas de los judíos y los romanos de la época le abocaron a un juicio en el que, con apenas 33 años, fue condenado a muerte. Desde su fallecimiento, la fe que predicó se extendió rápidamente y hoy en día el cristianismo es la religión mayoritaria de nuestro planeta.

Pero Jesús es ante todo la figura más influyente de Occidente, tanto desde el punto de vista histórico como filosófico. Su existencia transformó la vida de las siguientes generaciones hasta nuestros días. Sin su figura no puede entenderse ninguno de los grandes acontecimientos históricos de los últimos dos milenios. La importancia de la figura de Jesús es perceptible en cada pasaje de la Biblia. Los textos sagrados van clarificando el mensaje divino para ir prefigurando y anunciando la llegada de Jesús. Según la Iglesia, su nacimiento, muerte y resurrección suponen el fin de la revelación divina a los hombres.

Momentos clave en la vida de
JESÚS DE NAZARET

La Natividad • *Infancia de Jesús* • *La predicación* • *Los milagros* • *La Pasión* • *La Resurrección*

La Natividad

La Natividad es la fiesta religiosa que recuerda el nacimiento de Jesús. Solo dos de los cuatro Evangelios nos describen este episodio. Mateo y Lucas narran con gran detalle las vicisitudes y milagros que los padres de Jesús vivieron en aquellos días.

José y María vivían en Nazaret en la época en la que se produjo el milagroso embarazo de la Virgen. Cuando se acercaba el momento del parto, los esposos tuvieron que dirigirse a Belén porque el emperador Augusto había decretado la realización de un censo en todo el Imperio. Todo súbdito romano tuvo la obligación de acudir a su ciudad natal para quedar inscrito en el registro oficial. El estado de buena esperanza de la Virgen no pudo evitar esta imposición y los esposos partieron hacia Belén. La tradición relata que llegaron a la ciudad de noche y que en ese instante María comenzó a sentir los dolores que le anunciaban la inminente llegada del bebé. José buscó en cada rincón de Belén un lugar en el que dar cobijo a su esposa, pero nadie les recibía y, debido al censo, las pensiones se encontraban llenas. Agotados y con María de parto, la caridad de un conocido de José les permitió pasar la noche en un establo en el que, rodeada de animales, María dio a luz a Jesús.

La tradición nos cuenta que unos magos llegaron al pesebre del recién nacido guiados por una estrella; hoy en día se ha constatado que en aquella época un cometa pudo ser avistado desde la tierra. Los pastores de la ciudad de Belén fueron alertados por los ángeles que les anunciaron la Buena Nueva del nacimiento del Mesías prometido al pueblo de Israel, y lo que iba a ser un solitario nacimiento se convirtió en la primera adoración pública de Jesús.

Relato bíblico
«Mientras se encontraban en Belén, le llegó el tiempo de ser madre;
y María dio a luz a su Hijo primogénito, lo envolvió en pañales y lo acostó
en un pesebre, porque no había lugar para ellos en el albergue.» (Lc. 2, 6-7)

Infancia de Jesús

Los Evangelios han centrado su relato en los tres últimos años de la vida de Jesús, en el tiempo de su predicación. Apenas existen relatos canónicos que narren los acontecimientos que la Sagrada Familia vivió en los primeros 30 años de vida de Jesús. Son la tradición, junto a alguna referencia evangélica, y algunos escritos apócrifos los que nos han transmitido la información de la que hoy disponemos y que se centra únicamente en los momentos más importantes que Jesús, María y José vivieron en aquel tiempo.

En la época del nacimiento de Jesús una profecía advirtió al rey Herodes de que un recién nacido ocuparía su lugar como «el más importante de los judíos». Asustado y temiendo perder su trono, el monarca ordenó a sus tropas que recorrieran el país y dieran muerte a todo aquel varón recién nacido. Un ángel advirtió a San José del peligro que se cernía sobre la Sagrada Familia y huyeron a Egipto, donde pasarían los primeros años de la vida de Jesús.

La tradición indica que San José decidió acudir hasta Alejandría porque en esa ciudad vivían unos parientes que les ayudaron a establecer una nueva vida. En estos primeros años San José desarrolló su actividad de carpintero hasta que fue ascendido al puesto de capataz. María se dedicó al cuidado de Jesús, que gozó de una extraordinaria salud y vivió una infancia feliz rodeado de algunos parientes de su misma edad. Tras la muerte de Herodes, la Sagrada Familia consideró que el peligro de la persecución había cesado y decidieron volver a Israel. Llegaron a Belén para hacer saber a sus familiares que estaban sanos y salvos y que pensaban dirigirse a Nazaret, donde José había tenido su taller y le sería fácil retomar el contacto con sus clientes.

De su vida en Nazaret apenas encontramos referencias en los Evangelios. La tradición ha conservado algunos episodios de esta época en los que, guiado por la innata bondad infantil, Jesús realiza sus primeros milagros y prodigios. Cuando con-

taba con cinco años jugaba en la orilla de un arroyo y realizó unos gorrioncillos con barro. Cuando otro niño se acercó a Él y le reprendió por haber profanado el sábado trabajando la arcilla, Jesús dio una palmada y las figuras cobraron vida convirtiéndose en pájaros que desaparecieron volando.

San Lucas nos relata que Jesús fue presentado en el Templo como mandaba la tradición judía y que numerosas personas, iluminadas por el Espíritu Santo, se acercaban a él para adorarle. Destacan entre todas ellas el encuentro con la profetisa Ana, una viuda entregada al servicio del Templo, que al ver a Jesús sufrió un arrebato premonitorio y advirtió a la Virgen María de que su hijo sería el que consumaría la redención de Israel.

Jesús vivió su primera Pascua con 12 años, cuando sus padres consideraron que ya tenía la edad suficiente para acompañarlos a Jerusalén. Celebraron la fiesta con sus familiares y cuando todos volvían a Nazaret descubrieron que el niño no se encontraba entre ellos. Asustados, José y María regresaron a Jerusalén donde buscaron desesperadamente a su hijo durante todo un día sin dar con él. Fue a la mañana siguiente cuando gracias a un conocido supieron que Jesús se hallaba en el Templo. El niño había permanecido allí los dos días, orando y charlando con los doctores y sacerdotes. Todos estaban maravillados de la inteligencia y clarividencia de las respuestas de aquel niño. Al verlo, María reprendió a Jesús por la angustia que les había causado y él respondió que «debía ocuparme de los asuntos de mi Padre». El relato bíblico nos muestra a una Virgen María asombrada por los acontecimientos que tienen lugar alrededor de Jesús y que no llegaba a comprender en toda su extensión las acciones del niño, pero que «guardaba todas estas cosas en su corazón».

Relato bíblico

«[...] Volvieron a su ciudad de Nazaret, en Galilea. Allí el niño iba creciendo y se fortalecía, lleno de sabiduría, y la gracia de Dios estaba con él.» (Lc. 2, 39-40)

La predicación

Jesús decidió comenzar su predicación a los 30 años. A este trienio que transcurre hasta su muerte se le denomina vida pública. Las Sagradas Escrituras han centrado sus relatos en esta parte de la vida de Jesús y en los cuatro Evangelios encontramos una detallada descripción de las enseñanzas que Cristo transmitió y que se han convertido en el núcleo central de la fe cristiana.

Dando cumplimiento a la tradición judía de la purificación e instituyendo el primero de los sacramentos cristianos, Jesús se dirigió al río Jordán para que San Juan el Bautista lo bautizara. Allí, una vez que recibió las aguas, San Mateo nos cuenta que el cielo se abrió y el Espíritu Santo con forma de paloma descendió sobre Jesús mientras que se oía una voz que anunciaba: «Este es mi Hijo muy querido, en quien tengo puesta toda mi predilección».

Inmediatamente tras el bautismo, Jesús se retiró 40 días al desierto para purificar su cuerpo según la tradición judía. En esta cuaresma realizó un ayuno absoluto y dedicó su tiempo a la oración. El episodio se conoce como las «Tentaciones de Cristo» porque el relato bíblico indica que Satanás, aprovechando la debilidad física de Jesús, intentó seducirle pidiéndole que utilizara su poder para salvarse de esa calamidad. Puso delante de él manjares, reinos y todo tipo de comodidades, pero Jesús rechazó todo esto y cumplió con la expiación.

Preparado para predicar el Reino de Dios, Jesús comenzó una peregrinación desde Cafarnaún que le llevó a recorrer todo Israel. En cada pueblo o ciudad nuevos discípulos se acercaban a él. Jesús pedía que si en verdad creían en lo que predicaba,

19

dejaran todo y se unieran a su causa. Uno a uno, los principales discípulos se convirtieron y pasaron a ser llamados los Apóstoles, que constituyeron el grupo más cercano a Jesús. Ellos le ayudaban en la logística de su misión y eran testigos directos de la predicación. Dicen los Evangelios que día a día grandes multitudes que llegaban de Galilea, Decápolis, Judea o Transjordania se acercaban a ellos para conocer a Jesús y escuchar sus palabras.

A lo largo de los tres años de predicación, Jesús forja el núcleo de la fe que permanece inalterable a lo largo del tiempo y que constituye la base común de las iglesias cristianas. Cristo, partiendo de la tradición judía, redefine las normas que los israelitas observaban desde los tiempos de Moisés y predica una nueva ética del amor con vocación universal de dicho amor. Entre sus catequesis más recordadas, por la transcendencia que ha adquirido en el mensaje cristiano, encontramos el Sermón de la Montaña. Junto al mar de Galilea, frente a una multitud incontable de fieles, Jesús da a conocer gran parte de su doctrina. En este episodio Cristo predica las Bienaventuranzas, en las que reconoce los comportamientos y personas preferidas por Dios: los pobres, los mansos, los misericordiosos, los pacificadores, los que sufren persecución... San Mateo también refleja en este sermón cómo Jesús reza por primera vez el Padrenuestro y lo pone de ejemplo de oración simple y directa que es del gusto de Dios. Por último, Jesús da a conocer la llamada regla de oro de la ética universal: «Haz a otros lo que quieras que te hagan a ti».

Relato bíblico
«Jesús recorría toda la Galilea, enseñando
en las sinagogas, proclamando
la Buena Noticia del Reino de Dios.» (Mt. 4, 23)

Los milagros

Jesús es el Hijo de Dios para los cristianos y como tal su poder sobre la naturaleza no alcanzaba límite alguno. Desde su infancia Jesús realizó innumerables hechos sobrenaturales que maravillaban a aquellos que los presenciaban y que eran transmitidos de boca en boca para que fueran conocidos por todos.

Para la Iglesia los milagros son hechos sobrenaturales inexplicables por las leyes naturales en los que se muestra una clara intervención divina, sin la cual nunca hubieran tenido lugar. Jesús acompañó su predicación oral con la realización de gran número de milagros que expresaban su bondad, reforzaban su discurso o transmitían la realidad de su poder sin que hubiera lugar a duda alguna. Los estudiosos de las Sagradas Escrituras han tomado la decisión de dividir el número de milagros que realizó Jesús en cuatro grandes categorías: las curaciones, el control sobre las fuerzas de la naturaleza, la expulsión de espíritus malignos y la resurrección de los muertos.

Los Evangelios nos relatan 17 curaciones que Jesús realizó durante su peregrinación por Israel; curó a paralíticos, ciegos y leprosos. Uno de los episodios más conocidos lo refiere San Juan y detalla el momento en que Jesús eliminó la ceguera de nacimiento de un pobre al imponer sobre sus ojos barro hecho con arena de la calle y su propia saliva. El poder de expulsar demonios, es decir, exorcismo, fue utilizado por Jesús hasta en siete ocasiones. En todas ellas Cristo hace referencia a que el mal engendrado por el pecado ha tomado posesión del cuerpo de los afligidos y les impone numerosas calamidades físicas. En este sentido, San Lucas nos relata la curación de un niño epiléptico o la famosa expulsión de los siete demonios que atormentaban a María Magdalena.

El Antiguo Testamento ya hace referencia a unas cuantas resurrecciones milagrosas realizadas por la directa intervención divina. Pero no es hasta la llegada de Jesús cuando los tres milagros de resurrección que él practicó toman un sentido al servir de explicación y parábola de la propia resurrección de Jesús. Es el Evangelio de San Juan el que nos transmite la famosa resurrección de Lázaro, el de Betania, que tras llevar cuatro días muerto y sepultado en una cueva es llamado por Jesús para que vuelva al mundo de los vivos. La fama de este milagro ha traspasado la frontera del cristianismo y el Corán se hace eco de él para destacar la figura de Jesús.

Jesús también mostró su poder dominando las fuerzas de la naturaleza, realizando maravillas que desafiaban a las leyes de la Física. Los Evangelios hacen referencia a una decena de milagros dentro de esta categoría: la multiplicación de los panes y los peces, la conversión del agua en vino, la pesca milagrosa en el lago de Tiberíades o la desaparición de la tempestad y posterior caminar sobre las aguas son algunos de los más destacados.

Los milagros siempre respondían a una intención directa de Jesús. San Mateo nos indica que Cristo realizó la mayor parte de sus milagros en Cafarnaún y Betsaida porque en esa región vivía un mayor número de pecadores e incrédulos a los que no bastaba con su predicación para convencerles de que él era el Mesías que Israel esperaba. Según la Iglesia católica, es desde la predicación de Jesús cuando el poder para realizar milagros se extiende a todos los creyentes. Jesús ratifica a los Apóstoles que con el poder de la fe en él todo creyente puede obrar estas maravillas.

Relato bíblico

«Jesús dijo "Padre, te doy gracias porque me oyes […] pero lo hago para que esta gente que me rodea crean que tú me has enviado" y después dijo "Lázaro, ven afuera". El muerto salió con los pies y las manos atados con vendas […]» (Jn. 11, 40-44)

La Pasión

Los cuatro Evangelios y la mayor parte de los textos religiosos posteriores a la vida de Jesús centran su relato en la Pasión y la muerte de Cristo. Este significativo episodio es presentado por todos los autores como el acto central de la existencia de Jesús. La muerte en la cruz da cumplimiento a las profecías judías que desde los tiempos de Isaías habían indicado que el Mesías sería rechazado por su pueblo y matado de una manera humillante, como un simple delincuente.

En los capítulos de la Sagrada Escritura que narran la Pasión de Jesús no solo encontramos el relato de su muerte, sino que también podemos conocer de primera mano los últimos siete días de su vida. En ellos Jesús instituye la Eucaristía, anuncia la traición de Judas o enseña a sus discípulos cómo afrontar el nacimiento de la Iglesia una vez que él haya desaparecido.

Los cuatro evangelistas coinciden en situar el inicio de la Pasión con la llegada de Jesús y sus discípulos a Jerusalén para cumplir con el precepto judío de la celebración de la Pascua. Jesús ya era un predicador famoso y arrastraba tras de sí gran número de fieles y acompañantes. Todos ellos hicieron una entrada triunfal en Jerusalén. Montado sobre un pollino, Jesús fue recibido como un líder no solo religioso, sino también político tal y como profetizó Zacarías. Hay que destacar que, pese a las diferencias de enfoque de los cuatro Evangelios, en todos ellos se aprecia un inusitado interés en destacar las profecías de la tradición hebrea que se cumplían en la persona de Jesús y que le ratificaban como el Mesías de Israel.

Tras la preparación en el Templo y los rituales propios de ese tiempo litúrgico judío, los principales discípulos prepararon la que sería llamada la Última Cena. En realidad se trataba de la cena de la Pascua, en la que los 12 Apóstoles y Jesús

celebraron el final de la fiesta hebrea. En esta cena Jesús lavó los pies a sus discípulos para indicarles que pese al alto papel que estaban llamados a ocupar deberían ser los siervos de Dios.

Llegado el momento de la bendición del pan ácimo y del vino de la tradición de Moisés, Jesús instituyó la Eucaristía. Los católicos consideran que desde ese momento en cada misa se vuelve a repetir este milagro en el que el pan se transforma en la carne de Jesús y el vino en su sangre. Por el contrario, las iglesias protestantes celebran el recuerdo de la Cena del Señor. Independientemente del credo cristiano que se profese, la Última Cena es un punto álgido en la vida de Jesús porque termina con la tradición hebrea de la Pascua e instaura nuevos ritos que desde ese momento serían adoptados por sus fieles.

En el transcurso de la cena Jesús advirtió a los presentes que uno de ellos iba a traicionarle. Con este gesto se muestra la capacidad de clarividencia de Jesús y se destaca que era plenamente consciente del destino que le esperaba. Finalizada la cena pascual todos se retiraron al huerto de Getsemaní donde debían aguardar orando la llegada del alba. Los Apóstoles cedieron ante el cansancio y, mientras Jesús oraba, los guardias del Sumo Sacerdote aparecieron armados con la intención de detenerle. Judas Iscariote recibió su premio de 30 monedas de plata por haberles indicado el lugar en el que pasarían la noche y se cumplió así la profecía realizada por Jesús unas horas antes.

Tras el prendimiento, Jesús fue llevado ante las autoridades religiosas judías. Caifás, el Sumo Sacerdote, presidiendo el Sanedrín dirigió un juicio amañado con falsos testigos en el que acusaban a Jesús de blasfemo por hacerse llamar Hijo de Dios. Pese a ser declarado culpable, el poder religioso hebreo carecía de la potestad de condenar a muerte a Jesús y por eso a la mañana siguiente fue llevado ante el gobernador Poncio Pilatos para que dictaminara la más severa de las sentencias. El romano, acostumbrado a las tensiones religiosas entre las

diferentes sectas judías, no quiso tomar partido y solo condenó a Jesús a un escarnio público. Finalmente, presionado por la aristocracia judía y el pueblo que se congregó ante las puertas de su palacio, el gobernador Poncio Pilatos condenó a muerte a Jesús.

Desde ese instante Jesús es vilipendiado por los soldados romanos. Ya era un reo de muerte y como tal fue tratado. Azotado, apaleado mientras permanecía atado a una columna, los soldados le incrustaron en su cabeza una corona de espinas a modo de mofa contra él y contra todos los judíos que le consideraban su Rey.

La crucifixión era una de las fórmulas de ejecución más común en aquella época en el mundo romano. Los reos debían cargar con su propio madero y dirigirse a pie hasta el lugar, normalmente a las afueras de las ciudades, donde tendría lugar la crucifixión. Jesús realizó el Via Crucis por las calles de Jerusalén hasta llegar al lugar llamado Gólgota. Los soldados romanos le crucificaron junto a dos ladrones. Solo María, las siervas de Jesús y el discípulo amado le acompañaron en los instantes finales de su muerte. Unas horas después de su crucifixión, y tras haber perdonado a sus verdugos, Jesús expiró.

Relato bíblico

«[…] *Le golpeaban la cabeza con una caña, le escupían y, doblando la rodilla, le rendían homenaje. Después de haberse burlado de él, […] lo hicieron salir para crucificarlo.*» (Mc. 15, 20)

La Resurrección

Jesús destaca entre los fundadores de las principales religiones del mundo por su importante papel en la fe que predicaba. A diferencia de los profetas judíos, o de Mahoma, los cristianos consideran que Jesús no es uno más ni siquiera el más especial de los enviados por Dios para anunciar su Palabra, sino que es el mismo Hijo de Dios hecho hombre. Este mensaje se ve reforzado con el relato bíblico de la resurrección de Jesús.

Sin el episodio por el que Jesús mismo vence a la muerte, el cristianismo hubiera sido una más de las sectas judías que existían en aquella época. La figura de Cristo habría sido considerada al mismo nivel que otros hombres relevantes del judaísmo que tuvieron una especial relación con Dios y que mostraron el camino de la fe a sus iguales, pero no habría trascendido de manera especial ni relevante.

Pero el hecho de que Jesús anuncie y cumpla con su resurrección es la verdadera piedra de toque del cristianismo, el eje alrededor del que se vertebra la fe. Cristo prometió en sus últimos sermones que aquellos que creyeran en él vivirían eternamente y el relato de la resurrección pretende afianzar esta creencia que Él transmitió.

Jesús fue crucificado un viernes por la tarde. El *sabbat*, el día sagrado de la semana que observan los judíos comienza tras la caída del sol del viernes, por lo que los discípulos de Jesús tuvieron muy poco tiempo para trasladar el cuerpo. Sus restos fueron llevados temporalmente al sepulcro que cedió José de Arimatea. Allí se depositó envuelto en una sábana con la intención de que pasado el *sabbat* pudiera realizarse el ritual de unción y lavado del cuerpo para aplicarle los óleos que lo embalsamarían definitivamente.

Los Evangelios difieren en los nombres concretos de los discípulos que acudieron el domingo a visitar el cuerpo de Jesús para darle el trato que la ley judía prescribía

antes del definitivo entierro, pero todos ellos coinciden en que María Magdalena era la que lideraba el grupo de hasta cuatro discípulos que acudieron a la tumba a ofrecer a Cristo sus últimos cuidados.

Cuando llegaron, observaron que la piedra que tapaba la oquedad estaba movida y la entrada se encontraba accesible. En el interior, un joven vestido con una prístina capa blanca les esperaba y les anunció que Jesús había resucitado. Los discípulos, temerosos de que el cuerpo hubiera sido robado y aquello respondiera a un engaño, no hablaron con nadie. Jesús, según San Marcos, se apareció de nuevo a María Magdalena, esta vez a solas, y le indicó que transmitiera a todos la buena noticia de su resurrección. María Magdalena así lo hizo, pero no la creyeron. Finalmente, Jesús se apareció a los discípulos de Emaús, los acompañó en su camino de vuelta a casa desde Jerusalén y, cuando se detuvieron a descansar y tomar un refrigerio, todos se dieron cuenta de que era Jesús al verle partir el pan tal y como lo hizo en la Última Cena.

Los otros Evangelios también narran diferentes apariciones de Jesús durante los días que siguieron a su muerte, pero es ya solo en los de Marcos y Mateo y en el libro de los Hechos de los Apóstoles cuando se da plena cuenta de la resurrección de Jesús y de la firme convicción de sus discípulos de anunciar sus enseñanzas.

Relato bíblico
«Se apareció a los Once, mientras estaban comiendo,
y les reprendió por su incredulidad y su obstinación
porque no habían creído
a quienes lo habían visto resucitado.» (Mt. 16, 14)

ANTIGUO Testamento

Los textos que se recogen en las páginas del Antiguo Testamento fueron redactados durante casi un milenio, por lo que los personajes bíblicos que en ellos descubrimos son un fiel reflejo de la época en la que cada uno de los libros de esta recopilación fue escrito. En el Antiguo Testamento encontramos una evolución en la definición y tratamiento de sus personajes. En los primeros libros, especialmente en el Génesis, y más tarde en la época del primer éxodo a Babilonia, observamos unos personajes con características propias de los mitos de las religiones ancestrales. En ocasiones se nos indica que su vida se alargaba durante centenares de años, o poseían un conjunto de virtudes que claramente deseaban reflejar una idea, y no describir una realidad exacta. Con la aparición de Moisés y tras la conquista de la Tierra Prometida, se inicia el periodo de libros llamados históricos, en los que los personajes bíblicos son retratados desde un punto de vista más realista, aportando fechas, relaciones con otros reinos o imperios y situaciones de las que se han encontrado evidencias históricas que los corroboran.

Más tarde, los libros poéticos y místicos retoman la tradición original y nos presentan personajes que quedan matizados por la influencia de mitos propios y de religiones de pueblos vecinos. Gran parte de los personajes, especialmente los menores o episódicos, del Antiguo Testamento comparte características que en la tradición judía se consideraban como signos de presencia divina: los padres tenían problemas para concebir y el personaje nace fruto de un milagro que trae la bendición de un hijo al hogar. En otros casos se nos presenta la vida como una epopeya, al estilo helénico, en la que el personaje supera multitud de pruebas físicas, intelectuales y religiosas. Por último, hay que destacar que la relación con Dios de los personajes del Antiguo Testamento se narra de forma habitual como una conversación directa en la que el Señor se presenta o habla al personaje de una manera muy humanizada.

Adán y Eva

LOS PRIMEROS POBLADORES

Judaísmo, cristianismo e islam coinciden en un mismo relato de la Creación y para todos ellos Adán y Eva son los primeros pobladores, creados por la mano de Dios e iniciadores de la extirpe humana. El libro del Génesis nos cuenta el plan divino de crear el mundo tal y como lo conocemos. Dedicó a esta tarea siete días en los que dio forma a los astros celestes, los ríos, las montañas, los animales y las plantas… El sexto día Dios tomó un poco de barro y modeló el cuerpo de Adán a imagen y semejanza suya. Más tarde insufló vida al cuerpo con un soplo que le transmitió el Espíritu Santo para que habitara en su alma. Adán se encontraba solo y reclamó al Creador una compañía. Dios aceptó que «no es bueno que el hombre esté solo» y adormeció a Adán para tomar de su cuerpo una costilla de la que creó a Eva, su compañera.

Dios otorgó a Adán y Eva el privilegio de vivir eternamente en el Jardín del Edén, una suerte de paraíso terrenal en el que toda la Creación estaba a su servicio. Dios solo puso una condición en esta alianza: no podían comer del Árbol del Bien y del Mal. Durante un tiempo indeterminado la pareja vivió feliz cumpliendo los designios divinos y en armonía con el resto de la Creación. Pero Satanás, bajo la forma de una serpiente, tentó a Eva, y esta convenció a Adán para que incumplieran el mandato divino y probaran el fruto del árbol prohibido. Esta acción, el Pecado Original, les abrió su mente al conocimiento, pero les cerró las puertas de la vida eterna. Dios los expulsó del Paraíso, condenó a la mujer a sufrir los dolores del parto y al hombre a tener que trabajar para proveerse de alimento. Desde ese instante sufrirían enfermedades, peligros y calamidades.

La pareja, expulsada del Jardín del Edén, inició la colonización del mundo y tuvo como descendientes a sus hijos Caín y Abel.

Relato bíblico

«Y Dios creó al hombre a su imagen […] los creó varón y mujer
y los bendijo para que fueran fecundos y se multiplicaran […]» (Gn. 1, 27-28)

Caín y Abel

EL PECADO QUE CONDUCE A LA MUERTE

Los hijos de Adán y Eva son los primeros hombres nacidos en este mundo. Sus padres fueron creados por Dios, pero ellos recibieron la vida de sus progenitores.

El Génesis y también el Corán hacen referencia a los hijos de Adán y Eva. Caín fue el primer hombre en nacer tras la Creación. Más tarde nació Abel. Ambos convivieron con sus padres. Caín y Abel buscaron de nuevo el favor divino y ambos presentaron ofrendas a Dios. Caín ofreció los frutos que había recogido del suelo, pero Abel presentó a Dios los primeros frutos de su cosechas y las mejores piezas de su ganado. Dios miró con mejores ojos a Abel, por lo que Caín sintió una envidia irrefrenable que le llevó a abalanzarse sobre su hermano y darle muerte. Se produjo así el primer asesinato de la Historia, que tuvo como resultado que Abel se convirtiera en la primera persona en morir, siendo considerado el primer mártir. Caín ha sido señalado como el primer asesino, y el pecado de la envidia es uno de los peores que puede sufrir el hombre.

Tras el fratricidio Dios maldijo a Caín y lo expulsó de las tierras fértiles que habitaba, pero como Caín temió por su vida ante el pecado que había cometido, Dios se apiadó de él y le concedió una marca por la que todo aquel que le viera supiera que no podía matarle. Caín se retiró junto a su familia a las tierras al este del Edén. Fundó una ciudad a la que puso el hombre de su hijo Henoc. Consternado por el episodio que habían vivido sus hijos, Adán decidió aumentar su descendencia y a los 35 años tuvo un tercer hijo: Set.

Relato bíblico

«Caín dijo a su hermano "Vamos fuera" y, cuando estuvieron en el campo, se abalanzó sobre su hermano y lo mató.» (Gn. 4, 8)

Noé

Noé fue el hombre elegido por Dios para sobrevivir al Diluvio Universal y recibió el encargo de volver a colonizar el planeta desde un mayor respeto a las leyes divinas. Las tradiciones mesopotámicas, chinas, babilónicas y aztecas también reflejan en sus libros sagrados cataclismos parecidos al relato bíblico que nos ocupa. Las Sagradas Escrituras llaman al cataclismo Diluvio Universal. Noé era descendiente de Adán. El libro del Génesis le retrata como un hombre justo, irreprochable y seguidor de los caminos de Dios. En su larga vida tuvo tres hijos: Sem, Cam y Jafet. Su conducta irreprochable llegó a los ojos de Dios, que consideraba que el hombre se había pervertido de nuevo con el pecado. La decepción por la deriva de su Creación llevó a Dios a anunciar al único justo de entre los hombres, Noé, que se disponía a exterminar a la humanidad entera para comenzar de cero la vida. Dios encargó a Noé construir un arca de madera en el que debía acomodar una pareja de cada especie animal y un ejemplar de cada planta. Cuando Noé finalizó con todos los preparativos, recibió la orden de entrar en el arca y sellar la escotilla de acceso. La lluvia comenzó a caer ininterrumpidamente durante 40 días y 40 noches. El agua arrasó todo lo que se encontraba a su paso. La vida sobre la tierra desapareció. Noé esperó 150 días hasta que por medio de una paloma recibió la señal de que las aguas habían descendido y la tierra era de nuevo habitable.

Dios estableció con Noé una alianza que significaba un nuevo comienzo para la vida del hombre. Como símbolo de la misma, le regaló el arco iris y le ordenó que creciera y se multiplicara para colonizar de nuevo todos los rincones del orbe.

Relato bíblico

«Yo voy a enviar a la tierra las aguas del Diluvio, para destruir completamente a todos los seres que tienen un aliento de vida.» (Gn. 6, 17)

Abrahán

Abrahán es descendiente de la décima generación de Noé. Según algunas investigaciones, vivió en el siglo XV a.C. y es considerado el primero de los patriarcas bíblicos tras el Diluvio Universal y la tradición le atribuye la fundación del judaísmo.

Nacido en Ur de Caldea con el nombre de Abram fue un pastor trashumante durante la mayor parte de su vida hasta que, cuando contaba con 75 años, Dios le pidió que saliera de su tierra, confiara en su palabra y se dejara guiar a lo largo de un gran viaje que finalizaría en una nueva tierra donde sería recordado como el padre del pueblo más importante de la Historia. Este pastor, que todavía no había concebido ningún hijo con su mujer Sara porque ella era estéril, confió en la palabra de Dios e inició un recorrido que le llevó hasta Egipto y las tierras interiores de Israel.

El libro del Génesis narra la vida de Abrahán intercalada con la de algunos de sus descendientes, Isaac, Lot, o personajes famosos como Melquisedec. Es en la última parte del relato cuando las Sagradas Escrituras describen dos de los momentos más importantes de la vida de Abrahán. El primero se produce cuando Dios le pide que cambie su nombre de Abram a Abrahán en señal de obediencia a él y que para confirmar esta alianza les sea practicada la circuncisión a todos los varones que le acompañan. Poco tiempo después Dios le concede a Abrahán su mayor bendición, un hijo de su mujer Sara, que era estéril. Siendo Isaac solo un niño, Dios puso a prueba la lealtad de Abrahán: le pidió que tomara a Isaac, lo llevara hasta el monte Moirah y allí lo sacrificara en su honor. Abrahán accedió sin poner ningún impedimento. Su fe conmovió a Dios e instantes antes de proceder al ritual se apiadó de él y perdonó la vida de Isaac. En recompensa por su infinita lealtad Dios prometió a Abrahán una fecunda descendencia. Abrahán murió cuando contaba con 175 años y fue enterrado en el Valle de Hebrón.

Relato bíblico

«Deja tu tierra natal y la casa de tu padre, ve al país que yo te mostraré. Y yo haré de ti una gran nación.» (Gn. 12, 1-2)

Ismael

EL PADRE DEL ISLAM

Ismael fue el primer hijo natural de Abrahán, pero no su primogénito legal. Su estirpe dio lugar a los ismaelitas, tribu en la que siglos más tarde nacería el profeta Mahoma.

Dios había prometido a Abrahán una gran descendencia. El viejo profeta contaba ya con 86 años cuando todavía no había podido engendrar ningún hijo con su mujer Sara. La necesidad de perpetuar su estirpe le llevó a tomar como concubina a Agar, una sirvienta egipcia de la que nació Ismael. La tradición judía no reconoce pues a Ismael como primogénito y concede este honor a Isaac, el hijo de Abrahán y su esposa legal Sara. Ismael creció junto a sus padres y fue circuncidado cuando Dios pidió a Abrahán que instituyera este símbolo. Con la llegada de Isaac a la familia, Agar y su hijo Ismael, que ya contaba con 14 años, cayeron en desgracia y fueron expulsados de la tribu comandada por Abrahán.

La tradición relata que vagaron durante días por el desierto hasta que, cuando estaban a punto de morir de sed, un ángel les guió hasta una fuente en la que pudieron sobreponerse. Ismael y su madre se establecieron en Canaán y él contrajo matrimonio con una egipcia. Tuvo 12 hijos y murió a los 127 años.

Los primeros capítulos del Génesis son textos sagrados para judíos, cristianos y musulmanes. El nacimiento de Ismael es el punto de inflexión en el que la tradición islámica se desvincula del resto del relato bíblico. Los musulmanes centran su historia sagrada en la vida de los descendientes de Ismael hasta el profeta Mahoma. Hoy en día gran número de las monarquías árabes todavía destacan que su linaje proviene por vía directa de Mahoma e Ismael.

Relato bíblico

«También te escucharé en lo que respecta a Ismael: lo bendeciré,
lo haré fecundo y le daré una descendencia muy numerosa; será padre
de 12 príncipes y haré de él una gran nación.» (Gn. 17, 20)

Melquisedec
El primer sacerdote

Melquisedec es un personaje bíblico menor en cuanto al espacio que ocupa en los textos sagrados, pero para la tradición cristiana su importancia reside en que es considerado el primer sacerdote de la Historia. El Génesis relata que en vida de los monarcas de Senaar, Elasaar, Elam y Goím lucharon contra los reyes de Sodoma, Gomorra, Admá, Seboím y Belá. En la batalla Lot, pariente de Abrahán, fue hecho prisionero. Abrahán reclutó entre sus acompañantes un pequeño ejército de más de 300 hombres que, tras una emboscada en la noche, consiguió recuperar el botín de los ganadores y liberar a Lot.

Cuando Abrahán volvía de derrotar al rey de Senaar y los cuatro reyes de su liga bélica, salió a su encuentro Melquisedec, rey de Salem y «sacerdote de Dios, el Altísimo». Melquisedec le ofreció pan y vino y bendijo a Abrahán en nombre de Dios. Reconociendo el poder de Melquisedec, el profeta le otorgó una décima parte del botín ganado.

Quedó así constancia del primer diezmo religioso de la Historia. El relato bíblico finaliza en este punto, pero es la tradición cristiana la que abunda en el personaje de Melquisedec. Por una parte, se cree que Salem, la ciudad que gobernaba Melquisedec, es el pequeño asentamiento que siglos más tarde daría lugar a Jerusalén. También se abunda en el simbolismo de las ofrendas de pan y vino, como una anticipación de la Eucaristía.

Teólogos medievales consideran que Melquisedec es una cristofanía, o aparición de Jesús previa a su encarnación o posterior a su muerte. La Iglesia considera a Melquisedec como el primer sacerdote cristiano y así lo reconoce al ungir a sus postulantes bajo «el sacerdocio de Melquisedec».

Relato bíblico

«Y Melquisedec, rey de Salem, que era sacerdote de Dios, el Altísimo, hizo traer pan y vino y bendijo a Abrahán […]» (Gn. 14, 18-19)

Lot

EL PECADO DE SODOMA Y GOMORRA

———— ⬤ ————

Lot ha pasado a la Historia como el único hombre justo que Dios salvó del castigo divino impuesto a las ciudades de Sodoma y Gomorra.

El relato de Lot aparece reflejado en el Génesis como uno de los capítulos intermedios de la historia de la vida de su tío Abrahán. Lot era hijo de Matías y hermano de Iscá y Mildá. Su familia acompañó a Abrahán en el viaje a Canaán. La Biblia no aclara los motivos que llevaron a tío y sobrino a disputar por una zona de asentamiento y ambos tomaron caminos distintos con sus familias. Lot se estableció en la fértil llanura que separaba Sodoma de Gomorra. Las Sagradas Escrituras narran que tiempo después Abrahán conoció que su sobrino había sido hecho prisionero y organizó una expedición para liberarlo. El plan tuvo éxito y Lot regresó a Sodoma con su familia y sus bienes. Tiempo después los habitantes de Sodoma y Gomorra cometieron un gran pecado al intentar aprovecharse de dos ángeles que Dios había enviado a Lot. Dios decidió terminar con ambas ciudades y Lot le pidió que se apiadara de ellas en nombre de los justos que allí habitaban. El relato bíblico refleja la negociación que Lot estableció con Dios para librar a Sodoma y Gomorra del castigo que se avecinaba. Pero Dios no encontró un solo habitante ejemplar en Sodoma y Gomorra y la sentencia contra ambas ciudades y sus gentes se ejecutaría.

Dios permitió a Lot escapar junto a su familia de la devastación de Sodoma y Gomorra con la única condición de que, mientras se alejaban de la ciudad, no miraran nunca hacia atrás. La mujer de Lot incumplió el mandato divino y quedó convertida en estatua de sal. Lot vivió desde entonces en una cueva en el monte con sus hijas. Los días de Lot finalizan tras engendrar dos descendientes con sus propias hijas, quienes lo emborracharon y sedujeron con la intención de perpetuar su linaje.

Isaac

EL PRIMER CORDERO PASCUAL

Isaac es el primogénito de Abrahán y Sara. Su figura ha simbolizado la primera alianza de Dios con los hombres tras el Diluvio Universal.

Abrahán partió de su hogar con la promesa divina de convertirse en padre de una gran nación. Pero su mujer Sara era mayor y estéril. Ambos confiaron en la palabra de Dios y dos décadas después Sara concibió a Isaac. El Señor, después de concederle el nacimiento de su hijo legítimo, pidió a Abrahán que lo sacrificara en su nombre. Abrahán obedeció a Dios, preparó el viaje y partió con su hijo. Isaac cargaba con la leña para la pira y durante tres días y tres noches recorrió junto a su padre el camino que les separaba del punto indicado por Dios. Isaac preguntaba continuamente a su padre que dónde se encontraba el animal que tenían que sacrificar y Abrahán le contestaba que Dios lo proveería. Llegado el momento crucial, ambos prepararon el altar, colocaron la leña y cuando Abrahán iba a clavar el cuchillo en el cuello de su hijo Isaac, un ángel enviado por Dios detuvo su mano y evitó que el sacrificio fuera consumado. Como premio, un carnero apareció enredado en una zarza y padre e hijo lo sacrificaron en el altar que habían preparado. La tradición cristiana considera que Isaac es el primer cordero pascual, más tarde llegaría el de la Pascua de Moisés y finalmente Jesús, que se sacrificó siguiendo los designios divinos. Isaac vivió después con su padre hasta que se casó, a los 40 años, con Rebeca. La historia volvió a repetirse y su mujer resultó estéril, por lo que Isaac solicitó el favor divino para tener descendencia y Dios le concedió el nacimiento de sus dos hijos gemelos, Esaú y Jacob.

Relato bíblico

«El ángel le dijo "No pongas tu mano sobre el muchacho
ni le hagas ningún daño. Ahora sé que temes a Dios porque no me has
negado ni siquiera a tu hijo único".» (Gn. 22, 12)

Sara

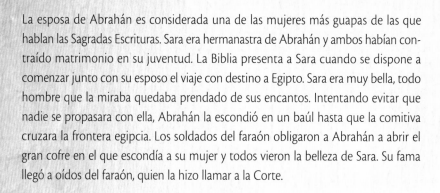

La esposa de Abrahán es considerada una de las mujeres más guapas de las que hablan las Sagradas Escrituras. Sara era hermanastra de Abrahán y ambos habían contraído matrimonio en su juventud. La Biblia presenta a Sara cuando se dispone a comenzar junto con su esposo el viaje con destino a Egipto. Sara era muy bella, todo hombre que la miraba quedaba prendado de sus encantos. Intentando evitar que nadie se propasara con ella, Abrahán la escondió en un baúl hasta que la comitiva cruzara la frontera egipcia. Los soldados del faraón obligaron a Abrahán a abrir el gran cofre en el que escondía a su mujer y todos vieron la belleza de Sara. Su fama llegó a oídos del faraón, quien la hizo llamar a la Corte.

También el monarca egipcio sucumbió a sus encantos y para conquistarla le entregó a su propia hija como esclava y puso a su nombre toda una región egipcia limítrofe con Israel. Los esposos estaban asustados porque el faraón quería poseer a Sara y esta pidió a Dios que les sacara de Egipto. Un ángel se le apareció al faraón para ordenarle que dejara marchar a Abrahán y Sara.

Fuera de Egipto los esposos sufren una crisis porque ella continúa estéril y el hijo anunciado por Dios no es concebido. Abrahán tomó como concubina a la esclava Agar y de su unión nació Ismael, lo que separó a la pareja. Finalmente, el milagro se obró y Sara concibió a un hijo, Isaac. La gente no creía que Sara hubiera dado a luz, consideraban que el hijo era un huérfano adoptado por el matrimonio. Para demostrar que había estado en cinta sacó sus pechos y dio de mamar a todos los recién nacidos que le presentaban. La tradición relaciona la muerte de Sara con el sacrificio fallido de Isaac. La mujer enfermó al conocer el destino de su hijo y tan fuerte fue la alegría de su salvación que falleció de un colapso cuando contaba con más de 100 años.

Relato bíblico

«Cuando Abrahán llegó a Egipto, los egipcios vieron
que su mujer era muy hermosa […] y los oficiales la vieron
y la elogiaron ante el faraón.» (Gn. 17, 15-16)

55

Jacob

La historia de Jacob, hijo de Isaac, y patriarca de Israel es una de las más apasionantes que se reflejan en el libro del Génesis.

Intriga, religión, historia y aventura se entremezclan en el épico relato que retrata a un inteligente joven hecho a sí mismo que se convertirá en padre de las 12 tribus de Israel. Isaac tuvo dos hijos gemelos, Esaú (al que iba a corresponder la primogenitura) y Jacob. La inteligencia de Jacob superaba la de su hermano. Siendo todavía niños, Esaú llegó un día a casa después de cazar, estaba hambriento y Jacob aprovechó la oportunidad para venderle a su hermano un plato de lentejas a cambio de la primogenitura que ostentaba y que le otorgaba numerosos derechos y dos tercios de la herencia paterna. Isaac no reconoció el trato entre los hermanos y quiso bendecir a Esaú nombrándolo solemnemente su heredero. Jacob de nuevo utilizó una argucia: aprovechando la escasa visión de su anciano padre, se disfrazó de su hermano ayudado por su madre. Isaac le bendijo como primogénito y cuando el truco fue descubierto Isaac ya no podía deshacer la unción solemne. Jacob tuvo que huir porque su hermano quería matarlo. En su camino hacia las tierras de su tío tuvo la famosa visión de «la escalera de Jacob» en la que vio una escala que unía el cielo y la tierra y cómo los ángeles discurrían por ella, mientras una voz le prometía numerosas bendiciones. Jacob se enamoró de su prima Raquel y, como no tenía dote que ofrecerle, prometió a su tío que trabajaría gratis para él durante siete años. Las intrigas familiares y los engaños se sucedieron hasta que Jacob tuvo que volver a Israel.

Jacob tuvo 12 hijos de los que descienden cada una de las tribus de Israel. También concibió a José, el mítico patriarca que llegaría a ser mano derecha del faraón. Murió a los 147 años rodeado de sus hijos.

Relato bíblico

«Jacob le dio entonces pan y guiso de lentejas. Esaú comió y bebió y se fue.
Así menospreció Esaú el derecho que le correspondía
por ser el hijo primogénito.» (Gn. 25, 34)

José el Patriarca

EL INTÉRPRETE DE LOS SUEÑOS

José fue el hijo predilecto de Jacob. Su azarosa vida transcurrió entre la envidia de sus hermanos hasta que, expulsado a Egipto, llegó a ser la mano derecha del faraón.

Jacob tuvo 12 hijos que darían lugar a las tribus de Israel. El undécimo de ellos, José, fue el favorito de sus progenitores y por eso el resto de hermanos le envidiaban. Movidos por el odio, los hermanos planearon deshacerse de José y un día que pastoreaban en el monte metieron a José en un pozo muy profundo hasta que aparecieron unos mercaderes egipcios a los que lo vendieron como esclavo. Los hijos inventaron ante su padre que su hermano había muerto atacado por una bestia. José fue llevado a Egipto donde trabajó a las órdenes de Potifar, un reputado terrateniente. Un día la esposa de Potifar intentó seducir a José, pero como no aceptó su propuesta ella lo acusó de haber intentado violarla. José fue condenado y llevado a la cárcel. En el penal comienza a forjarse su fama como intérprete de sueños. Allí descifró el sueño del copero del faraón que, gracias a su ayuda, quedó libre de la falsa acusación que pesaba sobre él.

La noticia llegó a la Corte y el faraón le llamó para que interpretara sus sueños. José descifró que a Egipto le esperaban siete años de abundancia y otros siete de sequía. Asombrado por su inteligencia, el faraón le nombró gobernador de sus tierras. Siendo la mano derecha del monarca, José volvió a encontrarse con sus hermanos cuando ellos viajaban a Egipto para comprar trigo con el que mitigar el hambre de sus familias. Los hermanos no reconocieron a José y este les puso una prueba para ver si seguían siendo los villanos que él había conocido. Como todos los hermanos habían cambiado, José se descubrió ante ellos y juntos acudieron a presentarse a su padre Jacob. El faraón honró a José cediendo tierras para su padre Jacob y sus hermanos en Egipto, país al que todos se trasladaron.

Relato bíblico

«Y el faraón siguió diciendo a José: "
Ahora mismo te pongo al frente
de todo el territorio de Egipto".» (Gn. 41, 41)

Benjamín

El nombre de Benjamín, hijo de Jacob y hermano de José, ha pasado a la Historia como la palabra que se utiliza para designar al más pequeño de los que conforman un grupo, especialmente una familia.

José, el hijo favorito de Jacob, se había convertido en gobernador de Egipto gracias a su poder para interpretar los sueños del faraón. Los hijos de Jacob fueron en una expedición comercial a las tierras del Nilo para comprar grano con el que alimentar a sus familias. José les reconoció, pero ellos a él no.

Deseoso de conocer el destino de sus familiares, José les preguntó por sus padres. Ellos le contaron la historia de su familia y le relataron que solo tenían dos hermanos más, uno que había muerto hace años, el propio José, y otro pequeño llamado Benjamín que no les había acompañado. Como quería conocer a su hermano menor, José urdió un plan: acusó a sus hermanos de espionaje y les permitió volver con el grano a su tierra a cambio de que uno de ellos quedara en prenda hasta que todos volvieran a Egipto junto a su hermano menor. Los hijos de Jacob accedieron al canje. Benjamín se convirtió en la moneda de cambio entre sus hermanos.

Cuando volvieron con Benjamín, José les puso a prueba de nuevo. Escondió una copa de plata en las alforjas de su hermano Benjamín y, cuando todos partían, les acusó de robo. José les amenazó e indicó que quien tuviera la copa en su equipaje sería condenado a muerte. Cuando la copa apareció en las alforjas de Benjamín, todos los hermanos salieron en su defensa y ofrecieron su vida por la de su hermano. José entonces descubrió que sus hermanos habían cambiado y se descubrió ante ellos. La familia, gracias al canje del pequeño Benjamín, se reunió feliz de nuevo.

Relato bíblico

«Ellos […] bajaron a Egipto llevándose a Benjamín.
En seguida fueron a presentarse delante de José
y este vio que venían con Benjamín.» (Gn. 43, 15-16)

Moisés

Moisés es el personaje bíblico más importante del judaísmo. El profeta por excelencia para los hebreos recibió de Dios las Tablas de la Ley y terminó con el destierro de los judíos en Egipto hasta conducirlos a la Tierra Prometida. La historia de Moisés es una de las grandes epopeyas bíblicas. Su nacimiento, hazañas y muerte nos ofrecen un relato épico que elevó a Moisés por encima del resto de personajes del Antiguo Testamento. El nombre de Moisés significa «nacido de las aguas» y, efectivamente, así puede considerarse el inicio de su vida. Los judíos vivían en Egipto trabajando en su mayoría como esclavos para la clase dirigente. Asustado por una antigua profecía, el faraón mandó matar a todos los recién nacidos de origen judío. La tía de Moisés fabricó una cuna de juncos y se deshizo del bebé en el Nilo, esperando que alguien lo recogiera y adoptara. Fue Batía, la hija del faraón, la que encontró la cesta y adoptó al niño. Como ama de cría, la princesa eligió a una judía que resultó ser la madre biológica de Moisés. Su infancia transcurrió en la Corte egipcia. Su vida cambió por primera vez cuando asesinó a un capataz egipcio del faraón tras ver cómo mataba a los esclavos judíos. Moisés tuvo que exiliarse y vivió su vida como pastor.

Llevando a su ganado al monte Horeb, Moisés vio una zarza que ardía y no se consumía. Maravillado por el extraño hecho, se acercó a la planta y permaneció un rato observando con extrañeza. Cuando el profeta se acercó, Dios le habló desde la zarza, reveló por primera vez en la historia sagrada su nombre, Yahvé, y encomendó a Moisés la tarea de liberar a su pueblo de la esclavitud y guiarlo de nuevo hasta la Tierra Prometida. Moisés se dirigió a la comunidad judía y se valió de milagros para que todos creyeran que era el enviado de Dios. El profeta se dirigió entonces a la Corte del faraón. Se entrevistó con el monarca y le pidió que dejara marchar a su pueblo. La negativa del faraón trajo consigo la amenaza de terribles consecuencias para los egipcios. Moisés le advirtió que Dios enviaría plagas y calamidades hasta que

su voluntad cediera y les permitiera abandonar el país. El monarca no cedió hasta pasadas las famosas diez plagas: una convirtió el Nilo en sangre; otra trajo ranas; una tercera llenó el país de mosquitos; la cuarta llegó en forma de insectos que dañaban al ganado; la quinta fueron unas enfermedades epidémicas; la sexta aportó úlceras y sarpullidos cutáneos; la séptima supuso el granizo de fuego y hielo; la octava fue la plaga de las langostas que terminaron con las cosechas; la novena trajo la oscuridad, y la décima supuso la muerte de los primogénitos de hombres y animales.

El faraón derrotado permitió a Moisés y su pueblo abandonar Egipto. Comenzó así una de las peregrinaciones más largas de la Historia. Durante 40 años los judíos vagaron por el desierto y el Sinaí. En la huida de Egipto Moisés realizó numerosos prodigios y milagros: las aguas del mar Rojo se abrieron para que pasaran los judíos y se cerraron cuando cruzaba por ellas el ejército del faraón. Durante el largo tiempo que duró el éxodo, el pueblo de Israel pasó por numerosas vicisitudes históricas y religiosas. Cayeron en la adoración a dioses extranjeros, no encontraban unas normas de conductas moral y cívica que poder aplicar a los problemas que surgían en su convivencia diaria… Moisés entonces recibió el encargo de Dios de subir al monte Sinaí. Allí recibió las Tablas de la Ley, los Diez Mandamientos, que también heredaría el cristianismo y sobre los que se basan algunos de los principios de la ley islámica. Las Tablas fueron guardadas en el Arca de la Alianza, que se construyó al efecto y que junto a otros nuevos elementos litúrgicos abrían la caravana tribal que dirigía Moisés. El Profeta Moisés terminó sus días antes de llegar a la Tierra Prometida; los pecados que había cometido impidieron su entrada en Israel y solo pudo observar desde una montaña la tierra a la que conducía a su pueblo.

Moisés es la figura de referencia para el judaísmo. Su fe es llamada, en ocasiones, la «fe de Moisés». Los cristianos le consideran el más importante de los profetas y lo utilizan como símbolo del antiguo judaísmo y la nueva alianza que Jesús, en el Nuevo Testamento, trajo a los hombres. Son las antiguas leyes del Pueblo Elegido frente a la nueva norma del amor de Jesús.

The tablets held by the figure read:

ECOVTE ISRAEL
I
IE SVIS LE SEIGNE
TON DIEV. QVI T'AY
TIRE DE LA TERRE
D'EGIPTE DE LA MAIS
DE SERVITVDE. TV
N'AVRAS POINT D'AV
TRES DIEVX DEVANT
MA FACE. TV NE TE
FERAS POINT D'IDOLE
NI D'IMAGE TAILLEE
NY AVCVNE FIGVRE
POVR LES ADORER.
II
TV NE PRANDRAS PO
LE NOM DV SEIGNE
TON DIEV EN VAIN CA
LE SEIGNEVR TON DI
EV NE TIENDRA PO
INT POVR INNOCENT
CELVY QVI AVRA PRIS
LE NOM DV SEIGNE
SON DIEV EN VAIN.
III
SOVVIENS-TOY DE
SANCTIFIER LE IOV
DV SABATH.

IV
HONORE TON PERE ET
TA MERE. AFIN QVE T
SOIS HVREVX. ET Q
TV VIVES LOG-TE
SVR LA TERRE.
V
TV NE TVERAS P
VI
TV NE COMMETTRA
POINT FONICATION
VII
TV NE DEROBERA
POINT
VIII
TV NE DIRAS POINT
FAVX TESMOIGNAG
CONTRE TON PROCH
IX
TV NE DESIRERAS
POINT LA FEMME DE
TON PROCHAIN
X
TV NE DESIRERAS
POINT SA MAISON. N
SON SERVITEVR. N
SA SERVANTE NI S
BOEVF NY SON
NY AVTRE
LVY APP

<u>Relato bíblico</u>
«El Señor dijo a Moisés: "Sube hasta mí, a la montaña, y quédate aquí.
Yo te daré las tablas de piedra, con la ley y los mandamientos
que escribí para instruirlos".» (Ex. 24, 12)

Aarón

Aarón era el hermano mayor de Moisés, su mano derecha durante los años del éxodo y su heredero al cargo del pueblo de Israel para asentarlo en la Tierra Prometida. La Biblia nos indica que Moisés tuvo desde pequeño problemas de tartamudez. Su hermano Aarón fue la persona que le asistió y le sirvió de traductor. Desde entonces desarrollaron una gran relación que duró el resto de sus vidas. Aarón y Moisés lideraron a los israelitas durante el éxodo de Egipto. Aarón, de la tribu de Leví, fue elegido por Dios como Sumo Sacerdote de Israel; desde ese momento todos los sacerdotes judíos pertenecerían a su misma tribu. Entre sus funciones como Sumo Sacerdote, estaba ser el encargado de custodiar los elementos litúrgicos del rito judío, como las Tablas de la Ley que se guardaron en el Arca de la Alianza.

Con el sacerdocio de Aarón se inicia la tradición litúrgica judía. Nacen los ritos, se crean numerosos objetos sagrados, como el Menorah de oro, y se diseña un tabernáculo móvil, que se desmontaba con facilidad, para poder acompañar a los judíos en su viaje, y se transformará unos siglos después en el Templo de Jerusalén. Aarón era un hombre de paz, sencillo y que aplacaba el carácter de su hermano. Su aversión al conflicto le valió la reprimenda divina por no detener a los judíos cuando fundieron un becerro de oro para adorarlo mientras Moisés se encontraba en el monte Sinaí recibiendo las indicaciones de Dios. La tradición relata que su bastón era la fuente de sus milagros: se transformó en serpiente frente al faraón y floreció espontáneamente. El bastón se convirtió en objeto de culto y se custodió también en el Arca de la Alianza junto a las Tablas de la Ley y el Maná. Murió a los 123 años.

Relato bíblico

«[…] Aarón arrojó su cayado frente al faraón y sus servidores,
y el cayado se transformó en una serpiente.» (Éx. 7, 6)

Balaán

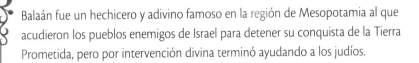

Balaán fue un hechicero y adivino famoso en la región de Mesopotamia al que acudieron los pueblos enemigos de Israel para detener su conquista de la Tierra Prometida, pero por intervención divina terminó ayudando a los judíos.

Los israelitas habían reanudado su marcha cerca de Jericó. Los reyes de las tierras que todavía no habían sido tomadas por los judíos temían perder sus posesiones a manos israelitas. Impotentes ante la sucesión de victorias de los judíos, los monarcas acudieron desesperados a Balaán, famoso por sus dotes mágicas, para solicitarle que maldijera a los judíos. Balaán les indicó que antes debía consultarlo con Dios. El Señor le dijo que no debería ir con los enviados reales; aunque si insistían y temía por su vida, les acompañara pero no hiciera nada sin antes consultárselo. Balaán finalmente partió de viaje y el libro de los Números nos relata un curioso episodio en el que un ángel enviado por Dios entorpece el camino de la burra que transportaba a Balaán.

Por tres veces el mago, que no veía al ángel, instigó con un palo al animal que se negaba a seguir andando al ver frente a ellos al ángel. Los golpes no causaron ningún efecto en la bestia y, cuando Balaán se disponía a infligir un castigo mayor al animal, el ángel hizo que el asno pudiera hablar. Balaán quedó asombrado y juró solo adorar a Dios y seguir fielmente sus órdenes. Cuando Balaán llegó ante los reyes, les engañó para que realizaran con él tres oráculos en los que en lugar de maldecir a los israelitas los bendijeron.

Relato bíblico

«Balac dijo a Balaán "¿Qué me has hecho? Yo te traje
para que maldijeras a mis enemigos,
y tú los has bendecido".» (Núm. 23, 11)

Josué

El profeta Josué fue el sucesor de Moisés como caudillo militar de los israelitas. Lideró al pueblo judío en las batallas que le llevaron a conquistar los diferentes reinos que habitaban en la Tierra Prometida.

Moisés acumuló el poder religioso, político y militar como líder indiscutible de los judíos. Preparando su sucesión, y por indicación divina, dividió las áreas de influencia entre sus dos manos derechas: Aarón y Josué. Aarón quedó revestido del poder religioso como Sumo Sacerdote y en su mano estaba también la aplicación de la recientemente promulgada ley divina. Josué recibió el encargo de liderar el ejército hebreo que debía presentar batalla. En vida de Moisés fue elegido para realizar algunas de las misiones más difíciles, como acudir a Canaán para espiar a los habitantes de aquella región y con la información obtenida diseñar la estrategia que permitiera la conquista de la Tierra Prometida. Cuando tomó posesión como caudillo de los judíos, todos ellos se disponían a atravesar el río Jordán para acceder a la tierra de Canaán.

El libro de Josué nos indica que las aguas se abrieron al paso del Arca de la Alianza para permitir que las tropas y el pueblo de Israel accedieran por fin a la tierra de sus ancestros. Al cruzar el Jordán, tuvieron que hacer frente a los enemigos para tomar la ciudad de Jericó. Tras un duro asedio, las tropas hebreas portaron el Arca de la Alianza abriendo el séquito y el sonido de las trompetas litúrgicas hizo que las murallas de Jericó cayeran, entregando la ciudad a los israelitas. En la batalla de Gabaón, Josué pidió a Dios que detuviera el discurrir del sol y la luna; el fenómeno asombró a los enemigos, y desde ese instante muchos se rendían directamente al paso de los israelitas, rehuyendo toda batalla.

«Entonces el pueblo lanzó un fuerte grito, y se tocaron las trompetas […]
y el muro se desplomó sobre sí mismo. En seguida el pueblo
acometió contra la ciudad, y la tomaron.» (Jos. 5, 20)

Débora

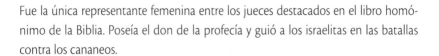

Fue la única representante femenina entre los jueces destacados en el libro homónimo de la Biblia. Poseía el don de la profecía y guió a los israelitas en las batallas contra los cananeos.

Nacida en la tribu de Efraín, conocemos pocos detalles acerca de su vida antes de ser considerada jueza de Israel. Casada con Lapidoth, un comerciante de antorchas, ella dedicaba su tiempo a emitir los juicios o profecías por los que era conocida. Cada día se dirigía hacia una palmera en el camino entre las ciudades de Ramah y Betel, se sentaba y esperaba a que los viandantes se acercaran a ella y le consultaran su opinión sobre un tema o le reclamaran una profecía. Tras el fallecimiento de Josué, la guerra en Canaán continuó y los reyes que todavía mantenían sus posesiones frente a los israelitas se coaligaron contra los que consideraban intrusos.

Una de las batallas cruciales se produjo contra el ejército comandado por Sísara. En una de sus profecías, Débora indicó que el enemigo Sísara sería derrotado, pero no a manos de otro militar, sino de una mujer. La batalla se celebró, y una milagrosa lluvia torrencial inutilizó los 900 carros de guerra que Sísara había situado en primera línea de combate. Aunque la balanza se decantó del lado de los israelitas, la hazaña no finalizó hasta la muerte de Sísara, que fue asesinado por una judía, Jael, cuando el general huía del campo de batalla buscando refugio.

Débora es considerada por algunos autores como «la madre de Israel» porque el poema que protagoniza en el libro de los Jueces es uno de los escritos bíblicos hebreos más antiguos jamás descubierto, por lo que es considerado el origen de toda una tradición.

Relato bíblico

«En aquel tiempo juzgaba a Israel una profetisa llamada Débora. […]
se sentaba debajo de una palmera […] y los israelitas
acudían a ella para resolver sus litigios.» (Jc. 4, 4-5)

Jael

VERDUGA DIVINA

La joven Jael fue una heroína judía cuya historia aparece retratada en el libro de los Jueces y está ligada a la vida de la jueza y profetisa Débora. Los hebreos libraron importantes batallas hasta que consiguieron reunir bajo su poder la totalidad de la Tierra Prometida. Las huestes judías se repartieron las zonas de ataque y la guerra se tornaba cada vez más cruenta puesto que las partes implicadas querían conseguir una victoria rápida y definitiva sobre el enemigo. En los tiempos de los jueces de Israel, la profetisa Débora era la líder moral de los judíos; a ella se acercaban gentes de toda la región para que solucionara sus problemas emitiendo sabios juicios o acertadas profecías. Barak era el líder militar que debía luchar contra los cananeos en la batalla de Esdraelon.

El general buscó el favor divino consultando su suerte a la profetisa Débora. La profecía de Débora no fue plenamente del gusto de Barak puesto que le advertía que el final de su batalla, y por lo tanto su victoria, no vendría de su fuerza, sino de la mano de una mujer. Barak pensó que esa mujer sería Débora y la conminó a que le acompañara al campo de batalla. Débora accedió y, cuando la contienda comenzaba a tornarse favorable para los judíos, el líder del ejército cananeo, Sísara, huyó temeroso de ser capturado por los judíos. La joven hebrea Jael, nómada de aquellas tierras, salió a su encuentro y le dio refugio en su tienda de campaña. Ella lo agasajó con leche de cabra caliente y cuando Sísara cedió al cansancio que lo azotaba y comenzó a dormir, Jael lo asesinó clavándole con una maza una estaca en su cabeza. La muerte de Sísara supuso la victoria definitiva sobre los cananeos que Débora había profetizado.

Relato bíblico

«Sísara pidió agua, ella le dio leche […] ella martilló a Sísara, le partió la cabeza, le machacó y le atravesó la sien.» (Jc. 5, 25-26)

Sansón y Dalila

LA FUERZA DE DIOS

Sansón y Dalila constituyen una de las parejas del Antiguo Testamento que más eco ha tenido en la cultura popular. La fuerza milagrosa de Sansón y el encanto cautivador de Dalila han inspirado decenas de obras pictóricas, musicales y dramáticas a lo largo de los siglos. Sansón fue consagrado desde su nacimiento a Yahvé, siguiendo el rito del nazareato, por el que el pequeño de una familia no podría jamás cortarse el cabello.

Desde joven su fuerza fue famosa en su tierra. Se casó con una filistea y durante sus nupcias el joven propuso un acertijo a los filisteos: ofreció un premio a quien adivinara la cuestión planteada. Nadie conseguía resolver el acertijo y se acercaba el plazo límite dado por Sansón. La esposa de Sansón, chantajeada por sus compatriotas, consiguió la respuesta y se la facilitó a los filisteos. Cuando Sansón descubrió el engaño, cazó 30 zorras, las ató de las colas en parejas y les prendió fuego. Los animales quemaron las cosechas filisteas con sus colas que ardían como teas.

Tiempo después se enamoró de Dalila, otra filistea, de belleza embaucadora. La mujer fue sobornada para que descubriera el secreto de la fuerza de Sansón. Tras varios intentos fallidos, finalmente consiguió conocer que su pelo le aportaba la fuerza sobrehumana. Un sirviente de la casa se lo cortó y Sansón perdió toda su milagrosa fuerza. Sansón fue capturado por los filisteos y se decidió que debía ser sacrificado. Los filisteos llenaban el templo para presenciar el sacrificio. Arrepentido de haber contado su secreto, Sansón rogó a Dios que le devolviera solo una vez más su fuerza para terminar con aquellos enemigos de su pueblo. Dios le concedió el milagro y Sansón consiguió derrumbar las columnas del templo y allí perecieron todos, incluido Sansón, quien con su muerte consiguió esquilmar las defensas filisteas, por lo que finalmente consiguió su objetivo inicial.

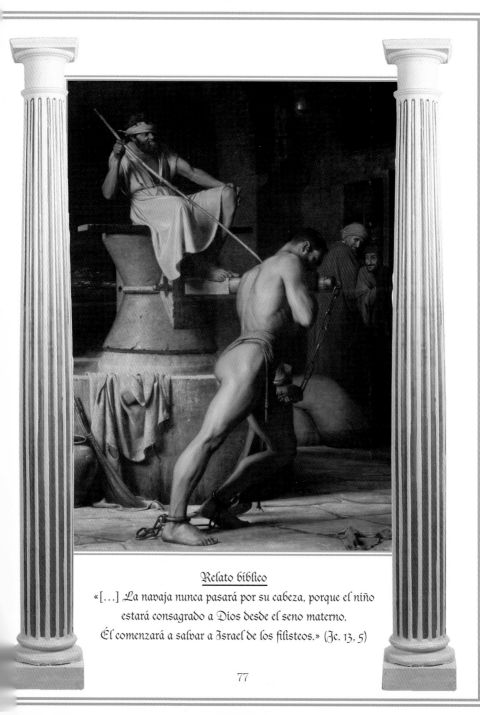

Relato bíblico

«[...] La navaja nunca pasará por su cabeza, porque el niño
estará consagrado a Dios desde el seno materno.
Él comenzará a salvar a Israel de los filisteos.» (Jc. 13, 5)

Samuel

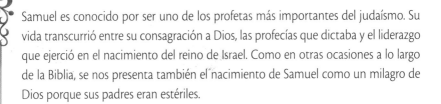

Samuel es conocido por ser uno de los profetas más importantes del judaísmo. Su vida transcurrió entre su consagración a Dios, las profecías que dictaba y el liderazgo que ejerció en el nacimiento del reino de Israel. Como en otras ocasiones a lo largo de la Biblia, se nos presenta también el nacimiento de Samuel como un milagro de Dios porque sus padres eran estériles.

Perteneciente a la tribu de Leví, la de la casta sacerdotal, desde joven fue consagrado al Señor y pasó su infancia junto al sacerdote Elí. Cerca de los 12 años recibió la llamada de Dios. El niño no entendía quién le llamaba en la noche y acudía a la cama de Elí, su preceptor, pero el sacerdote le decía que él no le había llamado. Así ocurrió en tres ocasiones, hasta que Elí se dio cuenta que era Dios el que llamaba a Samuel y le enseñó cómo debía contestar al Señor. Desde ese momento el niño fue elegido profeta de Israel. Su fama se acrecentó por momentos y llegó a liderar el ejército judío ante las últimas batallas que le permitirían convertirse en un reino independiente. Precisamente su poder como profeta le llevó a ser él, por indicación divina, quien eligiera al primer Rey de Israel, Saúl. Por estas circunstancias es conocido como sacerdote, profeta y rey, aunque formalmente no ostentara la corona judía. Sus interpretaciones de la ley de Moisés son, todavía hoy, aceptadas como una de las normas válidas para los hebreos.

Relato bíblico

«Samuel creció; el Señor estaba con él, y no dejó que cayera por tierra ninguna de sus palabras. Todo Israel [...] supo que Samuel estaba acreditado como profeta del Señor.» (1 S. 3, 19-20)

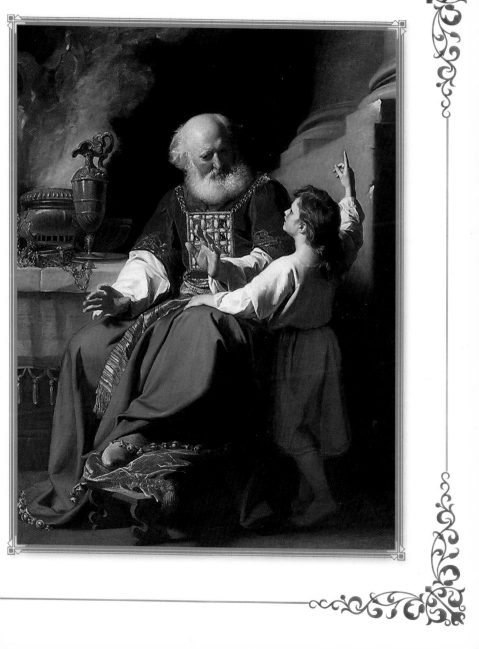

Saúl

Primer Rey de Israel

La historia y las Sagradas Escrituras indican que Saúl fue el primer Rey de Israel. Su reinado ha quedado a la sombra de sus predecesores, David y Salomón, pero es reconocido por la labor de unión de todas las tribus bajo una misma corona.

El pueblo judío se encontraba cansado de años de interminables guerras que habían diezmado la población y minado su moral. El profeta Samuel supuso un soplo de aire fresco que renovó las esperanzas de los israelitas en un futuro más halagüeño. Cuando la vida del profeta se encontraba cerca de su fin, y debido a que alguno de sus hijos podría intentar ocupar la posición del padre, los líderes de las tribus le suplicaron que ungiera un rey para todos ellos que fuera capaz de aunar bajo un mismo reino a todos los hebreos.

Saúl, un joven israelí que ayudaba a cuidar a los burros de su padre, fue el elegido por Dios y por Samuel. Aunque el libro de Samuel no se refiere a Saúl como rey, sino líder o comandante, finalmente le es otorgado este título. Saúl disfrutó del favor de Dios, mientras que siguió sus órdenes o las de su profeta.

Durante años trajo el bienestar a su pueblo, pero el engreimiento y la codicia fueron minando su corazón y finalmente se alejó de la tutela divina y Dios decidió rechazarlo como rey. El libro de Samuel nos cuenta cómo Dios decidió no continuar el linaje de Saúl y eligió a David como nuevo rey. Saúl, ignorando su destino, aceptó a David en su Corte y observó cómo su fama se acrecentaba como caudillo militar y líder popular. Cegado por su interés de ganar el favor divino saliendo victorioso del campo de batalla, se enfrentó a los filisteos. Enajenado, convocó al espíritu del profeta Samuel, que se le apareció y le profetizó la derrota total de su ejército y su muerte. La batalla cumplió la profecía del espectro y Saúl se suicidó tras matar a sus hijos.

Relato bíblico

«Samuel tomó el frasco de aceite y lo derramó
sobre la cabeza de Saúl: luego lo besó y dijo
"¡El Señor te ha ungido como jefe de su herencia"!» (1 S. 10, 1)

David y Goliat

El pequeño contra el grande, David y Goliat representan en las páginas de la Biblia la eterna lucha entre la inteligencia y la fuerza física que también mitos de otras religiones han reflejado en fábulas y leyendas.

David, cuyo nombre significa el «elegido por Dios», fue el segundo Rey de Israel. Fue el menor de ocho hermanos y, con escaso tamaño, desde joven había pasado inadvertido para los que le rodeaban. Siguiendo las órdenes de Dios, el profeta Samuel viajó a Belén para elegir al sucesor de Saúl, que había perdido el favor divino. Samuel se entrevistó con los hijos de Isaí, pero ninguno cumplía sus expectativas, hasta que por fin le trajeron a David, que estaba pastoreando en el campo. David fue ungido rey antes de fallecer Saúl; su nombramiento solo lo conocían Dios, Samuel y el propio David. Durante años convivió en la Corte con el monarca formal de Israel, Saúl, sin poder revelar su destino. Debido a su aspecto débil, David fue encargado del arpa en la Corte israelí, demostrando un gran talento entre quienes lo escuchaban.

En plena guerra con los filisteos, Goliat, el líder enemigo de Israel que estaba dotado de una impresionante fuerza física, retó a que los israelitas eligieran un representante que se enfrentara a él en lucha libre y aquel que resultara vencedor haría ganar la guerra a todo su pueblo. Los israelitas encomendaron esta tarea a David. El joven pastor y arpista se dirigió al campo de batalla y allí, gracias a su astucia, le bastó con una honda, un cayado y cinco piedras poder derribar al líder filisteo. La victoria le granjeó el favor del pueblo y la envidia del rey Saúl. David tuvo que huir hasta que finalmente los líderes de las tribus, a la muerte de Saúl, le reconocieron como verdadero rey. La Biblia también narra que David perdió el favor de Dios al cometer adulterio.

Relato bíblico

«[…] David enfiló velozmente en dirección a Goliat, se metió la mano
en su bolsa, sacó de ella una piedra y la arrojó con la honda,
hiriendo al filisteo en la frente […] Así venció David […]
sin tener una espada en su mano.» (1 S. 17, 49-51)

Salomón y la Reina de Saba

El rey de la sabiduría

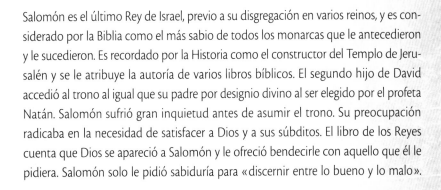

Salomón es el último Rey de Israel, previo a su disgregación en varios reinos, y es considerado por la Biblia como el más sabio de todos los monarcas que le antecedieron y le sucedieron. Es recordado por la Historia como el constructor del Templo de Jerusalén y se le atribuye la autoría de varios libros bíblicos. El segundo hijo de David accedió al trono al igual que su padre por designio divino al ser elegido por el profeta Natán. Salomón sufrió gran inquietud antes de asumir el trono. Su preocupación radicaba en la necesidad de satisfacer a Dios y a sus súbditos. El libro de los Reyes cuenta que Dios se apareció a Salomón y le ofreció bendecirle con aquello que él le pidiera. Salomón solo le pidió sabiduría para «discernir entre lo bueno y lo malo».

El reinado de Salomón es reflejado como uno de los más fructíferos de la historia de Israel. Las guerras fueron prácticamente eliminadas, floreció el comercio y las cosechas resultaron excelentes. El progreso de su reino llegó a oídos de la Reina de Saba, que viajó a la Corte israelita con gran cantidad de presentes para el famoso rey. Ella quedó prendada del monarca, se convirtió al monoteísmo y le regaló varias toneladas de oro. Por su parte, Salomón compuso para ella algunos de los poemas del Cantar de los Cantares. Ella volvió a su reino, pero su amor duró para siempre. Salomón quiso honrar a Dios por los años de gloria que Israel disfrutaba y decidió construir un templo que sustituyera al tabernáculo en el que se realizaba el servicio religioso judío en Jerusalén. Salomón recibió precisas instrucciones divinas sobre la construcción del Templo de Jerusalén. Salomón también desarrolló una intensa actividad diplomática, que incluía tomar por esposas a las hijas de aquellos monarcas que se lo ofrecían. Las esposas trajeron ideas nuevas al reino, como priorizar el comercio sobre la ley de Moisés, o introducir sus dioses paganos. La Biblia indica que estas cuestiones le valieron el rechazo divino y la maldición de la división de su reino.

Relato bíblico

«480 años después de que los israelitas salieron del país de Egipto,
en el cuarto año del reinado de Salomón,
comenzó a construir la Casa del Señor.» (1 R. 6, 1)

Elías

Elías es uno de los grandes profetas de la historia sagrada. Judaísmo y cristianismo reconocen los numerosos milagros que realizó, entre los que se incluye la primera resurrección de la que nos habla la Biblia. Al igual que otros profetas, la misión divina de Elías consistía en predicar su palabra y remover el corazón de todos aquellos que lo escuchaban, en especial los gobernantes, para que practicaran la máxima virtud y se ajustaran a las leyes hebreas. La primera misión de Elías la realiza anunciando la gran sequía que se avecinaba sobre Acab. Elías se escondió en una cueva del Jordán hasta que esta pasara, y allí fue alimentado por unos cuervos que le traían comida cada día y no dejaron que desfalleciera durante todo ese tiempo.

Cuando Dios lo indicó, Elías abandonó su retiro y se dirigió a la población más cercana y, al entrar a la casa de una viuda que le ofreció su máxima hospitalidad, el profeta multiplicó la comida para que ambos se saciaran. El libro de los Reyes nos indica que Elías resucitó al hijo de la viuda.

La Biblia también nos refiere el episodio en el que Elías retó a los sacerdotes de Baal, dios pagano, a que ofrecieran un buey a su dios y que este en señal de aceptación del sacrificio lo incinerara en la pira preparada al efecto. Los sacerdotes dedicaron horas a las oraciones frente al altar y nada ocurría. Elías entonces invocó a Yahvé y una columna de fuego consumió el altar.

Relato bíblico

«El Señor escuchó el clamor de Elías: el aliento
vital volvió al niño y este revivió. Elías tomó al niño,
lo bajó de la habitación alta de la casa y se lo entregó
a su madre.» (1 R. 17, 22-23)

Tobías

El matrimonio y la vida virtuosa

El profeta Tobías es el protagonista del libro bíblico que lleva su nombre. Destaca por haber mostrado por primera vez en la Sagrada Escritura la conjunción de las futuras virtudes cristianas en una misma persona. El relato rompe con la tradición más historicista de los escritos bíblicos que le precedían y vuelve a utilizar un tono metafórico, parecido al del Génesis, con la intención de transmitir una fe más que reflejar estrictamente una realidad concreta.

Tobías era hijo de Tobit, un judío que había quedado ciego al caerle en sus ojos excrementos de ave. La Biblia lo describe como un joven lleno de fe. El arcángel San Rafael se le aparece para guiarle en el camino de su progreso espiritual, inculcarle la vida en las virtudes y ayudarle en la búsqueda de esposa. El relato nos presenta el proceso por el que Tobías sale de su pueblo en busca de Sara, la joven de belleza y comportamiento idílicos que sufría el hechizo del demonio Asmodeo. Sara se había casado hasta en siete ocasiones, habiendo enviudado todas ellas durante la misma noche de bodas, sin poder llegar a consumar el matrimonio, debido a la maldición de Asmodeo. Al igual que en la literatura caballeresca de la Edad Media, Tobías, que ya ama a Sara por la mera descripción que el arcángel San Rafael le ha hecho de la joven, aparece en la vida de Sara para rescatarla de su destino. Tobías prepara por indicación de San Rafael una cataplasma de hígado y corazón de pez con la que consigue ahuyentar al demonio. Esa misma mezcla la aplicará también en los ojos de su padre, que quedará curado de su ceguera.

Relato bíblico

«El ángel le respondió: "Si se quema el corazón y el hígado
del pez delante de un hombre o una mujer atacados por un demonio,
cesarán los ataques [...]".» (Tb 6, 8)

Judit

Pocas mujeres aparecen retratadas en la Biblia con la fuerza y la inteligencia de Judit, la viuda hebrea que con sus encantos y astucia consiguió descabezar al ejército babilónico que azotaba a Israel. Judit era una viuda judía que vivió en la época en la que los israelitas luchaban contra las invasiones del ejército babilónico. La Biblia cuenta a modo de relato histórico novelado las vicisitudes que le ocurrieron a Judit durante la guerra contra Babilonia. Judit fue llamada por Dios para que se desplazara junto a su criada hasta la primera línea del frente bélico. Allí vivió en la ciudad judía de Betulia, que había sido sitiada por el ejército babilónico. Las gentes sufrían enfermedades y la villa se encontraba a punto de caer en manos enemigas. Judit, que contaba con gran belleza, se las ingenió para salir del recinto amurallado y llegar hasta la tienda del general Holofernes. Sus encantos cautivaron al babilonio, que cayó rendido ante ella. Holofernes se sintió enamorado y creyó que la hebrea también lo estaba. Judit emborrachó a Holofernes hasta que sucumbió al sueño, y ella aprovechó la oportunidad para degollarlo. La muerte del caudillo causó gran revuelo entre el ejército de Babilonia y las tropas se dispersaron presas del pánico, dando la victoria a los israelitas y liberando la ciudad de Betulia.

Como los libros de Tobías, Ester o Job, su fundamento no responde a un interés puramente historicista, sino al de incentivar el sentimiento nacional y religioso en quienes leyeran sus páginas. Los historiadores han descrito un cierto paralelismo entre el carisma de Juana de Arco y la Judit del Antiguo Testamento.

Relato bíblico
«Holofernes, completamente ebrio, yacía en su lecho.
Judit [...] le asestó dos golpes en el cuello con todas sus fuerzas
y le cortó la cabeza.» (Jdt. 13, 2-8)

Ester

La Reina judía de Persia

Ester fue coronada Reina de Persia mientras los judíos se encontraban desterrados en la tierra de Babilonia. Las vicisitudes de su vida, ascensión al trono y finalmente cómo salvó a los judíos del exterminio constituyen el núcleo central del libro homónimo incluido en la Biblia. Tras las guerras que relatan diferentes libros bíblicos, el ejército de Babilonia venció definitivamente a los judíos, que según la Biblia habían perdido el favor divino por sus pecados, y se inició un tiempo de prolongado dominio sobre las tierras que pertenecían a Palestina. Gran parte de la población fue exiliada a las tierras persas para trabajar como esclavos, aunque a las élites se les permitió trabajar para la administración imperial y no sufrir mayor castigo que ese.

Ester había sido adoptada por su primo Mardoqueo, un alto funcionario en la Corte de Susa. Este acceso al palacio real le permitió proponer a Ester como una de las candidatas a esposa del rey Asuero que acababa de enviudar. La belleza de Ester sedujo al monarca, que accedió a desposarla convirtiéndola en reina. Estando en la Corte, su primo Mardoqueo escandalizó a los persas al no inclinar su cabeza ante el rey y su esposa, debido a que los judíos solo se postraban ante Dios. El conflicto se convirtió en una oportunidad para que el sátrapa Amán, que gobernaba el reino en nombre del monarca, dictara la muerte de todos los judíos que no se postraran ante la imagen del monarca.

El objetivo real era confiscar todos los bienes de la floreciente clase comercial judía. Pero Amán desconocía que la Reina Ester era judía. Ester encandiló al rey y preparó un banquete en el que descubrir a Amán y pedir al monarca que perdonara a todo su pueblo y condenara al sátrapa. Su inteligencia al trazar el plan dio como resultado que los judíos fueran salvados del exterminio.

«La Reina Ester tomó la palabra y dijo: "Rey, si estás dispuesto
a hacerme un favor, y si esto es lo que te agrada, mi petición
es que me concedas la vida y mi deseo es que perdones
la vida a mi pueblo".» (Est. 7, 3)

Job
LA PACIENCIA COMO VIRTUD

Job es uno más de los personajes bíblicos que ha transcendido del ámbito religioso para convertirse en un símbolo de la cultura popular durante siglos y hasta nuestros días. La paciencia, la sumisión y la fe absoluta en los designios de Dios definen la vida de este icono bíblico.

La Biblia nos presenta a Job como un próspero ganadero judío que había engendrado a siete hijos y tres hijas. Era propietario de una heredad que daba trabajo a decenas de siervos. Job se ve involucrado de manera involuntaria en una de las eternas disputas entre Dios y Satanás. El demonio reta a Dios para demostrar la naturaleza pecadora del hombre. Satanás creía que la integridad y la fidelidad del hombre hacia Dios solo se producían en la gente que era bendecida con numerosos dones. Dios pretende demostrar su error y permite a Satanás que envíe cuantas calamidades considere para poner a prueba a Job, a excepción de tocar su vida.

Durante años Job sufrió enfermedades, la pérdida de todo su poder económico, el repudio de su mujer e incluso el fallecimiento de sus hijos. Pueblos extranjeros atacaron sus propiedades y Job se quedó sin nada, absolutamente nada que le atara a este mundo. No obstante, Job nunca repudió su fe, aceptó con resignación su destino y no puso en duda la bondad de Dios. Cuando la disputa terminó, Dios había vuelto a ganar a Satanás y premió a Job devolviéndole todo aquello de lo que había sido privado en una cuantía superior al doble de lo que antes disfrutaba.

Relato bíblico
«Después el Señor cambió la suerte de Job,
porque él había intercedido a favor de sus amigos,
y duplicó todo lo que Job tenía.» (Jb. 42, 12)

Isaías

Isaías es el profeta hebreo que dedicó la mayor parte de su predicación a anunciar la llegada de un Mesías para el pueblo de Israel que traería el Reino de Dios a los hombres. El libro de Isaías destaca entre las Sagradas Escrituras como uno de los textos de mayor profundidad religiosa y mayor poder profético. En sus versículos encontramos el anuncio de que el Mesías sería descendiente del rey David, que su reino moral se haría sobre el reino de Judá, así mismo tendría el privilegio de nacer de una virgen y su fuerza le llevaría a fundar un verdadero imperio de paz.

En el contexto religioso del momento Isaías supuso una vuelta a los orígenes del judaísmo. Los israelitas vivían influidos por costumbres y tradiciones paganas que se introducían en su vida diaria minando la estricta ley de Moisés.

El pueblo de Israel había sido deportado a Babilonia y poco a poco perdía la conexión con sus tradiciones y costumbres. El profeta Isaías pretende reafirmar el poder de Dios y atemorizar con grandes calamidades a aquellos que no sigan fielmente sus enseñanzas. Isaías dedicó gran parte de sus escritos a realizar oráculos contra las naciones extranjeras que «contaminaban» al pueblo de Dios, en clara alusión a los babilonios y otros pueblos orientales. También anunció la liberación de Israel y la vuelta a la Tierra Prometida, dando fin al exilio. Pero Isaías es destacado por el cristianismo por su gran dedicación a anunciar no solo la llegada del Mesías, sino un futuro Juicio Final en el que todos deberían expiar sus pecados.

Relato bíblico
«Porque nos ha nacido, un hijo nos ha sido dado.
La soberanía reposa sobre sus hombros y se le da por nombre […]
Príncipe de la Paz.» (Is. 9, 5-6)

Jeremías

El profeta Jeremías destaca entre sus iguales por la férrea disciplina religiosa y moral que trató de imponer a los reyes que gobernaron Judea durante su vida. Durante siglos los profetas habían gozado de una gran estimación entre los judíos. Sus indicaciones eran escuchadas, se les dispensaba un trato reverencial y el poder político (los monarcas) acataba las indicaciones de los enviados de Dios que los ungían en su nombre. Las guerras, las invasiones y el exilio motivaron importantes cambios culturales entre el pueblo judío que prestaba cada vez menor interés a las proclamas religiosas de sus profetas. Jeremías vivió bajo el reinado de Josías, Joaquín y Sedecías.

El profeta Jeremías transmitió a los monarcas el lamento de Dios ante la corrupción de los creyentes, y les advirtió que los caldeos tomarían el poder en Judá si no volvían de inmediato a la fe y la tradición de sus antepasados. Los monarcas, cuyas cortes cada vez se parecían más a las satrapías orientales, instigaban al pueblo contra Jeremías porque su discurso socavaba el poder real.

Los tres monarcas persiguieron a Jeremías, que se tuvo que esconder e incluso exiliar, llegando a dudar de su misión profética. Jeremías realizó un último intento de acercamiento entre Dios y Judá: pidió que fuera abolida la esclavitud como muestra de una verdadera conversión del corazón del monarca. Como su petición no fue atendida, anunció el castigo divino: el nuevo exilio que vendría de manos de Nabucodonosor II.

Relato bíblico

«A causa de los pecados que habéis cometido contra Dios, seréis llevados cautivos a Babilonia por Nabucodonosor, rey de los babilonios, [...] por siete generaciones, pero después de esto Dios les hará salir de allí en paz.» (Ct.J. 1-2)

Ezequiel

En el último periodo antes del segundo destierro a Babilonia, hasta cuatro profetas convivieron en la misma época en Israel: Jeremías, Daniel, Esdras y Ezequiel. Las visiones de Ezequiel han dado lugar a numerosas producciones artísticas y a estudios de angeología. Su capacidad como profeta estaba centrada en advertir al pueblo de Israel de la inminente caída de la ciudad de Jerusalén, de la destrucción del Templo y del largo exilio que todos iban a vivir. Las profecías se cumplieron y primero Nabucodonosor conquistó Judá, llevó a numerosos judíos deportados a Babilonia e instaló en el trono como marioneta a Sedecías.

Ezequiel fue de los primeros exiliados y en el nuevo país trató de reconfortar a sus fieles. Los judíos pensaban que el exilio apenas duraría unos meses, quizá años, pero que pronto regresarían a su tierra. La noticia de la destrucción de Jerusalén por culpa de la rebelión de Sedecías cayó como un mazazo entre los exiliados.

Desde ese instante se sucedieron muchos falsos profetas contra los que Ezequiel luchó dialécticamente para evitar que confundieran a los judíos de buena fe. Una de las visiones más famosas de Ezequiel es aquella en la que se le dan a conocer algunos de los diferentes tipos de ángeles, como los tronos, a la vez que se anuncia por primera vez el tetramorfos, con cabezas de águila, toro, león y hombre, que luego identificaría a los cuatro Evangelistas.

Relato bíblico

«Yo miré a los seres vivientes y observé que en el suelo,
al lado de cada uno de ellos había una rueda […]
de aspecto brillante como el topacio.» (Ez. 1, 15-16)

EZECHIEL

Daniel

PROFETA Y SABIO ARROJADO A LOS LEONES

Daniel fue el más conocido profeta de la época del exilio en Babilonia. Su inteligencia y capacidad para poder descifrar los sueños le convirtieron en gobernador de la capital babilónica.

Cuando solo contaba con 14 años, Daniel partió hacia el exilio tras la derrota judía a manos de Nabucodonosor. El monarca de Babilonia buscaba entre las élites judías algunas personas para integrarlas en la estructura administrativa del reino. Daniel fue uno de los elegidos y se trasladó a vivir al palacio real donde su astucia maravilló al monarca. La Biblia nos cuenta que una noche Nabucodonosor sufrió una pesadilla que le causó gran perturbación. El monarca convocó a sus expertos y pidió que le interpretaran su sueño. La dificultad estribaba en que Nabucodonosor había olvidado el sueño. Nadie consiguió descifrarlo y el rey ordenó asesinar a los sabios. Daniel pidió más tiempo y rogó a Dios que le iluminara. Por la noche tuvo una visión en la que Dios le concedía su petición. Daniel aclaró a Nabucodonosor su angustia y desde entonces gozó de gran fama y fue nombrado gobernador de la capital. Daniel continuó como alto burócrata en la corte de los nuevos reyes. Su poder le granjeó la envidia de los sátrapas que asistían al monarca y todos realizaron un contubernio contra Daniel, que fue condenado a morir devorado por leones. El profeta fue arrojado a un pozo con las bestias que debían matarlo. Pero al día siguiente cuando los guardias fueron a recoger su cuerpo, lo encontraron vivo y con los leones mansos. Este gesto fue interpretado por el rey como una señal divina y condenó a los sátrapas al foso de los leones en el que todos ellos perecieron.

Relato bíblico

«El rey dijo a Daniel:"[…]¿Ha podido tu Dios, al que sirves con tanta constancia, salvarte de los leones?" y Daniel dijo "¡Viva el rey eternamente!".» (Dn. 6, 21-22)

Susana

La belleza de la inocencia

Susana era una joven judía, esposa de uno de los más potentados mercaderes judíos que, pese al exilio, había acumulado una gran riqueza. El exilio judío en Babilonia fue una de las épocas más oscuras de la historia de Israel. En ese tiempo destacó la figura del profeta Daniel, y de varias de las personas que aparecen en su libro homónimo de la Biblia. Los esposos vivían en una lujosa casa con jardín y piscina. Cada día la joven Susana salía a bañarse en el jardín, y su belleza era conocida por toda la comunidad judía. Entonces las visitas se multiplicaban en la casa de su esposo. Un día unos ancianos judíos, llevados por la lujuria, concertaron abusar de Susana. Desde esa jornada acudían diariamente a la casa hasta que una tarde encontraron la posibilidad de llevar a cabo su macabro plan. Susana había pedido a sus sirvientas que abandonaran el jardín para quedarse sola durante su baño. Los ancianos accedieron a la zona de la piscina y retuvieron a la joven. Los gritos de Susana comenzaron a alertar a los sirvientes y los ancianos se vieron descubiertos. Dispuestos a salir del paso de aquel delito ambos decidieron inventarse que habían accedido al jardín porque habían observado que Susana recibía a un joven amante. La pobre Susana quedó devastada cuando los sirvientes y su marido creyeron la versión de los ancianos.

Se celebró un juicio rápido cuya sentencia fue la condena a muerte de Susana. Toda la comunidad judía de la localidad había acudido a la vista y al escucharse la sentencia se alzó la voz de Daniel que indicó: «Yo soy inocente de la sangre de esta mujer». Dios había hablado por su boca. Daniel, para demostrar la inocencia de Susana y guiado por el Ángel del Señor, mandó encerrar a los acusadores en estancias separadas y allí realizó a cada uno la misma pregunta: «¿Debajo de qué árbol se encontraba la pareja de supuestos amantes?». Uno de los ancianos contestó que una acacia, y otro de ellos dijo que un ciprés. El hecho sirvió para demostrar que ambos mentían y que Susana era inocente.

Relato bíblico

«Dieron gracias a Dios por su hija Susana, lo mismo que Joaquín,
su marido y todos sus parientes porque nada indigno
se había hallado finalmente en ella. Desde ese día,
Daniel fue grande a los ojos del pueblo». (Dn. 13, 63-64)

Jonás

EL PROFETA Y LA BALLENA

Jonás fue un profeta del Reino de Israel que desarrolló su actividad en torno al siglo VIII a.C. Según el Libro que lleva su nombre, Jonás recibió de Yahvé la orden de ir a predicar a la ciudad de Nínive, que se había entregado al pecado. El profeta intenta huir del mandato divino, y se embarca en dirección contraria, hacia Tarsis. Una terrible tempestad asola al navío, y Jonás acaba confesando que no se trata de una tormenta corriente: es el castigo de Dios por no cumplir sus órdenes. Los marineros lanzan a su tripulante al mar, la tempestad se calma de inmediato y un gigantesco pez enviado por Yahvé devora al profeta. Este permanece tres días y tres noches orando en su interior, hasta que Dios ordena al pez que lo libere.

Una vez más, Jonás recibe el mandato de ir a profetizar a Nínive. En esta ocasión decide obedecer y entra en la ciudad proclamando que esta será destruida en el plazo de 40 días. Los habitantes de la ciudad creen la palabra del profeta, por lo que se arrepienten, ayunan y piden clemencia hasta que Dios decide perdonarlos. Jonás no entiende la misericordia de Yahvé y, furioso porque no se ha cumplido su profecía, se marcha al desierto para convertirse en eremita.

En el Evangelio de San Mateo, Jesús habla del tiempo que Jonás pasó en el vientre de la ballena y afirma que, del mismo modo, «el Hijo del Hombre pasará tres días y tres noches en el corazón de la tierra».

Relato bíblico
«Entonces el Señor dio orden al pez, y este arrojó a Jonás
sobre la tierra firme.» (Jon. 2, 11)

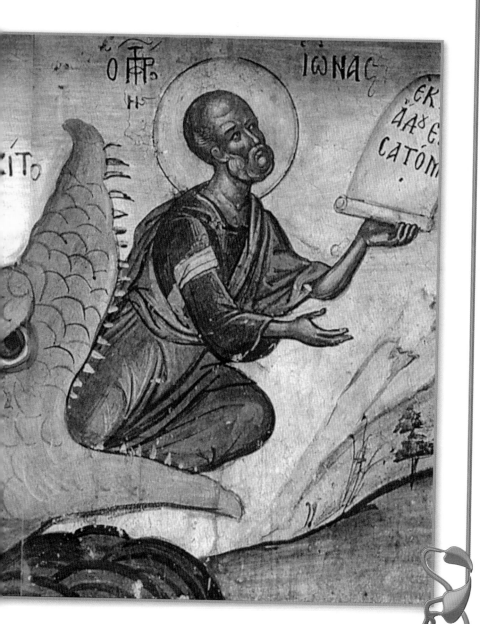

Joel

Yahvé es Dios

Es el segundo de los 12 profetas menores. El libro de Joel no ofrece muchos detalles sobre su autor. Solo se nos informa que escribió tras una terrible sequía y una plaga de langosta, lo cual, considerando el contenido de las profecías, puede haber ocurrido en cualquier momento entre los siglos IX y IV a.C.

Las profecías de Joel afirman que la plaga de langosta y la sequía eran un castigo de Yahvé; sin embargo, el pueblo no reconoce el castigo, por lo cual el profeta llama al arrepentimiento. En el capítulo segundo se muestra un ejército de extranjeros que debía acabar con el Reino de Judá: se ha interpretado que este ejército pertenecía a Nabucodonosor, que derrotó a los judíos y los llevó al exilio en Babilonia. Sin embargo, Joel vaticina que el pueblo de Israel regresará de ese exilio y obtendrá venganza contra los babilonios, haciendo gran hincapié en «el día de Yahvé», que podría compararse con el Juicio Final. Joel describe cómo Dios promete que derramará Su Espíritu sobre todos los hombres.

En los Hechos de los Apóstoles, San Pedro cita la profecía de Joel como un vaticinio de la venida del Espíritu Santo. Y otros autores interpretan el mensaje de Joel como un aviso ante la inevitable llegada del fin del mundo y el consecuente Juicio Final al que se deberán someter todos los hombres.

Relato bíblico

«Haré prodigios en el cielo y la tierra: sangre, fuego
y columnas de humo. El sol se convertirá en tinieblas
y la luna en sangre.» (Jl. 3, 3-4)

Zacarías
EL PROFETA MESIÁNICO

Zacarías es considerado el undécimo de los 12 profetas menores. Ejerció su ministerio en el Reino de Judá poco después del regreso del exilio en Babilonia, durante el reinado de Darío I, alrededor del año 520 a.C.

Según él mismo proclama en el libro que lleva su nombre, Zacarías era hijo de Berekías, hijo de Idó, y pertenecía a la casta sacerdotal. Su actividad profética comenzó cuando aún era muy joven, tan solo 17 años después del regreso del exilio. Mientras su contemporáneo el profeta Hageo llamaba al pueblo al arrepentimiento y a impulsar la reconstrucción del Templo, Zacarías en su primer libro realizó una historia del pueblo elegido con especial énfasis en la ciudad sagrada de Jerusalén. Más adelante,

Zacarías se centrará en proclamar la venida del Mesías, que será rechazado por el pueblo de Israel. Al fin el pueblo se arrepentirá de sus pecados, y el Mesías volverá para traer la paz. El profeta Zacarías es citado en el Nuevo Testamento, en concreto en los Evangelios de San Mateo y de San Lucas. En ellos, Jesús recuerda que Zacarías perdió la vida porque fue asesinado entre el templo y el altar.

Relato bíblico
«En tiempos de Herodes, rey de Judea, había un sacerdote
llamado Zacarías, de la clase sacerdotal de Abías.
Su mujer llamada Isabel era descendiente de Aarón.» (Lc. 1, 5)

NUEVO Testamento

A diferencia del Antiguo Testamento, los textos que se inician con los Evangelios y finalizan con el Apocalipsis, el llamado Nuevo Testamento, se escribió en su mayoría con apenas tres siglos de diferencia entre el primer texto y el último, en orden cronológico. También se ha de destacar que Jesucristo es el personaje central y que acapara el protagonismo de los textos del Nuevo Testamento.

Estas dos circunstancias favorecen la unidad del texto. El Nuevo Testamento destaca por la uniformidad en el tratamiento de los personajes, dentro de la variedad de estilos literarios y de las claras diferencias en los motivos y el público al que cada autor destinó sus textos. En todos los escritos, a excepción del Apocalipsis de San Juan, se puede observar un claro espíritu historicista y didáctico cuyo objetivo es presentar el punto del inflexión que Jesús significó para el judaísmo, así como comenzar la acción de magisterio y enseñanza de la nueva fe del perdón y del amor que Cristo instituyó.

Los milagros que podemos encontrar protagonizados por los personajes bíblicos del Nuevo Testamento concuerdan con la definición posterior que la Iglesia realizó («hecho no explicable por las leyes naturales que se atribuye a la intervención divina»), pero en cambio dichos personajes sí aparecen presentados de una manera más realista que abunda en la credibilidad de estas situaciones milagrosas.

Desde un punto de vista literario, frente a las características mitológicas y heroicas de tradición helenística de muchos de los personajes del Antiguo Testamento, vemos una mayor descripción de la personalidad de los personajes del Nuevo Testamento. Se nos describe con claridad su evolución psicológica y su tránsito y progreso en la fe, consiguiendo una mayor empatía y realismo con el lector.

San Mateo

Mateo, también conocido como Leví, era un recaudador de impuestos para los romanos hasta que se convirtió en uno de los 12 Apóstoles de Jesús. La tradición canónica le atribuye la redacción del Evangelio que lleva su nombre.

Los Evangelios sitúan a Mateo como hijo de un hombre llamado Alfaro. Mateo era todavía recaudador de impuestos cuando conoció a Jesucristo, quien le dijo «Sígueme», y Mateo lo abandonó todo por seguirlo. Ese mismo día organizó una gran fiesta para celebrar su nueva vocación, a la que asistieron Jesús y el resto de los Apóstoles. Según la tradición, Mateo habría escrito un primer protoevangelio en arameo al poco de la muerte de Jesús.

Este consistiría en una recopilación de frases y dichos del maestro. Más tarde, sería el propio Mateo el que tradujo el protoevangelio al griego, ordenándolo cronológicamente y dándole la forma que hoy conocemos como Evangelio de San Mateo.

En este queda claro que el Apóstol perseguía un objetivo muy definido: demostrar que en Jesús de Nazaret se cumplían todas las profecías relativas al Mesías de los judíos. Se cree que San Mateo sufrió martirio en Etiopía tiempo después de la muerte de Jesús.

Relato bíblico
«Genealogía de Jesucristo, hijo de David,
hijo de Abrahán […]» (Mt. 1, 1)

San Marcos

EL LEÓN DE ALEJANDRÍA

Juan, llamado Marcos, es considerado tradicionalmente como el autor del Evangelio que lleva su nombre, así como fundador y primer obispo de la Iglesia de Alejandría.

San Marcos no fue discípulo directo de Jesucristo. Según se desprende de los Hechos de los Apóstoles, podría ser un sobrino de Bernabé, o incluso un hijo (natural o espiritual) de San Pedro.

El Evangelio que lleva su nombre afirma que, cuando Jesús fue apresado en el Huerto de los Olivos, había un joven envuelto en una sábana: algunos teólogos han especulado sobre la posibilidad de que podría tratarse del propio San Marcos. Los Hechos de los Apóstoles recogen una disputa entre San Pablo y San Bernabé a propósito de Juan, llamado Marcos.

Este fue finalmente enviado a Alejandría, donde fundó la primera iglesia cristiana y nombró obispos y diáconos. Se cree que fue entonces cuando redactó el Evangelio, rememorando fielmente lo que le habían transmitido Pedro y Bernabé. Sufrió el martirio el día 25 de abril del año 68, y sus restos fueron trasladados siglos después a la Basílica de San Marcos, en Venecia, la cual fue construida precisamente para albergar sus restos.

Relato bíblico
«Comienzo de la Buena Nueva de Jesús, Mesías,
Hijo de Dios [...]» (Mc. 1, 1)

San Lucas

EL TORO DE ANTIOQUÍA

De origen griego y médico de profesión, Lucas fue discípulo de San Pablo y, según la tradición, autor del Evangelio que lleva su nombre así como del libro de los Hechos de los Apóstoles. San Lucas no era judío, sino que era originario de Antioquía. Se convirtió al cristianismo de manos de su maestro, San Pablo, a quien siguió a lo largo de sus numerosos viajes para asistirle en calidad de médico y para ayudarlo en la labor evangelizadora. Su Evangelio es el más erudito de los cuatro, el que está escrito en un griego más perfecto y el que aporta mayor exactitud y rigor. Para componer su obra, Lucas se entrevistó con los Apóstoles, así como con María, la madre de Jesús. Es gracias a esto que San Lucas puede contar de forma tan detallada la infancia que tuvo Jesucristo, aportando detalles sobre la Anunciación, la Visitación, la Natividad o los propios sentimientos de la Virgen sobre todo lo que estaba ocurriendo con su hijo Jesucristo.

Lucas fue también el autor de los Hechos de los Apóstoles, que están escritos en el mismo estilo riguroso y erudito que le caracteriza. Aunque algunas tradiciones aseguran que murió martirizado, los eruditos opinan de forma mayoritaria que murió en Beocia siendo un anciano.

Relato bíblico

«Muchos han tratado de relatar ordenadamente
los acontecimientos que se cumplieron
entre nosotros […]» (Lc. 1, 1)

San Juan Evangelista

EL ÁGUILA DE PATMOS

No existe acuerdo entre los eruditos y expertos en la materia sobre si Juan el Evangelista, autor del Evangelio que lleva su nombre y del Libro del Apocalipsis, fue o no la misma persona que Juan, el discípulo amado de Jesús. Sin embargo, la tradición pía suele identificar a los dos personajes como uno solo. Juan era hermano de Santiago el Mayor e hijo de Zebedeo, y el discípulo más joven de Jesús.

Era pescador en Galilea hasta que Jesús lo llamó. Desde entonces pasó a formar parte del círculo más íntimo de seguidores de su maestro, estando presente en hechos tan relevantes como la resurrección de la hija de Jairo, la multiplicación de los panes y los peces o la Transfiguración de Jesús.

El Evangelio de San Juan le da el apelativo de «el discípulo amado», asegurando que estaba reclinado sobre el pecho del maestro durante la Última Cena. Estando en la cruz, Jesús le encargó a Juan que cuidara de su madre, María.

En su faceta de Evangelista, Juan es el más poético y conceptual. Tras el martirio de Pedro y Pablo, Juan se estableció en Éfeso cuidando de la Virgen. Fue llevado a Roma para sufrir martirio por orden del emperador Domiciano, pero consiguió escapar del castigo y fue exiliado a la isla de Patmos, donde compuso el Apocalipsis. En sus últimos años regresó a Éfeso, donde falleció siendo muy anciano.

Relato bíblico

«Al principio existía la Palabra,
y la Palabra estaba junto a Dios,
y la Palabra era Dios [...]» (Jn. 1, 1)

S·JOHN

Arcángeles: San Miguel, San Gabriel y San Rafael

ARCÁNGELES DE DIOS

Aunque el Libro del Apocalipsis parece hablar de la existencia de siete arcángeles, la Iglesia católica solo reconoce a los tres que aparecen mencionados por sus nombres en las Sagradas Escrituras: Miguel, Gabriel y Rafael. El término arcángel significa «príncipe de ángeles». San Miguel, cuyo nombre significa «Quién como Dios», aparece mencionado en el Libro del Apocalipsis. La Iglesia católica le reconoce cuatro oficios: el de ser el principal contendiente contra Satanás, el de rescatar de las garras de Satanás las almas de los fieles, el de patrono de la Iglesia Universal y el de encargado de llamar a las almas para su juicio.

El nombre de Gabriel significa «la fuerza de Dios», y su función es la de mensajero del Altísimo. En el Antiguo Testamento encontramos referencias a San Gabriel en numerosas ocasiones, como es el anuncio a Noé del Diluvio Universal y la orden para que construyera un arca con una pareja de cada especie animal de la Tierra. Pero sin duda el episodio más importante protagonizado por San Gabriel es la Anunciación a la Virgen María. El arcángel se aparece a la Virgen, y más tarde a San José, para anunciar que ella ha sido la elegida por Dios para alumbrar al Mesías, al Hijo de Dios.

El nombre de San Rafael aparece en el libro de Tobías y significa «Medicina de Dios». Dios lo envió para sanar la ceguera de Tobías. Pero también, como el resto de arcángeles, es la punta de lanza de la lucha de Dios contra el demonio: fue enviado para realizarle un exorcismo a Sara.

Relato bíblico

«El ángel entró en la casa y la saludó diciendo:
"¡Alégrate!, llena de gracia, el Señor está contigo".» (Lc. 1, 28)

San José

San José fue, según los Evangelios, el esposo de la Virgen María y, por tanto, el padre terrenal de Jesús. Se ignora la fecha de su muerte: se estima que tuvo lugar cuando Jesús tenía más de 12 años, aunque antes de que iniciara su ministerio público.

Aunque de origen humilde, los Evangelios de San Lucas y San Mateo lo presentan como perteneciente a la estirpe del rey David. Siendo ya viudo y de avanzada edad, se desposó con María. El matrimonio judío constaba de dos partes: el desposorio, en el que los cónyuges seguían viviendo separados y manteniendo castidad, y el matrimonio, cuando comenzaban de hecho su vida marital. Cuando supo que María estaba embarazada sin haber tenido ambos trato carnal, José estuvo a punto de repudiarla en secreto, con el objeto de que ella escapara a la lapidación, castigo tradicional para la mujer adúltera según la ley judía. Sin embargo, un ángel de Dios se le apareció para explicarle que María había concebido por obra y gracia del Espíritu Santo, y que su hijo sería un salvador para todos los hombres. José siguió adelante con su matrimonio con María y, desde ese momento, adoptó a Jesús como hijo propio.

Asistió a María durante la Natividad y, cuando se decretó la matanza de Herodes, fue José quien recibió el mensaje del Ángel para sacar a su esposa y a su hijo de Belén y guiarlos en la huida a Egipto. Cuando murió Herodes, trajo a su familia de vuelta a Nazaret. José aparece mencionado por última vez cuando Jesús tiene 12 años, se pierde y es encontrado en el Templo hablando con los doctores de la Ley.

Relato bíblico

«José, hijo de David, no temas recibir a María,
tu esposa, porque lo que ha sido engendrado en ella
proviene del Espíritu Santo.» (Mt. 1, 20)

Virgen María

MADRE DE DIOS

La Virgen María es reverenciada por todas las Iglesias cristianas como la madre de Jesús. La Iglesia católica le reserva una forma especial de devoción, la hiperdulía, y le dedica el dogma de la Inmaculada Concepción, que significa que María nació sin la mancha del pecado original. María aparece por primera vez en los Evangelios al narrarse la concepción milagrosa de Jesús. Lucas nos cuenta que María estaba desposada (es decir, prometida) con un viudo llamado José. En el episodio de la Anunciación, María recibe la visita del arcángel San Gabriel, que le comunica que ha sido elegida para ser la madre del Hijo de Dios, a pesar de no haber conocido varón. María acepta con la famosa frase: «He aquí la esclava del Señor, hágase en mí según tu palabra». Después viene el episodio de la Visitación, en el cual María visita a su prima Santa Isabel, embaraza del que habría de ser San Juan Bautista.

Tras el nacimiento de Jesús en la localidad de Belén, la familia debe huir del mandato de Herodes de asesinar a todos los bebés nacidos en la comarca para refugiarse en Egipto. Regresan a Nazaret siendo Jesús aún un niño. Al contrario que su esposo San José, María aparece mencionada en varias ocasiones durante la vida pública de Jesús. Su primer milagro, la transformación del agua en vino, lo hace precisamente a petición de su madre. María acompaña a su hijo durante la Pasión, y estando este en la cruz le encarga a Juan que cuide de ella. Los Hechos de los Apóstoles nos cuentan cómo María formó parte de la primera comunidad de cristianos. Según los Apócrifos, se marchó a vivir a Éfeso con San Juan, y estando próxima su muerte, fue llevada por los ángeles en cuerpo y alma al Cielo.

Relato bíblico

«Llevó a María a su casa, y sin que hubieran hecho vida en común,
ella dio a luz a un hijo, y él le puso de nombre Jesús.» (Mt. 1, 25)

Melchor, Gaspar y Baltasar

LOS TRES REYES MAGOS

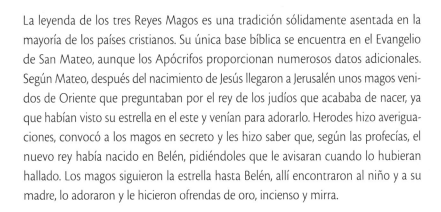

La leyenda de los tres Reyes Magos es una tradición sólidamente asentada en la mayoría de los países cristianos. Su única base bíblica se encuentra en el Evangelio de San Mateo, aunque los Apócrifos proporcionan numerosos datos adicionales. Según Mateo, después del nacimiento de Jesús llegaron a Jerusalén unos magos venidos de Oriente que preguntaban por el rey de los judíos que acababa de nacer, ya que habían visto su estrella en el este y venían para adorarlo. Herodes hizo averiguaciones, convocó a los magos en secreto y les hizo saber que, según las profecías, el nuevo rey había nacido en Belén, pidiéndoles que le avisaran cuando lo hubieran hallado. Los magos siguieron la estrella hasta Belén, allí encontraron al niño y a su madre, lo adoraron y le hicieron ofrendas de oro, incienso y mirra.

La Iglesia católica llama a este episodio la Epifanía, que es considerada un símbolo de la adoración de Jesús por todas las naciones de la Tierra. Los magos fueron advertidos en sueños de que no debían darle noticias a Herodes, de modo que volvieron a su hogar en secreto. Ninguna fuente evangélica sitúa en tres el número de magos llegados de Oriente; probablemente la cifra se deba a los tres presentes, oro, incienso y mirra. Respecto al título de reyes, es atribuible únicamente a la tradición piadosa.

Relato bíblico

«[…] los magos partieron. La estrella que habían
visto en Oriente los precedía, hasta que se detuvo en el lugar
donde estaba el niño Jesús.» (Mt. 2, 11)

Herodes el Grande

EL AUTOR DE LA MATANZA DE LOS INOCENTES

Herodes el Grande fue rey de Judea, Galilea, Samaria e Idumea desde el año 40 a.C. hasta su muerte, el año 4 a.c. El Evangelio de San Mateo le atribuye el célebre episodio de la matanza de los inocentes, que sin embargo no aparece recogido por ninguna de las fuentes historiográficas que analizan la figura de Herodes.

De origen griego, Herodes fue nombrado procurador de Judea por Julio César en el año 47 a.C. Fue Marco Antonio quien le concedió el título de rey de Judea en el año 40 a.C. Para legitimarse ante los ojos de los judíos, que desconfiaban de él por tratarse de un extranjero, contrajo matrimonio con Mariamna, que pertenecía a la familia real. Con el objeto de asegurarse en el poder, mandó asesinar a todos sus posibles adversarios, entre ellos su propia esposa junto con toda su familia, lo cual le valió fama de sanguinario entre los judíos.

Según San Mateo, Herodes recibió de los tres Reyes Magos de Oriente la noticia de que había nacido un nuevo rey de los judíos. Temeroso de que este pudiera atentar contra su posición, mandó asesinar a todos los niños menores de dos años que había en la comarca de Belén, lo cual motivó la huida a Egipto de la Sagrada Familia. María, José y el niño no volvieron a Nazaret hasta que Herodes hubo muerto, lo cual ocurrió el año 4 a.C. La discrepancia de fechas se debe a un error de cálculo en el origen del calendario gregoriano.

Relato bíblico

«[…] huye a Egipto y permanece allí hasta que yo te avise,
porque Herodes va a buscar al niño para matarlo.» (Mt. 2, 13)

San Joaquín y Santa Ana

San Joaquín y Santa Ana fueron, según los Evangelios Apócrifos, los padres de la Virgen María y, por tanto, abuelos de Jesús. Ninguno de ellos aparece mencionado en los Evangelios Canónicos.

Los Apócrifos narran que Ana y Joaquín formaban una pareja de posición acomodada (ambos pertenecían a la estirpe del rey David), pero estériles. Joaquín sufría mucho debido a la ausencia de descendencia, de modo que un día decidió retirarse a una montaña y ayunar durante 40 días y 40 noches para pedirle a Dios que les enviara un hijo. Un ángel se les apareció simultáneamente a ambos esposos y les comunicó que Dios había escuchado su ruego y que concebirían una hija, María. Cuando ella nació, fue consagrada a Dios y entregada al Templo de Jerusalén. El protoevangelio de Santiago narra cómo la Virgen niña bailó en las escaleras del templo el día que fue llevada allí al sentir ante ella la presencia del Altísimo. María permaneció al servicio de Dios desde los tres hasta los 12 años, momento de su desposorio con San José.

Relato bíblico

«El total de las generaciones es, por lo tanto,
desde Abrahán hasta David, 14 generaciones;
desde David hasta el destierro en Babilonia, 14 generaciones;
desde el destierro en Babilonia hasta Cristo,
14 generaciones.» (Mt. 1, 17)

Isabel y Zacarías

LOS PADRES DE JUAN EL BAUTISTA

Zacarías e Isabel fueron los padres de Juan el Bautista. Según San Lucas, Isabel era prima de la Virgen María. El Evangelio de San Lucas nos narra que Zacarías era un sacerdote judío de avanzada edad. Él y su esposa Isabel eran estériles, lo cual les provocaba un gran pesar. El arcángel San Gabriel se le apareció a Zacarías anunciándole que su mujer daría a luz un hijo. Sin embargo, Zacarías no creyó el mensaje del ángel y sintió temor, por lo que fue castigado sin poder hablar hasta que el nacimiento del niño tuvo lugar.

En efecto, Isabel quedó embarazada, y Lucas cuenta que la Anunciación a María ocurrió cuando Isabel estaba ya de seis meses. La Virgen visitó a su prima Isabel cuando ambas estaban embarazadas: Isabel reconoció en su prima a la madre del Salvador, y esta respondió con las célebres palabras del Magníficat: «Mi alma glorifica al Señor y se alegra mi espíritu en Dios mi salvador, porque se ha fijado en la humildad de su esclava».

Zacarías no recuperó el uso de la voz hasta la circuncisión de su hijo, que tenía lugar ocho días después del nacimiento, según la tradición. Estaban debatiendo el nombre que habría llevar y no acababan de ponerse de acuerdo. Entonces Zacarías escribió en una pizarra que había cerca: «Se llama Juan». En ese preciso momento recuperó el habla.

Relato bíblico

«Entonces se le apareció el ángel del Señor, de pie, a la derecha del altar del incienso. Al verlo, Zacarías quedó desconcertado.» (*Lc.* 1, 11-12)

San Juan el Bautista

EL PRECURSOR DE CRISTO

Hijo de Zacarías y de Isabel (la prima de la Virgen María), Juan el Bautista fue un predicador judío que anunció la llegada inminente del Mesías. San Lucas determina con gran precisión el año en que comenzó la actividad profética de San Juan: el año decimoquinto del reinado del emperador Tiberio, es decir, alrededor del año 28 d.C. Los Evangelios consideran que Juan vino a cumplir las profecías de Isaías, siendo «la voz que clama en el desierto», preparando el camino para la llegada del Señor.

Además de predicar, Juan bautizaba a las gentes utilizando el agua del río Jordán. También escuchaba sus pecados y se los perdonaba. Juan bautizó al propio Jesús; los Evangelios nos cuentan cómo, en ese momento, se abrieron los Cielos y una voz gritó: «Tú eres mi hijo amado, mi predilecto».

San Juan Bautista criticó en numerosas ocasiones el carácter sanguinario del rey Herodes, y le negó el derecho a desposarse con Herodías, la mujer de su hermano Filipo, motivo por el cual fue encarcelado. Desde su prisión, envió a sus discípulos a preguntar a Jesús si él era el Mesías. El propio Jesús elogió a Juan diciendo que, de entre los nacidos de mujer, él era el más grande. Mateo y Marcos nos cuentan cómo, al llegar el cumpleaños de Herodes, la hija de Herodías, Salomé, pidió como regalo la cabeza de Juan el Bautista, que le fue entregada en una bandeja de plata.

Relato bíblico

«Dios dirigió su palabra a Juan, el hijo de Zacarías,
que estaba en el desierto. Este comenzó entonces a recorrer
el Jordán anunciando un bautismo de conversión para el perdón
de los pecados.» (Lc. 3, 3-4)

Salomé

La decapitación de San Juan el Bautista

La Biblia hace referencia a tres diferentes Salomé. Una de ellas fue Reina de Judea, otra discípula de Jesús y finalmente la más conocida de todas ellas: la hija de Herodías que consiguió acabar con la vida del San Juan el Bautista. De origen idumeo, era hija de la princesa Herodías. La boda de su madre con Herodes Antipas causó un gran revuelo en la conservadora sociedad israelí de la época. La Corte y los habitantes de Jerusalén la consideraron una pecadora y la causante del repudio de la anterior esposa de Herodes. Entre los judíos que más denunció esta unión, se encontraba San Juan el Bautista, primo de Jesús, que dedicó gran parte de su predicación a denunciar la corrupción en la Corte de Herodes Antipas. El discurso de San Juan el Bautista se radicalizó cuando Salomé se divorció de su esposo para casarse con Herodes, su hermano por línea paterna.

Salomé gozó de una gran belleza que llegó a cautivar a su padrastro. Una noche la Corte celebraba una fiesta y ella preparó un exótico baile para homenajear al soberano, su padrastro. El quedó prendado de los encantos de la joven y como regalo le ofreció «cualquier cosa que ella deseara». La influencia de su madre y el odio acumulado durante años le llevó a solicitar que le fuera entregada la cabeza de San Juan el Bautista en bandeja de plata. El rey trató de llegar a un acuerdo con la joven, pero su postura fue firme y la muerte del Bautista fue su recompensa.

Relato bíblico

«En seguida mandó a un guardia que trajera la cabeza de Juan.
El guardia fue a la cárcel, le cortó la cabeza.
Después la trajo sobre una bandeja,
la entregó a la joven y esta
se la dio a su madre.» (Mc. 6, 27-28)

San Pedro

Simón Pedro era un pescador de Galilea que poseía un barco junto a su hermano Andrés. Cuando conoció a Jesús, decidió dejarlo todo para seguirlo. La tradición hace de él el Príncipe de los Apóstoles, y el primer Papa o Vicario de Jesucristo en la Tierra. Nacido en un pequeño pueblo de Galilea, Simón tenía mujer e hijos cuando conoció a Jesús. Siendo pescador de profesión, Jesús le ofreció convertirle en «pescador de hombres». No obstante, la versión de Juan es que tanto Pedro como Andrés eran ya discípulos de Juan el Bautista.

Simón fue el primero en reconocer a Jesús como el Cristo, el Hijo de Dios, ante lo cual Jesús le respondió dándole el nombre de Pedro y diciéndole: «Sobre esta piedra edificaré mi iglesia». Simón también fue uno de los pocos discípulos que asistieron a la Transfiguración. Tras la oración en el huerto, cuando los soldados acudieron a prender a Jesús, Simón trató de defenderlo con una espada, con la que llegó a cortarle la oreja al criado del Sumo Sacerdote; sin embargo, Jesús le impidió usar la violencia. Jesús vaticinó que, antes de que cantara el gallo, Pedro le negaría tres veces. En efecto, cuando Jesús estaba siendo sometido a juicio, una portera reconoció a Simón como uno de los discípulos, pero este negó tres veces ser amigo de Jesús.

Tras la muerte y resurrección de Jesús, Pedro se convirtió en una figura central para la comunidad de los primeros cristianos, tal y como recoge el Libro de los Hechos de los Apóstoles. Tras fundar la Iglesia de Antioquía, se trasladó a Roma, donde sufrió martirio por orden del emperador Nerón.

Relato bíblico

«Simón Pedro permanecía junto al fuego. Los que estaban con él le dijeron: "¿No eres tú también uno de sus discípulos?". Él lo negó.» (Jn. 18, 25)

Santiago Zebedeo, Andrés y Felipe

APÓSTOLES DE JESÚS

Santiago Zebedeo, conocido también como Santiago el Mayor, era hermano de San Juan, el discípulo amado. Jesús los llamó a ambos «hijos del trueno» por la impetuosidad de su carácter. Santiago formó parte del círculo íntimo de Jesús y estuvo presente en los momentos más relevantes como la Transfiguración o la oración en el huerto de Getsemaní. Los Hechos de los Apóstoles aseguran que sufrió martirio en Jerusalén, después de haber proclamado allí el Evangelio.

Sin embargo, la tradición católica hace de él el Apóstol de España. La leyenda asegura que, encontrándose en la Península Ibérica, se le apareció la Virgen María «en carne mortal» (es decir, antes de la Asunción) para insuflarle ánimos. Se cree que sus restos reposan en la catedral de Santiago de Compostela.

Andrés es conocido como el Protocletos, «el primer llamado». Hermano de Simón Pedro, fue el primero en recibir la llamada de Jesús para convertirse en pescador de hombres. La tradición asegura que fue martirizado en Patrás, Grecia. Por su parte, el Apóstol Felipe aparece especialmente retratado en el Evangelio de San Juan, en el episodio de la multiplicación de los panes y los peces. Murió en Hierápolis siendo un anciano.

Relato bíblico

«Felipe le dijo "Maestro, doscientos denarios no bastarán si queremos dar a cada uno un trozo de pan".» (Jn. 6, 7)

Bartolomé, Tomás, Santiago el Menor y Simón Zelote

APÓSTOLES DE JESÚS

El Apóstol llamado Bartolomé en los Evangelios Sinópticos y Nathanael en el de San Juan aparece siempre asociado con Felipe. Se sabe que Bartolomé fue testigo de la Ascensión de Jesús. Según la tradición se marchó a predicar a la India, y murió martirizado en Armenia, tras mucho sufrimiento. Por su parte, Tomás es conocido por ser el «Apóstol incrédulo». Cuando sus compañeros le cuentan que Jesús ha resucitado, él se resiste a creerlo y afirma que no quedará convencido hasta que meta los dedos en las heridas de los clavos. Ocho días después, Jesús se le aparece y le permite tocar con sus propias manos las llagas de su Pasión. Existe un apócrifo llamado el Evangelio de Tomás, donde se recoge su viaje de evangelización en territorios de Siria y de la India.

Santiago el Menor era sobrino de José el carpintero y, por tanto, primo de Jesús. Los Hechos de los Apóstoles destacan su papel como líder de la comunidad de los primeros cristianos en Jerusalén. Santiago el Menor intervino en el Concilio de Jerusalén para defender que los gentiles pudieran ser bautizados. San Pablo le llama «columna de la Iglesia» en una de sus cartas. Por su parte, Simón recibe el apelativo de Zelote porque formaba parte de esta facción política de tintes nacionalistas. En ese sentido, es todo lo opuesto a Mateo: mientras que este era publicano, por lo tanto favorable a la ocupación romana, Simón defendía la independencia de los judíos frente al Imperio.

Relato bíblico

«Jesús le dijo a Tomás:
"Trae aquí tu dedo: aquí están mis manos [...] en adelante
no seas incrédulo, sino hombre de fe".» (Jn. 20, 27)

145

Judas Iscariote

EL APÓSTOL TRAIDOR

Judas Iscariote fue uno de los 12 Apóstoles de Jesús y ha pasado a la Historia por haber sido el que le traicionó, vendiéndolo al Sanedrín por 30 monedas de plata. Judas siguió a Jesús durante su predicación en Judea y Galilea. San Juan nos pone en antecedentes de su traición: él era el tesorero del grupo, pero robaba el dinero destinado a los pobres.

Durante la Última Cena, Jesús vaticina que uno de los 12 va a traicionarlo. Todos lo niegan fervorosamente. Sin embargo, Judas hace un pacto con los sacerdotes del Sanedrín: a cambio de 30 monedas de plata, les guiará hasta donde se encuentre Jesús y se lo entregará. Será esa misma noche, durante la oración el huerto de Getsemaní, cuando Judas delate a su maestro, señalándolo con un beso.

Tanto Mateo como los Hechos de los Apóstoles nos relatan que Judas, arrepentido de su acción, intentó devolver las monedas y acabó por suicidarse. En el año 2006 se publicó el Evangelio de Judas, un texto gnóstico que data del siglo II d.C. y que no tiene ningún carácter canónico. Según este apócrifo, fue Jesús el que le habría pedido a Judas en secreto que le entregara para que pudiera cumplirse su Pasión, y Judas lo habría hecho como acto de suprema obediencia y amor.

Relato bíblico

«Judas Iscariote, uno de los 12, fue a ver a los sumos sacerdotes para entregarles a Jesús.» (Mc. 14, 10)

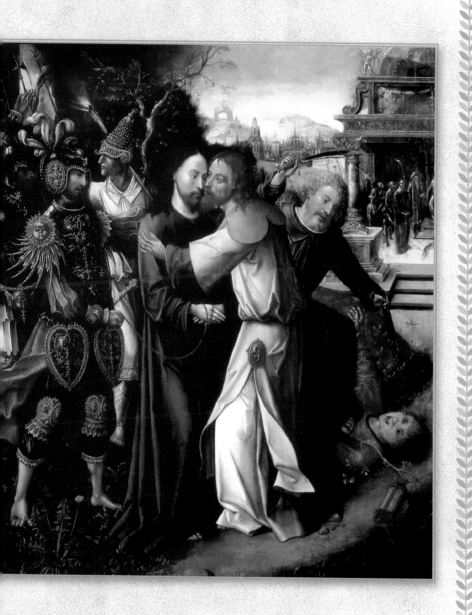

Judas Tadeo y Matías

Apóstoles de Jesús

Judas Tadeo era hermano de Santiago el Menor, por tanto primo de Jesús. Su nombre apenas aparece mencionado en los Evangelios, solo en las listas de los Apóstoles y una vez en el Evangelio de San Juan, durante la Última Cena, cuando le pregunta al maestro por qué ha elegido manifestarse solo a ellos y no al mundo entero que desea escuchar su mensaje de amor. El Nuevo Testamento incluye una carta que se le atribuye a él. La tradición considera que evangelizó Siria y Persia, donde murió martirizado.

Según se desprende de los textos bíblicos de los Hechos de los Apóstoles, Matías era uno de los 72 discípulos originales de Jesús, a quien siguió a lo largo de su predicación. Cuando Judas Iscariote traicionó a Jesús y murió sin arrepentimiento, dejó una «vacante» entre los 12 Apóstoles. Según preveían los Salmos, este hueco debía ser cubierto. San Pedro reunió a los primeros cristianos tras la Ascensión de Jesús, y tras elevar una oración al Señor, propuso sacar a sorteo uno de los siguientes dos nombres: Matías o José, llamado el Justo. Mediante este sistema, Matías fue el elegido. La tradición asegura que Matías partió a evangelizar hacia Etiopía, donde sufrió un martirio terrible. También existen diferentes escritos apócrifos cuya autoría es atribuida precisamente a Matías.

Relato bíblico

«Se propusieron dos: José, llamado Barsabás, y Matías. [...]
Echaron suertes, y la elección cayó sobre Matías,
que fue agregado a los 11 Apóstoles.» (Hc. 1, 23-25)

San Pablo

A pesar de no haber conocido nunca a Jesús, Pablo de Tarso se considera uno de los principales Apóstoles. A él se le debe la apertura de la evangelización a los que no eran judíos, es decir, a los gentiles. Saulo era un judío ortodoxo, ciudadano romano y de gran influencia helenística, que nació en la ciudad de Cilicia. Durante su primera juventud presentó una posición muy combatiente contra el cristianismo, abogando por el cumplimiento estricto de la ley mosaica y participando activamente en la persecución y captura de los primeros cristianos.

Según narran los Hechos de los Apóstoles, aprobó el martirio de San Esteban. Yendo de camino a Damasco, vio una luz intensa y una voz tan potente que le hizo caer del caballo y le decía: «Saulo, ¿por qué me persigues?». La voz se identificó como Jesús. Saulo estuvo tres días sin ver, sin comer y sin beber, al cabo de los cuales se convirtió al cristianismo. San Pablo realizó tres grandes viajes misionales, que le llevarían a Chipre, Siria, Grecia y Asia Menor. Es autor de numerosas epístolas que forman parte del canon del Nuevo Testamento, hasta que fue decapitado en Roma por orden del emperador Nerón.

Relato bíblico

«Pablo, Apóstol de Jesucristo por la voluntad de Dios, [...] saludan a la Iglesia de Dios que reside en Corintio, junto con todos los santos que viven en la provincia de Acaya». (2 Co. 1, 1)

228
336

María Magdalena

La primera discípula de Jesús

María Magdalena fue una de las discípulas más importantes de Jesús. Su nombre proviene de la ciudad de Magdala, de donde era originaria, que está en el lado occidental del lago Tiberíades. Las menciones a María Magdalena en el Nuevo Testamento son escasas. Lucas nos cuenta que había sido curada por Jesús, y que de ella salieron siete demonios. También asegura que ella dio alojamiento y comida a Jesús y a sus discípulos durante su predicación en Galilea. Marcos y Juan explican que estuvo presente durante la crucifixión. Los cuatro Evangelios concuerdan en que ella estuvo presente cuando se descubre que Jesús ha resucitado y, según sus testimonios, ella es la primera persona a la que se aparece.

María Magdalena aparece también mencionada en diversos Evangelios Apócrifos, que hacen de ella o bien una discípula señalada o el propio Jesús, o bien la «compañera» del maestro. A partir del siglo v, la Iglesia católica comenzó a identificar a María Magdalena con otros personajes bíblicos, como la prostituta arrepentida o María de Betania, la hermana de Lázaro, lo que ha creado mucha confusión entre los creyentes. Sin embargo, la literalidad del texto bíblico parece indicar que se trata de personas diferentes. De todas formas, para la Iglesia católica es Santa María Magdalena.

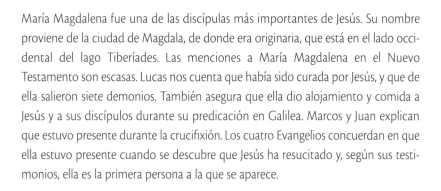

Relato bíblico

«Cuando regresaron del sepulcro,
refirieron a los 11 lo que habían visto.
Eran María Magdalena, Juana y María.» (Lc. 24, 10)

María de Betania

LA PECADORA ARREPENTIDA

Se trata de una mujer que se convirtió. Según el Evangelio de San Lucas, Jesús se encontraba cenando en casa de un fariseo cuando una mujer se presentó ante él. Llevaba un frasco de alabastro lleno de perfume. Poniéndose de rodillas, enjugó los pies del maestro con sus lágrimas, se los secó con su cabello, se los besó y los ungió con perfume. Jesús aprovecha la ocasión para contar la parábola del prestamista, y acto seguido le dice a la mujer «tus pecados te son perdonados». De la descripción de la escena se entiende que la mujer era una prostituta.

Mateo y Marcos cuentan un episodio muy similar, aunque no hablan de ninguna mujer pecadora ni se insinúa en modo alguno que se tratara de una prostituta. Lo denominan «unción en Betania». Estando Jesús en Betania, en casa de Simón el Leproso, se acercó una mujer con un frasco de perfume y lo derramó sobre su cabeza. Los discípulos empezaron a discutir si no hubiera sido mejor venderlo y darle el dinero a los pobres, pero el maestro responde: «A los pobres siempre los tendréis con vosotros, y a mí no me tendréis siempre». San Juan cuenta también este último episodio aunque identifica a la mujer con María de Betania, la hermana de Lázaro. Según el cuarto Evangelio, María ungió los pies de Jesús con el perfume y los secó con sus cabellos. También puntualiza que fue Judas Iscariote el que la criticó, argumentando que hubiera sido preferible vender el perfume para ayudar a los pobres.

Relato bíblico

«Entonces una mujer pecadora que vivía en la ciudad,
al enterarse de que Jesús estaba comiendo en casa del fariseo,
se presentó con un frasco de perfume. […] se puso a llorar a sus pies
y comenzó a bañarlos con sus lágrimas; los secaba con sus cabellos
y lo ungía con perfume.» (Lc. 7, 36-38)

Anás y Caifás

Los Sumos Sacerdotes

Anás y Caifás fueron los Sumos Sacerdotes responsables de la condena a muerte de Jesús. Normalmente, solo existía un Sumo Sacerdote, que era el responsable de presidir el Sanedrín. En tiempos de la Pasión el Sumo Sacerdote era Caifás. Sin embargo, Anás había ostentado el cargo antes que él y conservaba la facultad de dirigir las reuniones del Sanedrín.

Anás y Caifás pertenecían a la secta de los saduceos que, al contrario que los fariseos, no creían en la resurrección. Por ello estaban especialmente escandalizados con el episodio de la resurrección de Lázaro, cuya noticia se había extendido entre los judíos haciendo que Jesús cada vez contara con más seguidores.

Los Evangelios nos cuentan que los Sumos Sacerdotes prepararon una conspiración para prender a Jesús «y quitarlo de en medio». Cuando Judas se lo hubo entregado por medio de la traición, lo llevaron ante Anás y Caifás y lo interrogaron hasta preguntarle si era el Mesías. Él dijo: «Yo soy, y veréis al hijo del hombre a la derecha del todopoderoso». Los Sumos Sacerdotes decidieron que era culpable de blasfemia y que, por tanto, era reo de muerte, por lo que decidieron llevarlo ante Poncio Pilato.

Relato bíblico

«Después dijo a los Sumos Sacerdotes, a los jefes de la guardia del Templo
y a los ancianos que habían venido a arrestarlo: "¿Soy acaso
un ladrón para que vengan con espadas y palos?".» (Lc. 22, 52)

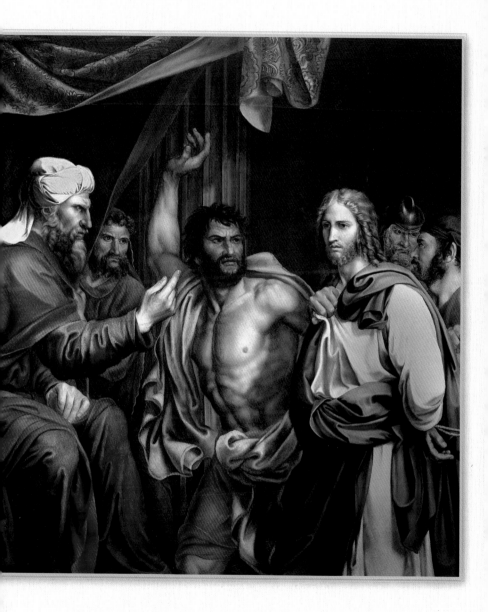

Poncio Pilato

EL ROMANO QUE SE LAVÓ LAS MANOS

Poncio Pilato (o Pilatos) era el prefecto de la provincia romana de Judea en tiempos de la muerte de Jesús. Según los Evangelios, fue él quien, a pesar de no encontrarle culpable de ningún crimen, sentenció a muerte a Jesús por seguir los deseos de los Sumos Sacerdotes y del pueblo en general. Cuando Jesús fue encontrado culpable de blasfemia por los Sumos Sacerdotes, estos lo llevaron ante Poncio Pilato, que como prefecto era el único que tenía autoridad para condenarlo a muerte. Este le preguntó si él era el rey de los judíos, a lo que Jesús respondió: «Mi reino no es de este mundo». Tras el interrogatorio, Pilato aseguró que no encontraba ninguna culpa en él, pero ante la insistencia de los Sumos Sacerdotes lo mandó llevar ante Herodes Antipas, puesto que era galileo. Herodes trató con desprecio a Jesús y se rió de él, vistiéndolo como a un rey, pero tampoco encontró culpa en él y se lo devolvió a Pilato, quien trató de liberarlo según la tradición de soltar a un reo por Pascua, pero los judíos prefirieron a Barrabás. Poncio Pilato accedió y condenó a muerte a Jesús.

Los Evangelios no hablan de Poncio Pilato ni antes ni después de la Pasión, por lo que cualquier detalle sobre su biografía es pura especulación. No obstante, sí existe evidencia arqueológica de que Pilato fue en efecto el prefecto de Judea en torno al año 30 d.C.

Relato bíblico

«Pilato dijo a los Sumos Sacerdotes: "No encuentro en este hombre ningún motivo de condena".» (Lc. 23, 4)

Simón de Cirene

EL PORTADOR DE LA CRUZ

Simón, llamado el Cirineo, aparece en los Evangelios en un solo episodio: cuando ayuda a Jesús a cargar la cruz. Según nos cuentan Mateo, Marcos y Lucas, tras ponerle a Jesús la corona de espinas y burlarse de él, lo llevaron a crucificar. Pasaba por allí un hombre llamado Simón, nativo de Cirene, que venía del campo, y le obligaron a cargar con la cruz de Jesús hasta la cima del Gólgota, donde iba a ser crucificado. Simón marchaba detrás de Jesús, y los seguía una gran multitud. San Marcos aporta el detalle adicional de que Simón era el padre de Alejandro y de Rufo. Por su parte, San Juan no menciona a Simón de Cirene en sus textos.

Algunas tradiciones cristianas aseguran que Alejandro y Rufo (los hijos de Simón de Cirene) se convirtieron en misioneros después de la resurrección de Jesús. El hecho de que se les mencione por sus nombres podría indicar que se trataba de personas relevantes en aquella época.

Por otro lado, algunas sectas musulmanas piensan que Jesús logró escapar de la crucifixión, sufriendo el martirio en su lugar Simón el Cirineo. La Iglesia ve en Simón una metáfora de lo que significa compartir el sufrimiento de Jesús, siendo la propia cruz un símbolo de todos los pecados que hay en el mundo.

Relato bíblico

«Al salir, se encontraron con un hombre
de Cirene, llamado Simón
y le obligaron a llevar la cruz.» (Mt. 27, 32)

José de Arimatea

EL DISCÍPULO OCULTO

Según los Evangelios, José de Arimatea era un seguidor de Jesús y el propietario del sepulcro en el que fue enterrado. El nombre de José de Arimatea aparece recogido en los cuatro Evangelios. Mateo nos cuenta que era un hombre rico, mientras que Lucas y Marcos afirman que era un miembro ilustre del Sanedrín. Lo que todos explican es que era discípulo de Jesús, pero lo mantenía en secreto por miedo a la represalia de las autoridades judías.

José era propietario de un sepulcro nuevo excavado en la roca, cerca del Gólgota. En el momento de la crucifixión le pide a Pilato que le entregue el cuerpo del maestro para darle sepultura. Fallecido Jesús, José lo descuelga, lo envuelve en una sábana limpia y, con ayuda de Nicodemo, lo traslada hasta el sepulcro. Lo cierran con una gran roca y ambos se marchan. La tradición cristiana asegura que, después de la Resurrección, José partió con María Magdalena para predicar en Francia y en las costas del Mediterráneo. Todos los datos apuntan que fueron ellos quienes se llevaron la Sábana Santa a Europa. Las leyendas artúricas aseguran también que José de Arimatea llevó consigo el Santo Grial hasta Glastonbury, Inglaterra, protegiéndolo en todo momento.

Relato bíblico

«José, hombre recto y justo, […] era de Arimatea, ciudad de Judea,
fue a ver a Pilato para pedirle el cuerpo de Jesús […]
lo colocó en un sepulcro cavado en la roca.» (Lc. 23, 50-53)

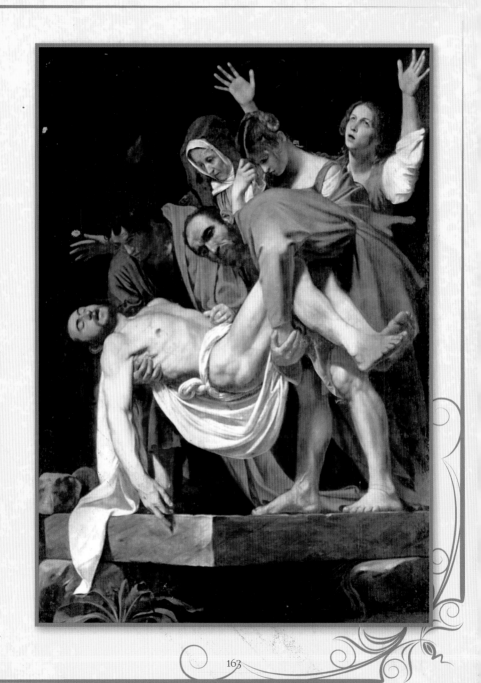

Los discípulos de Emaús

TESTIGOS DE HONOR DE LA RESURRECCIÓN

Los discípulos de Emaús constituían un grupo indeterminado de discípulos, no pertenecientes al círculo de los 12 Apóstoles, que reconocieron a Jesús resucitado cuando este hizo el gesto de partir el pan.

San Lucas nos cuenta que, después de la muerte de Jesús, los discípulos estaban atemorizados y desconcertados. Un grupo de ellos marchaba un día de Jerusalén a Emaús, a una distancia de unos 13 kilómetros, cuando se encontraron con un forastero que les preguntó qué les ocurría. Uno de ellos, llamado Cleofás, le habló de Jesús de Nazaret, que había sido un gran profeta pero que había sido entregado por los Sumos Sacerdotes para que fuera ajusticiado. Los discípulos esperaban que Jesús fuera el libertador que había sido anunciado en las Sagradas Escrituras, pero ahora que había muerto sentían miedo. Las mujeres de su grupo y algunos de ellos aseguraban que había resucitado, pero ellos no lo habían visto.

El forastero procedió a explicarles cómo las Escrituras preveían la resurrección del profeta. Cuando llegaron a Emaús, los discípulos le insistieron en que se quedara a cenar con ellos. El forastero tomó pan, lo partió, lo bendijo y lo repartió entre ellos. Los discípulos lo reconocieron de inmediato como Jesús, pero este desapareció al instante de su lado.

Relato bíblico

«Y estando a la mesa, tomó el pan y pronunció la bendición; luego lo partió
y se lo dio. Entonces los ojos de los discípulos se abrieron
y lo reconocieron, pero él había desaparecido de su vista.» (Lc. 24, 30-31)

La samaritana

EL POZO DE AGUA VIVA

Según la tradición, los samaritanos son descendientes de Manasés y de Efraím, los hijos de José. Se separaron de los judíos en tiempos del rey Saúl a propósito del lugar donde había que venerar a Yahvé: en el monte Garizim o en el Templo de Jerusalén. En tiempos de Jesús, judíos y samaritanos no se dirigían la palabra.

San Juan nos narra que Jesús se dirigía a Galilea pasando por Samaria cuando se detuvo en el pozo de Jacob. Allí se encontró con una mujer samaritana y le pidió agua. Ella se mostró sorprendida de que un judío se dirigiera a ella, pero Jesús le dijo que él podía darle de beber un agua viva que calmaba para siempre la sed. A continuación, Jesús le pidió que trajera a su marido, pero ella replicó que no tenía. Jesús le contestó que había dicho la verdad, ya que había tenido cinco maridos, y el que tenía en ese momento, no era en realidad su marido. La mujer lo reconoció como un profeta, y Jesús se reveló ante ella como el Mesías que había sido anunciado, el Cristo. La predicación de Jesús tuvo gran éxito entre la población samaritana.

Relato bíblico

«La mujer le dijo: "Yo sé que el Mesías […]
nos anunciará todo" y Jesús le respondió:
"Soy yo, el que habla contigo".» (Jn. 4, 25-26)

Lázaro, Marta y María

LOS AMIGOS DE JESÚS

Según los Evangelios, Lázaro fue un discípulo y amigo de Jesús al cual este resucitó, a petición de sus hermanas Marta y María. Según los Evangelios, Jesús se habría hospedado en su casa de Betania al menos en tres ocasiones. El episodio más famoso es el de la resurrección de Lázaro. San Juan nos cuenta que Lázaro era el hermano de Marta y de María, la que había ungido a Jesús con perfume. Ellas mandaron decir a su maestro: «Tu amigo está enfermo». Cuando Jesús llegó a Betania, Lázaro llevaba cuatro días muerto.

Marta y María le reprocharon que si él hubiera estado allí, su hermano no habría muerto. Jesús se hace llevar al sepulcro, manda apartar la piedra que lo tapa y, tras darle las gracias al Padre, le grita a Lázaro: «Sal fuera». Y el que había estado muerto salió caminando, aún amortajado. La resurrección de Lázaro tuvo un doble efecto: por un lado, mucha gente creyó en Jesús, y por el otro, los Sumos Sacerdotes se decidieron a matarlo.

Existe otro episodio que implica a Marta y María. Según San Lucas, en una ocasión en que Jesús se hospedaba en casa de sus amigos de Betania, Marta se afanaba haciendo las labores de la casa, mientras que María estaba sentada a sus pies, escuchándole. Marta le preguntó a su maestro si no le parecía mal que María le dejara a ella todo el peso del trabajo doméstico, pero Jesús le replicó que Marta se ocupaba de demasiadas cosas, cuando solo una era importante.

Relato bíblico

«Jesús le dijo: "Marta, Marta, te inquietas y te agitas por muchas cosas y, sin embargo, pocas cosas o más bien una sola es necesaria.
María eligió la mejor parte, que no le será quitada".» (Lc. 10, 41-42)

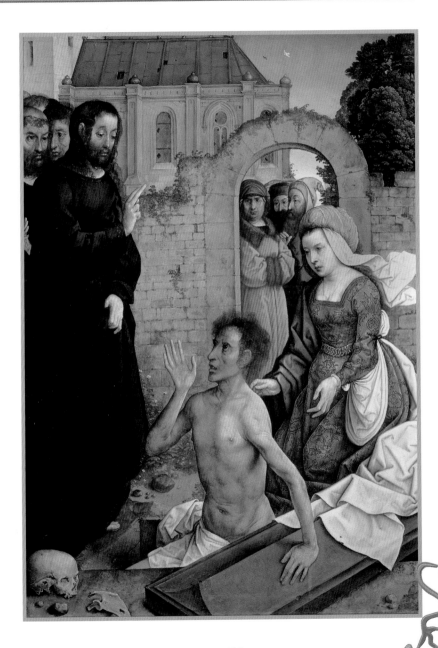

San Dimas

El buen ladrón

Según los Evangelios, Jesús fue crucificado junto a dos ladrones. Mientras el de la izquierda se burlaba de él, el de la derecha le pidió que se acordara de él cuando llegara a su reino.

San Lucas indica que de camino al Calvario llevaban a dos criminales para ejecutarlos con él. Cuando llegaron, crucificaron a Jesús con un criminal a la izquierda y otro a la derecha. El primero se reía de él y le decía que si él era el Mesías, se salvara a sí mismo y les salvara a ellos.

Pero el otro aseguraba que el castigo de Jesús era injusto porque él no había hecho ningún daño, y le rogó que lo tuviera en cuenta al llegar a su reino. Según la Iglesia, al decirle que esa misma noche estaría con él en el Paraíso, Jesús proclamó al primer santo de la Historia.

Los Evangelios no dan detalles sobre los nombres ni las circunstancias de los dos criminales que murieron junto a Jesús. Los Apócrifos aseguran que el buen ladrón se llamaba Dimas, y el mal ladrón, Gestas, y afirman que ambos eran forajidos y personas impías.

Relato bíblico

«Uno de los malhechores crucificado lo insultaba [...]
pero el otro lo increpaba, diciéndole: "
¿No tienes temor de Dios, tú que sufres
la misma pena que él?".» (Lc. 23, 41)

Bernabé
El Apóstol de Antioquía

Aunque no fue uno de los 12 Apóstoles elegidos por Jesús, la Iglesia lo venera como tal, al igual que a San Pablo, debido a sus múltiples virtudes y a la evangelización de Antioquía.

El nombre de nacimiento de Bernabé fue José. Era judío y originario de Chipre. Cuando se convirtió, vendió todo lo que tenía y lo puso a los pies de los Apóstoles, que le dieron el sobrenombre de Bernabé (según los Hechos de los Apóstoles, significa «hijo de la consolación»). Junto con San Pablo, fue enviado a Antioquía para evangelizar. El Nuevo Testamento indica que en Antioquía fue donde los seguidores de Jesús comenzaron a ser llamados cristianos.

En compañía de San Pablo, Bernabé realizó diferentes viajes. El primero de ellos fue a Chipre. El primo de Bernabé, llamado Juan Marcos y probablemente el autor del Evangelio de San Marcos, los acompañó. En el segundo viaje, con destino a Asia Menor, Juan Marcos los abandonó debido a los peligros a los que se enfrentarían. Fue precisamente a propósito de San Marcos por lo que Pablo y Bernabé discutieron y acabaron por separarse.

La tradición asegura que viajó a Roma y que fue lapidado en Salamina. Algunos eruditos lo señalan como posible autor de la Epístola a los Hebreos.

Relato bíblico
«Después toda la asamblea hizo el silencio para oír
a Bernabé y Pablo que comenzaron a relatar los signos
y prodigios que Dios había realizado
entre los paganos por intermedio de ellos.» (Hch. 15, 12)

173

Cornelio, el centurión

El primer gentil

El centurión llamado Cornelio fue el primer gentil en convertirse al cristianismo y en recibir el sacramento del bautismo. Según los Hechos de los Apóstoles, Cornelio era un hombre piadoso y temeroso de Dios que vivía en Cesarea. Un día recibió una visión en la que se le ordenaba llamar a Simón Pedro, cosa que hizo de inmediato y sin dudarlo en ningún momento.

Pedro, a su vez, había recibido otra visión. Un lienzo con reptiles y otras alimañas pintadas en él descendía del cielo. Una vez le ordenaba matar y comerse a uno de los animales, pero Pedro se negaba alegando que nunca había comido ningún alimento impuro. La voz replicó: «Lo que Dios ha purificado no lo llames impuro». Poco después, los enviados de Cornelio vinieron para llevarlo junto a él. Cuando Pedro llegó a su casa, el centurión se arrojó a sus pies y le relató su visión. En ese momento, el Espíritu Santo se posó sobre todos ellos transmitiéndoles toda su fuerza. Los apóstoles discutieron a continuación si era legítimo bautizar a los gentiles, dado que Jesús solo había predicado entre los judíos. Pedro, recordando su visión, alegó que si el Espíritu Santo había descendido sobre unos gentiles, ellos no eran nadie para llamar impuro a lo que Dios había purificado. A partir de ese momento, Pedro defendió la tesis de la evangelización a los gentiles, que más tarde continuaría San Pablo y que sería adoptada firme y definitivamente en el Concilio de Jerusalén.

Relato bíblico

«Había en Cesarea un hombre llamado Cornelio,
centurión de la cohorte itálica. [...] tuvo una visión
un día cerca de las tres de la tarde,
y vio claramente al ángel de Dios.» (Hch. 10, 1-3)

Longinos

EL VERDUGO ARREPENTIDO

Según la tradición cristiana, Longinos fue el centurión romano que atravesó el costado de Jesús con su lanza y más tarde se convirtió al cristianismo para seguir el mensaje del Mesías. El Evangelio de San Juan nos cuenta cómo Jesús expiró justo después de que le dieran de beber vinagre con una esponja. Sin embargo, como al día siguiente era Pascua, los judíos le pidieron a Pilato que les quebrara las piernas a todos los condenados, para asegurarse de que morían y poder bajar sus cuerpos antes de que comenzara la fiesta. Así lo hicieron con los dos ladrones que murieron crucificados junto a Jesús. Cuando llegaron junto a él, descubrieron que ya había fallecido. Para comprobarlo, un centurión romano le atravesó el costado con una lanza, y de la herida manó sangre y agua, por lo que quedó confirmado que Jesucristo había fallecido y no hacía falta quebrarle las piernas.

Los Evangelios Sinópticos no recogen este episodio. No obstante, Mateo, Marcos y Lucas narran que, hacia el mediodía, las tinieblas cubrieron la tierra, el sol se eclipsó y el velo del Templo se rasgó por la mitad. En ese momento, Jesús expiró, encomendando su espíritu a las manos de Dios, su Padre. Al ver todo esto, el centurión dio gloria a Dios y dijo: «Verdaderamente, este hombre era hijo de Dios». Fue entonces cuando, arrepentido, Longinos se convirtió y decidió abrazar la nueva fe. El nombre de Longinos no aparece en los Evangelios, ni siquiera en los Apócrifos, sino que proviene de una tradición medieval que se ha ido conservando a pesar del paso de los siglos y que ha llegado hasta nuestros días. A pesar de no figurar en las Sagradas Escrituras, la Iglesia católica venera a San Longinos como mártir y le reserva un lugar entre los que han sufrido por seguir a Cristo.

Relato bíblico
«[...] sino que uno de los soldados le atravesó
el costado con una lanza, y enseguida brotó sangre y agua.» (Jn. 19, 34)

Simón el Mago

LA FE NO SE COMPRA CON DINERO

Simón el Mago fue un samaritano convertido al cristianismo que intentó comprar a los Apóstoles el don de transmitir el Espíritu Santo. De su nombre viene el pecado de simonía, que consiste precisamente en pagar por obtener prebendas o beneficios eclesiásticos. Los Hechos de los Apóstoles registran en sus páginas que había en Samaria un hechicero llamado Simón, que tenía al pueblo maravillado con sus trucos y poderes mágicos. Cuando la palabra de Jesús llegó a su territorio, sus seguidores lo abandonaron para convertirse al cristianismo, y él mismo se convirtió de corazón y decidió adoptar el mensaje de Jesús. El autor de los Hechos explica que, aunque Simón y sus antiguos seguidores habían sido bautizados por los Apóstoles, el Espíritu Santo no había descendido sobre ninguno de ellos.

El antiguo mago, al ver que los Apóstoles tenían el poder de imponer las manos y hacer que bajara el Espíritu Santo, les ofreció dinero a los Apóstoles por tener ese poder él mismo. Pedro lo reprendió duramente por intentar comprar los dones de Dios, y Simón se arrepintió de haberlo intentado. Según algunos cronistas del cristianismo primitivo, Simón el Mago fue también el creador de una secta gnóstica que se conocía como simonaísmo.

Relato bíblico

«Al ver que por la imposición de las manos a los Apóstoles se confería el Espíritu Santo, Simón les ofreció dinero.» (Hch. 8, 18)

San Esteban

PROTOMÁRTIR DE LA IGLESIA

San Esteban es venerado como el primer mártir del cristianismo; de ahí el sobrenombre que se le ha otorgado de «protomártir». Según los Hechos de los Apóstoles, poco después de la Resurrección no dejaba de aumentar el número de discípulos que se unían a la nueva fe, por lo que se decidió nombrar a siete diáconos para atender a las masas y evitar conflictos innecesarios. Uno de ellos fue Esteban, quien predicaba demostrando mucha pasión, hasta el punto de que despertó la inquina de «unos cuantos de la sinagoga llamada de los Libertos», de modo que sobornaron a unos hombres para que levantaran falso testimonio contra él, afirmando que había blasfemado contra Moisés y contra Dios con la intención de que se dudara de él.

Los ancianos y los doctores de la ley interrogaron a Esteban, que les respondió con un hermoso discurso que los Hechos de los Apóstoles recogen íntegro. La muchedumbre se lanzó contra él, lo desnudó, lo arrastró por las calles y al fin lo apedreó hasta matarlo. Mientras era asesinado por una masa de gente enloquecida, Esteban rogaba a Jesús que lo recibiera en su reino, y que no tuviera en cuenta el pecado de los que estaban acabando con su vida a pesar del terrible sufrimiento que estaba padeciendo.

El Nuevo Testamento especifica que Saulo, futuro San Pablo, aprobó este asesinato, el primer martirio del cristianismo, que desató la persecución general contra la Iglesia a partir de ese mismo momento.

Relato bíblico

«Esteban, lleno del Espíritu Santo y con los ojos fijos
en el cielo, vio la gloria de Dios, y a Jesús
que estaba de pie a la derecha de Dios.» (Hch. 7, 55)

Satanás

EL ÁNGEL CAÍDO

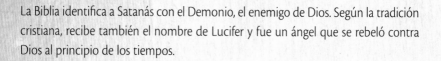

La Biblia identifica a Satanás con el Demonio, el enemigo de Dios. Según la tradición cristiana, recibe también el nombre de Lucifer y fue un ángel que se rebeló contra Dios al principio de los tiempos.

Satanás aparece mencionado en pocas ocasiones en el Antiguo Testamento como un ser que incita al mal y al pecado; por ejemplo, se cita en el Libro de Job. En los Evangelios se menciona especialmente al hablar de las tentaciones de Cristo. Tras haber recibido el bautismo de manos de Juan el Bautista, Jesús se retira al desierto para ser tentado. Tras haber ayunado 40 días y 40 noches, sintió hambre. Satanás se le apareció y le retó a que si en verdad era hijo de Dios, convirtiera las piedras en panes. Después lo llevó a Jerusalén y le dijo que se tirara desde una muralla, ya que los ángeles acudirían a salvarlo. Por fin le ofreció todos los reinos del mundo y su esplendor si se sometía a él y lo adoraba. Jesús resistió a todas estas tentaciones y mandó a Satanás que se alejara de él. También se menciona a Satanás en los diferentes episodios en que Jesús realiza exorcismos.

La doctrina cristiana identifica a Satanás con la Bestia que aparece en el Apocalipsis de San Juan.

Relato bíblico

«Jesús, lleno del Espíritu Santo, regresó de las orillas del Jordán,
y fue conducido por el Espíritu al desierto.
Allí fue tentado por Satanás durante 40 días.» (Lc. 4, 1-2)

ÍNDICE

Aarón	66
Abel	40
Abrahán	44
Adán	38
Anás	156
Andrés	142
Arcángeles: San Miguel, San Gabriel y San Rafael	122
Balaán	68
Baltasar	128
Bartolomé	144
Benjamín	60
Bernabé	172
Caifás	156
Caín	40
Cornelio, el centurión	174
Dalila	76
Daniel	102
David	82
Débora	72
Elías	86
Ester	92
Eva	38
Ezequiel	100
Felipe	142
Gaspar	128
Goliat	82
Herodes el Grande	130
Isaac	52
Isabel	134
Isaías	96
Ismael	46
Jacob	56
Jael	74
Jeremías	98
Jesús de Nazaret	10-35
Job	94
Joel	108
Jonás	106
José de Arimatea	162
José el Patriarca	58
Josué	70
Judas Iscariote	146
Judas Tadeo	148
Judit	90
La samaritana	166
Lázaro	168
Longinos	176
Los discípulos de Emaús	164
Lot	50
María	168
María de Betania	154
María Magdalena	152
Marta	168
Matías	148
Melchor	128
Melquisedec	48
Moisés	62
Noé	42
Poncio Pilato	158
Reina de Saba	84
Salomé	138
Salomón	84
Samuel	78
San Dimas	170
San Esteban	180
San Joaquín	132
San José	124
San Juan el Bautista	136
San Juan Evangelista	120
San Lucas	118
San Marcos	116
San Mateo	114
San Pablo	150
San Pedro	140
Santa Ana	132
Sansón	76
Santiago el Menor	144
Santiago Zebedeo	142
Sara	54
Satanás	182
Saúl	80
Simón de Cirene	160
Simón el Mago	178
Simón Zelote	144
Susana	104
Tobías	88
Tomás	144
Virgen María	126
Zacarías (profeta)	110
Zacarías	134